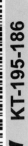

Abigail Tarttelin, an actress and writer, was born in Grimsby in 1987. Her first novel, *Flick*, published when she was twenty-two, was heralded as a 'cult classic' by *GQ*. She blogs for the *Huffington Post*, is books editor of *Phoenix* magazine and was named one of London's hottest 25 under-25s by the *Evening Standard* in 2013. Follow her on Twitter @abigailsbrain

Also by Abigail Tarttelin

Flick

GOLDEN BOY

ABIGAIL TARTTELIN

WEIDENFELD & NICOLSON

A W&N PAPERBACK

First published in Great Britain in 2013
by Weidenfeld & Nicolson
This paperback edition published in 2014
by Weidenfeld & Nicolson,
an imprint of the Orion Publishing Group Ltd,
Carmelite House, 50 Victoria Embankment,
London EC4Y 0DZ

An Hachette UK company

5 7 9 10 8 6 4

A CIP catalogue record for this book
is available from the British Library.

ISBN 978-1-78022-459-6

Printed and bound in Great Britain by
Clays Ltd, St Ives plc

MIX
Paper from
responsible sources
FSC® C104740

www.orionbooks.co.uk

For my parents

PART ONE

Daniel

My brother gets all As at school, and is generally always nice to everybody. He is on the county football team that trains and plays at his high school, and they rotate captain between the three best players, which is him and his best friends, so for one month out of every three, he is captain of the team. People like him because he is fair and always calls out the names of the other players to support them and claps when they win, plus if they won because of someone else's goal, he will always make sure that that person holds the trophy in the picture for the paper.

He is like the perfect one of the two of us. Whenever my family is in the paper, they show pictures of my brother. Mostly they cut me out. My brother is much taller than me, and he also has lighter hair and straighter hair than me, and mine is quite curly and a darker yellow that some people say is ginger, which I have been teased about at school. Mum says he looks like an angel and I look like a little imp, but I don't think she was trying to be insulting because she was smiling like I'd be pleased when she said it. My brother has proper muscles and can run really fast and wins all the races at school sports days. He is also doing an entrance exam for the big school that goes after secondary school so Mum and Dad don't have to pay any money for him to go, and he is probably going to get that, Mum says, because he works very hard and is naturally bright.

His friends Marc and Carl are funny. They are humorous-funny, but also strange-funny. When they are at our house sometimes they all go quiet when I walk in a room, and I say, 'Hey! You were talking about me!'

And they say, 'We weren't.'

And I say, 'What were you talking about then?'

3

And sometimes they make silly excuses but sometimes one of them will say, 'We were talking about girls.'

And then I say, 'No you weren't! You were talking about me!'

And my brother will say, 'No, really, Daniel, I promise we were talking about girls.'

And then I believe them because my brother would never, ever lie to me, because we are brothers and we have a blood pact never to lie to one another. A blood pact means you would die before you lied to each other.

My brother is also really popular with girls. Carl told me so and so did Marc, and so did Mum. I also deduced this fact because a few times we have picked him up from school in the car and he has been talking to a girl and holding hands and then once . . . once he was kissing a girl and I was shocked and horrified and Mum laughed at my mouth, which was wide open, and beeped the horn and waved at him and my brother smiled and went red and got in the car and when he got in the car I said, 'Why are you so red?'

And he said, 'Shuddurrrp, Daniel.'

And Mum laughed again, even harder.

The best thing about my brother is that he is the most amazing player of *World of War* ever. He doesn't even play it that often! He only plays it with me. He plays more on the Xbox with Marc and Carl usually, and we play on the Wii downstairs with Mum and Dad sometimes and he also occasionally plays on the Sega, but really he doesn't play many games because he is out playing football. But he does play *World of War* with me most nights and we play until eight or eight-thirty and then I have to either have a bath and go to bed or just go to bed, but usually have a bath and go to bed. Then I will read to Mum before bed, or sometimes I will read to Dad, but usually Dad is not home yet. Sometimes my brother comes in and we have our talks, which are very interesting conversations about life. My brother says I am very wise and he is right. I always have advice for him.

We are very different people. Some different things about the two of us are good, though, like he is best at English and

Geography and History, and he doesn't know what he wants to be when he grows up, but I am a very advanced robot designer for my age and I know exactly what I want to be when I grow up: a robotic engineer. I will do all the designs on the robots and I will oversee the construction of the prototype and then I will make an entire robot race, or I will use my robot powers to add robotic extensions to normal human beings, so they can be whatever they want to be. Like if you couldn't see but wanted to be a fighter pilot then I could add robot eyes, which could give you 20:20 vision, or even better 40:40 vision and night vision, with the ability to detect both infra-red and ultra-violet light. You would have a dial on your head and you could turn it to see which one you wanted to see. People would come into my workshop and I would look at them, and I would improve them until they were absolutely perfect and couldn't be improved further. I would work on my brother and make him really big and muscly and fast as a cheetah, and I would give him a really deep voice and a buzz cut and a gun that formed from his left arm when his heightened senses told him we were in danger.

I told my brother what I wanted to be, and he said that it was cool but unfortunately he wouldn't let me add extensions to him, because he wanted to be who he was and see how that played out. I said that was stupid. Who wouldn't want to be perfect? Or a robot?

And this is why I have chosen to write my class essay about my brother.

Sincerely,
Daniel Alexander Walker, age nine and four-fifths.

Karen

My parents were each other's antithesis. My mother was a beautiful, sad woman; dark, small and quick to anger. She would mutter about sacrifice and everything she had given up for us. She died when I was sixteen and now I wish I had known her better. My father was tall, with golden hair swept from a side-parting, and had a gentle, mild temperament. Dad used to practise law, and would leave for York very early in the morning, every day, to go to his office. Later, he became a politician. He saw enough of the world to have dreams for us, and when I could go – when it was still free to go study for a degree – he sent me to Oxford University.

I was three years older than my sister Cheryl, and I didn't want to go alone, so my friend Leah applied to train as a nurse in Oxford and followed me there. Two years after we moved to Oxford she met Edward, a philosophy student, while out rowing on the river. I was surprised she liked him so much, because Leah was so down to earth, and Edward was prone to arrogance. He felt too cold for warm Leah. Six months later, he took her for a picnic on that same river and proposed in front of all his friends. They married and moved to Hemingway for Edward's work. The houses were better value and roomier, and the town was quiet and safe. A few years after that, they found out they were going to have a baby – a boy.

Leah had moved to the suburbs, but I loved Oxford. The city was where I became a lawyer, where I met my husband, where we bought our first flat, where the buzz of energy took on a unique momentum and propelled even the most mundane start to an evening forward into something new, something different and unexpected. My boyfriend, Steve, was two years ahead of me in law school. After he graduated we would meet at the pub around six most nights, then either stay there until late, drinking and talking, or walk home together. He was from London, tall, leanly muscular, earnest, blithely good-looking and deliciously self-righteous. He was passionate. We argued a lot but had the same values. We both strove for independence and control, but somehow imagined success was already waiting for us. We were healthy and young and full of promise. We had no problems and no doubts.

We got married in Oxford a few weeks after I graduated. Afterwards we went for a meal at an Indian restaurant we both loved.

We found out I was pregnant just before we exchanged on the flat in Oxford, and we moved to Hemingway a few months after the birth of our first child. Steve was twenty-eight and I was twenty-six. The move was unexpected, but suddenly Oxford was too claustrophic. Our friends would drop by at all times, without calling ahead, and above all we wanted privacy.

We took a long time, a few weeks, to decide on a name for the baby. Steve kept suggesting ones I hated: Jamie, Taylor, Rowan. In the end he grew impatient with me, and starting calling the baby 'Max'. After a while, it stuck.

Later, when we had Daniel, our second child, my sister moved to Hemingway to be closer to me. Cheryl's life is very different from mine. She travelled instead of going to university. Cheryl has had several long-term boyfriends but only got married last year, at 38, to Charlie, who has a wide, boyish grin and wild, curly hair.

I know it sounds irrational, but sometimes I feel jealous of all the freedom and solitude she has experienced. As a barrister for the court and a mother of two, my own free time is precious. I spend it with my family, and when I get the chance I see Cheryl or Leah, but even these occasions seem to be few and far between. I call them both regularly but we only manage perhaps one lunch or dinner a month.

Perhaps because we made similar choices in life, Leah and I are closer than my sister and I. I know if anything happened to me, Leah would be there for my children, and if anything happened to Leah, I would be there for her son, Hunter, who, like many children without siblings, can be moody and controlling. I don't share that thought with Leah, obviously, because we all like to believe that our children are perfect, and personally, I wouldn't want to be disabused of that notion.

Despite Hunter's bossiness, Max and he have been best friends since they were little, and Leah and I have always been glad of this because on shared holidays they are good at entertaining themselves. They are both resourceful, playing football together, exploring, swimming, surfing, fighting and making up without our input. Max is always the first, and sometimes the only one, to forgive, ever the peacemaker.

Leah was the first person I confided in about Max's condition, and Hunter has known since he was four. He was young when he found out, sharing a bath with Max before bedtime, but he seemed to understand as much as a child could. We just told him Max is different. Max is special.

Max

It is eleven-ten on a Sunday night in late September and I am meant to be asleep, but I'm not. My parents are having a dinner party. It is obvious, by the sounds of the dizzy, hysterical laughter that you start to exhale when you're an adult and you have very few friends and only rarely have fun, that they are caught in a bubble of their own awesomeness, and won't be leaving the living room any time soon.

So I'm not asleep. I'm doing what I suspect most 15-year-olds do when there's a guarantee no parent is going to come into the room. I stroke a hand down my thigh, with my eyes closed. I'm thinking about kissing someone. This is all I've ever thought about when I've done this so far, in case I never get to go further than kissing in real life. I mean, obviously I want to. But, you know . . . I may never. Get laid, I mean. So I don't want to really think about it.

Hence the dreaming about kissing. Kissing is good. I can definitely score kissing. I have had some awesome kissing in my time. Thinking about kissing does not come with twinges of 'but what if I never . . . ?' attached. I love kissing.

So in my head my lips touch someone else's and I lean back onto the grass of the school playing field. My hands travel up my legs and roam around my crotch. I never know what's going to make me come. Usually it's really hard to get there, so I just settle for feeling good and a general touch around that area.

I roll over onto my side and my hair moves silkily across my face, and this is also erotic. I decide to do what I almost never do, and I suck my little finger, then reach down past my stomach.

It always gets me. Probably because I do it so rarely, and probably also because it's quite new. It's like a secret. I grin into my pillow and breathe harder.

'What are you doing?'

'Shit!' I look over my shoulder and grab at my duvet.

'Oh fuck!' The figure silhouetted by the light from the hall stands in my doorway, lets out a low laugh and claps its hand to its mouth.

It pushes the door closed and walks forward into the light, where the figure becomes Hunter Fulsom, son of my parents' friends Leah and Edward. Hunter attends the local sixth form college and we used to be on the same football squad, before he dropped out earlier this year. Now he just hangs around the town hall, where everybody underage goes to party, smoking weed and drinking. Leah told my mum that Hunter's grades have dropped off and he was cautioned by the police for egging someone's house over the summer.

I don't smoke pot. I can't anyway, even if I wanted to, because of Dad and Mum. They need me to keep out of trouble; to be good. They are lawyers, and they work hard and are in the paper a lot. There's a certain amount of pressure being in my family. People would write about us if I did something like that. Mum and I call it 'doing a Prince Harry'.

'Don't do a Prince Harry on me,' she says.

I wouldn't do it anyway. But it seems Hunter would, and has.

Hunter's tall, dark and, I suppose, handsome. His eyes look hooded and in shadow in the relative dark of my bedroom. I see the outline of his features only due to the moonlight outside. Everything about him is either black or grey. He smirks at me.

'Hey you,' he says.

Hunter's mum and my mum have been best friends since they were little kids. This makes Hunter a non-genetic 'cousin' and, purely by default, one of my best friends growing up. He knows all my secrets, including *the* secret, the one only my family knows, which means that, on some level, I always had to be on his good side when we were little. A year older than me, he was the one in charge in our relationship. He was the dark-haired, dark-eyed one who remained mysterious and guarded, and I was the sunny, blond one who was open and honest, and had inadvertently stumbled into a situation where I had to do Hunter's bidding in all our childhood games, because he had info on me and I had nothing on him. Despite this, I always thought of Hunter as one of my best friends and, in a way, my hero, because he did the things I wanted to do, but first and way better. It was Hunter that I had wanted on my team when I read *Swallows and Amazons*. It was Hunter I thought of when I saw the young John Connor in *Terminator 2*. It was Hunter who hand-carved me a wooden boat to sail on the lakes when we visited the scene of our mums' childhoods in Yorkshire, and it was Hunter who taught me to play pooh sticks, and held me in bed at night when the howling of the wind sounded like ghosts. He was a big brother for as long as I remained an only child and afterwards, a forever friend, for better, for worse, etc.

I'm surprised to see him now, though. We haven't spoken in months, not since a drunken conversation about sex at New Year, when we were staying with our families on a skiing holiday in Switzerland and where, for no obvious reason, Hunter had become angry and subdued and told me to 'fuck off, pretty-boy'.

'How many people have you slept with?' was the last thing I remembered saying to him. I was smiling conspiratorially, whispering this in his ear out of necessity – our parents were in the next room.

'People?' he asked suspiciously, then stood up and lurched for the door of the cabin that led outside. With a husky tone in his throat he had spat the words at me, 'Fuck off, pretty-boy.'

It's been nine months.

'What are you doing here?'

'I came to pick up my parents.' Hunter holds a car key aloft. 'They're pretty drunk. So are yours.'

Hunter walks towards me. The darkness makes his gait appear threatening. He drops his hips in a strange, wolf-like way. He stops about a metre away from me, holding a black rucksack. 'I said I'd say hi to you before I left. And your parents said it was alright.'

'Oh.'

Hunter grins. 'You were—'

'No,' I say, for no reason at all, because it's so obvious.

'I saw you.' He is silent for a moment. He wets his lips. 'Can you?'

'Of course I can!' I say crossly.

'Sorry. Didn't mean to insult you. It's just . . . it's more a boy thing to do, isn't it?'

'Oh,' I mumble, blushing. 'Err, I guess.'

'It's OK.' He comes to sit on the edge of my bed, and I subtly try, again ineffectually, to move the duvet and sheet a bit more to cover my exposed leg. 'It's nothing to be ashamed about.'

'I know.' I frown.

'I meant touching the bit you were touching.'

'What? How long were you at the door?'

He smirks. 'Can I see?'

'Um, no!'

'Forget it,' he laughs. 'I don't really want to. I just . . . 'cause I saw you touching it.' He pauses, watching my face.

My throat tightens at the 'it' word. 'It' is not a word I like.

For a while, there is just the sound of both of us breathing heavily, and cautiously in the quiet room. A car passes outside.

'I'm not going to tell anyone,' he says, sounding threatening. I look up at him and he smiles.

'Fuck off,' I murmur.

'Ooo!' He holds his hands up in mock protest, then rests them on his knees and shrugs. 'I'm just surprised. I just didn't think you would touch yourself.' He emphasises the 'you'.

I think about this, shrug and colour red. 'Oh. OK. Sorry.' (*Why did I say sorry?* I think.)

Hunter looks around my room with the proprietary air he has always had regarding my life and possessions. He's always been the leader and, sometimes, the bully. He's tall and muscular and masculine. I feel small next to him, wearing just a T-shirt, covered by the duvet. Hunter's wearing a T-shirt with a band logo on it and jeans, with a heavy metal key chain attached to his belt loops. His arms are strong and hairy. He smells of musky deodorant and beer. I probably smell of shampoo.

'D'you want a Stella?' he asks suddenly, as if he has been searching for something to say. 'I have some in my bag.'

I shrug. 'Sure.'

He takes two bottles out of his black rucksack and passes me one.

'Are you alright drinking and driving?' I say.

Hunter puts his left leg up on the bed and turns to me. I manage to get my leg under the cover and I sit up, sipping the beer.

'It's just Stella. Not everybody's a complete lightweight like you,' Hunter says, swigging from the bottle like it's Coke.

'So . . . what have you been up to? I haven't seen you in ages,' I say, careful not to bring up New Year.

Hunter just looks at me from under his eyelashes and rolls his eyes. 'I grew up.'

I raise my eyebrows. 'So getting stoned and egging houses is grown up now?'

'Fuck off, what do you know?' Hunter mutters, grumpily, but he shoves me as if we were playing, and he keeps his hands on my stomach and moves closer to me on the bed, curling up to me like we used to when we were little. 'You haven't changed,' he says, tousling my hair. He leans on my shoulder.

I smile with the bottle in my mouth and feel beer wetting my bottom lip and chin.

'Oops,' I say. Hunter watches me closely, like he's concentrating, while I wipe it away. 'Are you drunk?' I ask.

'No.' He looks down and chugs his bottle, then takes the tops off two more. 'I'm really thirsty.'

I take the bottle he hands me and put it on my bedside table. I can already feel my head going woozy from drinking too fast. Hunter wriggles around on the bed and leans back against the wall, his legs on my lap pinning me down.

'So . . .' I try to think of something to talk about. 'Are you still going out with Kelly Morez?'

'We weren't really going out.'

I wait. 'And that's all you're gonna say about it? I know you did it with her, you told me at—'

'Yeah, I know, at New Year.' Hunter runs a hand through his hair. 'It's not properly sex if you don't fancy the person.'

'You didn't fancy her?'

Hunter shrugs. 'I like other people more.' He takes another gulp of Stella. 'How about you? Seeing anyone?'

I shake my head. 'No.'

'I hear you've got with loads of people from your year.'

'Where d'you hear that?'

'Around. I'm supposed to keep tabs on you. You're my little cousin. Sort of.'

'Not really,' I point out. 'And I'm only a year younger than you.'

'Whatever. Loads of people at college like you too.'

'Seriously?'

'Yeah.' He snorts, kind of like a laugh, but not quite. 'They think you're pretty.'

'Pretty?' I frown.

'Well, you know. Whatever. Fit.'

I shrug. 'Well, I've never even been all the way. I stop before it gets that far.'

'I know, I heard,' says Hunter.

'Huh? From who? Who's telling you all this stuff?' I ask, laughing. 'Where are you getting your information, Gestapo?'

Hunter just smiles mysteriously. 'Well—' He chinks his bottle against mine as I pick up the second. 'I get it, anyway. You can't help it if sometimes you just don't want to, right?'

'Umm, well, it's not really—' I begin.

'And sometimes you . . . just do,' Hunter says quietly, studying the label of his bottle. He sips his beer and looks around my room. 'Cool games,' he mutters, staring at my consoles.

I frown. 'Are you alright, Hunter?'

For a moment he looks really miserable. But instead of talking he leans back onto my shoulder.

'Nothing,' he says, after a minute. 'Tired.'

And then he breathes in quickly, and I realise he's crying.

'What's wrong?' I exclaim, wrapping my arms around him. He buries his face into my neck and I feel his lips, open and wet on my skin. His throat makes a choking noise.

'Hey, hey,' I murmur softly, and, holding his cheeks with my hands, I gently push back his face so I can look at him. I stroke away his tears. 'What's the matter?'

Hunter manages to calm himself. He looks at me fiercely, almost angrily. His lip trembles. He presses both lips together as if considering something, as if he's confused, then he leans forward and kisses me. The fingers of his right hand knit with the hair at the back of my head. I'm so used to letting Hunter have his way that for a moment I don't react. I feel his tongue flick in between my lips.

'Woah,' I murmur, struggling to pull away from the considerably stronger force of Hunter.

His dark eyes are black now. They track over my face.

'What are you doing?'

He looks sullen. 'You're supposed to like me.'

'I'm *supposed* to like you?' I say.

'You're more girl than boy,' Hunter mumbles, and I realise he's very drunk. How he drove here without crashing and is going to drive his parents back I have no idea. 'When we were growing up I always thought . . . Max . . .' he whispers. 'Please, Max.'

'You're . . . Hunter, you're drunk.'

'I was just nervous,' he mumbles. 'Because I knew I was gonna see you. Please, Max.'

He leans in again but I turn away slightly, so his lips brush my cheek.

'I'm not gay. I'm sorry,' I say. I sound like I'm pleading with him. 'It's not a bad thing to be, it's just . . . I'm not.'

'You don't have to be,' he says, matter of factly.

I look to the side, trying to mull over this, my mouth forming the word 'what'. 'Um,' I eventually say. 'But . . . you are.'

'No I'm not,' he says. 'I don't like boys. Or girls. Just you.'

'You shouldn't drive home,' I say nervously. 'You don't look good.'

Hunter withdraws his hand and his eyes mist up, but it's a hard mist, like the frost on a car window in winter. They become opaque.

'Hunter,' I whisper softly. 'I'm sorry.'

He looks at me, then reaches for my throat with his hands and grips my neck. It's not really aggressive. It's intimate, like we're the best friends we used to be. His eyes are set on me – primal, feral. I watch Hunter like an animal, like prey gauging the intentions of a predator. He stares back at me. My eyes flicker down his chest. Taking in how much bigger than me he is.

'I'm not the freak,' he growls. 'There's nothing wrong with me. There's something wrong with you and you're making me feel this way.'

I look down and feel my bottom lip bump out, embarrassed to have him bring my condition up.

'You've always made me feel this way,' he says. 'You're a little cocktease. You're the freak. I'm not . . . I'm not . . .'

'Gay?' I murmur.

'No, I'm not that, because you're not even . . . because you're . . .'

His eyes roam over me. He looks like he's trying to prevent himself from having a panic attack.

I raise my arm and put a hand on his shoulder to calm him, and he takes advantage of this to move his arm below mine, wrap it around my waist and pull me, with one quick, easy move, from a sitting position to flat on my back, on the mattress below him. He moves forward and kisses me again briefly, before mumbling, 'You'll like it. I swear.'

He looks towards the door, rises slightly, unbuckles his belt and hops up onto the bed, leaning on my right leg so it's pressed down and pushing the other leg down with his arms. It happens so quickly I'm still feeling sorry for him as he does it. The tone of my voice flips from consoling and soft, to sudden panic.

'Hey! Wait, wait! What are you doing?'

'Shhh.' He hisses a warning. 'Your brother.'

He is referring to Daniel, who is almost ten, and asleep in the next room. No, I don't want Daniel to wake up and hear us and walk in right now. While I think about this, Hunter has cleared the duvet away from me in one quick swipe. It lands between my body and the wall to the right of me, pressing against my leg. He kneels painfully, right on my thighs, holding me down with his weight.

'Shit!' I cry out and cover myself with my hands. 'What the fuck? Hunter! Get off me!'

'Shut up.' Hunter comes forward, puts one hand on my mouth and one hand on my neck and shakes me hard, my brain feeling like it's thudding up against my skull, until I'm quiet and my head is aching. He leans low to my face and his lips brush against my skin. 'Shut up,' he says again, looking, even as he says it, unsure.

He takes his hands away and I lie there, unmoving, my hands still up by my face where I tried to break his hold on my neck. I cough gently, the air coming back into my lungs. I'm not scared. This is Hunter. I can remember what he looked like when he was five. In my head, he's five.

I lie still. I feel like my physical self, my ability to move, is floating above my body. I feel dizzy and light. Inside my head, my brain-self yells at me to come back.

Then the sensation of being within my own body returns. I breathe it in with two short breaths and realise I have been staring at the ceiling; hands up like a convict in front of the police, not breathing, for about thirty seconds. Some fumbling is going on further down the bed. I look down to my waist.

'Jesus,' I murmur in complete disbelief, as if I'm watching something awful on *CSI*. Hunter's penis is pointing at me. He takes his hands and rubs around my crotch roughly.

'Is this your pussy?' he whispers, shocked. 'Fuck.'

'No!' I regain my voice. 'Stop it!' I try to sit up but he leans forward and pushes me back, easily, with a hand on my chest.

'Don't move, OK? Please,' he mumbles. 'Just don't move.'

This is when the shock dissipates, and I get what's coming. It seems a long time to take to comprehend the situation. I mean, things like this never happen. They happen to other people, but not to you, not to me. Not with moody-but-harmless Hunter. Not with the son of your parents' best friends. Not with your best, true, forever friend when you were a kid. Not in sleepy, small town Hemingway. This happens to people in dark alleyways, at night, with strangers. This happens when you're lost in a city. More to the point, this happens to girls. So I've been thinking so far, *This isn't happening.* This is a situation I can control.

Now I'm lying on my back silently, while Hunter feels around my naked skin, and I can feel him, so heavy, his strong footballer's legs pressing down my thighs, and I realise what he's going to do. I realise I'm not going to be able to stop him. I realise too late.

'Ow! Get off me! Get the fuck off me!' I struggle but he's already pushing at it, me, it, pulling at the sides with his fingers. 'No! OW!'

I feel something roughly forced – shoved – inside me. A pain worse than anything I've ever felt shoots through me. It's too big.

My eyes and mouth open wide, I almost shriek in panic. 'No! Oh god! NO! Please! Hunter! Please!'

'Oi!' He hisses at me. 'Shh! Just shut up!'

'It hurts! No!' Tears are falling down my face and I feel ashamed of myself for being such a wimp that I'm crying already. I'm gasping and squirming and pleading with him with my eyes, and panicking and whining on one constant note like a dog that's been kicked. 'Please! Please, Hunter! PLEASE!'

'It'll get better!' he hisses, and pushes himself further in.

I hear a roar of laughter from downstairs. I hear the explosions of a video game and realise Daniel isn't asleep. He's awake, playing *World of War*, and I'm in the next room, with Hunter. Hunter grunts and I feel the skin pulling painfully and call out.

'NO! Please, please, please! Stop, please stop! Please!'

'Oi! Listen to me! Stop it! Listen!' He grabs my shoulders and shakes me again so my head is bouncing around on the pillow and I feel like an object, a thing, unable to move, pinned down, plugged and useless, and then he holds me so I'm looking straight at him. His dark eyes stare coldly into mine. I watch him struggle to keep them cold.

Hunter's fingers pinch my upper arms. His breath is hot on my skin. He moves towards me and kisses me, licking my mouth when I won't move my lips. He leans fully on me, his weight bearing down on my chest, and wraps his arms around my waist and neck. I can't breathe. He continues to push into me. His lips press against my cheek. I open my mouth but can't form any words. I moan. It's too painful.

'Hey,' he lifts his head. 'Do you really want your mum and dad to hear you?' he whispers. 'Do you want them to come in your room and see your little he-she dick?'

I shut up, shocked, and stare at him.

'Do you?' he asks, almost matter-of-factly. 'Do you want your mum and dad to see your little he-she dick?' His lips part, close. He swallows. He shakes his head minutely, still inside me. 'I'm not gay,' he murmurs. 'You're not a guy. You're . . . you're not anything.'

My lips tremble. Our eyes are locked on to each other's. Hunter's face grows more cold and angry as he convinces himself with his own words. I watch him disbelievingly.

'You're a freak,' Hunter murmurs, breathing quickly. 'You're a he-she.'

This is the worst moment of my life.

I have never been spoken to like this.

Those words, the word, burn in my cheeks, uprooting shame from my nervous system, causing tears to prick suddenly, immediately, at the corners of my eyes.

We wait together, in silence, for me to come round. My mouth is open. My eyelids blink. I swallow. I sweat.

I look at my penis. I look towards the door. I look at him, above me, inside me.

'Do you?' he whispers. 'Do you want them to see?'

I shake my head and close my lips and wait, watching him.

Hunter nods. 'Of course you don't. Nobody wants to see that, do they?'

I wait. He pinches the skin of my waist hard between his forefinger and thumb. 'Do they, Max?'

I shake my head again and mouth, '*No*.'

We have reached a sort of impasse. We understand I'm not to move, and I'm not to call out. Or in any case, I don't move. I don't call out. We stare at each other, straight in the eye, as Hunter moves forward, on top of me. He bends my legs into V-shapes and presses the knees down so I'm flat on the bed, my legs far apart. It feels so strange to be so exposed. It's the first time, I realise, in my entire life, I have lain in this way, utterly spread beneath someone.

He moves his hips forward quickly, and stuffs something hard and long further into me. His penis – I think, as if it could have been something else and the thought has just come to me. I feel a horrible stretching in my crotch and sick rises in my stomach and throat.

I let out a staggered cry, the breath escaping over my teeth. 'Uh-oh-oh.'

'Tight,' Hunter mutters coldly, like a scientist. Then, almost apologetically: 'Bit dry. Don't suppose you get wet, do you?' He's trying to keep his cool. But his lips are trembling.

I speak without thinking. 'I don't know.'

'It'll get better.'

He shoves again, deeper, and I gasp in pain. The pain is . . . unbearable. Explicit. Nauseating. Constant. Rising and falling slightly with each thrust.

I'm not made for this. I'm not built wide enough. He's too big. He's too big. The stretching snaps, stops, and turns to splitting. I can feel skin tearing down there. He leans over me, his breath hot, smelling of breath mints and beer. I feel sicker.

Hunter closes his eyes, turns his face into my neck and moans. 'Oh,' he mutters, moving in and out of me. 'Oh my god.'

I can't close my eyes. I just don't do anything. I lie there, a blank. I lie there as he kisses my neck, sucking at my skin. I lie there like a blow-up doll, my mouth open, moving up and down on the bedsheets while Hunter presses my legs down and moves back and forth into me. He raises his head and looks down to where he is entering me. I can't see it. I'm lying back. I don't want to see it, but I look where he's looking instinctually. My dick is flopping lifelessly as he pounds at me. I think about how it must feel to be a big, strong guy with a big dick and the ability to walk into any room and know you could overpower and take anyone you wanted. I wonder if I'd want that, given the choice. It seems a weird thing to be. It seems alien.

Hunter's watching our parts come together. He lets out another, 'Oh my god', rising in tone as he thrusts faster. He takes my arm and pushes it above my head, then holds it there. He seems to smell my shoulder. He puts both hands in my hair again, stroking it, tousling it, and moans, rocking back and forth. My hair's really soft. He used to stroke it like that, when we were little. I didn't think anything of it. Everyone strokes my hair.

I look at him, look at the ceiling, look across the room to my posters – the England Football Team, Dakota Fanning, Saoirse Ronan, the Hemingway Area 1st Football Team's Junior League victory with me in the centre front row next to Marc and Carl. I look at my DVDs. I look at the dismantled LP player me and Carl found in a car boot sale that we've been trying to get to work for over a month. I look at the TV and the tangle of wires that lead to the Xbox live, Wii and old Sega, which is funny to play when you're drunk late at night. *Halo 4* is on the floor, out of its case, next to a pile of dirty boxers and T-shirts.

'Oh, Max,' Hunter groans and ruts at me, his eyes closed. I feel my skin ripping more and squeak, gasp, let out an 'aah', pull the pillow over my head, trying to be quiet. His arms enclose my body. I roll to my right a little. He sits up, stops for a moment and takes hold of my legs.

Now he is above me, his torso at a right angle to the bed. I hear the smack of his thighs hitting against mine. A horrible squelching sound is getting louder. He's sliding in and out freely now, but still roughly, because I'm too tight and small for this. Not made for this. Pain travels up my legs and numbs my toes. I'm embarrassed at the way my body bends, embarrassed at the way it shakes and opens for him. I'm embarrassed and confused as to why I care that I feel ugly, why I want to put my hands over my penis and stop it lolling around. The pain is sharp at the entrance point and dull further inside me. I worry. I wonder what it's touching. It seems to hit against my stomach. The disbelief and shock shake off a little and the pain mutates into something so strong I have to speak. I slowly take the pillow off my head and grip it tightly above me on the mattress. My throat opens and my voice joins the cacophony of quiet sounds.

'Oh my god, please!' I beg him, earnestly. 'Oh my god, please. Hunter. Please.'

'Shh, shh,' he breathes, not looking at my face, his mouth open, his hips moving fast, a strange, confused, flickering spark in his eye. Intent. Excitement. Curiosity. Awe. Desperation. Embarrassment. Realisation. Shame. Want. Need. That opaque gleam. Then, the furious frown and movements of someone who wants to get something over with, get it done. I can hear a slapping sound, I can hear wetness, I can hear the *whomp whomp whomp* of concave things hitting other concave things and the air passing between them. I can hear the quiet creak of the bed. I can hear and smell and feel Hunter's breath on me.

'Oh my god,' he murmurs to himself. 'I'm gonna . . .'

His body buckles and crouches over me. Hunter lets out a long, low moan. His face is against my chest. His arms stretch out, feeling blindly for my shoulders, then hold them. I wait, while he hugs me.

Maybe twenty seconds pass, and he looks up, not quite meeting my eye. He looks surprised, tearful, and kind of grateful. Grateful and desperate. He wipes a shaking hand around his face.

'Sorry,' he mutters. He moves up the bed. I'm lying on my back. He lays on my left side, still inside me, his arm across my chest, his face turned towards me on the pillow, lips next to my ear. I am staring at the ceiling, but I can feel him watching me.

22

I frown, my breathing slowing, and look down my body. 'Did you come in me?'

I look over at him, and I see him panic again, then that cloak of anger going up. The petulant lip comes out. 'What do you care?'

Hunter moves down the bed. He pulls his penis out of me quickly and I let out an 'errr', a strange, sick, stuttering, reproachful, apologetic noise. He buckles up.

'What are you complaining about?' He pulls on his jumper, which he gets out of his bag. 'Don't tell and I won't tell about you. Don't tell your mum, either. She's got enough problems with you and your spacker brother to begin with.'

For some reason, I shake my head and whisper, calmly: 'I won't.'

Hunter packs up the empty beer bottles.

'He's not a spacker,' I say.

Hunter looks at me like he's five years old again, like I'm being mean to him in the playground. It's his look for when I've done something he doesn't like.

'Whatever,' he says.

Then Hunter isn't there anymore, and it's just me, lying, legs apart, like a dead bug, flattened to the mattress by pain, and blinking rapidly with my mouth open. Like I can't believe what just happened, happened. Like I don't know where I am. Like I am in some alternate reality where there is a possibility that Hunter is a bad person, that my average little bedroom is the scene of a crime, that I could be quietly forced into something so abhorrent I can't even think the word in my mind and that it could all be over in five minutes.

I hear the creak of the stairs as Hunter's shoes tap down them. The living room door opens, letting a gale of laughter drift upstairs. I let my aching legs lower to the mattress.

I can hear him saying something to Mum and Dad and Uncle Charlie and Auntie Cheryl, thanking them, saying goodnight, making a joke. They burst out laughing again, my dad's deep voice roaring beneath my mum's high-pitched giggle. I hear his mum and dad shuffle out with him, call goodbye. Then the front door closes and footsteps walk down the gravel drive, the gate creaking, the sound of an engine starting, and the crunch of tyres on gravel signals his departure.

A lorry rumbles by on the road outside. My posters are on the walls. *Halo 4* is still on the floor. The night still passes behind the blinds. I am still and quiet and dizzy and shaking. I feel cold and wet and a draft between my legs. I feel sick and vomity. I feel embarrassed and strange and in pain. Voices drift up the stairway.

I sit up slowly, painfully, and pull the covers over myself, with my eyes tight shut.

Daniel

Dad and Mum and Auntie Cheryl and Uncle Charlie and Auntie Leah and Uncle Edward are still going on downstairs and talking and stuff. I don't understand what they have to talk about. Everything they do is so boring. It's all law and rules and court cases and I told Mum she should do something fun like play video games otherwise she just has a boring life and is boring all the time and then she shouted at me. I don't understand that woman. I wasn't being rude. I was being helpful.

They are being so loud it becomes difficult to sleep, so I secretly play my game in my room with the sound turned down. It's a very complicated game, and it is actually for ages ten and up, but I'm extremely advanced at computing, so it's easy for me. There are sounds outside my door twice but no one comes in. Sometimes I think they all forget about me. I get angry with them a lot. Max doesn't forget about me, but sometimes I get angry with him anyway because Mum and Dad think he is so much better than me. They think I don't know, but I do. I'll show them when I'm older and am a billionaire robot engineer like that ugly little geek in that film. I won't be ugly or a geek though. If I am a billionaire I'll do the smart thing and use my powers to build myself into a super-robot, then buy really cool friends.

There, they are laughing again. It sounds like screaming, like on level thirty when you get to the massacre and take out all the aliens.

Well, if they are going to forget about me I am going to stay up and play my game. So I play and play and play until I hear the cars going home and I get to level twenty-two before I am so tired I cannot play anymore, and I also kill a total of three hundred and thirty-five evil dwarflords.

Sylvie

My head hurts from the music at Toby's all night. He lives in Oxford and goes to the uni. I made him drive me back but he was totally stoned. It was pretty scary.

I don't do drugs. I tried a few when I was younger, but only idiots like Toby spend their entire lives stoned. I'm dumping him tomorrow. I'll call him up.

Tonight I made him drop me at the church, because he's the type that, if he knew where I lived, would come round and play guitar badly outside the window. I've been there before and I don't think my parents can take it again. It's best, I always think, to compartmentalise.

It's really quiet at night, and the town looks like someone has sketched it in black and white. All the living people sleep just like the dead, and we share the quiet. I'm in the graveyard. The graves look so sweet in the dark. They're not scary. They're not eerie or anything. They're weird and cute and freaky. I like hanging out here, but you can't talk at night, because you wake the spirits, and you can't step on a grave, because that is sacrilege. You don't want to wake the dead. They sleep on, just like the living. Well, all the living people sleep apart from me, I guess.

A car drives past. I hear the engine humming when it's still out of sight and I sink into the shadow of a grave.

The car swerves a little on the road, slows, speeds up. I'm close enough to see through the glass, and the car is going slow enough through the town centre for me to recognise the face. It's a dark-haired guy from the sixth form college. He's hot. I remember him from parties but I don't know his name. A man is seated beside him. He looks like a smaller, older version of the driver so it's probably his dad. A woman is in the back.

Somehow the car spooked me, appearing so suddenly, and

when it's gone I slip out of the church gates and start walking home.

I wish I wasn't like this. So scared all the time. I feel like the older I get, the more scared I become. I think it's because you realise, as you grow up, that the world is a worse place than you thought when you were a kid and the worst thing was being pushed by a bully or peeing your pants in class. Now I realise there's a lot more to fear than that. I get scared of walking around on my own in the dark, scared of guys lurking in the shadows, too scared to live fully, freely. There are all these things that I want to do before I die, and what if I die now, or soon? Another thing that scares me is my life taking shape and solidifying. We're taking our GCSEs and deciding on AS Level options this year, and in two years we're off to uni. What if I make the wrong choices?

I get these panic attacks sometimes. I keep a brown paper bag by my bed. That's why I sometimes stay out at night on my own, like this. It's to prove to myself that the night is only the world in shadow, that my fears can't control me, that I have courage.

The dark isn't even a loss of visibility. It's just a change of colour, of tone. It's the same as day, it's just a different hue.

You need courage to do anything. It's the same courage you need to take an exam or make choices or write a poem when your last one was shit, as it is to go out at night without feeling terrified. If you fear, you'll never live. You need courage to do it.

Before I turn into my lane I hear the car one last time: a squeal of wheels and the engine of the car cuts through the stillness of the night as it turns left on Grove Street. Tyre burn. Dude thinks he's cool. Idiot.

Karen

It's this time of morning, just before dawn, that I love the most. It's the quiet. I didn't used to notice it, when I was a child, or at college. Now these minutes are the only ones during my day that are not full of noise. It's funny what we miss about being young, but I miss the proliferation of silence, unfolding before me on a long Sunday afternoon. I remember in our first house in Hemingway, slipping downstairs for a glass of water and looking out the bay window as the sun moved across the garden, or sitting propped up against my pillows in bed, still in the silent waking of the morning, just before the birdsong began and woke Max up. I remember the silences in the flat we used to have just after finishing uni, in the early days of my pregnancy, my bare-chested new husband reading next to me, while I read cheesy crime dramas and thrillers – my guilty pleasure – enjoying the peace before I started my daily ritual of throwing up and aching.

I try to imagine Steve that young, that skinny. Imagine Steve as a lanky boy in those old ripped jeans with no hair on his chest. I can't quite do it.

I rub my head to stave off the slight hangover I feel brewing from last night's dinner party. We used up the last of the wine Cheryl brought us from France this summer.

Life turned out differently from what I had predicted. I do understand what my own mother meant now, that you give up things for your children's sake, and perhaps there are lines that I wouldn't be able to cross in terms of sacrifice, but I haven't reached them yet and I hope I don't. I wanted my family to be close, like my childhood family never was, and it is. I'm not always the best parent, but I try very, very hard.

The greatest difference between how I dreamed my life would be, and what it became, has everything to do with what

I didn't know about love. I saw it as romantic, something apart from me. I didn't realise how much it would take as well as add to my life, how completely drained of it I would feel, how I would have to plumb reserves I didn't know I had to nurture it. I had no idea when I was younger about what love really was, what it does, how it moves, how it grows, what it feels like, why you value it.

How I feel about my children, in particular, is different from how I imagined it would feel to have children. I don't think I had thought it through well enough. I did not understand that my body and soul were about to be entirely claimed, that I would feel physical pain when I heard them crying, and that I would love them beyond all reason, even when they were being terrible. I'll admit that I wasn't ready. Being a parent meant having to make definite choices, rather than meander around possible options. It means having to live the way you wanted to live but could never be bothered to, prioritising things you never used to consider – boundaries and rules and plans. It means living in a school catchment area and saving for university. It means constriction in your chest, and worry all the time, and if not all the time, at least once a day. It means feeling responsible for the every move of two autonomous beings that I cannot control.

Particularly now that they are older. I keep waiting for something to happen, something to come in and crush us all.

Last month, a girl in Max's school, a couple of years older than Max, killed herself by jumping off a bridge. One of Daniel's classmates died during during an asthma attack the other summer. Am I giving them too much milk to drink? Am I one day going to get a call at work about drugs? Sex? Drunken violence?

Is it strange that I think of Daniel, my nine-year-old, when I worry about drugs, sex and violence?

Max has never done anything like that. Still, I have worried about Max every day since he was born. He must have lived in an atmosphere of constant panic for the first five years of his life. It was because of his problem. You hear about things going wrong during a birth, but when you're pregnant and in labour, you never think it will happen to you. No one thinks theirs will be the baby with the problem. And then it *was* my baby, and it made me worry all the more acutely for the rest of his life, because I had been right to worry before, because when it had been time to give birth, to do the most important thing I could do for Max, something had gone wrong. And I could not shake the feeling, despite logic and reasoning and common sense, that it had been my fault. And I wondered what else I would get wrong in the years to come.

But as he grew up, Max himself never did anything wrong. Not really. Sometimes I think the one problem was enough with Max. Sometimes I think we bore our burden; we had the terrified early years when we didn't know how he was going to grow or what would happen, and now we just get to enjoy him.

This is how the business of the day first breaks into my beautiful silence and sweeps me forward: these fretful thoughts, combined with a sharp tinge of a headache breaking through to my consciousness from last night. I look over at the wardrobe, where today's suit is hanging, pressed, ready.

The suits. I get caught up in the suits. I always liked fashion, but this is an obsession. Sourcing them, buying them, pressing them, fitting into them, throwing out the old suits to make space for the new ones – it all takes up far too much of my time. I suspect I am aiming for the perfect wardrobe for my roles in life, to make up for the fact that I am never quite sure what these roles require of me. On the left-hand side rail in the built-in wardrobe are the Good-Barrister work suits; on the right, there are the Good-Mother casual clothes, mostly slim-fitting trousers with plain blouses or T-shirts or casual but expensive white shirts with blazers to go over them. I wear the Good-Mother outfits to PTA meetings, cake sales, football matches, play dates. I am a Good Parent, and you can tell by my Good-Parent suit. Slim-fitting jeans work well. People can see you keep yourself healthy, you keep your kids healthy, you set a good example. A white T-shirt, tucked in, is sexy and cute but still conservative. Your outfit has to say: *I took a while deciding on*

*this because my house was clean and my kids were fed and mentally
stimulated, so I had plenty of time to pamper myself.* A cardigan is
appropriate; a jacket is better. No hoodies. No jumpers. No
bulk that says you have gained weight.

Today's suit stares me down.

I get up at six. I run. We have a gym in the basement. I
wanted it upstairs so I could look out the window while on the
treadmill. Steve couldn't understand: why would his crazy wife
want the treadmill upstairs? Why would she need to look out
the window?

*It's boring! Running and running on the same spot and not going
anywhere, ever, is boring!* I wanted to scream this at him, not
angrily, just loudly enough so he would hear, but he had a
conference call and I had a case going to court to prepare for
and there was Max's football gear to iron, and something with
Daniel, and so it goes, and so I didn't scream at him. We don't
scream at each other anymore. It sets a bad example. The
heated arguments are held in now, and then we forget about
them later, too tired to remember how irritated we were with
each other. We slide into bed after the lights are out, turn to
each other ready to continue to bicker, and then both sigh,
bereft of energy. We still make love most nights. It's always
been good. That has never changed.

Steve has free access to the gym at Hemingway City Hall,
which is part of the package for the local councillors and our
Member of Parliament, Bart Garrett.

Bart is tipped to resign soon, because the newspapers have
featured some fairly wild stories about his offspring drinking
and partying in expensive private schools, which turned out to
be true. Steve has been following his demise in the press with
a watchful eye, which makes me think about our agreement to
wait until Max was older before running for any form of
government. Steve is a Chief Crown Prosecutor. It's a worth-
while and interesting job, overseeing all the criminal prosecu-
tions in our area, and I work just under him as a barrister. It's
enough for me while the children are young, and I like being in

court, but I know Steve is hungry to be in politics. He always has been. And Max will be sixteen this year.

When I get back to the bedroom from the gym, there is a Steve-shaped emptiness in the bed. He'll be downstairs, putting on espresso to brew. In a few minutes I'll smell it, and be aroused enough to go down for a cup. Now though, I luxuriate in the shower for ten minutes, and then I discard the suit I set aside, and pick something else.

I choose the black skirt, high heels, sheer tights, and the pearl-grey blouse, adding a silver necklace, foundation, nude eyeshadow and a brief hint of mascara. My lips are plum. I check myself in the mirror. I look pretty good for forty-two.

I wake Daniel up, and he groans at me hatefully. 'Mum! I can't be bothered!'

I kiss his head and he wriggles out from under me, slides out of the bed and then pads down the stairs, sits at the table and stares at me with disdain as I pour milk onto his Shreddies. I smile beatifically back.

Daniel is not a morning person. We have all had to come to terms with this.

Steve is on the phone, a cup of black coffee in hand. We can hear him in the second reception room. I know, even without seeing, exactly what he is doing: gesturing, standing with his feet wide apart, one hand steadily weighing up an option to the side, before tossing it out, fist clenching, driving forward. He makes his point. He wins the point. Stephen Walker, everybody! Once second in his class at Oxford (I was first in mine), then barrister extraordinaire, now Chief Crown Prosecutor!

He comes in for a refill and we salute each other with our cups.

'Into the fray,' he says, nipping out to his car. 'Love you.'

We work in the same building but we take separate cars. I leave about half an hour after him in the morning and take Daniel to school, and I come home about an hour before him at night to sort out dinner.

It's seven-thirty. Max breezes into the kitchen in his uniform. He takes care of himself, always has. He whips past me, grabs a bagel from the cupboard and smears spread onto it, smiling briefly, slipping past me like a whisper, light on the feet.

'Light of my life,' I whisper, kissing Max's hair. 'Lights of my life,' I add, chucking Daniel under the chin.

'Your fingers smell of butter,' Daniel informs me.

'Thanks,' I reply.

Max's long fingers flip his tie end round and round and up through the loop efficiently. I lean across to fix his top collar button but he's already doing it.

I pack my leather bag. I have another cup of coffee. I read my case notes. I yell for Daniel, who has disappeared upstairs again, to get in the car. He yells back something I pretend not to hear.

Sipping from my cup, and surveying the room, I notice a shopping bag Steve brought home last night sitting on the seat across from mine at the table. Emblazoned on it are the words 'Mike's Printing Supplies and Services'. I purse my lips, put my coffee down and slip out of my chair. Inside the bag is shining bright red card. I move the plastic down to reveal blue lettering on a white stripe across the centre of the card. I stare at it, trying to decide how to react. It's a mock-up of a campaign placard, with the words: 'Stephen Walker, MP for Oxford West, Hemingway & Abingdon' emblazoned on it.

He's thinking about it seriously.

He's thinking about it seriously, I think again.

'But we talked about it,' I imagine myself saying.

'I know,' he will say. 'I know.'

Steve always says he knows. He knows, and he thinks that makes it OK.

When we spoke about this the other week, I told him I didn't feel that it's the right time to run, not while Max is still in school, but I do understand why he wants to run now. Steve would be a wonderful MP, and now would be a strategic time to stand. It's not a general election, so there will be fewer candidates, and Steve will get more financial support if less people are looking for backing from local businesses. We always discussed that it might happen someday. But we never really saw eye to eye on it actually happening.

How long does a card like this take to design and print? When did he arrange this?

The boys run past me, out the back door, and I pick up my bag and coat and follow them. There is no more time to think about the significance of the campaign card.

Before I go I leave a note for the cleaner to tidy away the piles of books and files from the front hallway. We don't use the front door, and we should. It doesn't look good to use the back door all the time. The detritus of our lives is here in the mud, the discarded footwear, the rucksacks. Plus we store all the wine at the back door. I don't want people to think we're heavy drinkers.

I slip my Bulgari coat about my shoulders. It's the first time I've used it in six months, and it smells faintly of the closet, but the material is rich and thick, and September is cooling off, the brief heat replaced all too soon by a chilling breeze. Max is talking to Daniel by the car and I give him a kiss before he leaves for the bus. The stop is at the end of our street, the opposite direction to Daniel's school.

'Got everything you need?'

'Yep.'

'Sure?'

'Yep.'

'Are you OK?' I touch Max's cheek. 'You're a little red.'

'No.' He lifts his eyes and beams at me. 'I'm great, thanks, Mum.'

'Work hard, have a good day.'

'I will.'

'Be good!' I call as he walks away.

I see him faintly roll his eyes at me, but he nods, good-natured, sunny, smiling, and slips out the gate at the end of the drive. And I remember the conversation with Steve a few months earlier.

'We would need to get an automatic one,' I told him.

'Why would we need an automatic gate?'

'Everybody has an automatic gate.'

'Do they?'

'Steve, you know what I'm saying makes sense. If you run for election, we'll need to protect Max and Daniel.'

'Protect them? From who? Kidnappers? The mafia? This is England. This is the countryside. This isn't London.'

'From prying eyes, Steve. We need to protect them from journalists and other people and—'

'Prying eyes? That's a rather antiquated expression.'

'Look, I can't stop you from running if that's what you choose to do. But this is the reality. The only reason you can run is because Bart Garrett is about to resign after the papers plagued his family.'

'Let them plague us. There's nothing wrong with our kids. They're not some ungrateful idiots at an overpriced school like Bart Garrett's kids. They don't go out and get drunk and smash up someone's car. They're smarter than that.'

'People will want to know about him, Steve.' I paused, sighed, and added quietly, 'Can you imagine what would happen if it got out?'

Max

The seats in English class are this eggshell blue fabric-cum-plastic. My fingernails scratch lightly over it. My nails are neat. Everything about me is so neat. Everything I do, I do well. I can't remember the last time I messed up. This is a big mess up. I feel like it's my fault. I know it's not, but that doesn't stop me feeling like it is.

'You got forty-six out of forty-seven on the first draft!'

'What?'

'You got the same thing last time. Dick.'

I look down to my English essay, scrawled all over in red pen: 'Excellent', 'eruditely, mellifluously communicated', 'fantastic', all followed by exclamation points larger than the words.

'Oh, no wait, you got forty-five last time.'

'Did I?'

'You're still a dick.'

I can feel Carl grinning at my left ear, but I can't turn to look at him. It's almost ten-fifteen in the morning. Carl is spouting the usual rubbish we spout in class and we're sitting at the back where we usually sit and we bought Coke cans and Maltesers on the way like we usually do, but today I'm not here. I'm thinking about STDs. I'm thinking about that splitting sound. I'm thinking about blood.

'So what's up?'

'What?'

'Are you pissed off at me?'

'No.'

'So, what's wrong?'

'Nothing.'

'You'd normally be gloating by now.' Carl nudges me. 'What is it?'

'Shut up. Nothing.'

I was thinking last night about how I live in the country just outside the town, but the town centre is ten minutes away by car. It's about five miles and that's where the doctor is, and they don't even take patients without an appointment. Then I realised it was going to be Monday in a few hours, and I'd be going to school. I could take the bus in and then walk off the grounds.

I didn't sleep after. How could you sleep? I lay in bed around 2 a.m., after I had dealt with it all as best as I could, washed myself off and changed the bedsheets, and I thought, *So what now? Do I go to sleep?* I turned over and started to wiggle my leg in my pyjamas in the way that you do when you're not tired, but then I realised it was hurting to move. It was stinging. I got still, and stared at the wall. The wall is a light blue. My dad painted it himself just before Daniel was born, so I didn't feel threatened. The new baby was getting a brand-new room. We had just moved from the centre of Hemingway to the suburbs, to this massive house on Oakland Drive. The house was big enough, but they built an extension over the garage to house the new baby, and Dad painted it yellow. I walked in the new room when it was done and felt really bummed, because they were getting a perfect new baby, after getting over the shock of me, their old, faulty one. I was worried they were going to forget about me.

Then Dad said, 'So, what do you want your room to look like?' and I grinned. Sometimes I've felt so close to my dad. Sometimes not so much.

I chose light blue and I got blinds, which at the time felt really grown up. I was five, almost six. Dad did the roller work, and then built me a cupboard for my games consoles, which back then just included the Sega and a PlayStation One. This was before he worked all the time. He just used to work normal hours then: nine to six like Mum does. I helped paint the delicate bits around the door and windows, joyously ripping the masking tape off afterwards to reveal perfect straight lines of paint. I can't remember Mum being around much when we were decorating, but I remember her teaching me how to make the straight lines on the walls, how not to go over the edge. She was round with pregnancy, a huge bump that pushed against me when she stood behind me, holding my hand as we painted, then, her voice stern and strained as if her throat were constricted, telling me off when I went wrong.

Then Daniel was born. He is an awkward little guy, but I'm glad I've got a brother. I can't remember life before him much now. That time seems so hushed and temporary and unstable, as if we weren't yet living, as if we were waiting for Daniel to secure us in space, to make whole a family that wasn't yet fully complete.

The wall is grey in the dark, the night that Hunter comes in, when I'm lying there afterwards, pressed against the wall, breathing in and out, trying not to think. The pain is heightened with nothing else there, no sound or colour. It hums and grows, gripping my back. I screw up my eyes and bury my face in the sheets. I sit up again and quietly open the drawer next to my bed. No pills. I take out a pair of socks and put them on. I pick up a jumper on the floor. It's green and knitted and from Topman. I open the door to my room slowly, so it doesn't creak, and I walk downstairs, the socks dampening the sound of my feet.

I go down to the large living room, where my parents entertain people. Mum used to smoke all the time, before we were born, but now she only does it socially. It stinks, and it makes all the cushions in the living room stink, so Daniel and I never hang out there after she has. I know she's smoked that night, with all her friends over, because the smell is hanging in the air at the half-open door. The coffee table has wine glasses and bowls of nuts on it from their evening, but the room is quiet now, the lights off. The door to the living room is wood, with two panes of frosted glass in the top two-thirds of it. Next to it, towards the back of the house, is the small living room, which is cosier and has the TV in it. Opposite the little living room is the kitchen, with a full wood door. I walk beneath the stairs to the kitchen door, push it open, reach to the wall on my left and turn on the light.

My ghostly reflection appears in the window over the sink.

I walk towards the other me, pull out a drawer and get some Ibuprofen out of it. I pour a glass of water and down two pills. I think of chucking down a third then decide not to be stupid and dramatic.

The other me looks across the kitchen to the first me.

We have changed. We have split into two. The me surrounded by the window frame looks a little tired, but otherwise healthy and happy, confident, OK, normal. A fit, unremarkable, soon-to-be-sixteen-year-old boy, wearing a forest green jumper. My slim frame has been ameliorated by football and weights and a short course of hormones when I was thirteen. Testosterone and something else. I don't know. Mum wrote everything down. My chest is a good size. Not large but not small. Well-developed compared to other boys in my year, which has a lot of skinny, scrawny and spotty guys who don't play sports. I'm an OK height for my age, and I think I'm still growing. I'm five foot nine, nearly ten.

The round neck of the jumper is kind of eighties, because right now those kind of jumpers are all over the shops and I like them because they're knitted and warm. It suits my neck, which is smooth and a light golden colour from spending hours outside in the summer playing footy on the school field and going to Spain before school started.

My face is soft-jawed for a boy, but not too much, not remarkably. Maybe I just notice it because that's what the doctors told me the last time we saw them, that I am soft-jawed for a boy. There is no facial hair there, not even any sprouting. My nose is small to medium, my eyes are a light green-blue. I used to have a lot of freckles as a kid and now I have just a few, on the tops of my cheeks. My eyelashes are quite long, but there's really no reason, right now, for anyone to suspect that I'm anything other than a teenage boy.

But wait until my facial hair doesn't grow. Wait until I don't look any manlier. Wait until all the other guys in my year become men, and I stay smooth-chinned, under-developed, androgynous. Wait a year.

I never think about these things, but now I am thinking about them, touching my chin, peering closely at the pores of the other me. My hair is blond, the yellow-blond colour of a newborn chick, and slightly fluffy. It hangs down from a very slight side-parting, not lank, but full and nicely. The hair at the back of my neck is cut closer.

I like how the other me looks. I mean, I know there's a clock ticking. I don't know what will happen after I reach eighteen, but we didn't know what would happen after puberty, after thirteen, and we got through that. Mum and Dad have always been OK about it. We don't talk about it much but I've never been made to feel that it was a huge deal. I mean, I know it is, I guess.

The other me touches the back of his hair, where lying on a pillow has fluffed it up and tangled it. The other me looks relaxed. The other me looks like he did yesterday.

But the first me, the flesh and blood me feels . . . weird. I'm hollow. I'm blank. I'm going through the motions of walking and getting and swallowing and rinsing the glass and putting it on the sideboard but I am just. Not. Here. I can't be, because any sane person would be freaking out, and I don't feel much right now. I've gone into survival mode. I'm tired, and shaky, and I know if I'm not a blank, if I allow myself to feel, I'll shake and shake and shake until my legs give way.

I think back to our Sex Ed classes. So far we've had:

1. How boys and girls work. Black and white line drawings on sheets of A4. I felt, understandably, left out. I wondered where I fitted in.
2. Checking for breast and testicular cancer. Foam models.
3. Where babies come from. Plastic models of different sized wombs, which we had to 'fit' to different sized babies. The clue: the bigger the womb, the larger the baby. We were twelve. I go to a grammar school. It wasn't rough, let me put it like that.

4. Rolling a condom onto a carrot or banana. The teacher tried to buy all bananas but the market had run out. The carrots were not shaped like penises. I know. I piss at urinals; I also have one.
5. STDs. This was a slide show our form tutor had to show us. We had to guess what they were. He then looked at a sheet he had been given with the slides and told us we were wrong, then frowned in amazement, not knowing himself what the slides were. Halfway through he ran out the room and never came back.

So. I have to go to the doctor. I could take the school bus in then walk away from it, towards town, towards the doctor's surgery. They can't tell anyone; I saw it on the clinic wall when I went there with Carl for him to have an STD test. If you're under sixteen it's confidential. Still confidential, I mean. I don't think if you're nineteen they run and shout it to the masses in the waiting room or ring your parents or anything.

In the kitchen, I open the treats cupboard, which is high up so Daniel can't get in, although obviously he just stands on a chair. There are Twixes and KitKats and raisin-and-biscuit Clubs, which I love, but I don't feel like eating. My stomach feels sick and bruised. I pad through in my socks to the small living room.

The couch is soft and inviting, a hand-me-down from Dad's parents. I slump in it and my feet hug each other on the floor. Across from me, family photos on the marble mantelpiece above the fireplace smile and, for some reason, make me feel guilty.

The clock above the photos says it's two forty-five. I switch on the TV. *High Stakes Poker* is on. Daniel Negreanu and a behooded Phil Laak are hunched over their cards. Both have queen/ten.

'Brilliant. Negreanu.'

I turn around. 'Hi, Dad.'

'I saw the light on, pal. What are you doing awake?' Dad says, sleepily.

'Couldn't sleep.'

'Anything wrong?'

I shrug and shake my head, staring at the TV.

He clears his throat and sits down at the other end of the sofa, reaching across with one hand and ruffling my hair. 'Turn it up,' he says, smiling. 'Guilty pleasure.'

This is how I end up sat with my dad on the night Hunter came into my room. Dad doesn't know what is wrong, or even if there is anything wrong, but he stays awake, and when poker finishes, he puts on an action movie from the nineties that I used to love when I was little, and we watch John Cusack and Nicholas Cage on motorbikes chase John Malkovich on a fire engine until Mum and Daniel get up and we go through to eat breakfast.

Then Monday morning, on the bus, the rattling around making my groin hurt and my tummy ache, off the bus, onto the school grounds, a quick walk towards the ground gates and freedom and safety, then—

'Max Walker!'

I was so close to the gate. The head teacher's voice called my name behind me.

I stood still and looked at my feet. I screwed up my face, once, and let out a few long, staggered breaths.

'Max Walker!'

I was so close to the gate.

'Is the infamous Max running out on us?' This is rhetorical. With her next question she squints at me severely. 'You're not leaving school grounds, are you?'

'No.'

'You're just taking a walk around the car park before getting yourself to registration on time, aren't you?'

'Yes.'

'Registration is at eight forty-five, isn't it?'

'Yes.'

'Yes. So you're going there now, aren't you?'

I turned and walked past her, my head down. Empathy is not in Mrs Green's arsenal. So you don't want to show her your worry. She'll only sneer at you. Don't give her the pleasure. I walked numbly across the tarmac and into the school building.

First period is after assembly, 9.25 – 10.15 a.m. So my second chance to leave is at 10.15 after English Literature, although now Mrs Green'll be on the lookout. Most of the teachers here are petty, stupid, small people who feel it's a victory in their sad, little lives to stop you from living yours.

In class I don't listen as Carl tells me about the Germany–Belarus match. I also don't listen, along with Carl, as we get a lecture on *Wuthering Heights*. Instead, I stare at the paper in front of me. I look out the window to where the trees on the field stretch away to the horizon in flames of orange, ochre, yellow, green, gold and red. I smell the mix of autumn air and dust the English lab emits. I pick my nails. I shift in my seat. I press the nib of my biro hard against the page and it makes a dull clunk and slides up inside the pen shaft.

I think about the splitting sound last night and worry. I think about future pleasure. I think about scarring. I think about how every one of us is different, how every intersex person is different from the other, about what the doctors said, about different problems. I think about contraception, and condoms and pills. I think about Hunter coming inside me.

Why didn't you fight more? says my brain.

It really hurt, I say.

Yeah. Why didn't you fight more?

I don't know. This is going to sound crazy but . . . I felt like it was his right.

You're right, that does sound crazy.

I know. I can't explain it. I mean, it's Hunter. I've always done everything he wanted. But it was more that I was shocked, because of what he said. So few people know. No one's ever said anything like that to me before. But also . . . I don't know. All the way through, I just felt like apologising.

Apologising?

For being disgusting, having messed-up junk, moving in the wrong way and not knowing what to do.

What is wrong with you?

43

I don't KNOW.
'Max?'
'Mm?' I look up. Carl is above me.
'Bell's gone.'
'Oh.'

Ten-fifteen is not my lucky break. The corridors drag us forward. I try to think of something to say to Carl, some excuse for why I want to go off alone, but my brain is mush. Too tired, in a daze, I end up in Biology. I figure, what's one more lesson?

I sit drumming my shoe against the desk leg. I sit blankly, staring at the board, the words unreadable, the shapes of the letters unrecognisable.

At first break there are two teachers standing by the gates. I run out of time finding another exit. And then Geography happens. And then Chemistry.

It is lunch by the time I get out. I climb over this tall wooden gate out on the school field, which leads to an alleyway. I take my bag. I'm guessing I won't be feeling like going back after the doctors.

My school is in Hemingway, which is a town next to Oxford that's referred to as a suburb of Oxford a lot. The centre is one large crossroad and a market square, but it is a pretty busy place with lots of its own suburbs. When you're in the centre, though, it feels quite small. It's basically a chocolate-box type of town that American tourists freak out over. It's very *Harry Potter*. There are some old buildings and there is an Oxford college that has its campus here. The building is huge and beautiful and five hundred years old. The place is full of ducks. We're often late to school because you have to drive really slowly behind them sometimes when they're with their duck-lings on the road. Or sometimes there'll be like this one stupid duck, like a mallard or sometimes a Canada goose, that will just waddle very slowly down the centre of the main road, and there will be a traffic jam for literally a mile until someone gets out of the car, lifts the duck up and puts it on the pavement. The buildings in the centre of town are around the square and along one road called The Promenade. The doctor's surgery is set back from the shops, and slightly tucked behind the church.

It's definitely autumn now. Summer wasn't that hot, but it seemed to stay warm for a long time. Today there's a breeze that spikes your skin with cold. The leaves are turning beautiful colours and the first have already fallen. I prefer summer to the other seasons, for the heat. You can be out all day playing football and not even have to worry about bringing a T-shirt. But autumn is loveable. It's summer's dying cousin. It's somehow vulnerable, for the world to die so publicly. You feel tender about autumn.

I wrote that in an essay for my teacher, Ms Marquesa. I wasn't there when she fed back on the essays but Carl said she (and I'm quoting him verbatim) 'basically creamed'.

I'm trying to hurry along The Promenade, partly because of the cold and partly because I don't want anyone to see me, the Walker kid, Stephen Walker's kid, out of school. Everybody knows Dad. Most people know Mum. I get stopped in the street all the time by people I don't know, talking about how great they are, how much they do for the community, how much more safe the area has been since Dad has been in charge, what it does for property prices. But if I'm stopped today I'll crack. I'll cry. I'll faint. I'm so tired and out of it, and the pain in between my legs is really uncomfortable.

Finally I walk up the public footpath, past the church, and onto tarmac. This is where I stop, under a tree, at the corner of the surgery car park.

The surgery is an ugly dirty-salmon-pink-red and the bricks are too squared off and flawless. The windows are plastic, and the whole place is fronted by a waiting room with one wall of floor-to-ceiling windows. I stay under the tree, shaded from the harsh light out in the car park. There are a lot of people in the waiting room. There are lots of eyes. The counter where you go up and tell the receptionist why you want to see the doctor is at the far end. It's set up so people don't hear what you're saying, but the door to the waiting room is often open and in any case there's a window behind the reception into the waiting room through which they dole out medication and call people for appointments, so you can hear what the patients at the desk are saying.

It's so much nicer outside. If I stand here, very still, then nothing is happening. My eyes drift over the building and I weigh up my options.

What are you going to say in there?

Shh. Don't talk about it.

You're just going to walk in there and blurt it out?

Shh.

You're going to end up saying nothing. You'll go in to tell her and you'll chicken out and leave the surgery with eye drops.

Would you shut up? I'm thinking.

Max . . .

Shh.

Max . . . We need to go inside.

Sylvie

I only notice him because he's there for so long, just standing under a tree, completely still, frozen like ice. I noticed him when the clock was chiming quarter past one. I didn't think anything of it, then at twenty to two, I see him still there.

It's pretty cold, but he's just standing broodingly under this tree and staring at the surgery. I know him. I know this guy enough to know that Max Walker just isn't the brooding type. He's the football-playing-wonder-boy type. He's one of the most popular of the popular crowd. He's the son of the wondrous Walkers, the barristers who were in the newspapers because they prosecuted that media billionaire. Max Walker is the boring, bland, blond, golden boy type. He's the sort of person who will always be referred to as 'Max Walker' and never as 'Max'. I don't usually go for schoolboys, but if I did, it wouldn't be Max Walker. There are a few guys in school who are older-looking and dark-haired, a bit taller and more muscular. But I know Max Walker has his share of skinny bambi-legged admirers. They trail around after him during lunch. Whenever I see him in the corridor someone is saying hi to him. He always says hi back, but you can't read too much into that.

I watch him not moving. He's a few feet away, but I almost don't talk to him. I almost get caught up in all that nervousness about talking to the popular kid, but then I tell myself off, I tell myself to stop being so scared, stop judging people before I know them, stop being scared of taking a chance, and just freaking say

'Hi.'

He looks up.

'Oh, hello.'

I don't read anything into it.

47

I look down at him, intrigued despite myself. The graveyard is to the side of and sort of above the surgery, on a little hill. So I'm sat on the grass, next to the wall, but I'm above Max, looking at him through the branches of the little tree.

'It's Max Walker, right?' I say, because for some reason it's good etiquette to pretend you don't really know someone's name, even when you've been at school with them for four years.

'Yeah. Hello, Sylvie.'

'Hey!' I say, surprised that Golden Boy Walker has even registered me. 'How do you know my name?'

'You sat behind me in statistics last year.'

'Ohhhh, yeahhhh,' I say, remembering how badly I messed up that exam. I got drunk with Toby the night before and have to retake it this year. This thing, it sucks: if you're smart you get put ahead in Maths, so you take GCSE Statistics in Year Ten and GCSE Maths in Year Eleven. Believe me, they do not expect smart people to be drunk during the exam and fail in the way that I did. Super fail.

'How did you do in the GCSE?' I ask.

'Um, good.' He nods and swallows, tossing his blond hair out of his eyes like Justin-freaking-Bieber.

'Wait, I remember. You got an A star, didn't you?' I say with a grin. 'That's so sickening. I flunked it.'

He smiles pleasantly, but kind of blankly, like he doesn't know what to say but wants to be polite.

'So, how are you?' he asks, as if he hasn't been listening to anything I've said before.

I raise my eyebrows. 'Great. What are you doing here?'

He looks over to the surgery. Then it is obvious to both of us what he's doing. Nobody is so nervous they stand for half an hour outside the surgery for a doctor's appointment they've been blasé enough about to schedule. Emergency appointment. Which means one thing for a guy in our year: STD check-up. He looks really uncomfortable and shifts his legs in an embarrassed way. I clock a look at his crotch to figure out if he's itching himself or not. Wow, I hope for his sake it's not crabs.

48

'Did you do someone without a condom?' I say, teasing to communicate this: that I'm cool to talk to, that I'm feeling sorry for him, that I understand, that I'm trying to make him feel less weird.

Instead of feeling better because of what I've said, he blushes red, his mouth turns down and he shrugs.

'Are you OK?' I ask.

He looks up and forces a smile that clearly takes a lot of effort. 'Yeah, I'll be fine. Just don't feel well.' He shrugs. 'So, why are you bunking off?'

'I'm bleeding and hormonal and I hate the world today.'

He laughs. 'I know that feeling.'

'I bet you don't, actually,' I say. 'You don't know pain until you've wanted to commit suicide because your back hurts so bad. Period pain is the worst.'

He continues to smile but it fades a little and he searches for something to say. 'Well, I hope you feel better. You should write more while you're bunking off. I really liked that poem you read in assembly last year about your ex-boyfriend.'

'That's so weird you remember that!' I exclaim, much too happily, and then I can't think of anything more to say.

'Yeah.' He nods.

There is an awkward silence.

'Pity you got cut off by the headmistress before you could finish.'

'Well, you know, censorship,' I say. I brandish my notebook and pen. 'I'm actually writing now.'

'Good. Cool.'

There's a pause and I say, 'Well, I'd better get going.'

'Other bunking-off spots to occupy?' he asks, in a sort of sugary way. I feel like he's teasing me.

'No, I'm going to go get something to eat. Do you want to, like . . . come?'

He hesitates. 'I can't.'

'What about after you're done?'

'Um . . .' He looks down again and chews his lip

absentmindedly. After a too-long pause, he says, 'I'm sorry, I shouldn't.'

'Suit yourself,' I say, kind of relieved. I'm not great with company. I wish I was. But I'm not. Hey, somebody's got to be the loner.

I scoot my legs over the wall and jump down beside him. He's standing next to my bike, and he steps back as I get on it. He does it to give me some space to get on, but then he does a little second take at what I'm wearing: leather hotpants, long black socks, white Converse, a see-through top with a black bra, and a long black velvet coat. I'm aware I don't dress like a sixteen-year-old. It's one reason my boyfriends all tend to be older. Plus I find it never helps to wear school clothes when you're bunking off, or shitty clothes when you're feeling like shit. Rookie mistakes, both.

'Good manners, haven't you?' I say, as he helps me put my backpack on. His fingers brush the fabric of my top and he gives a kind of embarrassed laugh, like I've caught him staring, which I have.

I push down my right foot and circle my bike once around the surgery car park.

'Hey, I saw your cousin driving through town yesterday night. Around midnight?'

'Oh,' he says, the smile dropping instantly from his face.

'What's his name?'

He seems to consider for a second, before answering, 'Hunter'.

'He's kind of a dick, isn't he?' I say casually. 'I've seen him around at parties. He gets way too stoned and he's pretty rude.'

Max Walker's face is very still. He shrugs.

'Don't you think he's a dick?'

He shrugs again and looks away towards the door of the surgery. 'I have to go in now,' he says quietly.

''Kay. See you around.' I hold up one hand in a salute, heading for the car park exit. I look back. He's looking over at me, getting smaller as I bike away.

'Bye,' he says, and lifts up his hand to wave, wagging it back and forth like little kids do. 'Bye,' he repeats.

I bike away, thinking maybe Max Walker isn't so bad after all. In my wing mirror he watches me ride, his head rolls down and he stares at his feet. His shoulders rise and fall and I realise he is sighing. He raises his head, bites his lip, regards the surgery in front of him solemnly, and he steps out onto the tarmac.

Archie

Medicine, my field of science, is always evolving and in flux. Some studies are bound to fail; methods of care we use today may be extinct in a few decades; people we treat still die. Approaches being used in busy centres like London and Manchester may not reach country hospitals for several years after their approval.

Most things here in Hemingway – including traffic, pedestrians, the passing of time and changes to medical care – are slow.

I moved here from Delhi almost twenty years ago to train as a general practitioner in London. During my studies, I spent six months in paediatrics at St Thomas' Hospital, and came into contact with birth defects, deformities and sometimes illnesses that were fatal in the early years of a person's life. The trick is to treat the sick like you treat the well. More than anything, they need to feel normal.

When I qualified as a GP, I moved to a practice in small, intimate Hemingway. Watching patients carefully, closely, over years makes an art out of diagnosis and prognosis. I am my patients' first point of contact for diagnosis, and I provide continuing treatment, advice and evaluation for all their medical conditions. Perhaps, if I tried, I could predict the health of Hemingway's individuals over the course of their lives. I could tell you who might be at high risk of cancer or diabetes or liver failure. I could tell you which children will become obese, which might develop eating disorders, and which might have problems with drugs.

Due to my experience, I take most of the patients who are under twenty-one. It has become evident to me, after twelve years at Hemingway, that I have most contact with my young patients before the age of five and between the ages of thirteen and eighteen. I see the under-fives for vaccinations, chicken pox, colic, whooping cough, scarlet fever, the mumps, diarrhoea and parental hypochondria. I see the teenagers because of sex.

Thirteen seems young to start talking about sex, but I have heard it said that children are getting older. I think adults are getting younger. I also suspect, however, that the sexuality of adolescents has not changed in nature since we were apes. In fact, I am certain that in medieval times, in Hippocrates' days and through the somewhat conservative Victorian era, thirteen-year-olds have been engaged in sexual activity, teenagers have procreated, and the LGBT issues we think of as contemporary existed in all their variations and multiplicity.

What has changed, perhaps, is that our ability to connect with these people in our society has grown via the internet. Some policy has advanced because of this, and is clearly outlined in best-practice documents and in medical school curricula, but some areas are still being debated. In particular, medical approaches to trans, intersex and asexual people can vary greatly between jurisdictions.

I know that our practice is ahead of most in our approach to these teenagers, but there are some areas where I do not know enough, and we need to improve. Like most clinics, like the curricula, like the policy-makers, we are struggling to keep up with scientific advancements, and also with our patients.

Between my list of patients and the adolescents who come to the drop-in sexual health sessions I run after hours at the clinic on Tuesdays and Thursdays, I look after about 700 adolescents, five of whom I know to experience some degree of gender dysphoria. About thirty have discussed a non-heterosexual preference with me. A number have come in to the after-hours clinic upset because they don't 'get' sex. One hundred and thirteen are on the pill. Three have had abortions in the past year. I treat the occasional sexually transmitted disease. About eighty per cent of all my patients come to the clinic for free condoms.

As I run the late night clinics, I often work from 2 p.m. until

10 p.m. Today I pull my car into the drive in the early afternoon and the leaves crunch as I walk towards the doors.

Ahead of me reception is busy as always. A blond boy, a Hemingway teen, dressed in the high school's uniform of suit trousers, white shirt, a black V-neck jumper, black tie and blazer, leans in close to the service window, his hand on the frame. The warmth of the low autumn sun is caught in his fair hair and on the skin of the other patients next to him, creating a blinding glow that makes it difficult to see. I lift my hand up to shade my eyes. As I move nearer a few of them turn hopefully towards me. To my left, the cluster of heads in the waiting room lifts, and I feel, as I usually do, bad that I can't see all of them, that I will only be taking one person through to my office to release them from the long wait and bland magazines. Then the blond boy steps forward, out of the light.

He moves towards me purposefully and his lips part.

'Can I help you?' I ask.

He smiles and glances at my nametag. 'Dr Verma? Can I talk to you?'

'Have you made an appointment? What's your name?'

He hesitates, then whispers softly as I pass by, my step brusque, 'Max Walker.'

I stop and turn around to look at him. As an older couple pass, Max ducks his head down and hair falls over his face.

The Walker family is a mainstay of the *Hemingway Post*, and all the local press. Max's father and mother both frequently appear on the evening news. His mother advises people who call in on legal matters and his father often gives statements about current cases. They are both lawyers of some kind, and Max's dad, particularly, is something big in local law enforcement. But I cannot recall having met Max before.

'Are you a patient of mine?' I ask.

'The receptionist says so.'

I look towards the waiting room. People watch Max over their magazines.

'It's urgent? Will it be quick?'

Max nods emphatically.

'Alright then,' I say. 'Let's be quick.'

'Thanks.' He smiles, visibly relieved.

I slip into the office and murmur to the receptionist, 'Hold my list, OK? And I need Max Walker's file.'

I escort Max briskly to my room and close the door, just as the office phone starts ringing. 'Let me just get that,' I say to Max, slinging my bag on the table. It's the receptionist.

'No, I said Max Walker.'

Max sits down in the chair opposite me.

'No, Walker. W-a-l-k-e-r.'

I roll my eyes at the phone for Max's benefit. He gives a weak grin and looks ready to burst into tears.

'Yes, that's it,' I say into the phone, and replace the receiver.

Max is staring worriedly at an appointment slip left on my desk and wriggling uncomfortably on the chair.

I sit in my chair opposite him. 'Now, what have you come to talk to me about today?'

Max takes a deep breath, but falters. 'Is this confidential?'

'Yes.'

This is not strictly true. There are various grounds on which I am able to break confidentiality, and I have done so before. But, by and large, confidentiality is key to being trusted, so I don't explain the nuances of that statement. Particularly when it comes to helping young people.

He looks doubtful, but swallows, attempting to smile. I watch it fading gradually from his face, beat by beat, coming back as he pushes for it, fading away as he loses faith.

'OK, um . . .' he says, wetting his lips. 'I need a morning-after pill.'

The click of the door interrupts us, and we are silent as the receptionist slips in and places Max's file on my desk. She leaves, closing the door behind her.

I nod. 'May I ask why?'

He swallows and shifts forward then backward in the chair.

'Is it for a girl? Because I'm afraid she has to come in.'

He shakes his head. 'No, it's for me.' He pauses. 'You should probably read my file.'

I reach for his file. The cover reads: Max Walker, D.O.B 25 September 1996. I look up.

'It's alright, I'll wait.' He looks over at the window. I watch him struggling to smile to himself, to grin, like it's a drag, like it's an irony. I close the file without reading it.

'Don't you just want to tell me what is relevant?'

He looks back at me, alarmed, then breathes out slowly, calming himself. 'Alright.' His hand brushes his hair behind his ear and he blinks. 'I'm intersex.'

'I see.'

'Like, a hermaphrodite.'

'I understand. I haven't seen you before, have I? We run a clinic on Tuesdays and Thur—'

He interrupts me. 'I had specialists. I mean, I have specialists. So I haven't seen you about . . . anything to do with this before. I came in once when I had a stomach bug, but I think you weren't here. I saw a nurse.'

I nod. 'Wouldn't you prefer to see your specialists now?'

'Well . . . I can't drive. They're in London. On Harley Street.'

'Do you want me to arrange for someone to take you to the train station in Oxford?'

'I don't want to see them. They're . . . they ask a lot of questions and stuff.'

'I see.'

'Can't I just see you?'

'Yes, of course you can. I deal with all sorts of conditions. I have to warn you, I haven't had too much experience with intersexuality.'

'Have you had any?'

'Yes, I have. I've worked with some cases featuring genital variations when I was training. But if you like we can talk about anything you want to and then if I feel I don't know enough to advise you, we can look at specialists – with your permission. Does that sound good?'

Max tucks a leg underneath himself, shifting nervously, and nods.

'I'm just going to scan your file, now I know what I'm looking for.'

''Kay,' he whispers.

I look down at his file again and open it. Max is quiet while I flip through. Most people have fairly slim A5 files. Max's is bulging out of the cardboard folder, most of it faxed over from several NHS hospitals and, later, a private clinic on Harley Street. The papers include: possible diagnoses from his birth, then final diagnosis with several addendums added in later years, advice and opinions of a number of doctors on operations, what should be done, what could be done, preserving fertility, later references to a consensus statement on management of intersex patients with a redefined diagnosis for Max, then a list of hormones advised and then used for treatment, including documentation of injections and courses of pills. Then there are the photos. Max as a baby, Max as a toddler, Max as a four-year-old with a piece of paper held in front of his face for anonymity, while green-gloved hands prise apart his legs. The photographs cease. There is a full page of notation on parental reaction to the diagnosis, starting from birth and ending two years ago, just before Max's fourteenth birthday. Most records seem to end at that time.

I make a note to scan Max's file into the computer. It's much too cumbersome in paper form, and we are trying, slowly, to make the move over to digital.

In my peripheral vision I notice Max watching me curiously and I look up from the files.

'Max, are you sure you need this pill?'

He nods, biting his fingernail. He notices me looking at it and lowers his hand. 'Sorry.'

I smile. 'I don't mind if you bite your nails.'

He shrugs.

'Did your specialists say you were fertile?'

'They said there was a slim chance.'

'You get periods?'

He blushes. 'Not very often.'

'This says you have a uterus?'

57

He shrugs. 'Yeah.'

'And you haven't had it removed at any time?'

Max shakes his head.

'Are you on any type of contraception?'

'No.'

'Just condoms?'

'No,' Max replies miserably. He opens his mouth, as if to say something, then shuts it firmly.

'Do your specialists know you're sexually active?'

'Um . . .' He does not continue, instead morosely ripping the top of his thumbnail off.

'Didn't they ask you about it?'

'I haven't seen them in ages and I . . . wasn't then. They usually talk to Mum, not to me, anyway.'

I point to the file. 'These notes seem to run out almost two years ago. Is that perhaps when you last saw them?'

'Maybe.'

'Right.' I nod and scan the last few pages.

Suddenly Max pipes up, louder than before, 'I'm not fertile in the . . . guy way.'

I frown, not understanding. 'So—'

'No!' Max is suddenly upset.

'What do you mean, "No"?' I ask, confused.

'It's not . . . I didn't . . . I can't *self* do it!'

'Self-fertilise? No, of course you can't, Max. I wasn't suggesting that.'

'Um, OK.' He swallows, calming down. 'Sorry. You . . . you can't be both, can you?'

'Fertile in two ways? I've haven't heard of it. Medicine isn't often a finite science, but I don't think it's possible. In humans,' I add.

I make a mental note to drag out my old textbooks at home and look up intersex diagnoses online. There are many, with many different causes. While most are classified as 'disorders', some are, to a certain extent, reversible, some are defects, caused by the body's lack of hormones, or faulty hormone receptor, and some are to do with the sex chromosomes.

Studying for a medical degree in England, our curriculum never went into much depth about intersex disorders. In fact, I recall when training that, on the odd instance they came up, we referred to them as hermaphroditism. The words have changed, and I wonder why.

I frown at the file. It is true that I have dealt with some patients with ambiguous genitalia, but not to this extent. I flick through it again, trying to find the notes on fertility, but nothing jumps out at me.

Max pulls his jumper over his fingers and wipes his face. His cheeks are red.

'Max? Are you OK?' I say to him. 'I'm sorry to ask all these questions, I'm just trying to ascertain—'

'I just need a pill! Can't I get one?'

'Of course you can. Of course.'

'Can I have the thing that makes you not get an STD too?'

'Excuse me?'

'Isn't there something that stops that?'

'You mean HIV prevention medication?'

'Yeah.'

'Do you think you might have been exposed to HIV?'

Max looks confused. 'I don't know. Probably not HIV.'

'There's nothing else that we have preventative medicine for.'

'Oh.'

'Would you like the medication?'

Max thinks. I can't see his eyes properly, behind his hair. He's looking down at his knees. He rubs an eye with his sleeve again. 'Probably not.'

'OK. Alright, let me get a Levonelle pack.'

I stand up and he looks at me, lost.

'The emergency contraceptive. I'll just be a minute.'

I put my hand reassuringly on his shoulder and sweep out the door.

Max

This is the most embarrassing, horrible day of my life, and if I can just get through it, stay blank, breathe in and out, keep smiling, keep nodding, it'll be over, and tomorrow will be better, and the next day will be better than that and soon it'll be like it never happened.

I'm never going to hang around with Hunter again and in less than two years he'll have gone to uni and I won't see him at all. Maybe our parents will stop being friends and drift apart. Maybe we'll move away. You never know what will happen in the future. Things often work out even when you really, really think they won't, like that time when I was little and I was convinced, utterly convinced, that Mum wasn't going to come home, and I didn't know why at the time but I knew she wasn't, whether she was dead, or had left us, I don't know, but she did come home, she did. Dad was angry at her, and I shouted at him not to be because I thought she would leave again, but she didn't, she stayed and everything I thought would happen didn't happen. Sometimes things just aren't what you think they are, and even when things seem really bad, it can work out. Everything can work out and go back to normal. If I can just get the pill, then I'll buy some more Ibuprofen on the way home at the chemists, or in Sainsburys, because then I can go through self-service and I won't have to talk to anyone to explain why a Walker kid is out of school during school time, then I can get home, say to Mum I'm ill and go to sleep.

Then maybe tomorrow I'll call in sick. No, I don't want to miss school tomorrow! I've been looking forward to tomorrow for ages. Fuck Hunter, I'm not going to let him ruin my day. OK, so tomorrow will be good and then I'll forget about it, minute by minute it'll trickle out of my brain until it means nothing, and it just hasn't happened.

So. First I get the pill, then Sainsburys. What if the pill is too late? No, it works up to twenty-four hours after, that's what they said in class. It's been . . . fourteen hours. That's OK. Besides, Dr Verma seems to think I'm not fertile. I think she thinks that anyway. She's a bit brusque and clinical. She's like, let's get to it, matter of fact. I guess that's good in a doctor but it makes me feel more shitty. I thought I'd be able to talk about everything, but I can't bring myself to tell her about Hunter.

I just have to get through today. Then things will go back to normal. Until next year, when maybe all the other guys will have facial hair, and then in two years, when everyone will be having sex but me, and then in ten years, when everyone will be getting married and having kids but me, and over the years, the kissing will dry up because I won't have sex with people, because I won't go out with people, because if I have sex with someone, they'll see, and then they won't want to go out with me anyway. Because I'm a freak. Because I'm freakish.

Archie

'Right. I have to ask you a few questions before I can give you the pill.'

The door swings shut and I take my seat opposite Max.

''K,' he mumbles.

'Oh!' I turn to face him and speak softly. 'Don't cry, it's OK.'

Max puts both hands, gripping sweater sleeves, over his face. His skin is red and tears fall onto his lap. He sobs something into his palms.

'Pardon?'

'I hate it.'

I hesitate, not knowing what to do. I end up reaching out and squeezing his arm. 'Do you mean being intersex? Do you get upset about your condition a lot?' I ask.

He shakes his head and his light hair swings back and forth. 'It never comes up.'

'At home?'

'Well, we never talk about it but . . . it's never been an issue. It's just a thing. I don't know. It's one of those things you just have to accept.'

'Haven't your doctors ever talked to you about operations or medication?'

'I don't know. Like I said, they usually talk to Mum and Dad. I did have some hormone injections and pills and stuff a few years ago.'

'OK. Well, if it makes you this upset, maybe . . . we should talk to your parents about it? Do you want me to call them?'

'NO!'

'OK, OK, sorry.'

'You won't, will you?'

'I'll only call them if you ask me.'

'OK. Well, no.'

'Sorry,' I say reassuringly, patting his arm. I open the Levonelle packet and take out a piece of paper. 'If you can just read this for me. It lists the possible side effects of the pill, and I just need you to sign here to say you understand. Did the unprotected sex occur in the last seventy-two hours?'

Max nods and reads the paper, holding his hands in his lap, occasionally lifting one up to wipe a stray line of moisture away from a cheek.

'Can I just have the pill now?' he mumbles. He's so wretched, it's upsetting even for an old-timer like me.

He's oddly despondent, actually. I study him carefully. Something just doesn't quite fit in this scene: an uncaring mood, a lack of eye contact, a blankness. As I watch him avoid my eyes, shuffling in his chair uncomfortably and worriedly chewing a nail, I remember seeing him before.

It was last summer, and I had recently read about his mother winning a landmark case in the paper. The article said that Karen Walker, if I recall her name correctly, was a barrister. The newspaper focused on Karen's career, rather than the case, and there was a picture of her family, including Max, at a black tie affair.

Later that day I had been at the cinema, and I recognised Max. He was holding hands with Olivia Wasikowski, another patient of mine who had come into the clinic to have an implant fitted a few weeks before. As I noticed them both, Max put his hands on Olivia's cheeks, leaned in and kissed her.

Looking at him now, remembering this, a thought rolls into my cerebral cortex like it belongs there, like a broken shoulder snapped back into place, and I feel so incredibly stupid I close my eyes and shake my head at myself.

I clear my throat. 'Max. I'm sorry to ask this so forwardly. Are you attracted to boys?'

Max's mouth opens. Then his hand reaches up to it and suppresses any words that were forming. He shakes his head.

'What I'm asking is, did you consent to sexual intercourse?'

Max's hair shakes again from side to side.

'That's why you're asking for the emergency contraceptive pill?'

His hair gives a tiny nod. He looks up nervously.

'Are you in any pain?'

A tear falls down his cheek and he wipes it away and sniffs.

'OK. Do you want to get up on the bed and let me have a look at you?'

Max sighs, as if he has seen this coming. A thought flickers through my mind: he must be used to having doctors looking at his genitals. An intersex diagnosis is not only something that must be studied for prognosis; to many doctors it's interesting. We see so few cases. My own curiosity is piqued, but I don't let on. Max's eyes slip to the side and dilate, becoming distant. He nods.

As a doctor, I've discovered the answers are always between the lines, somewhere in the landscape of the body. Physical evidence speaks louder than words. Evidence is all over Max's face. His bottom lip presses nervously against his top one. I nod, resolved.

'I'll just give you a minute to get undressed for me. Pop this sheet over yourself and sit up on the bed with your head back here, OK?'

I pat the bed and hand him the sheet. He nods again, almost wearily, and I step outside.

Daniel

It's my brother's birthday tomorrow so I want to make him a card, but the teacher, Miss Jameson, is saying that we have to pack up now, because it's story time.

Why should we have to pack up now? That is my question. It's completely ridiculous having to stick to a schedule like we're babies that need napping and feeding and our bottoms cleaned. It's stupid. I'm going to take these scissors and sit in the corner of the class, and I can listen to the stupid story while I do the card for Max. I'm doing one of those stupid cards where you fold a piece of A4 white paper into four and then you cut a boy shape in it so that you get four boys and they're all holding hands. Then I'm going to colour them in and I'll make them me, Mum, Dad and Max, although actually the Mum one will still look like a boy. Oh well, I'll just draw her in pink trousers and then I can stick some hair on from another bit of paper later. Anyway, this card is actually going to be awesome though, because here's the special bit: they're all going to be robots, and I'm giving them all a gun I've specially designed for them.

Hmm. Miss Jameson is waddling over to me, like a duck. Mum told me off for calling Miss Jameson a duck. We're not to say Miss Jameson is a duck. Anymore.

'Daniel, it's story time now.'

'Yes. I know.'

'Everybody's waiting. You don't want to ruin their story time, do you?'

'No. I'm not making my card *in front of them*.'

'Yes, but we can't do story time without everyone sitting in a circle, can we?'

'Yes.'

'No, we can't.'

'Yes, you can.'

'No, we can't.'

'Look, Miss Jameson, if anyone is ruining story time, it's you, because you can do it and you won't.'

'Well.' Miss Jameson puts her hands on her hips. 'I'm not going to because you're being a naughty boy. Now, you put down that card or I'll throw it in the bin!'

I frown and mutter very quietly, 'Duck.'

'Daniel Walker, put that card down! Do you want to keep it? I'll throw it away if you don't put it down now!'

She takes my hand and I shake it off.

'I'M JUST MAKING A CARD,' I say, really loudly so she'll understand and leave me alone. 'GET YOUR STUPID HANDS OFF ME.'

'Don't you dare yell at me, Daniel! Stop being a naughty boy! Look, everyone.' Miss Jameson turns to the class. 'Daniel is being naughty and so we can't have story time until he acts like a good boy and sits down with us all.'

All the other boys and girls look at me sympathetically. It's so unfair. It's Miss Jameson's fault that her stupid rules mean that for some stupid reason I can't make a card for my brother AND listen to a story at the same time.

I sit there in silence and I hold onto my card and I don't look at her until Miss Jameson says, 'Right!' She leans down and grabs my wrist really hard and I push her off with my right hand and she starts screaming just like me, but louder and hootier, as if she is both an owl and the victim of a shooting.

66

Max

I lie back on the bed. It's spongy and slender. I wait to feel her hands. I look at her nametag: Dr Archie Verma. When did they start putting first names on doctors' badges? I don't remember that from all the specialists. I never knew their first names. They always spoke over me, to Mum or Dad or to other doctors. They rarely asked me stuff, even when I could have just told them the answer. Dad said we had to be careful how much we told them, so I kept my mouth shut, while they pried around me, poking me with their stubby, plastic-gloved fingers. I was an interesting case study for them, an experiment. I've never thought about it before in great detail. But as I wait for Dr Verma to poke at me, I remember what it felt like on the cold, steel tables in the clinic in London. The eyes, the shaking heads. I just used to get a lollipop from Mum and look away.

When is Archie Verma going to touch me? I hold my breath, waiting for it.

She puts the sheet back over me.

'OK, Max, you've definitely had a tear down there, but I can't tell without cleaning where it is or if I need to put in any stitches. I'm going to take a few samples, and then I'm going to clean you up with some saline solution, OK? And then we'll find out where the bleeding is coming from.'

I nod compliantly and she goes away and comes back with a bottle of liquid and some other stuff, which makes a clank when she puts it down on the table.

Then I feel a pulling. 'Ow.'

'I'm sorry. This will hurt but it's important, OK?'

''Kay.'

I shut my eyes and try to think about football, running, the outdoors, fresh autumn air, leaves that crunch, girls' lips, bonfire night, and then the uncomfortable feeling stops and Dr Verma says, 'It's over.'

Then she uses a cloth to dab hesitantly at me. I watch, not saying anything still. She's much more gentle than the specialists. She looks up and crooks her mouth at me apologetically.

'Nearly done,' she says quietly. She takes the cloth away. 'I'm just going to press in a few places, and you tell me if it hurts, OK?'

I nod and she presses around me. 'No . . . no . . . no . . . YES . . . yes . . . no.'

'OK, I don't usually do this, but I'm going to put in one stitch. You're being very brave.'

She gets up, takes off her gloves and fetches a clean pair.

'Actually, Max,' she goes over to her desk and brings me a pill and then a glass of water from the tap, 'can you take this?'

I nod and swallow it.

'I'm going to prescribe you some strong painkillers as well, but you have to promise me you won't exceed the dose.'

' 'Kay.'

'This is a local anaesthetic.' She rubs a liquid on me and turns away for a minute, screwing tops onto some vials with sticks in them. She writes labels in tiny handwriting and sticks them on the vials. Then she turns back to me and asks me to close my eyes.

I feel a tugging and then she says it's done. I put my clothes back on behind the curtain, and she tells me what medicines she's going to give me. Before she lets me off the bed, she rolls up my sleeve and takes a blood sample in a needle from my arm.

She talks to me while she's doing it, giving me more instructions, but my head swims, and she gives me a look and says she'll write everything down so I don't forget.

'Max,' she says, business-like, rolling down my sleeve. 'I want to ask you something.'

I try to focus, as Dr Verma looks serious.

'Do you think it's going to happen again?'

'No.'

She stares at me, like she's trying to assess whether I'm telling the truth. 'Are you sure?'

I nod.

'Max, I have an obligation if I think you're likely to be assaulted again to go to the police.'

'No!' I shout, suddenly terrified.

'But I'm not going to,' she says. 'Not without your permission, because you've told me it's not going to happen again and I believe you. But . . . do you want me to contact the police?'

'Do I . . . ?' I'm surprised, weirdly I guess. I hadn't thought about it. 'No.'

'I could go with you.'

I shake my head. 'I don't want anyone to know.'

She sort of nibbles her lip.

'Your parents don't have to find out,' she says.

'My dad's the Crown Prosecutor.'

She takes a breath in and holds it for a second, then nods, letting it out. 'Yes. I see.'

My dad prosecutes all the criminals that the police pick up. He's in charge. He oversees every case that's tried in our area.

'I don't want even . . . I don't want anybody to know.'

Dr Verma nods, and says quietly, 'I took some samples. So I have his DNA.'

'You do?' I look over to the vials as she collects them and puts them on her desk.

'Definitely.'

I grimace, and don't ask her how she knows for sure.

'I can store them, and I can also get the samples analysed, so that if you wanted to go to the police, all the evidence would be here.'

She must see that I look uncomfortable, because she says, 'It can just be between us, unless you tell me otherwise.'

I nod.

'So? Do you want me to call someone from the local station? They could come see us here. We don't even have to leave the office. We could ask them not to tell your dad.'

She looks at me really nicely, but I'm just a blank. I'm just tired. I just want it to be over.

'I don't want anyone to know,' I say again.

Karen

The first thing out of my mouth when I arrive at Daniel's school to take him home is straight from the Book of Bad Parenting, 'What is wrong with you?'

Damn it, I think.

'What's wrong with you, Karen?' he asks immediately, and I resist an urge, a truly terrible urge, to slap him right across the mouth.

I am a terrible parent, I think. *I am not cut out for parenting.*

I try to gather myself together. The heat of the case I had been arguing, the indignation, the adrenaline from the win (fifteen years in prison), the frustration of having to leave to pick up Daniel, to pick up Daniel for something so callous, so beneath him, so disgusting, something that I will have to pay for in appearing to be calm and in control and fawning at parent–teacher conferences; everything is coursing through me, becoming forward momentum, and I have to remind myself to take everything a step at a time, not to look at the big picture, to breathe slowly, calm down and stop myself from reaching out, leaning forward and shaking him.

My mother grew up in Ireland before she moved to Yorkshire and met my father, and I am unhappy to say I sometimes fall back on her old Irish Catholic parental tactics when I am frustrated. It happens today, and I choose to inflict guilt upon Daniel in an attempt to make him sorry for hitting his teacher in the face with scissors.

'You know better than that, Daniel,' I say, shaking my head. 'I'm so, so disappointed in you.'

'I didn't *hit* her. I *touched* her.'

I grab at his arm, attempting to pull him up, to get him out of the school before someone sees us, and he pushes me away.

I often feel out of my depth with Daniel. It is possible that I would have felt exactly the same way had Max been normal, I suppose. But he wasn't. He was easy, if you didn't think about his problem. He was perfect and reasonable and sweet to a fault, and sometimes I wish Daniel could be like Max: cuddly, obedient, always close by.

Everything is a fight with Daniel, everything is a trial and it all makes me think I'm such a bad parent, such a bad mother. It reminds me of the conviction I had when we first found out Max was different from other babies – that I had failed as a mother, that I wasn't cut out for the job, – and I feel heart-broken again, like I'm back in the hospital sixteen years ago.

Steve says it's because I care so deeply about Daniel that I get so frustrated with him. If I didn't care, I wouldn't feel so irritated.

I sit next to Daniel, exhausted.

'I didn't hit her,' he says miserably.

I study the mural of staff photographs on the wall. When Max went to primary school there were four teachers in total: three class teachers and a headmaster. Now I count twenty-four teachers and 'support staff'. Have children become exponentially worse in the six years between Max and Daniel? I imagine the support staff in a milieu of screaming, shrieking, hitting little terrors.

'Do you believe me?' Daniel asks.

I turn to him. I think about this for a minute.

'Yes.'

Daniel turns sadly towards the mural. 'Thanks,' he says.

'We should go home,' I say suggestively, as if putting it on the table. *It's just an option,* my tone says. *We can sit here for the next five hours if you want.*

'OK,' he says.

Suddenly the irritation turns a corner and I feel a rush of empathy for Daniel. He's not easy, but it's not easy being him. He is awkward with everyone; he grew up too fast having a much older brother; he talks like a mini-politician because of his father; and he is quick to temper, which he gets from me. Max inherited all our best attributes, and Daniel all our worst.

He's bright, but he doesn't have Max's concentration in class. He's a B+ student. He's obsessive-compulsive. Physically he is small, inheriting his height perhaps from my mother's side, yet he is bony. He has my proliferation of childhood freckles and childhood scrapes, an inherited tendency towards being bitten by mosquitoes, tripping, accidents. He once shot himself in the eye with a friend's BB gun, resulting in a nightmare trip to the hospital for him and Steve, while Max and I waited anxiously at home for them.

My funny little man, I think, looking at Danny's curly strawberry-blond hair.

I put my arm out spontaneously. The bottom length of it touches his shoulders, just fractionally, just the start of a hug, gently. My right arm goes around his front. I lean in to kiss his hair.

'Get off!' Daniel shakes his head aggressively, hitting my teeth with his skull, lurching away from me.

I cry out, my hand flying to my mouth.

'Come on then,' Daniel says, sliding off the chair. He walks over towards the secure door.

I take a breath. I tell myself it's going to be OK. We're going to go home and I'll make dinner and he'll calm down.

I pick up my coat and walk over, touching the door release button, high up the wall above Daniel's head. The doors are released, we step through and head for my car in silence.

Archie

I sit back down at my desk as Max readies himself to leave, folding the information page from the Levonelle pack into his blazer pocket. I now feel a little helpless, although I know I've done all I can.

'Shall I write you a sick note for tomorrow?' I suggest. 'Or for the rest of the week?'

'Um . . . no.' He slips his rucksack onto his shoulders. 'Just today is fine.'

'It's no trouble, Max. Take a day off.'

'Um, I want to be in tomorrow.'

He smiles, and I nod and speak more lightly, following his lead to try to change the tone.

'Something exciting happening at school? Football match?'

He shakes his head and speaks shyly. 'It's my birthday.'

'Of course!' I hold aloft his file, with the date on it. 'Sixteen?'

'Yeah.'

'Sweet sixteen. That'll be fun.'

He turns towards the door. 'Yeah. I'm a grown up!' He gives a little, forced laugh.

'Are you going to be alright?'

Max nods. 'Thank you very much . . . for the pill and everything.'

'Remember not to exceed the dosage of the painkillers. Apply the anaesthetic three times a day. Come back if it keeps hurting, or if you change your mind about going to the police. I've got all the evidence here.' I gesture to the vials on my table.

Max shakes his head. 'I don't want to.' He hesitates. 'Please don't tell them. 'Cause of Dad. Please don't tell my mum.'

I frown. 'I understand why you don't want me to go to your dad's office, Max. But I really should. I have a duty of care.'

'No! Look, if it happens again, then that's different. I just . . . It was just a one-time thing.'

I think. 'Do you swear you'll come to me if this happens again?'

'I swear,' he says earnestly.

'OK.' I nod, still unsure. 'OK.'

''Kay. Thanks . . . thank you.' He smiles determinedly and then hurries out. I close the door behind him, and then it's just me, and the labelled vials of blood and DNA on my desk.

Karen

The house is cold and quiet when we get home, around three-thirty. We have a two-storey-high main hallway, and the heat often rises to the first floor from the ground. I switch the central heating on, setting the timer to go off after an hour.

'Can we have a fire?' Danny asks.

'No.'

'What is the point of the stupid woodburner if we never use it?'

'Honey, we'll roast if I start a fire. It's not cold enough.'

'Well, why get it put in in September?'

'I don't know,' I sigh, leaning heavily on the kitchen table. 'You have to go to your room now, OK?'

'Am I grounded? That's not fair. You said you believed me that I didn't hit her!'

'Daniel . . .' I begin. It's my fault. I phrased it as a question. I'm not a good disciplinarian. It either comes out imploring or aggressive.

'You'd believe Max,' he says darkly.

'That's not true, darling.' I shake my head. 'I don't treat you and Max any differently.'

Daniel appears about to scream at me in frustration when the back door opens, surprising us both into silence.

Max's head comes through the gap and he looks at me nervously. He looks exhausted, and dumps his schoolbag onto the floor by the coat rack. Before I say anything about cleaning up, I note the contents of my own handbag sprawled over the kitchen table.

'What are you doing home this early?' I frown.

His mop of hair shakes. 'No one showed up for Geography, so they let us go. I feel sick.'

'Do you believe him?' cries Daniel. 'You do!'

76

'What's happening?' Max asks. We sit down together at the table and he leans his head on his hands. I knit my fingers through his hair and stroke the baby softness.

'Daniel's grounded,' I murmur.

'I don't want to be bloody grounded!'

'Don't swear at Mum!' Max says softly, just as I take my hand out of his hair and say,

'You'll be grounded for longer if your dad hears what you just said, young man.'

'I'm going to get some water,' Max mumbles, standing up. He leans against the kitchen counter next to the kettle and rubs his eyes.

'Aren't you feeling well, honey?' I say, watching him. There is a loud crash and I turn around to see Daniel climbing onto the kitchen surface to get at the treat jar. 'Daniel!'

'I want a KitKat,' he says, grabbing at the cupboard handle.

'You are absolutely not allowed a treat today!' I stand up and pull him off the counter. 'Get to your room.'

'Fine,' Daniel growls, like the grumpy adolescent Max never became. 'I'll just play Xbox.'

'No, you won't, I'm confiscating it.'

'What? No!'

'Upstairs now!' I plant my hand on his back and guide him firmly towards the kitchen door.

'He was sent home today for hitting a teacher,' I say to Max, as the door swings shut and Daniel's steps recede.

'I didn't hit her,' Daniel yells, running back to the kitchen and poking his head through the door. 'I *touched* her!'

'Daniel, go upstairs,' I say, looking at Max.

Daniel bangs the door closed. I hear him thudding up the stairs dramatically. Max stares faintly at my waist from beneath the tips of his hair, his head slightly lowered.

'What's wrong, sweetie? You look terrible.'

'I dunno.'

I touch his forehead. His face is white. 'Are you coming down with something? You're not hot.'

'I dunno, Mum.'

77

Screeching rap music and gun blasts sound out from upstairs.

'Daniel! I can hear that Xbox! Turn it off!'

'No!'

I open the kitchen door and shout up the stairs. 'Turn it off now!'

The music stops.

I look around again at Max worriedly, and he catches my eye, whips around to face the sink, leans over, and is sick.

I rush over to him, holding his hair back from his face. His body buckles and retches. He moans, his jaw straining, the veins showing through the skin of his neck. We wait a minute to make sure it's over. He reaches for a kitchen towel and wipes his mouth with it.

A yellow liquid pools around the remains of food and three pills.

'Did you take some painkillers, honey?'

Max nods. 'Ibuprofen.'

'You're only supposed to take two. Don't take too much, OK?'

'Huh?'

I reach out, and touch Max's warm back and my hand moves up to his golden neck. I notice the veins, the lines, the older skin on my hand. Max's young skin smells like cinnamon.

'Mum,' he groans, shocked by being sick.

'OK,' I say, pulling him to me. 'Go lie down in the living room, darling. I'll be through in a minute. I'll just clear up.'

Max nods, wipes tears from his eyes and pads out the door. I start the hot tap and the waste disposal and the pills and thick, viscous liquid swirl down the drain. I look through the window, at my own reflection and beyond it, to the low fence at the back of the property. We have to get hedges planted before the campaign too, if Steve runs. There's so much to think about.

I nudge the laptop nearby. It wakes, and I tune in to the local radio station's live streamed programme. Bart Garrett's resignation was announced today, so the post is now officially open.

Paparazzi stalked Bart, twenty-four hours a day. They were savage. They were young reporters, looking to make a big splash, looking to unbuckle him. They went after his children first, and then uncovered some secrets, money he had slipped to people, not illegal, but inadvisable in his position. He voted to the right of the way Steve and I vote, but he wasn't a bad person, and they made him out to be. Tax-dodging allegations, accusations of affairs, his son drinking, his daughter made a racist joke.

If Steve runs, Daniel can't get sent home again, and Max has to go to Hemingway St Catherine's, the private sixth form where they keep a better eye on the kids. Leah and Edward sent Hunter there this year. Max is already booked in to take the entrance exam, but I haven't had a chance yet to call Leah and discuss the school. I promise myself I'll do it tonight.

Sometimes I see kids from Max's school smoking in town at lunchtime. I make a point of not looking for him, because I trust him. I know my son, and what is going on in his life. He'll have a better chance of getting into Oxford University if he goes to a private sixth form, instead of a state school in Abingdon or Oxford, and he deserves to go. He works so hard.

Steve was the same, but with a more directed ambition. Stephen Walker for Member of Parliament, Oxford West, Hemingway and Abingdon. Like so many things, I might have to get used to it.

Archie

It is ten at night, the end of my shift, by the time I am able to deal with the vials in my office. I shut up the clinic as fast as I can, and drive the specimens I took from Max out to a friend who works in a research lab at Oxford University. She works all our criminal cases, and usually I'd wait for the surgery to ship the samples over, but this time I can't.

'You want to come in?' Mia asks as soon as she opens the door. 'You look like you need a drink. Or three. I definitely do.'

'Sorry, I'm in again at eight,' I say, thrusting the samples at her. 'I have to get back. Are you sure you're OK to do this for me?'

Mia looks disappointed, but she nods. 'I'll call you with the results tomorrow. Anything I should know about this?'

I shake my head. 'It's a rape case but . . . other than that, I want you to find out what you find out and let me know. I also want chromosomal analysis on the blood sample, particularly the full vial. That's the victim. And if there are two kinds of DNA on the swabs, could you get both?'

Mia rolls her eyes. 'I knew there would be something more. You ask a lot, Archie. Karyotyping to get the chromosomal analysis will take a week.'

'I'm very grateful. Keep it quiet. It's for a young patient.'

'Poor thing.'

'Mm,' I murmur. 'Speak to you tomorrow?'

Mia smiles and goes to close the door. 'Drive safe.'

The roads are quiet on the way home, through the suburbs of Oxford, out onto the short stretch of connecting road, through the darkness of trees and fields and a cloudy night, and back into the human world, in the residential lanes of Hemingway.

I find myself thinking, in spite of my belief in leaving work at the office, about Max.

Max is sixteen. So much changes when you are a teenager. You become aware of sex and love. You rush things, because you think your friends are experiencing more than you are. That's one reason I see so many young kids coming in to talk to me about unprotected sex, about drugs, about alcohol. They all want to explore these new feelings. All the adolescents in Max's school are pairing off or experimenting, as far as I can tell from how many come in to the drop-in sessions for contraception. Max must be waking up to it, revisiting his feelings about his condition as he understands what a difference it will make to his ability to form relationships. I wonder if I should recommend a counsellor.

Does Max feel intersex, or more like a boy? He seems to identify as a boy. He certainly wears the suit well. Little heartbreaker.

I requested karyotyping from Mia because it will tell me what type of intersex Max is and whether it's in his chromosomes, written in his genetic make-up. This code dictates much of who Max will be, his health, how he functions, and his gender. Max's file is over-full and confusing, and with diagnoses of these gender variations in such flux, I want to make sure he has been properly diagnosed. Karyotyping is a test often done with blood, which evaluates whether Max is XX (a girl), XY (a boy), or a combination. It might be that he is not truly intersex at all, that he presents that way physically, but is chromosomally a boy, or even a girl. If he is a boy, it could offer some real comfort to Max.

Max's notes were all over the place, in all different types of handwriting. Not a lot was known about intersex conditions, even fifteen years ago, and I could not find his exact diagnosis in my quick scanning. I decide to read up on him, perhaps in my old textbooks, when I get time this week, while I wait for the karyotype.

One common type of intersexuality is Androgen Insensitivity Syndrome, where babies are genetically boys, but the body doesn't react to androgens, including testosterone, in the womb, so they present as baby girls. The only reason I remember this type is because I saw it on a documentary. I search my memory, but I cannot recall any specific types I learnt about in my training. I wonder what secrets Max's body is keeping.

Daniel

'Shouldn't you be in bed? It's eleven,' Max says, coming into my room. 'You upset Mum today.'

'Mum's always upset with me.' I shrug.

'She's never upset with you,' says Max, and I raise my eyebrows at him, because for an older person, he sure doesn't notice much.

'Me and her fight all the time now,' I tell him.

He sits down next to me. 'Oh. Do you?'

I kill three zombies and glance at him. 'What's wrong with you?'

He picks bits out of my carpet. 'Nothing. Why?'

'Don't do that,' I say.

'Sorry.'

'I thought Mum said you were sick. Aren't you supposed to be lying down somewhere?'

'No. I'm fine. I just . . . had a shock today. I told her I was fine. Didn't want to make her worry.'

'Suck up,' I say, teasing him like he teases me sometimes. Max just looks at me and his eyes roll around in his head like he's thinking. Not right back or anything, just from side to side.

'I'm only joking,' I say.

'I'm not a suck up,' he says.

I pause the game and put the controller down. 'What shock?'

Max shrugs. 'Nothing. I'm over it now,' he says, picking up the controller and turning the loud music back on. He instantly kills a Gnomobear, which is sixty-five points. That's triple the points you get for wiping out a zombie. He gives me a big, blank smile, like a line stretching across his face and showing one sliver of tooth. He giggles, promptly killing another Gnomobear, watching the frustration on my face because I have yet to kill any of them the whole game.

'Nothing,' he says again.

Sylvie

It beats and it beats and it beats,
This beast . . .

That's all I have. It just came to me this morning, while I was doing my homework on the computer in the IT room. It repeats in my head, along a rhythm, but no other words come. I love writing poetry, but it comes slow sometimes. I often write a bit while I do my homework in the IT room in the morning, or at lunchtime. I've noticed it's the place where all the kids without friends go.

Let's face it: I do not have friends. It's not by choice. I don't know why. I used to have one in primary school. We were tight, we used to make up all sorts of stories together and play imaginary games all the time. We had imaginary dogs and cats. Mine was a kitten called Tabby and she had a puppy called Max. I don't like to be arrogant, but I was a good friend. We used to swap presents we made for each other all the time. I always made a big deal out of birthdays. But then when we were twelve I moved away, here, to Hemingway. We lived in Islington in North London. Then my mum and dad moved jobs to ones in Oxford and we moved here.

I never see my old friend now. It's OK. It's been four years. I never really met anyone at this school who was like me. There were a few near hits, and a lot of misses. I don't mind it being just me now. I'm used to it, I guess, but I do miss knowing there's someone out there who can stand me, who maybe thinks I'm funny, and is funny back. I miss having someone to be ridiculous and piss myself for ages with; I miss having someone who makes me feel like I'm not weird, or maybe that, no matter how weird I am, there's someone out there who is just as weird as me. Sometimes I panic about that, but then that's crazy. I'm only sixteen. I'll meet someone cool.

After I've done my homework, I go to the common room. I sit alone as usual. Emma, Laura and Fay are nearby. They are halfway girls. Halfway pretty, halfway popular, halfway mean and halfway nice. Sometimes I hang out with them when I'm bored.

'OMG,' says Emma. 'Did he really? He's so hot.'

'Oh my god, yeah, totally.' Laura nods.

'But his girlfriend is such a slaaaaag,' Fay chimes in.

'Right, Sylvie?' says Emma, looking at me.

'Right.' I nod. I don't know who they're talking about. I don't know why they talk to me. My guess is that I make a good audience. Everyone here bitches about each other and talks about boys all day. I don't get it. I thought they were joking when I first came here, because who bitches so much about their friends behind their backs? And who would make boys like the ones at Hemingway the centre of their universe? Blah people. Small town blah people. So I don't say anything. I just listen.

Not that the boys are so bad, but . . . they're just people. In fact, the only people I've had fun hanging out with here have been boys. But here it is weird for boys to hang out with girls. In Hemingway, the boys hang out with the boys ('boy' = footballer who plays video games, drinks beer, wears blue, listens to rock music, likes tits, and will likely one day become a politician/work in finance and have a mild coke habit) and the girls hang out with the girls ('girl' = would-be accountant/footballer's wife/housewife who dyes her hair blonde, drinks wine, wears pink clothes and orange make-up, dances to light RnB, likes pretty-boys and will likely one day have a mild coke habit).

So mostly I just hang out by myself, and sometimes Emma Best will come over with Laura, Fay and a few other people and talk to me. She blatantly digs for dirt all the time. On anyone. I can only take so much of them. I'm just not built for it. It's not like I'm not incredibly observant and witty (and cocky); it's just

I'm not interested in bitching about or to people. But for some reason, Emma, Fay and Laura always come up to and sit right next to me. This morning I stuck my headphones in as soon as they arrived, to indicate I was busy.

If I'm not in the IT room, I usually like to hang out in the library to avoid them, but it's only open at lunchtime, so I have to come to the common room. Not many people from my year hang out there, and none of the boys come in the IT room or library, of course (the boys say: 'work = gay'). Max Walker doesn't come into the library either.

I think of Max Walker at this point because he is standing in the frame of the common room doors. The sun is shining on him. Doesn't it always.

Max moves out of the halo ray of sun in the doorway and moves slowly up to a group of the popular people. Carl turns around and notices him. He reaches out with his arms.

'HAPPY BIRTHDAY, KID!'

'Hi!' Max grins, and then Carl runs round him and jumps on his back and Max yelps and wriggles out. Max mumbles something, and looks half-pained and half-happy.

'I was just saying happy birthday.' Carl holds up his hands in mock reproach.

Max smiles at him. Max talks considerably quieter than Carl so I can't really hear what he's saying.

I don't know why I'm listening to the exchange. I'm so bored. B-o-r-e-d. I'm trying to zone out by watching YouTube videos of Ash Sarkar and Kate Tempest on my iPhone. They're badass performance poets, and they are just a few years older than me. I wish I still lived in London. If you come of age there, you're at the epicentre of the performance poetry scene already. But I notice, after a few minutes of listening to Max talk, that I have let the YouTube video play out and stop. Instead of searching for another one, I pretend I'm still listening to my iPhone, so no one talks to me, but I take one earphone out and try to listen to him instead.

He doesn't look as nervous as yesterday. I kind of want to go over and ask him if he was OK. He probably hasn't told anyone. He is the Walker offspring, after all. Must keep up appearances.

'Heyyy!' Marc Paulsson yells, running past me, over to Max. 'Happy sweet sixteen, mate!'

They high five and then they all sit down on the comfy chairs and talk more quietly, so I can't hear them. Maria and a few girls walk over in tiny pleated skirts and give Max hugs and wish him a happy birthday. He has a conversation with Suzanne and Nikki, which I give him a plus point for, because Suzanne and Nikki are cool. They are kind of bookish. Outside of school, they wear very fifties gear. Some of the other girls call them the Pink Ladies, after the girls in *Grease*. It's supposed to be an insult, but if I acted like Rizzo or looked like Sandy, I wouldn't complain.

I watch Max laughing with them, and waving to other people who wish him happy birthday, but he looks a little . . . subdued, or reserved, like he's trying to be excited but isn't, or doesn't have the energy. He smiles at everyone, like he is a sweet little eleven-year-old, who hasn't a clue how bitchy people can be at secondary school. I guess Max Walker wouldn't know how bitchy people can be. All the girls love him. But he seems so young to me. Weird, I know. But he seems young.

Watching him now, he looks the kind of happy where you're sad, but you're doing your best to be upbeat, and I wonder if any of his friends notice that. It always seems strange to me how little people notice about each other's lives. One good thing about being a loner is that I notice a lot, because I'm outside everything, with nothing to do but watch and write it down in poetry. It's clear to me that Max is miserable, but his friends don't seem to see. He shrugs at something Maria says, and laughs. She leans over and kisses him on the cheek and he blushes, looks at his lap, and smiles.

I frown and look away. I don't know why I frown. It's fine if he likes Maria. She's OK. A bit blah, but still OK. She is the type of blonde, swishy-haired girl who would be a golden boy's girlfriend. They are both normal, predictable and kind of boring: the golden people of school, and who knows in the life after school? Maybe golden people tarnish fast.

Later, on the school field, at lunch:

'His lips were gross and tiny. Like, there was almost no lip there,' Laura Narne says thoughtfully, pulling at her own full bottom lip, as I rub my stomach. I have period pains. Hate, hate, hate. Who cares about his lips? Whose lips? I'm not lips-ning.

'Why did you even kiss him, then?' Fay asks, sitting on the grass outside the art block, inspecting her legs in her gross polyester school skirt.

'He was cute otherwise.'

'He was the only one there who wasn't heinous,' Emma says with a smirk, and Laura punches her. 'Everyone else there was fug.'

'What's fug?' asks Laura.

'Fugly, you dick.' Emma sits up. 'Err, why is Wonder Boy Three walking over this way?'

Who is Wonder Boy 3? Who cares? My back is killing me and I feel totally grumpy from listening to Emma bleat on all lunch. But I have itchy feet for company. You can't talk to yourself alone for too long. You'll go crazy.

'Is Max Walker Wonder Boy Three?' asks Laura. 'I thought he was Number One?'

'Huh?' I look up, across the field. Max Walker is walking towards us.

'No, he's Three,' Emma says. 'Todd Z is Wonder Boy One, Marc Paulsson is Wonder Boy Two and Max Walker is Three.'

'Max Walker's way fitter than Marc Paulsson.' Laura frowns. 'And Todd Z.'

'It doesn't matter how attractive they are really. They are all dicks.'

'Ems, that's not true. Marc Paulsson's OK. I have him in Biology,' says Fay.

'Er, he is definitely walking this way.'

'OMG,' says Laura.

'He's a dick.'

'Shut up, Emma!' Fay nudges her.

'OMG!' Laura yelps, like she's pissed herself.

'Hi, Sylvie.'

'Err . . . hi,' I say awkwardly, putting my arm over my eyes to shield them from the sun. I squint up at Max Walker, and blink at him uncertainly.

'Hi guys,' Max says shyly to Laura, Emma and Fay.

'Hi Max,' says Fay.

'Hello, Max Walker,' says Emma, and giggles maliciously, staring at me like she wants me to catch her eye.

'What's up, Max?' I say, in the bored fashion you use when you are sitting next to a group of girls who will make it a *huge* deal if you seem at all interested in a guy.

Over the field I see Maria looking at us. She's standing next to the football field, watching the boys play with all the rest of her group of girls. She has long blonde hair that's perfectly straight. She's like an extra from *High School Musical*. No, the lead. Of an erotic version of the same. She turns back to watch the football. I don't know why. The players do the same thing every bloody lunchtime.

'I just wanted to see if, um . . .' Max is mumbling. He clears his throat. 'If maybe you wanted to hang out?'

'Oh,' I say, tearing my eyes slowly away from Maria. She flicks her hair away from her face and I remember Max blushing earlier. 'I'm kind of . . . busy,' I finish lamely.

'Oh, OK, that's cool.' Max shrugs and looks down at his feet. Then he takes a deep breath, lifts his head and gives me a big smile. It's his usual beam but it looks like it takes a lot of effort today. 'Maybe we could hang out another time. We're going to the cinema on Saturday for my birthday, if you wanted to come?'

'Who'll be there?'

'Um . . .' He looks around at the football pitch vaguely, like he's having difficulty remembering. 'Marc, Carl, Todd, Grant, Maria, Olivia, Karina . . . Some other people. I dunno.'

'And you're asking me because you need another girl whose name ends in "a"?'

'Oh yeah, Sylvia,' he says, as if he had never considered that this would be my full name before. Everyone calls me 'Sylvie'. I see a peak of a genuine grin. He laughs a little. 'Yeah, we need symmetry. The world is just . . . too illogical to handle without it. Your friends are welcome to come too,' he adds, gesturing to the girls. 'I think afterwards we're going to go to the Pancake Café.'

There's a silence while I think about going to the Pancake Café with that many people and being so awkward with them I don't know what to say and don't speak the entire time, and then when I'm at school we pass in the corridors and I don't know whether to wave so I don't, and then they think I'm a bitch.

Then Max says, 'I'll buy your popcorn!' which sounds a bit desperate, and may or may not mean that he really wants me to come.

I find this confusing, and am unsure how to react. I probably can't say 'I don't like people'. That would probably not be the right response. For some reason Max actually seems nervous asking me as well. He seems so freaking young, but he's only a week younger than me. My sixteenth birthday was last Wednesday. Toby and I went clubbing.

Max Walker makes me say things in my head that sound like I'm a grandma. Like 'bless him'. He has this very childlike quality of utter cheeriness. Like a puppy. Although today, he looks more like a kicked puppy, tail down and in the corner. I guess the word is 'cute'. It is almost distracting, this cuteness. He has this impossibly sunshine-like smile. Other girls, of course, find it utterly distracting. Not me. Because I am an individual.

I screw up my face. 'I don't actually think I can do Saturday.'

Emma and Laura both look at me like I'm crazy. Max smiles, but – and here I feel a little bad – looks truly disappointed. He obviously sees that I'm lying. He shrugs.

'Oh, OK, that's cool, no worries.' He puts his hands in his pockets. 'I'll get going, then. I think they need me on the field.' He gestures towards the football match. 'If you do get free, though, the film starts at six forty-five, at the Kinema. I'd love you to come, but no worries if you can't. Bye.'

He says this last bit kind of lamely and waves his hand, then turns away and heads up to the field.

'Max!' I call, then roll my eyes at myself. 'Listen, another time, OK?'

He grins, and suddenly his entire face lights up and I watch a group of Year Sevens passing him practically faint.

'OK! Bye, Sylvie.'

He wanders off slowly to the football field and runs a little bit up and down with his friends, kicking the ball half-heartedly. The girls are talking excitedly behind me, but I watch Max. He looks around the field, over to me, turns away again, says something to Maria, then picks up his jumper, and walks over the field and into the library building, head down, looking kind of lonely and glum.

'Sylvie! Isn't it his birthday today?' says Emma, in a tone that suggests they have been talking to me and I haven't been listening.

'Erm, maybe,' I say.

'He wanted to hang out with you on his birthday and you said no.' She giggles. 'You're such a freak, Sylvie. I love it. You're like, "No, I totally don't care whether you clearly fancy me or not".' She hugs me.

'He doesn't fancy me!' I protest between her breasts.

'He thinks he's the shit,' says Laura.

'Totally,' agrees Emma. 'He thinks he's hot.'

'Really?' I say slowly, getting my iPhone back out. 'I don't think so.'

'Oh my god, like so.'

'So.'

I groan audibly at them, but they won't understand what I'm

groaning at so it doesn't matter. I plug in my earphones and open the YouTube app again.

So Max Walker wants to hang out. I hope he was OK the other day at the clinic.

Max

I can't sleep.

I had a pretty good day today, I guess. Everyone was talking to me all day, because it was my birthday, and I got cards and some of the girls brought me presents at school. I didn't have time to think about anything, really. I was planning to be on auto-pilot, trying not to think about it. You know. *It.* But everyone was making jokes and hugging me anyway, so I didn't have to worry about it.

This late at night, there's no one here to force myself to feel OK for, to smile or hold it together for, and I feel pretty bad. I try to do what Mum always says to do, and think about how there's always someone worse off than me in the world and I should be grateful for what I have, but tonight it doesn't help me stop thinking about everything. I changed the sheets, but I had to do it Sunday night straight after it happened, so there is still a sheet with blood on it in a plastic bag in the bottom drawer. Quite a lot of blood. It's weird how blood pools out like that.

I still feel sore when I move too. I felt sore all day pretty much, even though I took the right doses of painkillers. I couldn't play football at lunch. I said my ankle was hurting. Liar, liar.

Sylvie Clark was sitting on the school field so I decided to go and say hello. She looked really pretty. I felt shyer than I have before. I usually am a tiny bit shy, but I just try to go for it with girls. But today I felt nervous after Sunday and everything. Anyway, I'm not sure that I feel that way about her. I mean, I don't even know her. But she was nice the other day at the clinic, and she's obviously really, really beautiful, so I thought maybe if I got to know her, we might get on.

Her hair today was like a curly mess of caramel around her

face and down onto her shoulders. She has caramel-coloured skin too. She looks like sweets. I wanted to stroke her skin. God.

She said she was busy.

I couldn't really think of what to say, because she didn't look at all busy, but I said OK and that maybe we could hang out another time. Today, language seems to have failed me. I kept smiling all day and looking excited and stuff, but I found that trying to talk that way was too much. I keep panicking, and thinking someone's going to find out. I'm avoiding Mum and Dad for the same reason. I just keep thinking they're going to look at me and know, or I'm going to bleed a bit or something. I kept going into the toilets to check my trousers at school, make sure there were no marks. If Mum and Dad found out about the other night, not only would I be their intersex kid, then I'd be the kid that everytime they looked at him, they would think of my crotch and Hunter doing that to me and how I didn't fight back. I tried but, like, how would they know? Would they believe me? If they knew it was Hunter, would they think I had been with him all along, ever since we were kids? Urgh.

After Sylvie said she was busy, I asked her if she wanted to come to the cinema on Saturday and she said she was busy then too. I think she was lying. She's a bit of a kook.

I smile to myself in the dark, in my bed, imagining stroking her hair. Kook.

After we talked I tried to play footie, but I was aching too bad, so I went to the library and did my homework so I didn't have to do it when I got home. When school finished, I went round to Marc's with Carl and got wasted. They gave me my present from them, which was *FIFA Soccer 12* (!!!) and a pack of condoms and some lubricant.

'For gay sex,' said Marc. 'Because you are gay.'

He was just joking, but I almost cried. Instead I grabbed him and buried my face in his shoulder and pretended I was expressing my undying love for him and said, 'Only for you, Marc. Only for you.'

I got home too late or I would have shown the game to

Daniel. He loves video games. He has an encyclopaedic knowledge of what is on release at the moment, and how many stars *Gaming Magazine* gave everything. He'll be excited. I'll get him to play with me tomorrow.

Marc, Carl and I played the game and we had to drink every time we scored a goal. They got a bit drunk but I got absolutely smashed, even though we had the same amount to drink. I always get drunk quicker than everyone else. I wonder if it's my build.

They had to smuggle me out when I left, so Marc's mum didn't see. When I got home I walked very carefully up the stairs and threw up in the toilet. I flushed it away and then cried in the bathroom, like an idiot, sat on the floor next to the bath. No one saw. Usually I'm not this emotional. I think I was just upset about what happened on Sunday even though I wasn't thinking about it.

How could Hunter do that? He was my best friend.

I carried it around all day.

Something really big happened, you douche, my brain says. *You're allowed to be upset. It's only Tuesday.*

I know. I just hate it. I'm bored with it.

You're bored?

Yep. I don't wanna think about it anymore. Why should I have to? I don't deserve to.

Nope. But it's only been forty-eight hours.

So? I don't deserve it anyway. I'm not going to think about it. Close my eyes and go to sleep. Think about something else.

Sylvie . . . ?

Maybe.

We could . . . you know . . .

Why does everything have to always be about sex?

Huh?

How can someone be friends with you for that long and always have been thinking about sex with you? It just ruins every memory you ever had with them. Was he always thinking about it? Even when we were little? Did he always want to touch me? Am I like this curiosity to him?

96

You said you weren't going to think about it.

I'm not thinking about it.

Yes, you are.

God, SHUT UP! Just shut up.

You are shouting to your own head. Retard.

I know. Urgh. Why would he do that?

Yep. Urgh. Hope we don't see him around any time soon.

Don't say that.

Sorry. Max? What if we do . . . ? Max?

Please stop talking.

OK.

Karen

'Hi,' I say, surprised when I walk in the kitchen after work on Wednesday.

Steve is home, sat at the kitchen table. The mock campaign posters are spread over it. There is a new one, a large one: 'Stephen Walker: the only independent Independent.'

'I didn't know you'd left the office,' I say.

He stands up from the kitchen table. 'I thought I'd come home and work on this. I heard the Murphy case went well today?'

He holds his arms open to me and pulls me in to his shoulder. It feels strange to have him so near after being colleagues all day. I'm still in work mode, strong and in control and ready for anything, but this – being held close by a body much larger than mine, feeling petite and protected – it's a change in roles and it always takes me a minute, each day, to switch between the two.

Steve never seems to notice my stiffness. I soon relax. I smell his familiar smell, I feel his familiar weight on me, his waist, his bulk, his warmth. But that first time we touch after work, I stiffen and he doesn't notice, and I think, *How do you not notice this? Do you know me at all?*

'Mm, it went well,' I say, and he kisses me.

'Sexy,' he murmurs. 'I like a powerful woman.'

'Steve,' I mutter, through his lips.

'Mm?'

'We need to get them to put in the automatic gate if you run.'

He stops, hesitates.

'I'm sorry,' I say. 'Maybe I mentioned it before. I'm just thinking about the children.'

He nods, licks his lips. '*If* I run?'

'Oh. You're definitely running?'

He steps back from me and sits on the edge of the table. He sighs. 'I don't think I can turn back now.'

I nod.

'I know the last time we talked we didn't agree on anything.'

'You know.' I shake my head, repeating the familiar line back to him.

'Yes, I know. Where are you going?'

I'm moving towards the kitchen door, automatically heading for the heart of the house.

'I don't know,' I say, turning back. He looks so tired. I smile at him.

'I love you,' he says.

'I love you too.'

'Are you . . .' He pauses. 'OK with me running?'

I think. 'Yes. As long as we prepare.'

'We can install a gate. I'll organise it.'

I nod. 'Have you spoken to your sister?'

'She's pleased. She did not like Bart,' he says, laughing.

'He's not a bad guy,' I mutter.

'I know. I told her that. Her pregnancy's coming along fine, by the way. She's looking well. I saw her for lunch on Monday.'

'Good,' I nod.

He smiles, putting his arm around me. 'I feel like we haven't talked for days about anything but work.'

'You've been late home every night.'

'I know, I'm sorry.'

I grimace at the 'I know', but hold my tongue.

'How are the kids?' Steve asks.

'Fine, I think. Max was sick in the sink Monday night but he's seemed better since. I forgot to mention it yesterday.'

'He didn't get in until late last night. Where was he?'

'Marc's or Carl's, I think. I knew you weren't going to be back for a while, so I said he could go with them when he called. We can have a family meal later this week to celebrate.'

'OK. So, the sickness was just a twenty-four-hour bug?'

'Probably. He seems fine now. Are you going to go watch his match on Saturday?'

'What time is it?' Steve says, picking up his slim black diary.

'Nine-thirty.'

He snaps the black book shut. 'I can make it.'

'Don't invite press,' I say quietly. 'It's not a photo opportunity.'

'I know. I wouldn't. They just show up.' Steve shrugs and runs his hand through his hair. 'Is he doing something with his friends for his birthday this weekend?'

'He's going to the cinema. Saturday night. With Marc, Carl and some girls.'

'Girls?'

I smile. 'He's growing up.'

Steve grins back. 'Maybe it's time to have a talk with him.'

'About what? He's just going to the cinema.'

'Karen,' Steve says, as if I'm supposed to know.

'What?'

'He's different.'

I tut. 'He's fine.'

'Mm.' Steve looks doubtful and I frown at him. 'Anything else?'

'Else?' I ask.

'Anything else . . . about me running? Anything you need me to do?'

I chew my lip, remember I'm wearing lipstick and run my tongue around my teeth. 'I wonder about Daniel . . .'

'Daniel?'

I look at him incredulously. Sometimes it seems like he doesn't see anything. 'His behaviour, Steve.'

'Don't say it like that. I'm not oblivious, Karen. I know I'm at work later than you, but I'm still aware of what's going on in my own house.'

'Don't snap at me. I'm just asking what you think.'

'About Daniel? It's a phase. He'll grow out of it.'

'Max was never like that.'

'Max was different. They're different people,' Steve says, reproachfully.

'I'm not saying . . .' I sigh, exasperated. 'You have to admit he's difficult. And Max is so easy.'

'Well, Daniel's got all sorts of hormones going through him. Max never had that.'

'Urgh!' I snap in frustration. 'Max isn't how he is because he's . . . you know.'

'I know, I know. I just mean . . .' Steve stops. 'Well, he is in a way. Isn't he?'

'Steve. That's so unfair.'

'I didn't mean it in a bad way,' he says, shaking his head. 'Just . . . it is what it is.'

'He's a good boy. He's always been good.'

'Well, he works for it. He wants to be perfect for you.'

I hear the tone in his voice. 'For me? What does *that* mean?'

'Karen, you have high standards. *We* have high standards. It's not a bad thing. Max . . . he doesn't want us to think of him as intersex.'

'Don't say that word, it's horrible. That's not it, anyway. He's just a good kid. Don't take that away from him because of his illness.'

Steve sighs. 'It's not an illness.'

'*I* have high standards?' I say, shaking my head. 'I have high standards?'

Do I?

He doesn't have to be perfect for me. I just want him to be perfect for him, because it will be easier for him. Is that having high standards? Are they unreachable standards? Suddenly I'm very tired. Steve has a way of doing this, of discussing me into confusion.

'This isn't what I wanted,' I state, without knowing whether I mean for this evening, for Max, or for me.

Steve laughs, suddenly. It lightens the air. He smiles at me and I melt a little, then feel angry at myself for giving up so easily.

'What do you mean? What did you want?' He stands and walks over to me. He touches my waist. 'Come upstairs,' he murmurs.

I nod as he nuzzles my neck. 'OK. In a minute.'

I watch him stride through the door, loosening his tie. I look back to the posters, strewn on the kitchen table. I look at the car bumper stickers, packs of them. Then I realise: these are not mocks. There are too many, and I knew before. I knew he would run. I should have talked to him earlier, but I let it slide. I let it happen. I went along with Steve's plan, as usual. I suppose I can't blame him if I didn't have an alternative one.

Max

Both Mum and Dad are on the sidelines when I score the winning goal on Saturday morning. Marc and Carl run towards me and hug me and we high-five. When the whistle goes two minutes later, we do it again.

I think for a moment after the game, when we get our oranges and are standing on the pitch talking about it, and my parents are waving across at me through the crowd, that my life is perfect. That I'm so lucky.

Then a light flashes across the pitch, and everything sort of breaks.

The photographer is standing close to Mum and Dad, taking pictures of them. It's the regular one from the newspaper that covers the matches. He's always here, but he normally just takes a picture of the winning team at the end. He says something to Dad and Dad leans in to him and shakes his hand. My eyes slide to the side and see Mum, and I notice the people she's talking to: Auntie Cheryl and Leah. I nervously scan the spectators for Hunter's face, but I don't see him.

I turn away for a minute when Matt, our coach, starts talking to me about next week's game and I nod and try to listen. But I am feeling suddenly more self-conscious. Everything broke when the light flashed, and I'm wondering if people can see it. Did part of me split open and show itself on my face? Can everyone tell about me? Can everyone tell what happened? It's such a fine, thin line between everyone knowing and everyone not. One little sentence, one word, a word like the word Hunter used, and it would be out. I could say it now, a Freudian slip, and everyone would know.

Hunter. I scan the crowd behind Matt, looking, searching for a dark-eyed face. But somehow I know he's not here. I'd be able to feel him. When Matt moves away, I circle the pitch again anyway, with a wary look, turning back towards Mum and Dad. A light temporarily blinds me. When it fades from the pools of my eyes, becoming pink, then disappearing, the face of the photographer is standing in front of me.

'Good-looking lad,' he says.

I blink. 'Excuse me?'

'You'll look good on the front of the paper. Great picture!' He smiles and holds the camera aloft. 'Be front page news next week. I hear your dad is announcing his candidacy for MP for Oxford West, Hemingway and Abingdon on Monday.'

I listen, I frown, I swallow. *I didn't know that*, I think.

And then I nod. 'Yeah,' I say, with my best smile. 'That'll be great.'

'Perfect,' he says, taking another picture. 'Perfect.'

Daniel

It's really, really late on Saturday night. I hear my brother come in from his birthday cinema treat, but I don't hear Carl or Marc, so I wait a bit, and then I hear him go to the bathroom and then the loo flushes and I hear the bathroom door open again.

'Max?'

The landing is quiet. I didn't hear Max open his door, so I guess that he is listening to see if he really heard me and I whisper again.

'Maaaax.'

My door opens.

'Hey, buddy,' says Max.

'Hi.'

'What are you doing up so late?'

'I cannot sleep,' I tell him. 'You smell like beer.'

'Are you accusing me of drinking?' he says in a funny voice, kneeling down at my bed. I have a bunk bed, but I'm sleeping on the bottom one tonight.

'Stop doing that silly voice,' I say.

'OK,' he says, and he sighs.

'Where are Marc and Carl?'

'Um, they both went home with girls. Or stayed out with girls. I don't know. So it begins, I guess.' He shrugs and looks a bit annoyed.

'Why?'

'Why what?'

'Why did they stay out or go home with girls and not with you?'

'Well, when people get older they like to pair up into men and women, um, or men and men, and women and women, and then at some point they choose one person to pair up

105

with for a really long time, and they become a mummy and daddy.'

'But mummy and daddy are silly names that babies use.'

'Alright then, a mother and father.'

'Or mum and dad.'

'Yeah.' Max groans a bit and buries his head in my cover. 'Or mum and dad.'

'But a man and a man can't be a mummy and daddy.'

'They can both be parents.'

'Can they?'

'Yeah,' Max says, like he is distracted and tired. 'It's normal. It's just less . . . often that you see it, I guess.'

'But that means it's not normal.'

'Well, it's not always great to be normal.'

'Are Marc and Carl normal?'

'Yes.'

'Are we normal?'

'No.'

'Oh,' I say, and I'm a bit sad. 'Is it because I'm weird?'

'Who said that to you?'

'Kelly at school.'

'You're not weird. Anyway, no,' Max says. 'It's because we're superheroes!' And he tickles me and I can't help laughing, even though he is being silly and smells of beer, which is horrible.

When we've settled down again, I say, 'Are you annoyed with Marc and Carl?'

Max thinks and then smiles and shakes his head. 'No, I'm not annoyed with them. It's good that they're having fun. Carl has always really liked Maria, and Marc and Olivia get on well, so . . .'

'So what's the problem?'

Max clears his throat and looks down, then looks up and shakes his head again. 'Nothing's the problem. I had a good night. A girl I hoped would come didn't come, that's all, but I wouldn't have been able to invite her home anyway.'

'Why not?'

'Um . . .'

'Max?'

'Sorry.' He groans again and folds his arms and puts his head on them on my bed. 'Girls want to do things that . . . I can't do or . . . they wouldn't want to do with me if they knew . . . stuff. I don't know. It's only this year everyone has started to pair up. It's weird. I guess I always knew it would happen.'

Max seems to be talking to himself and not explaining things properly.

'What things do girls want to do?' I say impatiently.

'Oh!' He laughs, looking up at my face like he is surprised to see me. 'I'm so smashed. Drunk, I mean. Um, like play certain computer games.'

'Like that *Dance Factor* thing that goes with that TV show?'

'Yeah, exactly, like *Dance Factor 2012*.'

'I understand. That show is awful.' I pat him consolingly.

'Thanks, Daniel,' Max says. 'So . . . would you like a ghost story?'

'Yes! Can I come in your bed?'

'No, because you'll get scared and then you won't want to walk in the dark to your own room, will you?'

'That wouldn't happen!'

'It happened last time. And then you screamed, and Mum told me off for keeping you up past ten.'

'What time is it now?'

'Midnight.'

I think. 'Fair enough, let's do the ghost story in my bed.'

'OK. Give me the torch.'

I give Max my green torch and he climbs under my duvet next to me.

'You're letting all the cold air in!'

'Shh! I'll tuck you in. There, is that better?'

'Yes.'

'OK.' He switches the torch on underneath his chin. 'It all began one dark, stormy night, shortly before Halloween, when a zombie mutant crawled from his grave with blood-sucking wounds . . .'

'Cool!' I shout.

'Shh!' Max laughs.

My brother tells the BEST ghost stories.

Archie

It's Sunday before Mia calls. I hear the phone ringing as I return from yoga, and I rush to answer it.

'Archie Verma,' I murmur breathily, slipping my bag off my shoulder and sinking onto the armchair in the hall.

'Why didn't you tell me the victim was intersex?' Mia blurts out.

'I didn't know what karyotype. I wanted you to tell me.'

'Sneaky.'

'Just easier.'

'I'll fax the entire analysis over to you. Did you get my email about the perpetrator?'

'Yes, thank you. Did anything come up in the police database?'

'The DNA wasn't a match to anyone, no. Are you going to go to the police now?'

'It's a very tricky situation, and I sort of want to see how it plays out.'

'Is this victim a minor?'

'No. Sixteen now. I was hoping we'd find a match in the database. It would have made things easier. I really don't want to do anything unless he asks.'

'The victim identifies as male?'

'Yes.'

'It's too bad he can't just go by intersex. You know there was a whole new shift a few years ago around what we're supposed to call them? Seems like all they talk about is definitions.'

'What are we supposed to call them? Not intersex?'

'No, it's still intersex. But now we call their variations DSDs.'

'DSD?'

'It stands for Disorders of Sexual Development.'

'Oh. I don't think I like that.'

'Why?'

'I'm not sure. I suppose "disorder" sounds like it affects their health. I know it does sometimes but . . .'

'Yeah, I guess,' says Mia. 'So what's the plan?'

'I'll talk to him about the police again if he comes back in. I hope he will.'

'Good luck.'

'Thank you. Was there any disease in the large vial of blood I gave you?'

'Nothing. It was clean.'

'Great. That's a relief.'

'Well, let me know what happens. I'll send you through the consensus for the redefinition of intersex conditions as DSDs, and a few other papers I found last night. Makes interesting reading.'

I put down the phone. Last night I read through my old text-books, expecting to find a whole section I had missed, but there was nothing. There wasn't even that much on sexuality itself. It came up in basic classes on endocrinology and anatomy, STDs were covered in infectious diseases, then erectile dysfunction was rather primly covered within sections on renal medicine, diabetes and drug side effects. Intersex itself seemed not to rate a mention in any of my books.

In my own lecture notes, there were a few references to genetic testing and genetics. It is perhaps too much of a specialist subject to cover in a medical degree, but it would be helpful in this case to know something about the psychology of growing up with an intersex condition, or the logistics of surgery, or support groups.

Suddenly I have a thought, and dial Greta Pettigrew's number. Our young district nurse picks up her mobile and greets me cheerily, but although she only finished training two years ago, she admits to never having covered intersexuality in any real depth. As I go to ring off, I hear her voice calling me.

'Wait, Archie? Archie?' blares the phone.

'Yes?'

'Have you tried Googling it?'

'I thought you might say that.'

Most doctors rely on Googling, but I am wary of the internet. Call me a technophobe, but it feels unreliable.

After changing and making myself a coffee, I sit in my office. About 3.8 million entries come up online when I Google 'intersex'. I am overwhelmed instantly by the number so I navigate instead to an online bookshop, but when I check, there really aren't any medical textbooks available on the site about intersexuality. I click guiltily on Wikipedia. I learn that the term 'intersex' came about in the mid-nineties as a result of activism. A large section of the article is dedicated to whether intersex conditions are normal or should be termed 'disorders', 'maldeveloped or undeveloped', 'errors of development', 'defective genitals', 'abnormal', or 'mistakes of nature'.

I baulk at this, but read on.

One doctor emphasises that all of these conditions are biologically understandable while statistically uncommon. Wikipedia claims research in the 20th century led to a growing medical consensus that this was true, and then immediately begins to talk about the intersex condition's redefinition as 'Disorders of Sexual Development', a term which seems to clash with their definition as biologically understandable. I am left confused.

I read about the history of hermaphroditism, I read about the Greeks, I read about Victorian-era hermaphrodites. I read about different approaches to gender norms, I read about surgery. I read that specialists in the UK began to advise the minimisation of childhood surgery in 2001. Max was born five years before.

In Max's file there were five pages of writing about his parents' reaction to his disorder and to everything the doctors said. They were encouraged to let Max be assigned as a girl, then later they were encouraged to assign him to a male gender. The notes stop two years ago. He was almost fourteen, and had just received a round of male hormones.

'Was he a girl at birth then?' I murmur to myself, scrolling through the Wikipedia page. 'What karyotype did Mia come up with?'

I can't wait until tomorrow, so I drive over to the clinic and let myself in with my key, quickly disabling the security system. There, in my fax machine, is the key to Max's intersexuality. I boot up my work computer, type Mia's analysis into a browser and click 'search'. Three hours later, I'm still trawling through websites, rapt.

I print out each document I find, a mass of paper amounting on my printer tray. I absent-mindedly staple leaves together, bind others in hole-punched folders. I daydream about giving them to Max, going to his school, perhaps dropping by his house. I sit and I wonder how much he knows about his condition.

From our meeting, it seemed to me like he knew very little. I wonder if his parents plan to tell him when he's older. I have a feeling that explaining everything to him would be for the best, but would it be going against their wishes?

Is it my duty as a doctor to tell him everything I know? I could tell him if he asks, but what if he never does? Is it better for him to go through life unaware, but relatively happy? Or does he only appear to be happy, but is silently searching for something, for a sense of belonging, of self, of home inside his own body?

I could give this all to Max and ruin his life. Or I could give this to him and he could feel relieved to know who and what he is. I might send his sixteenth year into turmoil, aggravate a fairly powerful local family, and ruin his vision of himself. What would Max want me to do?

A fortnight later, with the pile of papers in my office at the surgery still awaiting him, Max hasn't contacted me again. I take this as a cue, and I regretfully put all thoughts of spilling his parents' well-kept secrets to the back of my mind.

Max

The middle of October is entrance exam time for Hemingway St Catherine's, the private sixth form college. Other schools do them a bit later, but since I'm local, a space is reserved for me to take the exam early.

Everyone taking the exam has to go over to Hemingway St Catherine's and sit in a big hall. The exam determines who gets in, so I need to do really well. I'm one of the top people in my year, academically, but I still get nervous about exams.

Well, that's not completely true. I get nervous about the grades I'll get after I've done the exam! Actual exams are pretty good, because:

1. You get it over with and if it's a subject you're not taking when you're older, then you never have to remember what you've revised for again.
2. It beats lessons any day.
3. Because it takes a little time to get over to St Catherine's and settle into the exam hall, you basically get a whole afternoon off from school.

I don't, however, feel that great about today, because Hunter goes here. Despite the fact that his grades have dropped off this year and I know his parents are pissed at him about it, Hunter's actually really smart. He scored ninety-eight per cent on the entrance exam when he took it.

We wait in the corridor and I watch out for him anxiously, but I don't see him. I'm relieved as my group files into the big hall. We're called in alphabetically, so when I walk in, amongst the last there, Sylvie Clark is already sat near the front, in the first row. I smile at her as we pass. I've smiled at her a number of times in the last few weeks, but she always looks away. It's funny, outside of school she had no problem talking to me. Inside the school corridors, she seems to avoid everybody's eyes. Today she has her hair in two bunches either side of her face. When I smile at her, her irises roll down to the page in front of her and she chews the tip of her pen. She's wearing a grey skirt that's pleated and hangs low on her legs, grey tights, and some badges in her black jumper. The girls in my school have to wear grey, the boys wear black. We all wear black jumpers because you can't find V-neck grey jumpers and it's too cold to go without. She twirls her ankle like she's listening to music in her head.

I grin and whisper to myself, 'Kook.'

My seat is the second desk to the very last in the whole hall, in front of Todd Z. Todd used to do pretty well in class but recently he's been doing worse. So have most of the guys, because they're all going out with other people now. Marc was mumbling about Olivia to me the other day. I think he wants to go out with her, after what happened at my birthday thing on Saturday.

They left when we all did, and she went back to his house for a bit. They didn't go inside apparently, but they 'talked' outside. 'Talked' means made out, no matter how innocently Marc said it. I used to hang out with Olivia, so I think he feels bad. I don't mind though. I did really like her, but I couldn't go out with her properly, of course. So I told him it was OK if he wanted to, even though he hadn't asked. Then Olivia hung out with me yesterday on the football pitch. She said she really liked Marc, hoped I didn't feel bad, etc. I said that Marc really liked her, and she should go for it. I didn't tell her I used to really like her. It would only make her feel guilty. I do still really like her, actually, I just don't like to think about it. She's really nice and funny. I always liked hanging out with her. It was fun. I felt a pang of regret when I said she should go out with Marc. But they both like each other, and they're both free to go out, so. I said it wouldn't make things awkward between me and Marc, that I was the one who said I couldn't go out with her, so I couldn't say anything. I told them both. We'll see what happens.

The examiner tells us he's going to wait for five minutes so we start on the hour. We have to sit in silence, so I rest my head on my hand and think about yesterday evening, when Daniel kicked off about the exam.

It's then that I see him. He's walking past the window. Somehow I feel him before I see him. He's walking, talking to a friend. He's wearing the uniform: black suit, white shirt, and black tie. His head turns towards me, as if in slow motion. When he sees me he keeps walking, but Hunter touches the knot of his tie, his lips part, and his brow changes minutely, his eyes narrowing, checking it's me. Then he smiles.

115

Daniel

I only got angry because Max finds everything so easy and I
find everything so hard and I think it's unfair. I have to try
all the time to 'check my behaviour', like Miss Jameson says,
even though I don't know what it is that they don't like about
my behaviour. It just makes me so angry, and then they don't
like that I'm angry, but how can I not be angry if they are going
to be so stupid and treat me like a baby?

Then with this exam, Mum was saying how she was sure
Max would do really well and go to the good school, and I just
asked if she thought I would do the exam and go to the good
school.

And she said, 'There are lots of schools, honey.'

And I said, 'I want to go to the GOOD school.'

And then Mum sighed at me like it was my fault I find things
harder. I'm really good at Maths. I don't see why I wouldn't
pass the exam. Then she said sorry for sighing, because she was
tired and I shouted, 'MAX never tires you out.'

And then Max sighed and rubbed his hands over his face and
I said, 'Why are you sighing at me?'

And he said, 'Sorry, no, I wasn't sighing at you, Daniel. I'm
just trying to revise.'

I said, 'Fine, I'll go.'

And I went upstairs. Then later I came down and yelled at
Mum that I could do the exam and if Max finds everything so
easy why don't they just give him the scholarship without the
exam. I asked Max if I was any stupider than him and he said
no, but then he said he had to work and he'd talk to me later,
but then he never did and Mum wouldn't read me my bedtime
story because I kept asking when Max was going to come in
and talk to me. I told her I didn't want to hear what she had to

say to me, I wanted to hear what Max had to say, because we're brothers and he never lies to me.

Mum got hurt and she said, 'I never lie to you', but she said it sort of confused, like she didn't know.

Then she went to bed.

This morning I told Max I was disappointed with him for not coming in to see me at bedtime.

He said he was sorry. Then he said, 'I like talking to you about this stuff, but sometimes I really have to revise and do school work. Why don't you write it down during the day, if you think you're going to flip out at someone, and then you'll remember to talk about it to me in the evenings, and if there's an evening I miss, we'll make it up the day after.'

I frowned. 'Go on.'

'And we'll, like, work out solutions together. And talk about it. I don't mind,' he said, smiling. Mum looked at him like he was amazing. I rolled my eyes. But I like talking to Max.

So I thought about this for a minute and then I said, 'OK.'

Max gave me a big hug. He got the car in with us this morning, so that he could revise before he went. In the car Mum played Max's CD of The Strokes, which we all like, so we were happy when we got to school.

Mum gave me a kiss and I waved to them as the car went away. Then I turned and gave the school a once-over. Miss Jameson, my nemesis, was standing in the window. I was going to glare evilly at her, but then I remembered I promised Max I'd write stuff down rather than flip out. So I put my bag down on the tarmac of the car park, got out my workbook, and wrote: 'Miss Jameson nemesis looking at me from evil HQ (her office)'.

I saw a movement in the corner of my eye, and I noticed Miss Jameson walking down the path towards me, so I put everything in my school bag and put it on my back. Everyone at school has *Ben 10* backpacks but I have a *World of War* backpack.

'What are you doing out here, Daniel?' Miss Jameson says.

And I smile at her like an angel and say, 'Just making notes for a story for school, Miss Jameson', and she looks confused and I skip past her, grinning to myself, and go to my classroom.

Max

'Pens down,' I hear from the front of the exam hall.

I'm shaking and sweating. I still have to finish my answer. I go to put my pen down and have a thought: I'm so obedient. I just put my pen down. I just lie there for Hunter.

I look up to the front of the room. The adjudicator is picking up people's papers and not looking this way. I quickly scribble the rest of my answer. I put my pen in my pocket. Done.

I see Sylvie's copper-caramel head up front. Her chin rests on her hand, and she's looking out the window Hunter walked past earlier. I can see the outline of her lips and cheek. I look out the window.

'Thank you,' the adjudicator murmurs, when he walks past me. It's our cue to stand up. We file out from the back first, out a different door.

'Hey, it's your cousin,' says Todd.

Ahead of me, Hunter is leaning against the door of a classroom. He's waiting for me, just past the exit of the hall, in a corridor lined with light green flooring. It gives everything a cold hue. He looks sharp, tall, together, still. People part to let us walk towards each other. He raises a hand to Todd, who nods, then leaves us alone. They all know Hunter as my cousin. As I get closer, I feel like I'm being pulled on a track, that it's inevitable that I must walk up to him. How could it not be? Everyone is watching. Everyone knows we're close. They expect us to say hi. I feel eyes on us. Everyone stares. A metre away and he looks me up and down slowly, swallows and adjusts his tie again.

'Hi,' he murmurs, his voice deep, his hand touching the back of my blazer firmly, and reaching across my shoulders. I feel it stroking sideways from the back of my right shoulder to my left. I feel him pulling me closer. 'Y'alright?' he drawls.

I nod, not knowing what to say.

'Missed me?'

I don't reply. I notice some people watching us, so I put on a smile and nod at Hunter. I try to say something, but I find I can't. I chew on my lip, remembering to keep smiling, and feel my face getting hotter and hotter.

'Aren't you going to say anything?' he says.

I open my mouth. I look over to where people are watching us, as they walk by, dozens of strangers passing us in a stream on their way to classrooms. I try to speak. I try again. I shake my head. My whole body feels heated. I feel like I'm sweating in my armpits and my socks.

'I can't,' I say quietly.

He frowns. 'What's wrong with you? Why you being so uptight?'

I shrug, still grinning. Smiling and smiling like my mouth is cut into that shape. I imagine the corners sliced away at the sides, the lips locked into a perpetual clown grin.

He leans in and whispers in my ear. 'Is it because I saw your junk?' He darts out from my ear and grins at me. As if it's funny. As if it's no big deal.

I imagine Hunter again above me, looking at all that. All that mess. My cheeks burn and I feel my face about to buckle. I pull my hair in front of my eyes with my hand and turn in towards Hunter so the people passing can only see my back.

'Max, don't worry,' he says, his tone changing, lowering, his smile gone. 'I was so pissed I can hardly remember it.'

I look up. He seems genuine. He doesn't seem like he's lying. He looks concerned that I'm not talking.

'Really?' I say, swallowing. My throat feels like it's swollen.

He smiles slowly and his eyes go to my temple and across my forehead and down to my lips. 'Sure. Fun though, wasn't it?'

Is he crazy? I shake my head incredulously. 'No!' I whisper, my voice breaking.

Hunter grins and pokes me in the stomach. 'Come on, you loved it. All that moaning.'

'Shut up! No I didn't,' I hiss.

'Yes you did!' he scoffs, looking a little confused, half-smiling, half-frowning. He looks at my lips again and he swallows. He's nervous too. He shrugs, as if to say, 'Well, never mind, it was just a bit of fun'.

A thought crosses my mind and I mutter, quietly, in horror, 'You've not told anyone, have you?'

He shrugs.

'Please, Hunter, please don't, OK?'

He starts to grin, like he's teasing me, and shrugs again.

'Please!' I say too loudly, then look down, look around, fiddling with the bottom of my blazer. I meet his eyes and beg him. 'Please, please don't tell anyone. If you do, everyone will find out about me.'

'Shh, Max.' He shakes his head.

'Please, please, please,' I beg him, moving closer to him, about to cry.

He takes pity on me. 'Shh, quiet, OK?' He touches my arm lightly. 'I'm not going to tell anyone. Don't be crazy. This is me, Hunter. Your secret's safe with me, Max.'

It's when he says this last bit that the timbre of his voice goes dark and threatening. I stare at him, absolutely rooted to the spot with terror, but he just looks normal. He looks as if nothing's really wrong, as if he can't understand why I'm so frightened.

Hunter squints at me searchingly. 'We're alright, aren't we?' he asks. I feel his hand on the muscle of my upper arm. He squeezes it gently.

I bite my lip, studying him. I give him a big smile. 'Yeah, we're OK, Hunter.'

Sylvie

After the exam, bored, done, dusted, easy, I stare out the window at the day I'm missing.

'Up,' murmurs the dude at the front of the room, like I'm a dog heeling. I raise my eyebrows, and slowly, slowly, circle my feet around to the side of my chair, and lift myself out of it. I look back at him angrily and wander down through the hall to the door at the back of the room, which almost everyone but me has already left through.

I walk softly through it, opening it, and stop, holding the door. I feel like I'm in a movie, so cinematic is the scene in front of me. In the further reaches of the corridor, I see a river of uniformed older kids passing through from the corridor to a classroom. Another smaller river passes the other way, out of the corridor. These are people from the exam hall.

I am the only person at the end of the corridor, but between myself and the river are Max and his cousin. I am the observer, and I have the weirdest feeling, like this is a scene in a play and it's telling me something. Everything looks staged: Max and Hunter being right in the middle distance, having the other people in the far distance, me being equidistant to them as the far distance is from them. Max is standing straight and stiff and facing Hunter, and the low light is making his hair glow very yellow, very prettily. It's all over his face, a messy veil. Hunter is laughing, and his sharp face is turned into Max's. They look like they're sharing a secret joke. It just seems theatrical for a moment.

And then someone pushes through the door behind me and bumps my shoulder, and the moment is gone, the symmetry of the scene broken.

Hunter looks over at me, noticing I'm looking, and Max

notices Hunter noticing me. I watch him follow Hunter's gaze over to me, and I hold my hand up in a casual wave.

'Hi,' says Max, faltering, eyes on me.

Hunter looks away from me and smirks at Max. 'I'll catch you later.'

He starts to walk away, but then leans back, trying to catch Max's eye. 'Max, yes? OK?' He touches his arm. 'Max?'

'Yeah.' Max smiles weakly and shrugs. ''Kay.'

'Bye,' says Hunter, in exactly the same sweet tone Max said 'bye' to me on the field.

As Hunter walks away I walk up to Max. I know I look really steady, but I'm hiding nervousness. I'm really good at hiding nervousness.

'You don't look alike, but you can tell you're cousins,' I say, when I reach him.

Max frowns. 'We're not,' he says. 'Our parents are just friends.'

'Oh, I thought—'

'We're not,' he says again. He watches Hunter leave. I wonder if I can just walk around Max and run off. But then Max turns back to me. He beams sweetly.

'How are you?'

123

Max

On the Friday before Daniel's tenth birthday, I'm in a bad mood.

I've been getting these moods, on and off. Just occasionally dipping down into hate and depression, thinking of Hunter and being intersex and everything. I remember Hunter above me, using the 'he-she' word (horrible horrible horrible), and I feel like it matters more now. I feel like for years my family has been pretending I'm normal. And I'm really not.

Usually I can deal with it, put it to the back of my mind, smile at everybody. But with these moods I've been having, I don't feel like playing football or being around people. Being around people just means I have to make a huge effort to look happy when I feel really unhappy. I'm exhausted, but I'm sleeping heavily. I don't really feel like doing much of anything. So on Friday at lunch, I go to the library to do my homework, hoping to get it all out the way so I can just sleep when I get home.

Sylvie Clark is in there, to my surprise. I rarely ever see her at lunchtime. It's not like I've not looked, if you know what I mean. I've looked.

I put my books down gently on a table near hers and slump into my chair, picking up my History textbook. I'm taking English Literature, English Language, Maths, Information Technology, Physics, Chemistry and Biology. These are all compulsory at our school. You also have to take one language, so I'm doing Latin. Then you get three electives, so I chose Ancient History, Politics and Psychology. I wanted to do Art too, because I like sketching, but I'm not that great at it, so my careers advisor told me not to do it. He said if I got a B or a C in it, it would bring down my application to universities. At the time, this scared me into not doing it, but now I think he was talking a bunch of crap. It's only GCSEs. You have to do A Levels and then a degree before anybody takes anything you do seriously. But teachers live in school so they think it's the be-all and end-all. News flash for them: there are bigger things going on in life.

'Hey,' someone murmurs over my shoulder.

I look around. Sylvie Clark has moved closer to me. 'So, what are you doing?' she drawls in her husky voice.

I shrug and blush. 'Nothing,' I say, massaging my head.

'You alright?' she asks.

'Just a headache,' I say, and smile automatically.

'I saw you in the paper,' she says. 'So your dad's going to be our MP?'

'Oh.' I shrug and turn back to my book. 'I guess. He's running anyway. There's only one other candidate, and he's a Tory.'

'I bet your dad will win. You're gonna be famous,' she says, in a funny way.

'Not really.'

'Well, don't go being naughty like the last MP's kid did. Weren't they all over the paper for wearing some kind of fascist outfit to a fancy dress party?'

I close my eyes for a moment and think about what it would be like if Hunter went to the paper and it was all over the front page that I was intersex and I'd done it with him and everybody read it and no one could look at me without imagining Hunter inside me.

'Guess I shouldn't do that then.'

There's a minute of silence, and then the chair next to me is pulled out and she sits on it and brings her stuff over.

'You're not OK, are you?'

I frown and shrug. 'Why didn't you come to my birthday?' I ask.

Sylvie looks puzzled. 'Huh?'

'You weren't doing anything,' I whine. 'You lied. It was obvious.'

She purses her lips. 'Oh.'

'Did you think I couldn't tell?'

'I'm sorry, Max. I didn't mean to make you feel bad.'

'Why did you lie?'

'I . . . I'm not good around . . . people.'

I think for a minute. 'But you never smile at me in the corridor when I smile at you either. You ignore me.'

'Oh!' She laughs.

'I don't think it's that funny,' I mutter, confused.

'No, like, the main reason I don't say hi is because I have really bad eyesight.'

'Huh?'

'I need glasses, but I don't want to get them, because it's an acknowledgement of my vulnerability. Basically, I don't want to believe that I can't see stuff. So I keep my head low all the time in case someone waves and I don't know who it is.'

'That's a stupid reason! You should get some glasses!'

'I know, I've got an appointment. I hope I don't look weird in them.'

I put my classbook down and think about whether to say what I want to say. I look sideways at her. 'You couldn't look weird,' I say, despite myself.

Sylvie pauses. 'Re. the not saying hi thing . . . I'm also kind of awkward, in general. Like, shy.'

'You didn't seem shy or awkward when I met you in the churchyard, or after the exam,' I point out.

'Mm.' She shrugs. 'Didn't you notice I left when Marc and Carl came over?'

'I guess.' I think, remembering. 'Listen, if you're so awkward that you don't know normal social etiquette then . . . I think I should just give you some pointers.'

She frowns. 'Ohhhkaaay. I'm listening.'

'The rules are, if you know someone you say hi to them, and if you want to hang out with me alone and not with other people, you just tell me.' I smile, kind of shyly, a bit worried the teasing won't go down well. I can't tell with. Sylvie Clark. I murmur the last bit under my breath. 'You kook.'

She laughs. 'I didn't know those were the rules, but now you've told me, I promise I'll say hi, OK?'

'OK,' I murmur, grinning.

The librarian hisses at Sylvie to be quiet.

'Sorry,' I say to the librarian. She frowns.

'*Shh,*' she hisses, this time just at me.

'Don't worry,' Sylvie says, as the bell goes for fifth period. 'She hates everyone. Even your angelic charm won't work on her.'

I watch her pack up her bag and I gather my books in my arms.

Sylvie stands up, her shirt falling out of the front of her skirt. Her knees are scuffed, and the cuffs of her shirt are chewed.

I take a deep breath.

'Sylvie, do you like ten-year-olds?'

'Huh?'

'It's my brother's birthday party tomorrow. He gave me an invite for one friend,' I say, fishing it out of my pocket.

'Erm.' She bites her lip.

'Don't say you're busy,' I mutter, in a kind of too-miserable I-know-you're-going-to-say-no way, and she laughs at me. 'Sorry,' I say, embarrassed. I smile, as if to say 'I'm an idiot'. 'You don't have to come.'

'Sure, OK,' she says. 'I'll come.'

We head out the library.

'Cool!' I say, gratefully, letting out a sigh. 'You have to come as a ghost.'

'Hm. Did you wait to tell me that until after I consented, so I'd be more likely to agree to come?' Sylvie says to me as we walk down the stairs from the library to our form rooms.

I nod at her as we part. 'Yeah,' I laugh. 'Yeah, I did.'

Daniel

My brother brought his girlfriend to my birthday party today. At least, I think she is his girlfriend. That's what Mum says.

I don't get what the difference is between a girlfriend and a friend who is a girl. Max has said things about them being attractive, but is that the only difference? People have girl-friends and boyfriends at school, but they hang out just like normal friends do. Sometimes they hold hands. Sometimes I want to hold hands with Mouse at school, I guess, but she is just my friend. Her real name is Mel, but she is small with big ears, so I call her Mouse. She thinks it's funny, though. She doesn't get annoyed with me like stupid, old duckface, Miss Jameson.

But I think when you get older, it gets different, like Mum and Dad, so I suppose you would kiss and hug and stuff. And have sex and babies. I don't know why everyone is so obsessed with sex. It sounds gross.

Max didn't do anything girlfriendish with this Sylvie, though. He didn't even kiss her. They just watched me open presents and then they played on the Xbox with us for a bit, and then they helped Mum and Dad with getting dinner ready. Then Sylvie went home when my friends did. Max walked her home, and when he got back I asked if he kissed her.

And he grinned and went red, but he said no, he didn't.

I said, 'Why not?'

And Mum said, 'Daniel!'

And Max said, 'Maybe next time', but quietly, like he thought me and Mum couldn't hear. I don't think Mum heard, but I did.

Max

We roll over wet ground on a cold October day. Her lips taste of orange lip balm and fruit tea. Her tongue is hot. I bury my face in her honey hair, I bite her neck, she laughs out loud, we chase each other, we fall to the ground. Sylvie Clark is breathing life into me, and I haven't thought about September for over a day and the white autumn light bleaches her face out and sets her blue eyes electric, and I bend over her and tickle her skin with my hair and kiss her softly and smile.

Dreaming is as good as the real thing, without the risk.

Nothing happened at Daniel's birthday party, or when I walked her home. She looked so pretty; too pretty to just kiss and walk away and pretend like it was just a kiss. Her hair was gold in every pool of lamplight. The sun had already gone down. The breeze was still a little warm, but when I hugged her, her brown cheek was cool and soft against mine. I feel shy around Sylvie like I've never done with other girls. Maybe it's to do with the Hunter thing. Sometimes I wonder what she'd think of me if she knew. Anyway. She just looked too pretty.

She was quite quiet during the party. We were just hanging out, not talking much. She talked to Daniel, she was sweet with him. She brought him a card with some money in. I kept looking over at her, then when she looked over I would look away. I thought back to all the girls I've kissed and realised that I'm not exactly forward. They have always come a certain distance, and then I leant in to meet them. With Sylvie, she was just sitting back, being nice and friendly, but a little shy, and that made me more shy. I didn't want her to . . . I don't know, whatever. Reject me. Or kiss me. Kiss me, and then everything fast forward, and me have to stop doing whatever we were doing, because of what is in my pants.

I couldn't tell what she was thinking. I just remember

thinking it was enough, to just hang out with her, and occasionally brush my arm against hers, when we were setting the table or playing on the Xbox.

November goes by in a rush of schoolwork and winning matches. Sylvie continues to ignore me most days in the corridors, but now I know it's because she's awkward. And sometimes – sometimes – she smiles at me. And it makes me feel alive in every cell in my body.

I'm doing well in all my subjects, which bodes well for the GCSE mocks, which we're always reminded are getting closer and closer. We'll learn if I got the scholarship for St Catherine's in January, after my mock results come through. They base the scholarship on both the entrance exam and your GCSE mocks.

I spend November working really hard, revising in the evenings and getting all my coursework done, most of it ahead of time, all of it by the deadline, in any case. Sometimes I wonder why. I think a lot about being in the same school as Hunter, having to see him every day. I try not to think about it but I do, when I'm in bed at night.

Daniel doesn't have any more incidents at school and we talk pretty much every night about the things that have been bothering him. Sometimes the things that bother him are funny (for example: 'Andrew took the best colour paint in art'), some are alarming (e.g. 'wanted to push Mouse into a pond today after she spent entire day trip out of school talking to Rasheed instead of me'), but most, oddly, I can relate to. It's good to talk to him and it takes my mind off my own crap.

Dad's campaign was announced and is heating up. But by December, I guess it seems almost routine. It just feels like another of their big cases, with lawyers and assistants round at our house, always until late at night, ordering Chinese takeaway and making endless cups of coffee.

There's Lawrence, Dad's right-hand guy, and there are assistants and volunteers and a new intern, Debbie, who is nineteen and at university, and seems to always be around now. She's nice and quite hot, but I can't think about anyone but Sylvie.

The front living room is redone even nicer than before, and seems to have been redecorated by this black ops decorating team in a matter of hours. It's so Dad can bring people home to talk to them and convince them to give him money and support. People keep talking to me about it outside school, but no one in school cares much.

I'm still getting in bad moods, though. Sometimes I just don't want to get out of bed. I feel exhausted. I don't think it is all because of the Hunter thing. Maybe it's just winter, just a lack of sun and heat.

Nothing has happened since I saw Hunter at school. Hunter's parents, Leah and Edward, have only come over once in the past month, and I went to Carl's in case Hunter picked them up, but Daniel said he didn't. Sometimes Leah, Edward and Hunter come see us on Christmas day, but they're going to Leah's parents in Yorkshire for Christmas this year, and we're going to spend it at home with my granddad on my Mum's side, Auntie Cheryl and Charlie, Dad's sister Julie, Julie's boyfriend and Julie's new baby, which is due in a week and a half, on December the seventh. Dad's parents are going to Australia for Christmas, and Mum's mum died when Mum was my age.

We're all pretty excited about Auntie Julie having a baby. It'll be cool to have a cousin. We don't have any real ones. Plus it'll be really cute. I love babies. You can see them learning, listening, watching you, figuring you out behind their eyes. I've never been around a really tiny, just-born baby much before either.

They didn't find out the sex. I think it's because Auntie Julie knows about me. When she came round the other weekend, she said that she doesn't care if it's a boy or a girl. I didn't meet her eyes. I don't know if she was looking at me. I kind of hope it's a girl. We don't have one in the family yet. I think Julie secretly wants a girl. She just doesn't want to jinx it. I can understand that. But I think a little girl would be perfect. We'll know soon, I guess.

Karen

Friday morning. It's my fault the house is full of hassle today. Everyone is wound up. I suggested it: a family photo, one of the cheesy ones with a white background, everybody laughing. Steve said he could do it as part of the campaign, cover the cost, get a few different shots taken.

'I want to use them as Christmas cards, so we have to do them now,' I had said.

Whenever I receive similar ones in the mail from friends and colleagues this time of year, I usually go along with the boys as they describe them as 'cheesy' (Max), 'silly' (Daniel) and 'a bit nineties perhaps' (Steve), but secretly I think they're so cute. With this picture, I want to capture something, a moment in the life of our family when everything is perfect; some example of happiness we could all aspire to achieve every day, in case we forget how to do it or what we are aiming for. Maybe that's ridiculous. All I told Steve was that we needed it, so we took the boys out of school for the morning.

At any rate, Steve agreed.

'It'll look good blown up on the big wall in the entrance hall,' he said. 'United front. Family values. Maybe one on the stairs.'

'Mm,' I hummed. 'Well, that's not exactly . . .'

He swept away to get it booked.

Daniel seems to have turned over a new leaf. Max has been talking to him a lot recently about his frustrations at school. I think Max has been a bit ill. He's tired a lot and wants to stay at home after school rather than go out and play football, so it's good that he has Daniel as a little project. He's a good example and I can't help feeling overly proud of him, in a smug, motherly way. I don't know what I'd do without him.

The newly-sweet Daniel helps me with the washing up after breakfast and stays in the kitchen to talk. He is telling me about a project he is doing for History, about the Ancient Egyptians, when Max wanders in, in his jeans and an old flannel shirt. He slumps down next to me at the kitchen table and starts going through all the ironed clothes.

'Mum, where's my blue jumper?'

I look up from ironing my jeans. 'Oh, do you have to wear that, Max?'

'Huh?'

'That shirt's so old and those jeans are ripped. No, sorry,' I say firmly. 'You have to change.'

'OK,' he says dubiously, looking down at his clothes.

I pull a freshly ironed pair of khaki trousers from the pile, still warm. 'Put these on, and this shirt.'

'I wouldn't wear these with a shirt,' he mutters reproachfully.

'What would you wear with a shirt?'

He thinks. 'I guess I wouldn't wear a shirt.'

'Well, you'll have to one day for work, so get used to it.'

'Only if I do something like lawyer-ing,' he says grumpily.

I frown at him, too surprised to tell him off. Max is never moody. 'OK, well, pick a T-shirt.'

He hesitates and chooses one from the pile of ironing.

'Hand me what you're wearing for the wash. I'll just give these trousers another iron; they're still a bit creased.'

He looks down.

'Come on, we haven't got all day, Max,' I instruct, stressing. 'We have to be there by nine.'

Max obediently pulls the flannel shirt over his head, holding his hands over his chest. He pulls the T-shirt on.

'Come on.' I hurry him along.

He nods and unbuttons his jeans, still slowly. He takes them off.

'Which blue jumper was it?'

'Um . . .'

'Which one, honey?' I glance distractedly at the laundry basket.

'Why are you ironing Max's trousers and your jeans?' Daniel asks me.

133

Max asks me about getting the trousers, but I barely hear him. I'm thinking about not being late, about doing my make-up, about where Steve is, about elongating this precious bit of peace with Daniel.

'To get the creases out, sweetheart,' I reply to Daniel, sounding calmer than I feel. 'Do you want me to do yours?'

'Mm.' He thinks, sipping orange juice from a carton. 'No.'

'Can I have my—'

'Which blue jumper, Max?' I repeat impatiently.

'Mum, THE blue jumper, my only blue jumper,' Max snaps. 'Pass me my trousers!'

Daniel and I turn to stare at him.

'What's wrong with *you*?' asks Daniel.

'I just want the trousers,' Max whines, uncomfortably. He is crossing his arms over his boxers and looking stressed.

'Sweetie, I'm *ironing* them,' I say. 'Do you want to iron them?'

He shakes his head despondently.

'What's wrong?'

'Nothing,' Max mumbles. 'Just want my trousers and my jumper.'

'When did you last wear your jumper?'

'Urgh!' He runs his hands through his hair and repositions them over his boxers. 'OBVIOUSLY I've already thought of that. I can't find it!'

'Max! Don't talk to me like that!' I frown. 'Sweetie, what's wrong?'

'Nothing. Talk like what?'

'You're shouting,' I say soothingly. 'You never shout.'

'Daniel shouts all the time and way worse!'

'Yeah, but you don't,' says Daniel.

'I just want to put my fucking trousers on.' Max growls so comically that I laugh in spite of myself.

'I changed your nappies, Max. There's no need to be bashful! And don't say the eff word.'

'Hey, Max,' says Daniel.

'What?'

'You swore at Mum. You're the bad boy now.'

Max reaches out with one arm and shoves Daniel's chair. It's only a slight move of his arm, but the chair leans sideways for a moment, tilting as if it will right itself, then Daniel slips across it, the weight shifts, and it topples to the floor.

'Ahhh!' Daniel bursts into a sob. 'My head!'

'Max!' I cry, aghast, running round the table to help Daniel up.

Max's face creases up and I can't tell if he's about to cry or scream. He takes his trousers off the ironing board.

I watch him, incredulous, while I hug Daniel. 'What's come over you?'

'I didn't mean for the chair to fall over,' he mutters, pulling the trousers over his socks.

'You pushed him,' I say, shaking my head. 'I'm so disappointed in you.'

'What's happening?' says Steve, striding into the kitchen.

'Max pushed Daniel,' I hear myself say, uncomprehendingly, as if the laws of gravity have just been suspended.

'I'm sorry,' Max mutters, his trousers already on.

'Why did you do that, Max?' Steve's deep voice cuts through Daniel's crying. Steve picks up Daniel and holds him, big as he is, on his waist. Daniel puts his arms about him.

I turn my attention back to Max. He stares at Steve, attempting to speak, but not knowing what to say. His fingertips touch each other and he picks his nails anxiously.

'I'm sorry,' he says. Everything about the situation is alien to him, to us. Max toes the line. That's just who Max is.

I am suddenly so deflated. I wanted this day to be special for us. Max looks at me, crestfallen, reading my expression.

'Isn't it funny when Max is the bad one?' Daniel comments, sniffing.

Max looks from me to Steve as if he doesn't know what happens next.

'Did you push Daniel off his chair?' Steve asks.

Max doesn't say anything.

We stand in silence, a family portrait.

Finally I clear my throat. 'We have to go in ten minutes.'

'Max hasn't apologised to Daniel,' says Steve.

Max looks at Daniel in Steve's arms. His lips open. Daniel pulls closer to Steve. Max frowns. He doesn't speak.

'Max!' Steve snaps.

Max swallows. He looks at Daniel, but he can't apologise. We wait. Max looks at me. I switch the iron off.

'Sorry, Danny,' Max says softly.

'OK,' I say. 'I found your blue jumper. Let's go.'

Max

The day of the photographs, the last day in November, was freezing and I felt weird, unwell, unhappy. I got up, walked through to the bathroom to pee, looked at myself in the bathroom mirror and retched. Nothing came up, but I think it was just something about the way my hair and mouth looked. It was . . . I don't know. Seductive. Kind of innocent. It was too quick between the look and throwing up for conscious thought. I just gave myself a glance then turned to the toilet and my stomach heaved, just once, but I briefly thought about how people who knew about my condition might see me. Hunter's one of the only ones who does, and he couldn't stop himself from doing that to me. It's weird to think of yourself as this seductive thing, with no thought to you, how you are. It's as if my sexuality doesn't belong to or have anything to do with me, just Hunter, or the other people who look at me, and how they see me.

I looked so otherworldly for a moment in the mirror. It's not often that you really look at yourself, is it? It's not often that you stare in a mirror. In the bathroom this morning I saw an androgynous fullness to my lips, a softness to the long slope of my jaw, this ambiguous eye, full lashes and no make-up, coming out from behind my hair. I don't look girlish. I do look boyish. But I don't look like a man. I'm something in-between, and normally I don't see it. It was just that angle as I turned, as I looked up. It made me flinch. It made me wonder if I was the kind of person who turned perverts on.

It made me wonder, for a brief moment, if that was the only kind of person I could turn on. Then I remembered how Sylvie looks at me sometimes, and I felt OK again. This was after I'd thrown up, after I'd washed my face, while I was sitting on the closed toilet seat, the door locked, picking my nails, wondering. Feeling inadequate, lost and indefinable. There are no real words for me. Intersex means between two real things.

I stood up and turned around to pee. I pulled down my boxers and took my penis out. I've never had a real problem with my junk. It's the only junk I've ever had. I don't know any different. I wonder if it would gross Sylvie out, though.

When I was little, the doctors called me a hermaphrodite. It's got a lot of stigma, but as a word on its own, I like it better. It's a thing. It's not between things. It's an ancient Greek word. It makes me sound old, like we were always around. I like that.

After we get the photograph taken –

('Amazing, gorgeous, perfect,' the photographer, a woman, kept saying. Danny and I exchanged nervous looks.

'Incredible, amazing, perfect.'

I sighed and I saw his little shoulders in front of me lift and drop too. We smiled until our cheeks ached.)

– they drop us both back in school. I could have stayed home but I have Games in the afternoon. Didn't want to miss football. We're playing a friendly 5-a-side tourney.

'Oi, Captain, look out!'

I turn around and catch the ball on the tip of my shoe. I spin it around, and head upfield, dribbling and running with it.

'Big Tom, take it!' I kick it over to Tom, who is open on the other side of the field. He takes it out and towards the goal, passes to Tiny Tom, then I've run up near the goal on the other side of the field and Tiny Tom passes to me. I shoot, and we score.

'Nice one Big Tom and Tiny Tom!' I shout.

'Thanks, Captain!'

'Alright, you tosser, I'm gonna get you,' Marc laughs, running back to mark me.

Marc's captain of the other team. Me, Carl, Big Tom, Pete and Little Tom are doing well, up two goals to one with twenty minutes to go.

The regional coach, Matt Baxter, is on the sidelines, with our school coach, Mr Harvey.

My chest is aching and I think back, but can't remember getting hit by the ball. I look down my top to see if I'm bruised, but I can't see anything.

'Max, stop staring at your tits and chase down that ball!' yells Mr Harvey.

Matt says nothing, squatting at the sideline. I look over at Matt and make a face when Mr Harvey isn't looking. Matt nods.

Marc has the kick and taps the ball back to Jim, his best defender, who boots it up to Gary, who has raced ahead and is near the goal. Luckily, Carl is too and sends it back up our way.

I get it, pass it to Big Tom, who passes it straight back to me as Marc tears up to him. I pass back to Pete, who pops it up to Little Tom, who runs with it. Then Jim is all over him and the ball shoots back to Marc. I turn and run after him, then get in front and tackle him. The ball slips back to me, Marc tackles it out from under my feet, then turns, and tries to boot it down to their goal end. I dive in front of it and it hits me right in my chest.

'OW!'

It rebounds and I see Marc's feet whip away as I grab myself and bend over.

'Get it together, Walker!' Mr Harvey yells.

I try to stand up but my chest is sore. It feels bruised. I look over my shoulder. Marc pops the ball in the goal. We're drawing.

I stand still, trying to catch my breath.

Matt jogs up. 'You alright, Captain?'

I nod.

'What was up with your chest before?'

'Thought it was bruised,' I gasp. 'It wasn't.'

Matt gestures with his fingers and I let him look down my top.

'Has he hurt his tits?' says Mr Harvey, appearing from behind Matt.

'I'm fine,' I murmur.

Matt presses on my chest.

'Ow! Shit!'

'You're not fine,' says Matt. 'Substitute!' he calls.

Mr Harvey grumbles and rolls his eyes and I look up at them both.

'I'm fine, really.'

The school coach shakes his head. 'It's your bloody build, Max. I told you, you should bulk up or you won't survive the try-outs for the under-eighteen squad,' he says, trying to infuriate me. He turns and walks towards the sideline, getting ready to blow the whistle as Mike Dante comes on as my substitute. Mr Harvey calls to me over his shoulder, 'Man up, Max.'

I scowl at him.

'Don't listen, just come off the pitch,' murmurs Matt. 'You don't want to break your ribs just before Christmas.'

'He's a tosser.'

'Yeah, well, he doesn't decide who's on the team or what happens in the game, mate. You do.'

'Urgh,' I groan, sitting down on the grass next to Matt as everyone else starts to play. 'I can't wait to be out of this school.'

'How much longer have you got until study leave?'

'Six months.'

'Exciting,' says Matt. 'You going to St Catherine's?'

'Hopefully,' I say, kind of glumly. I think about the day of the exam, Hunter's hand touching my shoulder, like it's his to touch.

Marc kicks the ball wide and I follow it with my head as it flies off the pitch. Across the field I see Sylvie standing over by the fence of the netball courts, apart from the other girls.

I would go over, but I have to watch the match. It's not polite to walk away from it, especially with Matt here. But I lift my hand, and I wave at her.

Sylvie

'Hi, Sylvie!' Max Walker seems to come out of nowhere as I'm walking out the school gates. It's Friday, and school has just ended. He waved to me this afternoon, again, like a little kid. He seems in a better mood today. I wave back, smiling.

'Hi Max, how are you?' I say casually.

'Ooo,' Emma calls out as she walks past. 'Max Walker rejected but tries it on again with Sylvie Clark! Way to go, Maxwell!'

I turn to Max and roll my eyes. 'She's an idiot,' I murmur.

He grins. 'My name's not Maxwell, by the way.'

'I didn't think so.'

'So . . .' He shrugs, as if building up to something big.

'Are you going to ask me to hang out again?'

He lets out a breath and looks off into the distance, smiling. 'Oh my god, how did you know? Am I that transparent?'

'Like glass.' I give him a playful push and he gasps. 'Shit, did I hurt you?'

'No, sorry. Football injury.'

'You hurt your tits?'

'They like to play dirty.'

'I'll bet.' I shoot back a grin and we are caught for a moment in a bubble that is completely unfamiliar to me. *So this is it*, I think. *The golden boy bubble*. We smile at each other like we know what's going to happen.

Shit. Shit.

I watch his lips. His pretty hair flutters in the wind in front of one green eye.

Shit.

I like Max Walker.

Before I know it's coming out of my mouth, I say, 'We could go back to mine.'

Max hesitates, his eyes glancing to the side for a moment, and I guess I must look offended, because he seems to panic, smiles and then says, 'Um, OK.'

'Yeah?' I ask, unsure of what I want, of what I expect to happen, a bit worried about him looking panicked.

'Yeah, sounds good!' says Max. He beams at me kind of blankly and heads off in front of me down the path to town.

'You know where I live?' I ask, confused.

'Yeah, you told me.'

'When?'

'Like three years ago in swimming class.'

'What the eff, how do you remember this stuff?' I say incredulously, and Max giggles at me, and takes the lead, and I follow him, like a freaking lamb to the slaughter, like a horny teenage boy after any breathing girl, like a giggling Emma or Laura or Maria after a golden boy.

Shit.

142

Max

Sylvie's house is a beautiful semi-detached Victorian house that I know my dad would love. Like our house, they have a front door they don't really use, with a pretty grand stone surround. Around the back of the house, a door opens into the kitchen, again like ours. When we walk in, instead of kicking her boots off like we do the moment we step in the house, she heads through the kitchen, past a massive range cooker and a huge, bare oak dining table, and through to a small set of stairs that serve the back of the house. I later discover a much larger staircase in the front hall, and understand we are walking up what would have been the servants' stairs in Victorian times.

'Are your parents home?' I ask.

'Nah,' she says. 'But in case they come in, his name is David and her name is Bennu. They'll probably both be at the uni until late, though. Dad's doing a post-grad in Egyptology and Mum's an Archaeology professor.'

'Are your family Egyptian?'

'Um, yeah, my mum's family. But my dad's doing this super big research project on Ancient Egypt. He's obsessed with it.'

'Cool, what is it about?'

'The, um, role of Ma'at in Ancient Egypt applied to modern-day philosophy about democratic society.'

'Wow.'

'Ma'at is the concept of fate and universal balance. It's not an actual mat.'

'OK.' I grin.

She grins back, then frowns. 'Well, I *think*.'

We go into her room and I look around, before remembering not to be nosy. I take off my shoes and coat, then sit on her desk chair.

'You can sit on the bed,' she says.

'Oh, thanks.'

'You're just a nice, simple boy, aren't you, Max?' Sylvie says, smirking weirdly.

I smile, although I'm not sure what she means. 'You think I'm simple?' I say, and laugh.

'I didn't mean stupid,' she replies.

Then her eyes go misty and she leans towards me like she's about to kiss me and I say, 'Have you got any alcohol?'

'Huh?'

'We could play a game,' I say, looking around the room for a bottle of something. 'Like we have to drink every time Meg speaks in *Family Guy*. Do you have cable?'

'That could be a long game. I've seen you really wasted at parties. Do you drink a lot?'

'Not really. Just I . . . can't drink much.' I shrug, grinning. 'I'm a lightweight.'

She raises her eyebrows. 'I'm trying to cut back. But I love dark rum. I'll go get some.'

'OK,' I say, in an overly-cheery way, and she says,

'Wait there,' and leaves the room.

I put my arms around my knees and sit patiently, obediently on her bed.

It's a really nice room. The walls are the dark red of a cherry, with wood almost the same colour. It's not big but it's not small either – it's a good size. She has a double bed, which makes me slightly worried, and two windows: one over her desk and one the other side of the bed. That one has a window seat. She's got loads of poetry books and tons of clothes, all hanging on a rail. A black sphinx sits in the window, watching me.

I'm kind of anxious. I'm all healed up down there, that's not the problem. It's . . . obviously it's still weird. There's no way I would do anything, so that's OK, but it's just that girls always look so disappointed when we get into a situation where we should maybe be going for it, and then I pull away, or move their hand or don't let them kneel down, or whatever. That's happened a few times.

When I first started to get off with girls, sex and oral sex weren't a problem, because we were fourteen and no one was doing it. We would just kiss. I had a nice girlfriend called Anna for a whole year, and then she moved away and I went out with another girl called Lee for a couple of months. Then, about six months ago, everybody started to expect more.

Lee was so nice and funny and really quirky. She liked surfing and had long, hippy-like brown hair with natural light blonde streaks at the front. We used to go hang out a lot at the park, or the doughnut place in town, or at the Kinema, Hemingway's independent cinema. She also liked to play computer games. She swore all the time, and we weren't allowed to at home, so of course I loved that about her. She was great with Daniel too.

I was in the park with Lee on a February night. It would have been pitch black if it weren't for the light from the houses nearby. We were kissing as usual, and as usual, it was great, when suddenly she grabbed my hand off her breast and put it up her skirt. Naturally, I thought this was brilliant. We'd been going out for a while and I was ready. I tried to be really gentle. I'd never touched myself like I was doing to her at that point, so it was a surprise and so sexy. I got hard. Before I knew it, she had unzipped my pants and was pulling down my underwear. As her hand reached around my penis, I yelped and leapt away from her.

'What the fuck?' Lee said, her hair floating in the breeze, her breath visible.

I couldn't say anything. I wouldn't let her touch me, find out what was down there, find out what was missing. I had no way to explain it really, no terminology. At that point I had never even thought about how it would affect life with girls. All I knew was that I was intersex, but I didn't know what that meant. *I still don't, really*, I think, with a frown.

So Lee asked me again.

'What the fuck, Max? Did I hurt you?'

I shook my head.

'You don't want me to touch you? Say something.'

I couldn't meet her eye. I was so embarrassed. I was thinking,

145

Lee, if you knew what was down there, you would never have gone for it. It would gross you out.

Gay people get ridiculed in school, transvestites get ridiculed, boys who wear tight tops and girls that do sports are ridiculed. What would they do to me? I trusted Lee, but if I told her and somehow word got out, I'd have been dead. My life would have been over. No one would look at me the same way. Lee wouldn't. Her parents wouldn't. They'd hate me.

Lee was so angry.

'You know, this makes me feel really shitty,' she hissed at me. 'That was a pretty fuckin' intimate thing I was gonna do for you and you've just had your fingers up me, and now you don't want to fuckin' talk at all?'

I put my hand to my forehead to shield my eyes. I shook my head again, in a silent apology, and turned around and zipped up.

When I turned back, she was at the locked gate to the park, climbing over it, and landing outside.

After Lee, I decided to just fool around with people. I didn't want to break anyone's heart again, so I'd act friendly and then kiss the people I absolutely fancied so bad I HAD to kiss them at the end of the night. When I started to do this, I'd tell them, 'let's take it slow', but what I didn't realise was that that implied that I was a stud who'd been there, done that, and it was no big deal so I could wait. Everyone knew I'd been with Lee, so this made me look experienced. This was problematic on two counts:

1. Because it made it sound to people who were up for fooling around and didn't want to go out with me like I was definitely up for having sex with people, only after a couple of hours, days or weeks, when we had worked through kissing, hand jobs, oral etc.
2. Because even if I really, really liked the person I was getting off with, and especially if I thought they really liked me, I couldn't let myself fall in love with them, or them fall for me,

because then they would want to have sex anyway, because they would think I'd done it already, same as the others.

And if I had sex with them, everyone at school would find out what I was. And then everyone would crucify me, just like they crucified Samuel Collins, when he came out last year, or when Ellie Panger kissed Katie Fox at that party this summer and Katie told everyone Ellie was way too into it. It would be another sexuality/gender thing that would give people the creeps, and it's no use asking why questions of sexuality and gender give people the creeps, and it's no use blaming it on society and saying it should change, because nothing is going to change about high school, and bitches who gossip, and guys who get freaked out and think people like Samuel want to get off with the entire football team. Nothing is going to change my high school in the next year and make it OK for people to know the truth about me. Nothing is going to change that would stop everyone from wanting to know and from talking about it and from feeling . . . grossed out, I guess.

Now when I kiss a girl, I just move her hands away from that area, or stop kissing altogether and suggest we go inside, get a drink. I guess I've already lost my virginity anyway. I guess that's one bonus of the Hunter thing. I won't die a virgin. Fuck. I've lost my virginity. I didn't imagine it would go like that.

Understatement of the century.

I rest my head on my knees and turn to look at Sylvie's big red pillows and her teddy bear propped at the head of her bed. This thing with Sylvie has been different. She's different. I'm different with her. It's not that I don't want to kiss her, because I really do, but it's that I want other things more. I want to hang out with her. I want to talk. I want to be her best friend. And that complicates things so much more, because it means that she invites me home, and I go, my legs excitedly carrying me there even as my mind is apprehensive of what will happen. I don't want to offend her. I don't want her to hate me. And yeah, even though I won't take off my clothes, and I can't go further

147

than kissing, this time I really, really want to. My whole body is humming with it.

You're in Sylvie's bedroom, says my brain.

Yup.

Are you gonna do it with her?

No, how can I?

Oh, go on. You want to bury your face in her hair so bad. What's the worst that could happen?

She could scream and run away and tell everybody.

Come on, she likes you! Maybe it won't be like that. How do you know how she'll react?

I know.

But—

Please stop talking about it or you're gonna make me cry in her room.

You've been so emotional lately.

I know.

You've been emotional, you hurt your chest, you've been throwing up. Are you sure there isn't anything wrong? Are you thinking about that night in September again? With Hunter?

Shut up!

'Hey.' Sylvie comes back in. 'Rum and Coke?'

I nod, smile, hold my hand out for a cup and realise it is shaking.

'Definitely need one or three of those right now,' I say. I think she sees I look nervous, so she takes pity on me and turns on the TV.

'I was thinking about what we could do. Do you want to play *Tech Dog*?'

'Sure,' I say, watching her set it up. 'My brother loves video games. We play all the time.'

'Cool,' she says, and hands me a controller. We sit down together on the floor. Our knees are touching, I can smell her perfume, and I can't help thinking *It's really nice, and I don't want to leave.*

Sylvie

'You're so drunk!'
'I'm not!'

'Oh, Max . . .' I stroke the hair around his face and tease him. 'You're such a lightweight.'

It's after we've played *Tech Dog* and had a few rum and Cokes, and I'm surprised to see Max is pretty smashed. He's all floppy and cuddly and, during the last few games, he kept putting his head on my shoulder.

I was like, 'That's no way to play a game to beat me!'

He said, 'I'll never beat you, you're too good.'

'Are you tired?' I said.

'No.' Max shook his head. 'I like your hair.'

'You like my hair?'

He nods and looks studiously at the screen, a slow smile forming over his face. 'You're pretty.'

I laugh out loud at how shy he's being. 'I'm pretty? Where's the Max Walker who, like, makes out with everyone at Year Eleven parties? Aren't you gonna, like, pounce on me?'

'I don't pounce on people!'

'Yeah, right!'

'I don't! They pounce on me,' he says and laughs, not arrogantly, but joyfully and hysterically, like he knows it sounds obnoxious and that's why he's said it, as a joke.

'You know,' I murmur, looking over at him, 'people are wrong about you.'

'Why? What do they say?'

'Oh, you know. Just that . . . you're full of yourself.'

'What?' Max looks really offended. 'Who said that?'

'Err.' I shrug, thinking I shouldn't have said that. Why am I so prickly with everyone? 'Just people.'

'But I get along with everyone I talk to. I go out of my way to be nice to people and to do favours,' he mutters. 'Who said that?'

'Just . . . Emma and Laura.'

'Oh,' Max says sadly. 'That's not nice. Why do they think that?'

'Um . . .'

'Do I come across like that?'

'Well . . . no.'

'Then what? I don't get it.'

I look at him. He looks that kind of too-upset you get when you've had too much to drink.

'Look, honestly, um . . . fuck.' I blush, embarrassed, which doesn't suit me. 'I just think it's because you're . . . oo-ookin'.'

'What?'

'Um.' I clear my throat. 'Good-looking.'

Max suddenly breaks into a massive grin and turns to me. 'You think I'm good-looking?'

'Well . . . I meant that Emma and Laura do.'

'Oh,' he says, sitting back against the end of the bed and flicking his controller. His character jumps over a fence and eats a mushroom. He looks confused. 'Oh.'

I sigh. 'Max?'

'Yeah?'

Through gritted teeth I admit, 'I think you're good-looking too.'

Max looks over at me and does some mental arithmetic. 'Ohh,' he smiles with what seems like relief. 'Cool. I thought when you said they did that maybe you didn't.'

'Don't be crazy.' I watch him and he turns to me slowly and meets my eyes and then he looks down shyly and goes a bit red. I decide the time is now and I throw my controller to the side, take his away, and pull him up. I can be very forthright when I want to be. He scrambles to a standing position and then I push him back onto the bed and he giggles.

This is when I stroke his hair and tell him he's a lightweight.

This is where I suddenly feel that nervousness that you get when you go out with someone new, that fear of fucking it up, of opening yourself up to all that heartbreak again. I close my eyes and in my mind I run over that fear like a truck. I open my eyes again and look down at Max. I lean over him.

He grins at me and then his face gets all soft suddenly and vaguely nervous, like it's been doing on and off all evening, and he notices my hand moving away from his face, and we both watch it brush over his T-shirt on his flat stomach. I feel hard muscle beneath my hand and shiver excitedly. My fingers finish up over the zip of his school trousers. My palm rests on the thin fabric and then presses meaningfully down, cupping him. The fabric moves and reveals the shape beneath. I feel it halfway between hard and soft. Max lets out a small breath and I rub him softly.

He lies on his back on my double bed, his arms up, his fingers curled. His left arm stretches upwards and holds the edge of the mattress. His eyes move from my hand to my eyes and he swallows loudly, and we watch each other's face, then my hand again. His chest heaves as he breathes deeply and the T-shirt shows an outline of ribs, of a taut stomach, of slight pecs with a line down the middle of his chest. His eyes close momentarily and I watch his pink lips part and widen. He looks at me. His eyes are this amazing green. Like gold-green. His right hand moves to his forehead as my hand moves further down to the base of his thing and he frowns and turns towards me and props himself up on his right arm and his pink lips move into me and his left hand moves away from the mattress and touches my neck and Max Walker's lips close around mine and gently kiss my top lip, then the bottom one, then both. He tastes sweeter than Toby. His lips feel softer. No stubble. His fingers hold my neck softly, pressing me to him, and his thumb tracks across my cheek. He flicks his tongue just a little into my mouth, then a little more, then we're in a rhythm, passing kisses back and forth, his lips still soft and sweet and full. I press my tongue into his mouth and it opens, accepting, inviting, and as if he has no control over it. His forehead creases and he gasps slightly, before his hand on my neck moves to my hand on his pants, and knits our fingers together. He leans into me, our legs slip between each other, and he guides my hand to the pillow behind me, so I'm lying on my back. He does this seamlessly, without moving away from my lips. From above his blond hair strokes my skin. I put my left hand to his face and hold his cheek and the back of his hair. I feel his chest is hard against mine. I feel something else hard too. I make a move to touch it again with my right hand, but Max holds me gently but firmly to the pillow. I frown. I try to move my left hand, but he takes that too and holds it and smiles at me sweetly. I give in, quit trying to rub him off, and kiss him again.

Max

Uhh. Where am I?
 I wake up, feeling sluggish and nauseous.
 Oh, with Sylvie. She looks so pretty. She smells so good.
 Oh my god, it's eight-thirty in the morning! We slept for, like, eight hours. I still feel so tired. I don't want to move. She's asleep on my arm. Her hair is gold in the sunlight and beautifully curly. The house is quiet.
 I reach out for my phone with my free hand. Good – I text Mum last night and said I was at Carl's and she said it was OK. Wow, I must have drunk quite a lot to not remember that.
 I look down at the floor.
 Oh. Just a few rum and Cokes. There's plenty left of the rum. Wow. I feel sick. I'm gonna take my arm out . . . slowly . . . slowly. There. Do I feel really sick? Nah.
 Wait.
 Oh my god.
 I roll slowly off the bed and hold my hand to my mouth. I shakily stand up, feeling dizzy and weird. I open her bedroom door and see a tiled floor beneath the door opposite. Relieved, I throw myself through the doorway, pull up the toilet seat and puke into it.
 Uh oh. I retched the other morning too.
 I turn and put the seat down, sit on the lid and press down the flush.
 Uh oh.
 I think for a minute. I was groggy and tired a second ago but now I'm wide awake. I do a calculation in my mind.
 I lean over the sink and wash my mouth, then pad back quietly to Sylvie's room. She's just waking up.
 'I gotta go,' I whisper.
 'Oh.' She frowns. 'Are you OK?'

153

'Yeah. I just have to go. We're . . . seeing my grandparents today.'

She sits up, blinking sleepily. 'Really?'

I pause. 'Well, no, not really. I feel sick.' I pull my jumper on, pick up my school tie and blazer, and stuff them in my bag. 'Sorry.'

'Oh. I guess . . . too much to drink?'

'Err, yeah,' I say, swinging my bag onto my back.

'OK.' She looks uncertain.

I want to say more, but I'm in a hurry. I give her my best winning grin, holding my stomach, feeling like I might throw up again. I murmur, 'Bye. Sorry,' and I let myself out.

The pharmacy is on the way home. I could go to the supermarket, but there'd be loads of people there, people that know Dad and Mum. I might not even know them, but they'll know who I am. The pharmacy is tiny and hardly anyone ever goes there. The sick feeling gone, my stomach nevertheless feels tender. I slip inside the door of the pharmacy, looking around to make sure no one is watching.

The tests are in the aisle next to the condoms. I pick one up quickly and throw it on the counter, my head down.

'Hi, Max.'

I look straight up, shocked.

'Hi Emma,' I manage to say after a few seconds. I smile at her uncertainly.

Emma Best smirks at me, typing in the price. She picks up the test and produces a plastic bag from underneath the counter.

'Bag?'

'Yes, please.'

'So, who is this for?' She holds out the bag to me, then jerks it away when I reach out my hand. 'Are you, like, going out with Sylvie for real now, then?'

My jaw tenses. I stop smiling. 'Why d'you ask?'

'Yeah.' She rolls her eyes. 'Like, for no reason at all, Max, for no reason at all. The preggers test will be fourteen pounds ninety-nine, thank you very much.'

I hand her a twenty and she holds the bag while she puts it in the till.

'Just FYI, Max: we girls look out for each other, so don't expect to just leave her, and then be able to get with someone else.'

'What?' I say incredulously. 'I'm just buying a test, Emma. It's not conclusive evidence of anything.'

'I'm just saying. If Sylvie ends up *with child*, then everyone will know it was you.' She hands over the change and I reach over the counter and snatch the plastic bag with the test in it from her hand.

'Yeah, whatever, just don't tell anybody,' I say nastily. 'It's not for Sylvie, anyway,' I add, muttering.

'*What?* How many people are you *sleeping with*?' she shrieks, and I start walking out immediately, not able to deal with her. 'Let me run a few names of people you've hooked up with, Max, you total boy slut.' I hear her voice calling after me, reciting a list as I leave the store, practically running: 'Maria in form 11S, Marissa King, Sam Baines, Carla Hollis, Nats B, Karina C, Anita Singh, Olivia Wasikowski, Becky P, Anna Svensson, Coralie in 11B, Sarah M, Rosie C . . .'

Stupid bitch.

Karen

December's first few days bring the most honed shafts of light: delicate, pale, concentrated rays that strike the dust falling through the air and reveal it. I love this time of year: the low sun, the acute happiness of short days and cold air. The dust is my particular love. I read somewhere once that the dust in our houses is almost all dead human skin. The dust is us: Steve, my boys and I. We are living in a whirlwind of our own skin, making this house our home, giving it our fingerprint. Our DNA is at rest on the mantelpiece.

At least, until the cleaning lady comes tomorrow and dusts it.

On Saturday morning, I cannot help lying down in the small living room, sighing in exhaustion and with relief, locking the big, old door with the quirky metal key ever so quietly so Steve's staff cannot come in. I cannot help melting into the comfort of the old sofa, and taking a moment to watch the light drift across the room, the dust falling through it. Beyond the light is one of the new pictures of my family over the mantelpiece that we had such a rushed, hassled day to get. When I look at us all, I still can't quite believe that I made this family, that I am this old, that I am responsible for both those boys, one already a teenager.

Max was Max the moment he was born. He gave a startled cry, then smiled, and kept smiling. He slept through the night and rarely whined and was happy with so little. Steve worried about that sometimes. Max was happy with nothing. Steve wanted him to want things. I understand, but I think it's important to be grateful and not to make a fuss, and Max is very grateful and doesn't make a fuss.

Then Daniel came, and grizzled and grumbled and turned away from us and wouldn't take milk and threw toys.

It's true I see them a little differently: Daniel is a hormonal timebomb, Max . . . isn't.

Max is the gun that can't fire. He doesn't have the same hormonal problems as other teenagers; he's just steady and unchanging. In ways, he will never grow up. He'll never have kids. This is awful. It's awful that I see it that way, but I've never had cause to see it any other way. He is steady and unchanging and he has never let me down.

I take a tissue from my pocket and wipe away tears that have begun to stream down my cheeks. I have been thinking a lot lately about what could go wrong for my boys, and it is because I have detected a change of mood in Max that is frightening to me. I find any time I am alarmed about Max, my emotional state has reverted immediately to how I was the first year of his life, when I couldn't keep it together, when I was sick with worry about him. I feel like that mother who couldn't even give birth to a normal, functioning baby, as much as I know that's illogical. I remember the doctors' faces, aghast, concerned, serious.

Yes, Max has been moody lately. Perhaps it's testosterone finally kicking in naturally, but I find I don't want to accept it. I find myself shaking my head. I've never seen him miserable, I've never seen him mean. There was that one night when he was about fourteen, after all those hormone injections, but that was one of the reasons we stopped him taking them. If Max naturally doesn't have all those hormones coursing through him, then why add them? I don't want a moody child. I don't want him to hate me. I don't want to be the one that administers something that makes him upset. I like that he's not like other teenagers. I like that we're so close and I don't want to lose him to adolescence. He is not full of testosterone, he's not horny all the time, he doesn't feel the need to become the sort of rutting pack animal teenage boys usually are, taking drugs, getting girls into trouble. He's just Max. He's just my perfect, smiling, uncomplaining, clever, sweet, reliable Maxy. I hate that he's been in such a mood lately. I hate it to my core. It makes me feel uncomfortable, wrong, terrified. And I realise in thinking about it that, terribly, I don't want him to grow up. I don't want him to push away from me like Danny does.

I have to stop thinking about this, because I know that nothing I do can stop him from growing away from me in the end. I can resist it with every synapse under my skin, but one day Max will move away from us and I won't know him as well as I do now. I try to ignore my inner panic, to calm myself.

I listen to the sounds of my house. I become aware of the Saturday morning noises, which have changed very little over the years, but are beginning to become quite different. Instead of the kids, I can hear Lawrence and Debbie in the kitchen, discussing the campaign with Steve. The kettle boils and the clink of cups being set on the surface mixes with low murmuring. There is a plumber here taking out the old boiler. I hear quiet grunting, and the metallic sound of tools touching each other. The radio is on, softly, on the windowsill behind the sink. Upstairs, Max is missing, but football games mean this is often the case on a Saturday, and I either go to watch him or anticipate his return. I look forward to his hug, his cold cheeks, watching him walk in with mud on his socks and shirt, then watching him brush it out again. Above me now, I hear the sound of tinny guns and gruff voices cut out and I know Daniel has tired of playing his game. Sure enough, his feet bump lightly down the stairs – light and slow feet for Daniel; soft, quick, but heavier sounds for Max; loud, steady and thumping for Steve. I think I'm heavier-footed than I want to be.

There is a knock at the door.

'One minute, darling!' I call.

I check my face in the mirror, wipe streaked mascara from under my eye, and unlock the door. Daniel's curly haired head pops through.

'Hello, Robot Mum.'

'Hello, Robot Son,' I say, letting him in, locking the door after him. He looks around, as if he doesn't live here. 'Do you want a robot cuddle?' I ask hopefully.

'Robots do not respond to human affection.'

'I hear robots have energy systems which respond to the heat of a human body. Perhaps if you lie next to me, your energy will be recharged for the next level of *World of War*.'

I sit down on the sofa and pat the spot next to me.

'No, thank you,' he says. 'I'm actually playing *Living Dead 10: The Annihilator*.'

'Oh, I see.' I take my hand away from the couch and place it on my lap. 'How's it going?'

'I'm annihilating them and mutilating their families so they won't come for mine.'

'Goodness.'

'It's rather a violent game.'

'I guess you're doing well, then.'

'Yes, I am.'

'Well . . . thanks for the protection.'

'You're welcome, Mum.' Finally Daniel sits down next to me and curls up to my shoulder. I move my head over his and smell the minty shampoo in his hair.

'Could I maybe do football like Max when I'm older?'

'I don't see why not. You could go to practice now if you wanted.'

'With Max?'

'They arrange the practice groups according to age, darling.'

'Oh.'

There is another knock at the door, and Daniel gets up to open it. A blond head appears.

'Max?'

He pushes the door open tentatively, still wearing his rumpled school uniform. Behind him, Steve's intern raises her hand and waves at me.

'Good morning!'

'Hello,' I call to her, smiling, then address Max. 'I thought you were at football, honey?'

'No, I got in a while ago.'

'Why are you upset?' says Daniel loudly. Max looks over his shoulder at the intern and shuts the door.

'I'm not, I'm just tired.' Max rubs his face. His eyes are red.

I sit up and Daniel leaps off me and runs past Max. 'I'll get

World of War ready upstairs so we can play, Max!' He bangs through the door.

Max nods and looks at his feet.

'What's wrong, honey? Where have you been?'

He shakes his head and looks as if he's going to leave the room, then seems to change his mind and closes the door. He turns back to me.

'Mum . . .'

He pauses, then walks over to the couch and sits cross-legged on it, facing me. He bends his head and I reach over to his hair and run my fingers up his neck, and through the soft, fluffy yellow. 'You're so lovely,' I say.

Max raises his head. 'Mum. I can tell you anything, right?'

'What's wrong?'

'Mum,' he moans, letting out a sob that alarms me. It's the sob of someone who does not cry often, the half-held-back sob that has characterised all Max's infrequent outbursts of sadness. It stops, a second after it starts. This is how Max cries. This is the extent of Max's misery. He leans forward, wrapping his arms around me.

'Baby,' I croon, panicked on the inside, calm on the outside. 'Of course you can tell me anything. We can talk about anything. Mum's here.'

'Um,' he mumbles into my neck. 'Oh fuck, Mum. Sorry for swearing. I'm just . . .' He sits back, wipes tears from his green eyes and leans towards me again, tilting his head downwards so his hair tickles my neck and his forehead rests on my collarbone. 'I'm pregnant.'

'No.' My whole body stiffens, unwillingly and all at once. I raise my hands away from his shoulders, as quickly as if dropping something hot, and I repeat myself firmly, as if to stop him, as if to make him stop talking, stop doing this, just stop. 'No,' I say. 'You're not.'

PART TWO

Karen

I look at Max in the rear-view mirror. He's curled into the
door with his hands over his face. Despite this, I don't think
he's crying. He's just sitting there, not saying anything. I've
never seen him so silent and blank.

He takes his hands away and the look of sheer disbelief
mirrors my thoughts.

'This is unbelievable,' I mutter, looking at the road, gripping
the steering wheel. 'This is insanity.'

'Karen,' Steve murmurs from the passenger seat. 'Slow down.
You're at forty-five in a thirty.'

We pull up at a red light and I look over my shoulder. 'What
happened? What were you thinking?' I almost shriek.

Max's eyes trail around the car, avoiding mine. He shrugs.

'Did you just *shrug*?' I screech.

'Karen!' Steve says.

I turn back to the wheel, trying to calm myself down, but
racing towards hysteria. 'I just . . . I thought you liked girls.'

Steve makes a clucking sound with his mouth and looks
back at Max. 'Do you want to keep it?'

'Steve!'

'What?'

I frown, pressing down on the accelerator again. 'Don't ask
such bloody stupid questions.'

'We have to ask,' Steve murmurs.

'Um, no,' Max says in a tiny, clear voice from the back seat.

'Thank god,' I snap.

Whenever there is a problem in the lives of one of our children, my instinct is to run to Steve. I know this to be true and
I am aware that in some ways this is very unhealthy, but I do
it thinking of my mother, her inability to punish us without
being too severe, her inability to depersonalise our actions.

Everything that we did wrong she saw as an affront to her, and I never wanted to give that impression to Max or Danny, but I know that I take things too personally. I think back to Max's birth, and know that my first notion of myself as a mother was as a bad mother, and I panic.

True to form, as soon as Max told me, I went to Steve. Shrugging Max off me and grabbing his arm in the same instant, I practically ran out of the living room, looking frantically for his father, bowling past the stunned intern and up the stairs. I heard Danny as we rushed past his bedroom door, playing *World of War*.

'Max,' he yelled, hearing us outside. 'Are you coming?'

'Not right now, he's doing something with Mum,' I snapped hastily.

I turned around and Max was standing there, looking at me uncertainly.

'Come on.' I ushered him in to my room.

'I don't want Dad to know!' he said, panicked.

I shook my head at him, as if to say, 'Not now', opened the door, and nearly pushed him into the room, so strong was my need to get this off my chest, to not be the one adult solely responsible for my son.

Steve was shaving.

'What is it?' he said, seeing my face.

I gestured to him to follow me, and he washed off his chin with an anxious look. I picked up the phone from my nightstand and the three of us relocated to Max's room.

Max sat on his bed.

I stared at him. He looked at me in horror. He shook his head.

'Max, what is it?' asked Steve.

He itched his hair and whispered in a small, high voice, 'I'm pregnant.'

Steve sucked in a breath, rubbed his lips together, and blew the air out. I loved him for being so calm in that moment, but I was also jealous. I felt like falling to the floor and cracking up, sobbing, completely going to pieces.

But I had only had to bear the burden alone for all of three minutes. My limbs relaxed just a bit, and I brushed Max's clothes off a chair and sat down.

'Are you sure?' Steve asked.

Max nodded.

'OK,' said Steve. 'Have you seen a doctor?'

'I spoke to Dr Verma a few months ago. I took a morning-after pill.'

Why didn't the doctor call us? I think immediately, but then I realise: it's all confidential, so I can't help my son not make mistakes that might ruin his life.

'But it didn't work?' Steve says softly, his forehead creased.

'I think maybe I threw it up. I didn't realise at the time. In the sink, remember?' Max says quietly to me. I shake my head and look down at the floor.

'This cannot be happening,' I mutter.

Steve looks at me. He takes the phone out of my hand, gives my palm a squeeze, then turns back to Max. 'Did you like Dr Verma?'

Max nods.

'I'll call her then, and we'll go see her.'

'Today,' I say, raising my head. 'Let's get it over with.'

Thankfully the clinic is open on weekends now. We booked an appointment for three o'clock with Dr Verma.

As Steve spoke on the phone, I watched Max sitting on the bed. He was curled into the corner of the room, cross-legged, head bent over, his face hidden by hair. He blinked and looked up slowly, straight at me. We held each other's eyes, not saying anything, not letting our faces say anything.

'Yes,' Steve was saying on the phone. 'Thank you, that's so kind. Yes.'

Max's mouth stretched into a small smile.

I tried to smile back, to let him know it was OK, but I couldn't. I just couldn't do it without bursting into tears. I felt his head lower in my peripheral vision. His hand lifted to his cheek, brushed it and dropped again.

'If you could be discreet, that would be very kind,' said Steve. 'Yes, there has been lots of attention with the campaign.'

Max and I both looked at him. I watched Max roll his eyes in exactly the way I do, and felt sick.

This is my child. *This is my child*, I thought. I briefly, horrifically, imagined him having sex. 'Oh my god,' I murmured.

Max leant his head on the wall and started to bite his nails. Steve hung up.

'It was an accident,' Max said quietly.

Steve sat down on the end of the bed. 'It's OK, Max, these things happen.'

'What?' I turned to Steve incredulously.

'Teenagers get pregnant. It happens.'

'No,' I said coldly. 'It doesn't just happen.' I turned to Max. 'Who did you have sex with?'

Steve looked over at Max.

'I don't want to talk about it,' Max muttered quickly.

Before I could say anything, Steve nodded. 'OK, we're in at three with Dr Verma. Change your clothes and let's all get something to eat before we go.'

I stood up and headed for the door. I wanted to ask him more questions, but more than anything I wanted to get out of Max's bedroom. I couldn't get out of there quick enough.

'Max?' I heard Steve say. 'Do you want to come down for lunch? Can I bring you some toast?'

I shut the door behind me.

Steve sent the intern and Lawrence home, and we had a quiet conversation in the living room, about the campaign, about privacy, about what we would do if this got out to the press, if the situation somehow became worse.

'Do you think I should tell Lawrence about Max?' asked Steve.

'No!' I whispered. 'Why?'

'Crisis management, keeping it contained if it does come out?'

We sat in silence for a minute or so.

'How the fuck can you think of it like that?'

Steve looked up at me from his tea, surprised. I could feel myself shaking with anger.

'Like what?'

'He's our baby. We have to protect him, no matter what,' I hissed.

'Karen, he's an adult. He's not going to live the rest of his life under our protection. He's going to go out in the world, and he'll have to learn to not only live with this and be happy, but to cope if somehow people found out about him, if it became an issue. Avoiding discussing this with him now will only make things worse. I'm passionate about the campaign, about better government. We can't change who we are because of Max. It will only make him feel more different.'

'So we just let him make these mistakes, deal with the scrutiny of a public political campaign? We made his bed, now he has to lie in it?'

'This isn't our fault. These things happen.'

'They don't just happen.'

'This isn't your fault.'

I sat miserably, holding my cup in my hand, feeling the warmth leave it.

'He's too young to make his own choices. He's shown that today. We have to protect him better.'

'We can't protect him from everything. The campaign might not even—'

'*Fuck* your campaign,' I hissed. 'Stop talking about your campaign. I don't want to hear about it. I told you this was a bad idea. I told you.'

I started to sob, thinking about Max when he was born, so tiny and innocent of everything. Now he goes out into the world alone and I'm powerless. He doesn't know what it's like, how much the choices you make count, how much things will change if people know, if people find out.

What have I done? I thought. *What has Max done?*

I locked myself in the living room, unable to look at Steve, his calm strength transformed into a blasé attitude that made me want to lash out at him.

A few hours later Steve, Max and I slipped out. Max was sitting in the corner of his bed when I went to get him. He was ready. He had changed into his green jumper, jeans, trainers and a green coat.

'Are we going?' he said, as if he was asking what I was cooking for dinner.

'Yes, we're going,' I said sternly, and he followed me out.

On the way to the clinic, we dropped Daniel at Leah and Edward's house.

'Karen!' Steve warns, in the car. 'Stay at thirty, love.'

I nod absent-mindedly. I glance again at Max in the mirror.

'Max, don't chew the sleeves off that jumper.'

He looks back at my reflection angrily, takes his sleeve away from his mouth and slumps further down in the seat.

We pull in to the clinic car park and I turn the engine off.

We sit in silence for a minute.

'This cannot be happening,' I whisper.

Steve looks over at me, and I look back at him. For a moment, we both forget Max is in the car. 'He's only sixteen,' I whisper, tearing up. Steve reaches out and takes my hand. 'Who has he been sleeping with?'

'Karen . . .' Steve says admonishingly. I remember Max, and I know Steve is right. It's not something we need to know. We shouldn't push him. But then I think: *no*. This is my life too. This is our life, as a family, and Max has done something that has shaken us, shaken me to the core. We deserve to know how this happened to us, to our team. I turn to Max tearfully.

'Who have you been sleeping with?'

He rolls his eyes and looks out the window, biting his sleeve again.

'Do you have a boyfriend?'

He puts his hands over his eyes and doesn't reply.

'Why won't you tell us?'

'No reason, it's fine, let's just get it over with,' Max says quietly. 'No, I don't have a boyfriend.'

'Did you?'

'No! Can you stop firing off questions?' Max shouts.

'Don't shout at your mother, Max,' Steve says. 'Accidents happen, but you don't get away with being irresponsible and then yelling at your mother when she is upset. We are understandably upset, as much for you as with you, and she's dealing with it as best as she can.'

I shake my head, turn to my side of the car and lean against the window.

'So let's just stay calm, and see Dr Verma,' Steve is saying.

In the wing mirror, Max's eyes open and look at me. We stare at each other, as if we don't know each other. As if we are strangers. His bottom lip juts out like he's going to cry. I shake my head and I let a tear slip down my cheek.

'I'm so disappointed in you.'

169

Archie

It's been three months since I last saw Max Walker, so when I arrive in reception, I am already concerned. There is a lot of pointing and mouthing from the receptionist, before two heads rise to observe me from the waiting room. A third head, between the two raised, is still lowered, Max's blond hair hanging long in the front. I raise a hand in response and wait at the counter for the file.

Stephen Walker seems even more stolid and broad-shouldered than he looks on television. I remember when I first saw him on the BBC, talking about a case concerning media and privacy, where he had been the prosecutor. On television, he seemed very much like one might expect a barrister to look – a little self-righteous, and without much personality. Unexpectedly, in real life he has a likeable, attractive face, with a concerned but warm expression. He takes up much more room than Max, his legs longer, his body fit but larger. His coat is thick and expensive-looking, the coat of someone who is aware of his appearance on a daily basis. His hands are large. His hair is already grey, but handsomely so. His eyes seem grey too. In fact, it is hard to see any resemblance to Max, save that permanently affable half-smile, something warm in his eyes. They do both have charisma.

Stephen puts a protective hand on Max's neck to awaken him to my arrival. It's strange to see a different persona in a public person. This is Stephen Walker, the father.

Presuming Stephen called because Max wants to know more about his condition, I drove quickly back to my house to fetch all my research on intersexuality.

I gesture to my handbag, although the Walkers will not understand why, and they rise together.

Stephen is almost a head taller than Max, but when Karen

Walker stands, I notice she is tall too, the same height as her son. Max lifts himself off the chair slowly, then touches his stomach gently.

I watch through the glass as Stephen strides towards the door of the waiting room, opening it for his family. He takes my hand and shakes it.

'Thank you for seeing us on such short notice,' he says quietly, with a grateful and somewhat relieved smile.

'Of course, Mr Walker.'

'Call me Steve,' he says.

I nod, indicating the badge on my chest. 'Archie. Follow me.'

When we enter my office, Karen and Steve sit on the plastic chairs, moving them to be either side of Max, who perches on the bed where I cleaned him up almost three months ago.

The resemblance is much stronger between mother and son. Karen Walker crosses her legs at the ankles, her back straight, hair smoothed, make-up impeccable, cream shirt pressed, a dark green skirt revealing long, lean legs that look toned from possibly track or yoga. She wears low, elegant heels. Her hair is a tasteful, dark honey-blonde. Her nails are neat and painted nude, and her earrings are small diamond studs. The resemblance to Max begins with her long, lean legs, and continues up to her face. Her eyes are green, exactly the same as Max's, but they are surrounded by neat eyeliner, mascara, and a wisp of light brown eyeshadow. The lower half of her face is heart-shaped, like Max's, with a defined jaw and full lips. When she flicks her hair slowly off her face and settles it over her ears, she looks exactly like Max did in September. She casts a look down at herself as we sit, smoothing her shirt, skirt, crossing her feet, the ankles slim and coated in sheer tights. Her face is still, giving nothing away.

'We're so sorry to drag you away from your usual patients,' Karen says, in a smooth but firm voice.

'It's OK. We actually have a drop-in session on Saturday afternoons, for post-natal mothers and babies.'

A flash of something close to anger tears across Karen's face and then disappears. 'Oh,' she says politely.

Max rubs his nose, not listening.

'So . . .' Steve begins. 'We wanted to see you because we know Max came to see you a few months ago.'

I look over at Max, surprised. He is staring blankly at the floor.

'We are concerned, firstly, that this doesn't become . . . public knowledge.'

'Public?' I ask, confused.

Steve and Karen share a look and Steve sighs, minutely. Karen gives him a quick nod. Neither give anything away. I am starting to realise this is not about Max's condition, but I cannot think what else it could be.

'We're just worried for Max that this doesn't get out,' Steve says.

'This is about the campaign?' I ask, confused.

Steve clears his throat. 'Not exactly. Max is in trouble. The contraception you gave him didn't work. Not –' he says on my look, holding up a hand. '– that I'm saying there was anything wrong with the pill. Max just thinks he might have been sick and the pill may not have been digested first.'

I nod, understanding.

'We are here because we want to deal with this situation quickly and privately, and to find out what Max's options are,' Steve adds, patting Max on the knee.

Karen leans in and adds, 'I want to know how this could have happened, with Max's condition.'

I frown. 'I'm sorry, to clarify – Max is pregnant?'

'Yes.' Steve nods.

We all watch Max for a moment. He looks exhausted and uncomfortable, fidgeting slowly and dreamily, his eyes wandering around the room.

'How could this happen?' asks Karen.

I lean forward. 'Being intersex doesn't mean you're infertile. In fact, intersex people are more likely to become infertile if they have surgery to "correct" their genitals. Surgery is a lot more common now than it was in the past, so you're likely to hear of a lot fewer people with Max's condition being able to bear children.'

'We should have had the procedure,' Karen says immediately, addressing her lap with a little note of self-admonishment.

'Well,' I say. 'Not necessarily.'

I look over at Max, but he doesn't appear to be listening as Karen asks me how long it will take to schedule an abortion.

'About two weeks,' I reply, my eyes still on Max. 'No one should have to wait over three.'

'It could be three?'

'It . . .' I focus on Karen and Steve. 'It might be, but with Max, the doctors will probably decide to do it sooner rather than later.'

Karen nods. 'Good.'

Max rubs his eyes. His dad looks at him expectantly but he shrugs, his lips firmly closed. It is as if he has shut down the part of himself that cares to speak.

'Do you think it would be better to go through his specialists in London?' Karen asks. 'Will the doctors who do the abortion be specialists?'

'In general, doctors in the UK don't have much training in working with intersex people, but doctors who perform abortions will have lots of experience dealing with varied anatomical configurations. Having been over Max's files and researched his condition, I think they should be able to cope. If, however, it would make you feel more comfortable—'

'We're not working with the specialists anymore,' Steve interrupts.

Karen and Steve share a look over Max's head. He notices and glances at both of them questioningly.

'Well . . .' Karen murmurs, glancing at Steve. I detect a small frown on Steve's face.

'Approaches have changed a lot since Max was born, if that's what you're worried about,' I add. 'Corrective surgery is no longer advocated in all cases. They won't push anything more than an abortion.'

I notice the corners of Max's mouth twitch. He chews on his fingernail nervously.

Steve shakes his head. 'Thank you, but no. We don't want specialists. We didn't like the way they worked with Max. Their ideology was different to ours.'

Max finally raises his head in surprise. 'How?'

'We'll talk about it at home, honey,' Karen says.

Max flashes a quick look at me before focusing on picking his nails again.

'OK. So I'll contact both the clinics in Oxford and see which one can take Max.'

'Why can't I have it here?' Max asks quietly.

Karen shakes her head.

'I'm afraid,' I reply, looking directly at Max, 'we don't have the resources to do this safely in Hemingway, so it would be at either John Radcliffe or The Manor Hospital in Oxford.'

'Is there a possibility of having one operation to perform both an abortion and a hysterectomy?' Karen asks.

'That's not usually done together,' I say, as Steve says, 'We haven't talked about that.'

'We probably should have a long time ago,' Karen replies quietly.

'It's not necessary right now.'

'Right now? It's relevant.'

Steve makes a small humming sound, a warning note, with his mouth.

'So he can have a normal life,' mutters Karen.

'Whether or not you want to consider a hysterectomy, you should probably discuss this with Max in detail at home.' I attempt to catch Max's eye, to no avail. 'Do some research on the net, read some books.'

Karen shakes her head.

'Max,' I say. He finally looks me in the eye. 'You should know that there is, within the medical community and society as a whole, a lack of understanding for issues of gender and sexuality, and in a case like yours, doctors might be too willing to

174

force surgeries rather than help you decide on a gender without surgery. You need to be prepared.'

'Why does he have to decide on a gender?' Steve offers.

'Or not decide, whichever,' I agree, with a small smile.

Max seems to have zoned out again.

'That seems like good advice, Max,' Steve says, turning to him. 'Should we talk about this when we're home?'

Max nods weakly.

'When are we going to have time to talk about this?' Karen says, almost to herself, before turning to me. 'As you said, the doctors will probably be much better about that now, in any case, and they won't want to study him like an ape, hopefully,' she adds.

'*Mum*,' Max whines softly.

I purse my lips but press on. 'Policy has changed a lot since the nineties. I've been doing some research. It's hard to find information that relates to intersexuality. It usually gets buried in information about transsexuals. I've been looking for support groups in the area as well, but I'm only finding groups that cater to LGBT young people.'

Max clears his throat. 'LGBT?'

'Lesbian, gay, bisexual and transgender,' I reply.

'Yeah, I know, just . . .' Max looks at his feet. 'That's not me.'

'I know,' I say. He looks up at me and smiles slightly, for the first time. It's good to see.

'Do you want to see a psychiatrist?' Karen asks Max.

'Why?'

'To discuss things like sexuality, if you're confused.'

I bite my lip and look down at my files. One quick glance at Max's blank expression tells me he hasn't had the courage to tell them the sex wasn't consensual.

'I'm not confused,' murmurs Max.

'I always thought you liked girls but—'

Max cuts Karen off. 'I don't want to talk about it.'

'You could see one on the NHS.'

'No!'

'Karen,' says Steve. 'He doesn't want to talk about it.'

'Fine.' Karen nods calmly, smiling at me as if to say, 'Nothing wrong here'.

'So,' she says. 'We'll have the surgery in Oxford and we'll think about a hysterectomy.'

Steve nods. 'Yes, alright Max?'

Max bites his lip. 'OK.'

Max

There is a pause while Archie Verma types something into her computer and the whoosh of an email crackles through the nineties-looking speakers.

'So they'll get back to me about dates,' she says casually, like it's no big deal. I am so grateful to her right now. She's totally nonchalant about it. So calm. I feel like yelling at her, 'Take me home! Take me with you!'

Beside me I can feel Mum and Dad, starched like shirts, upright; Mum angry but deadly calm, Dad busily dealing with it, getting it done, shuffling the problem like paperwork. They argue it like a case, back and forth. It's so embarrassing.

I feel myself getting redder as I think about the hospital and everybody looking at me, reenacting this scene again, more questions, more explanations, the group of people knowing getting wider, getting easier to leak out, to end up on a blog somewhere like the last MP's kid with the Nazi outfit. Max Walker, cute teen son of the eminent Stephen Walker, a knocked-up he-she. *Lock up your sons and daughters, Oxford-shire, this kid is freaky, indiscriminate and, apparently, virile.*

I watch Archie typing and wish she could do the abortion. I wish we could just keep it between us. She's the only one that knows how it happened.

'I always wanted to ask this, but if Max did have a child, would it be likely to inherit his intersex condition?' my dad asks, out of the blue.

'What?' Mum and I say simultaneously.

'Just . . .' He looks at us both, as if he forgot for a second that we were here. 'Wondered.'

It's like this is *interesting* for him. I'd forgotten how shitty it was to be in a doctor's office with people talking about me. Everybody finds it so *interesting*. I look over at my dad, wondering if genetic engineering had been available then, would they have changed me. Or maybe if they'd found out before I was born, they would have got rid of me. I want to say to him, 'If you'd known I was like this, Dad, would you have had me?'

But this is just one in a long list of things during the appointment and in fact, now I think about it, over the years, that I don't say out loud. Because it would rock the boat of our perfect life.

'What does that matter?' Mum hisses. 'It's being aborted.'

It. A sexless, blank thing that is neither he nor she. I guess me and my child have that in common. Wow. My child. Shit.

'How likely is it that this would happen again?' Mum says to Archie.

'Why?' asks Dad.

'Because if it's likely, he'll probably need a hysterectomy.'

'Why?' asks Dad darkly.

'To be realistic –' Archie leans forward, thankfully butting in – 'Max has one fully-functioning ovary. There's no reason at all why he would be infertile.'

'Woh,' I whisper. 'Seriously?'

'Max,' Mum says firmly, meaning 'stop talking'.

I look down at my nails again and push the cuticles back.

Archie ignores Mum and answers me. 'Yes, Max. The big surprise is that we don't hear about this more often, but that's because babies with your type of intersexuality are often operated on at birth. Because they present as male physically, doctors try to turn them into boys, which would mean that the ovaries and uterus get taken out.'

I think about this and feel sick.

'As I explained earlier, quite often your intersex type is infertile, but not as a side effect of the condition, more as a side effect of surgery.'

I look up. 'What type am I?'

'Not now, Max, let's not get into that.' Mum shakes her head.

'Wait, but . . . am I like a normal type?'

'Max! Of course you're normal!' Dad lies, more to himself than me.

'How many types are there?'

'*Max*,' Dad says firmly, meaning *Enough*. 'This is something we can talk about at home.'

'What?' I feel my voice louder in the room. 'Why can't we talk about it now? I wanna know!'

Archie Verma's almond-shaped eyes move from me to Dad, to Mum, then back to me. We catch each other looking and I look away, blushing.

I feel like shit. 'Sorry,' I apologise.

'You know –' Archie says, leaning her elbow on the desk – 'I can talk about this at more length with Max another time, if he wants to.'

Mum and Dad look at each other doubtfully.

Archie tries again. 'It's important, as people get older, for them to know about their genitalia, for reasons of hygiene, and also to prevent accidents like this. Max needs the right contraception, perhaps some advice.'

Mum picks imaginary fluff off her skirt and looks at Dad. I feel Dad staring at me, and I busy myself looking at the wall charts and funny medical advice posters and imagining new ones. 'If you are experiencing the menopause, don't get in a hot flush – talk to your doctor . . .'; 'Feeling itchy and scratchy downstairs? Don't get your knickers in a twist – we can help . . .'; 'Getting older? Urinary dysfunction? Fill your underwear with something else – our deluxe new incontinence pads . . .'.

We are simultaneously pretending it's not happening, shirking the blame and avoiding responsibility. I wonder if I look more like Dad or Mum.

'I collect those posters,' Archie says with a smile. I look up at her and smile back. 'Max, would you like to come in one day after school and I'll explain about your condition?'

I nod. 'Yeah, OK.'

'OK, we'll check in the diary and sort something out for next week. Before the assessment.'

'What assessment?' Mum tuts.

'Max has to have an assessment at the hospital before he has the abortion.'

'Will that take long?'

'Not long. It's standard procedure. They might give him an ultrasound.'

'OK,' Dad says.

'Why's he having an ultrasound?' Mum keeps firing out calm, evil, lawyery questions like she's the Gestapo. I just want this day to be over.

'Because the doctors will probably want to determine, in Max's case, where the foetus is, and how big it is, and how that corresponds to Max's unique anatomy to decide what form of abortion to choose. Shall we go over the options now, so we're all aware?'

Archie

'If the foetus is up to nine weeks old, the procedure is quite simple, but I don't think this is an option, in terms of our time frame.'

Max shakes his head. He's still despondent but he's paying attention now.

'A surgical termination can be performed from nine weeks until thirteen weeks. Normally you'd be put under general anaesthetic. A tube goes into the womb through the cervix and suction is used to terminate the pregnancy. I think this would be the option to go for.'

Max stares at his knees, chewing his lip. 'What if . . . What if we wanted to wait a bit?'

'For what?' Karen looks alarmed.

'That's a good question Max,' I answer. 'Some people do want to have a bit more time to become comfortable with the idea of abortion, and so there are procedures for late-stage abortions. From fourteen to nineteen weeks, the procedure is basically the same, except we call it surgical dilation, where the neck of the womb is stretched open and the doctor uses forceps to get the foetus out.'

Everybody nods, heads down like schoolchildren being told off. Only Steve meets my eyes. He smiles regretfully.

'And after that?' Max mumbles.

'It probably won't come to that in your situation.'

'I just want to know.'

I hesitate, but continue. 'Between twenty and twenty-four weeks, you'd be given different pills, and the baby would pass vaginally. It can be quite painful.'

Max nods nervously.

'You'll be kept in the hospital if this happens and given pain relief. The very last option is surgery – this is if the foetus is quite large. And again, the foetus is suctioned from the uterus, but first the neck of the womb is softened and the foetus's heart-beat is stopped.'

'I don't want that one,' Max whispers.

'As I said, you shouldn't need to.'

'I don't want to do that one,' Max says, almost to himself.

'I think we just want an abortion as soon as possible,' interjects Karen.

'Are we definitely ruling out the first option? Has it been nine weeks?' says Steve, turning to Max.

Max shrugs.

'I think it's about ten weeks since Max came to see me.'

'Why did you wait that long, Max?' Steve asks him.

Max shrugs again. 'Didn't realise,' he mutters.

'Why didn't you use contraception?' Karen asks.

Max shrugs.

While Steve and Karen frown at each other, Max raises his head and looks at me through his hair.

I nod, meaning, 'No, I won't tell anyone'. He smiles gratefully, regretfully, relieved.

After a little while, Steve turns back to me. 'Well, I think while we're here with the doctor we should pick up some protection. Do you think so, Max?'

Max shrugs.

'Max?'

'Yeah, OK.'

'OK.' I turn to the computer, slipping some free Durex into the purple bags they provide for us, while I check my email. 'The hospital will probably get back to me this afternoon with a date for the assessment and a likely date for the surgery.'

'Great. Thank you, Dr Verma.' Steve stands up, and Max and Karen take this as their cue to follow.

'I'll be in touch,' I say, and I shake their hands.

As Max's palm slips into mine, I feel a sudden temptation to say more, to offer some comfort. He seems so frightened. He gives me a little nod, as if to reassure me, then Karen puts a hand on his shoulder as Steve opens the door. Karen and Max walk through it. Before she leaves, Karen gives me a smile. Steve does the same.

'Thanks again,' he says quietly, and shuts the door behind him.

Karen

When Max was diagnosed, I couldn't do anything but weep silently. I remember listening to doctors murmur to Steve about surgery. I nodded over and over again, hearing no real words, just hoping they could fix him, asking what I did, why it happened. They couldn't tell us.

Max was obviously a little baby boy. He looked so boyish when he was born, with bruises on his face from the forceps. Steve nicknamed him The Little Thug, and that was the name he used until he lost patience with me, and named him Max. I didn't want a gender neutral name. I thought they all sounded strange and on purpose, like we wanted to name him something else, but we only had so many choices. I liked 'Max' because it felt like a boy's name to me, but Steve felt it was gender neutral because it could always be short for 'Maxine', so we were both happy with it in the end.

The moment after Max was born, the nurse took him away from us. I knew something was wrong right then, because they usually put the baby on the mother's skin.

It was the young nurse who took him. She was about my age at the time, twenty-six, and her name was Anna. Anna, who had a brown ponytail, little silver hoop earrings, and a cheerleader-type zest during the labour, had only recently qualified. I wondered immediately if it was Anna who had done something wrong. As she cleaned the baby, she called the older nurse, Barbara, who was by my side. Anna waved her over like she didn't want to say anything out loud.

Barbara went to stand by her side and started to rub the baby and talk to him. They had their backs to me. He was still gurgling so I couldn't think what could be wrong. The doctor who had the forceps was still standing there, Dr Horvath, and he

184

was talking to me, and then Anna came over and the doctor went to the baby.

Everything became slow motion. Not for minutes, or hours, but for years. Everything became slow and sickly and improbable. First, they thought it might be one of the diseases that can kill the baby without treatment. I'll never forget the name: congenital adrenal hyperplasia. They said that the disease could present initially as ambiguous genitalia, then within weeks the baby could demonstrate poor feeding, lots of vomiting, dehydration. If untreated, it could die.

Then, after they had ruled CAH out, they thought he should be operated on to become a girl, because he had a small phallus, and internal sex organs. But we thought he looked enough like a boy. Steve baulked at them cutting him up. Then they wanted to give him hormones. They took pictures upon pictures. Later, they thought he should be a boy, because he seemed to identify that way. Above everything, they wanted us to choose. They said he would be mal-adjusted, sexually confused, or suffer from gender dysphoria. They said it was better to have the operations while he was young, that children were more resilient, that it was better we confirm his gender as soon as possible. I agreed with them, in part. Who would want their child to have to go through that? Shouldn't it be us that bore this burden for him? But Steve wouldn't hear it.

On the day of his birth, I remember I was on the bed, looking at the polystyrene tiles in the ceiling. Steve was holding me and I was shaking with fear and pain. My chest hurt. My stomach hurt. My ribcage felt broken, like every bone had caved in. I had failed the first task of being a mother. Something inside me had hurt my baby. I couldn't look as the doctor examined him.

'What is it?' Steve said, standing up, letting go of my hand.

The doctor turned around and took off some plastic gloves I hadn't seen him put on. He faced us both and spoke softly, but firmly – something about ambiguous genitalia. He said he was going to take Max and do some tests.

'Yes,' I nodded, anxious, terrified, still in pain. 'Just take him.'

'What tests?' Steve asked.

'Just some standard tests to decide if the baby is a boy or a girl. I wouldn't want to say right now whether we would need to do anything surgically to better fit baby to his or her assigned gender, but we want to just check and make sure that that doesn't have to happen.'

I nodded.

Steve spoke again. 'Does it have to be done now? She hasn't even held him.'

The doctor faltered, said something along the lines of, 'baby might have something wrong internally causing this external ambiguity. I would really like to take baby now. I can leave baby with you for a minute while I ask the nurse to prepare the tests, but I'll be back very soon.' He picked up his clipboard. 'Does baby have a name?'

He kept saying 'baby', like it was this thing, this monster, this anomaly that didn't have a soul, a sex, a definition.

'A name?' He repeated, looking at me.

Steve looked at me, then back at the doctor. 'We'll decide later,' he said.

Steve held Max for a bit, then sat on the edge of the bed. He tried to give him to me, but I couldn't stop crying.

'I know you're tired,' he said. 'But you have to hold him. Come on, Karen. Pull yourself together.'

I sat up, choking, my hand on my mouth. It was the first time I looked at him, and I can't see how, not in terms of height obviously, but in every other way, I can't see how he has changed. The Max I saw then was indistinguishable from the Max of today or, rather, of yesterday. He was quiet, he was sweet, he was watching me, waiting for my reaction. He was warm, a little surprised, but he was looking at me as if I was the centre of his world. Those first few years, I felt, some days, sick with responsibility for him. When we used to talk about surgery, I would just baulk at the thought that I had to make such a huge choice for him and nod along with whatever the doctors said, thinking they knew best. I think Steve thought it was part of an ideology I had, but it wasn't. We had huge fights

186

about it; we couldn't see eye to eye. But really, I just couldn't make that choice.

I had gotten pregnant, accidentally, the year before finals and had an abortion. The boys don't know that. After we graduated, I got pregnant again. I don't know if I could call it an accident, because things between Steve and me were so passionate, and carefree. We were the golden children at college: we had both got the best jobs we could possibly get and graduated with excellent marks. Nothing could go wrong, and that was why it was all the more unnerving when we had Max.

The shock of having Max hovered over me like a cloud, but in the end, he was so bright, so good, so happy, that you just couldn't be sad around him. We agreed that we would never let him become 'the issue'. We agreed not to talk about it around him. So we didn't, and we haven't, and the bomb that I thought I was waiting on never went off. So I stopped waiting for it. I thought we were passed it.

We did have a number of difficult conversations with Max, but Steve always took the lead. We told Max he was intersex when he was six. The doctors had just started using the term, instead of hermaphrodite, and we thought it sounded OK enough to tell him about it. That sounds like a stupid reason, but there you go, that was the reason.

He took it at face value. He was more concerned with Pokemon; being intersex didn't mean anything to him. He shrugged and said, 'OK, Mummy, it's alright', because I was obviously upset, so I hugged him and sent him off to play, and he ran straight out of the conversation into a game of football with Steve.

Then when he was thirteen we had one awful night. Steve and I had a row, we weren't agreeing on how to deal with it, and Max was upset. We came home from the hospital, from the hormone injections, and Steve starting shouting in the garden, roaring like he was losing his mind.

And I screamed at him, 'What the hell are you doing? All the neighbours can hear you!'

'What are we doing to him? What are we telling him with these injections? This isn't right! It isn't fair!'

'Steve, shut up!'

Max was crying in the kitchen.

'Steve!'

'I'm so frustrated, Karen. I'm so angry!'

'At who?'

'I don't know. At them, at us, at the world. What are we doing?'

'Shut up and come inside! Everyone can hear you.'

'Aren't you frustrated, Kaz? Aren't you? Don't you just want to let it out? Come on, babe. Let it out. Don't hold it in, talk to me about it, yell with me.'

I was walking in, waving him away. I was growing older, and I didn't want to talk about Max being intersex anymore.

That was the only time I've seen Steve act truly out of line, out of order. That was what I liked about him: the order. He has always been reliable, steadfast, strong. He was grateful but he never questioned our entitlement to the life we wanted. He never faltered. He was always sure of himself. It was what I had craved at home, when my father was away.

That night, Max cried and cried and wouldn't stop crying. We dipped in and out of his room all evening. Steve had to leave around ten for an emergency with a murder case. I held Max until about 4 a.m. He cried himself to sleep. The next day, he'd forgotten about it. That's been it. The extent of the drama. Until today.

I feel . . . so stupid. I thought he was going to become a terror teenager because of all the problems, but he never did. And then this happens, and I never – not once – expected this. Now Max is still uncomplaining, but he's confused, quiet, shy and awkward and miserable.

What did we do wrong? What did Max do to deserve this? Nothing. I didn't smoke or drink during my pregnancy. Max isn't a drug addict, or a brat, or a bastard. What did we do?

'Jesus,' I murmur, holding my hand over my mouth.

'Karen, that's the fifth time you've said that since we got in the car.'

'Steve, shut up.'

He tuts.

'Sorry,' I mutter.

'Let's not do this now,' he says, which infuriates me.

'Yes, you're right. Why don't we get back and you can go to work and then you can avoid dealing with this, and I'll have to?'

'I'm not going to work this weekend.'

'We've got that Rotary dinner tonight. We said we would go.'

'We can cancel.'

'Oh *god*, Steve, let's just go. It'll take our mind off it. We're not going to get parenting awards for staying home from one dinner. It's over. We lost the good parenting badge.'

'Don't be dramatic,' he says, taking my hand.

Oh no. The cracks are beginning to show. I feel like I'm back there again, waiting for them to tell me what's wrong with our baby. I can't relive that all again. I just can't do it.

I look at Max in the mirror. He has his iPhone headphones in and is staring out the window. He looks ahead and I catch his beautiful green eyes in the rear-view mirror. I look away tearfully.

Steve turns his head. 'You alright, Max?'

'Yeah, thanks Dad.' Max's mouth stretches at the corners and he nods compliantly, but I know this is only for us. His eyes are troubled and weak, flitting away from the mirror to the houses we're passing. All those people's lives being lived behind closed doors. I wonder what they would think if they could see my family. I wonder what the boys Max likes will think of him. I wonder what people will think if this gets out, what headlines the bloggers and YouTube videos and news sites will use. A tear escapes from the corner of my eye and I wipe it away.

Just leave him alone, I think fiercely, my mind flashing back to that happy, tiny thug holding my finger, my eyes watching the sun dance over Max's lovely, soft, golden skin in the back of the car. *Hasn't he dealt with enough? Leave my baby alone.*

Daniel

Two things are happening in our lives right now: firstly, Dad is running for Member of Parliament for our area.

This is extremely exciting. Debbie, who works for Dad, is around all the time, and so is Lawrence, who also works for Dad.

Lawrence is tall and old with a thin face and yellow hair, but not bright yellow like Max's, sort of dull grey-yellow. He did not appreciate me saying this when I observed this.

I know this because he told me, 'I do not appreciate you saying this, young Daniel.'

'OK,' I said. 'Whatever.'

Lawrence basically tells Dad what to do, or sometimes he gives Dad advice, which he doesn't follow. Mostly, though, it's like the two of them are running for MP together, but Dad is the more nice one who everybody likes, so he is the front man.

Like when Max and me play *World of War* and he goes ahead to take enemy fire because he's better at dodging. In the same way, Dad is better at saying things that dodge reporters' questions.

'Don't repeat that to anyone but me,' Lawrence said when I told him this theory.

Debbie is much, much younger. She is nineteen, and really nice, with curly brown hair and is thin but with a big bum and boobs.

'They are not that big,' she told me.

'What cup?' I said, but Mum made me leave the table after I said that and Debbie laughed and called me a 'liability'. I'm going to have to look that one up.

Debbie basically does a lot of the work Dad and Lawrence don't want to do, like photocopying, making phone calls, and running. Dad and Lawrence walk everywhere, but Debbie runs everywhere, like there isn't enough time to do everything she has to do.

'Why do you work for my dad?' I asked her.

And she said, 'I agree with his politics. I hate the other guy and your dad's the only guy who offered to pay me.'

'Hm, how much?' I asked.

I think he should probably pay Debbie more than Lawrence, because she does more running around.

'I'll make a note of that,' Lawrence said when I suggested this.

One exciting thing about Dad running for MP is that we get to go to lots of parties. I never knew people threw so many parties. This week, Mum, Dad, me and Max have been to the Rotary dinner (Saturday night) and a barbecue for some old dude (Sunday), the Lions dinner (Monday – no lions), and then yesterday Dad and me went to a party at an old folks' home, which had surprisingly good jelly and ice cream and music. Dad talked about somebody called Cold Train with some old lady. I just danced, and they all said my dancing was good. Mum stayed home from that one because she said she had a headache, and Max stayed home too, because of the second thing that is happening at our house at the moment.

The second thing is that Max is ill and even being sick sometimes. This morning, I was waiting in the car with Mum and then he came in and immediately ran out again, saying, 'Sorry.'

And then we waited ages.

I said, 'What if he's dead?'

And Mum didn't move, but stared out of the window like she was hypnotised.

'Go and see if he's OK, Mum!'

'Why?' Mum jumped and said this like she was angry, but then she unbuckled her seatbelt, but as soon as she opened the car door to get out, Max came back.

I asked, 'Are you alright, Max?'

Max said, 'Yeah, it's fine.'

Then nobody said anything for the entire time we were going

to school, except when we pulled up at my school and I said, 'Thanks for the conversation, folks.'

I poked my head back in the car.

'Daniel! Don't do that, honey. I could have run you over,' said Mum.

'I said, "thanks for the conversation, folks".'

'We heard you,' Mum said.

'I love you guys.'

'Love you too,' Mum said. 'Be good at school.'

I waited for Max to say something, but he didn't, so I said, 'I love you, Max.'

And he said, 'Love you', and smiled. He looked really sad, though.

Max doesn't usually come with us in the car, but this week he has been coming with us every day. Mum said nothing was wrong, he just didn't want to go on the bus because it smelt of petrol and it was making him feel sick. She said he has a bug.

I'm slightly worried Max will be weak for my army. What if he dies?

Children get cancer. I saw it on a programme on television. A boy became sick and threw up everything he ate and had no hair. Children get leukaemia. I don't want Max to have leukaemia. I don't want Max to have no hair. I don't want my brother to die. Thinking about it makes me nervous all day. I chew through the cuff of my jumper, because I remember this boy in Great Ormond Street Hospital on TV who looked a bit like Max and he got small and sick and had a tube in his face and he died. Then I go and sit in the little house in the playground because I am crying and I don't want anyone to see.

It's Wednesday today and Max hasn't even come in my room, even though I know he's in from school, because I can hear his music in his room. He hasn't spoken to me much at all, even though I keep asking him if he is OK. Max is never all rubbish and doesn't want to play. Something must be wrong.

Also, Mum and Dad are pretending not to notice that he is very quiet.

He didn't even finish his food at the dinners we went to. And we always finish our food because if we don't, Mum says children in Africa will die.

At the Lion's dinner, which was full of mostly old people, Mummy was talking about seeing Auntie Leah and Uncle Edward, and Hunter, our cousin, and how we haven't seen them for ages. She asked Max if he wanted to hang out with Hunter and Max said no, because Hunter takes drugs and stuff. Then Mum said 'shh' and looked at me. Like I don't know what drugs are! I'm not stupid.

Then she told Max to finish his food and Max nodded and tried to eat more, but he couldn't, so I said, 'He could box his up.'

'What's that, sweetheart?' Mum said.

'For the children.'

'What children?'

I frowned. 'In Africa.'

'Oh.' Mum looked confused and smiled like she was sorry about me being weird to the other people we were sat with.

'For the children in Africa, right Max?' I said, and he looked at me and nodded and smiled, but in a kind of not-really-smiling way. His eyes were sad, like dogs', except dog eyes are brown and Max's are green.

He said his tummy hurt. Tonight we are not going out. I don't know what we will have for dinner. I'm looking forward to it, though. I hope it's broccoli. I'm a fan of broccoli.

The music Max has been playing this week is sad music too. Usually we listen to rap and rock music because that is the soundtrack to *World of War*, but he has been listening to very slow, spacey music that makes me feel tired. I really hope he's not dying.

I decide to go and see him, because he always comes to see me when I'm feeling bad.

I knock on his door, one, two, three, like Mum showed me, and then when I don't hear anything, I open the door.

He is curled up under the duvet with his face in the pillow.

I walk up to him. He is very still.

'Max?' I say, and I reach out and poke him.

He does not move, so I check if he is breathing by putting my hand over his nose to feel the breath. I would usually do the mouth, but it is closed.

'Hey!' He moans. 'What are you doing?'

'Checking you're alive,' I say.

'I can't breathe when you do that.'

'Sorry,' I apologise politely. 'What's wrong with you?'

'Nothing,' he says into his pillow.

I narrow my eyes. 'I'm not stupid.'

He groans and turns over so he is facing the wall. 'This isn't about you, Daniel.'

'I know.' I frown, because Max is stating the obvious, like he says I do all the time. 'But I was worried about you.'

'I'm OK,' Max mumbles.

I start to worry a lot, because I've been worrying all day at school and for Max not to tell me something is a big deal, because we tell each other everything. If I ask him, he always tells me stuff.

'Please, Max,' I say, wiping my nose on my sleeve because it has started to run. 'Are you going to die?'

'What?' He turns over, and his hair is all fluffed up and his face is all red from the bed. I put my hand to it. It's very warm.

'You have a temperature!' I cry.

'No, no.' He rubs his eyes. 'I've just been asleep in a hot bed. Come here,' he says, and pulls me onto the bed next to him. 'I'm not going to die. I'm not even ill.'

'But you're sad and you're being sick!' I sniff.

'I'm just a bit tired,' he says, hugging me. 'My tummy is poorly but that's it.'

'Do you want to sleep?' I ask.

Max nods.

'Can I sleep in your bed with you?' I say.

'Sure,' he says, but then when I go to get under the covers, he looks around at the bed and says, 'Actually, let's go in yours.'

'Why?' I ask, as he takes my hand and pulls me after him through the bedroom door.

194

'Because I like your bed more. It's comfier,' Max says, and we both get in it.

He falls asleep very quickly and I stroke his fluffy hair on his forehead and then I wriggle out of the bed and I put Daniel The Bear under his arm so Max won't be alone. Then me, and Pingu, which is a penguin that I named after the penguin on telly, play *World of War* with the sound turned down so we don't wake Max.

Auntie Julie's baby was due today, but it didn't want to come out yet. I hope it will come soon. I'm going to recruit it for my army.

Max

I saw Sylvie when I was coming out of the door of the new school building with Marc and Carl earlier today. We had been in the music room. Carl plays guitar, so we were listening to him. Marc was mucking about on the drums. He's terrible. It was giving me a headache, but it was good too, to just mess about. It gets my mind off stuff. I just want to feel normal. I just want to feel kind of drunk. But I'm not really a bad boy. I was tubing Smarties instead of drinking. Tubing is where you put the whole tube in your mouth and basically drink the sweets.

So it was coming close to the end of lunchtime. I've been letting my homework slide a bit, I really should have been doing it. It's only two weeks, though, and then it'll be over. I'll be able to think clearly again without feeling in pain, like my brain is my twisted guts. We headed out of the music room towards afternoon registration. The bell starts ringing as Carl is pulling open the door of the new block.

'Heeeey Sylvie,' I hear him say. 'How you doing?'

'Err, alright,' she says, looking him up and down like he's an alien.

'Sylvie! Sister from another mister,' says Marc. 'Up high!' He raises his palm. Sylvie just looks at it.

'Sorry,' I say.

She does her funny, smirky, to-the-right-side-of-her-mouth grin and slaps Marc's palm with her own. 'S'OK,' she says to me.

I smile but I blush at the same time. Imagine if her parents knew what I was, what had happened. They'd throw up more than I've been doing.

'Hey, Marc, we have that thiiing,' Carl drawls.

'Ohhhh.' Marc nods. 'That thiiiiiiiing.' He draws it out

comically. They leave Sylvie and me standing by the door and run off across the quad. I rock back on my right foot.

'Hi,' I say shyly, not looking at her.

'Hi,' she says.

She looks me all over, my face, my hair, my eyes, my neck, my chest and all the way down my body. I don't like that. I shift on my feet and drop my head down, suddenly needing to swallow and finding it difficult.

She moves in closer to me, slowly. Her arm slides around my neck from the left side, her breasts meet my chest. She's warm and soft and inviting. I slip my hand automatically around her waist.

'I don't know why you're being so shy, but it's a frickin' massive turn-on,' she says.

I grin helplessly, as she leans in and slips her tongue between my lips. Her own lips close around my top one. I can feel myself getting hard. She presses her body against mine, pulling my head to her with her arm. Kissing Sylvie Clark is totally delicious. I wrap my other arm around her and pull her closer, then lift her up off the ground and towards me, leaning back. She shrieks and laughs in my mouth, still kissing me.

I drop her to the ground and she backs away a little.

'You look so pretty today,' she says.

'Pretty?' I say.

'Pretty,' she confirms.

We look at each other for a little. I study her skin, the little freckles on her nose, the wide lips.

If she knew what you are, says my brain, *she would freak out. She would tell people. She would tell her next boyfriend, the one after you.*

No, I say.

Yes. The one after you.

Shh.

Max, you're disgusting.

How come it's 'you' and not 'us' all of a sudden? I ask my brain.

There's no answer.

'Max?' Sylvie is looking at me quizzically. She laughs. 'Dreaming of me, are we?'

I press my lips together. I have to tell her I can't see her. It's not fair to her. If she knew what I was, she wouldn't want to go out with me. If this gets out – if it blows up – everyone will talk about her too. She'll be the person who went out with the knocked-up hermaphrodite.

Oh god, I think, the thought making me feel like being sick.

'You want to come round tonight?' she says.

I open my mouth. I close it again. 'Um, I can't. Another dinner thing with my dad.'

'Ah, the wining and dining phase ·of the campaign. Are you schmooze-ready?'

I shrug and smile.

'Well . . .' She leans in to me. 'You just tell me when you want to hang out again, OK?'

I swallow and keep my mouth shut. But our faces are close together, and I look into her lovely eyes and she looks back at mine and I nod.

She leans away slightly, then screws up her nose. 'I was trying not to ask you this, but can I just grab your arse?'

I let out a quick, shocked laugh, then blush. 'Yeah.'

'Yeah?' she says teasingly. She leans in, checking down the corridor behind me to make sure nobody is coming, puts her arms around me and gropes my bum.

'Mmm,' I say, suddenly feeling really turned on. I drop my head to her shoulder and hug the top of her back, my arms over her arms. I giggle into her neck.

'Oh my god!' she shouts, whirling away from me, passing by me into the new block. 'So hot. SO hot!'

I laugh, watching her go.

She turns towards me, walking backwards. 'Bye,' she says.

'Bye,' I say, helplessly, and give her a little wave.

You didn't tell her, my brain says.

No.

I watch her go, biting my lip. Sylvie Clark is phenomenally

sexy. I press my head against the door handle and moan in frustration. Fuck.

I think about it in bed later that afternoon, which I go to as soon as I get home, like I have every day this week. I've been so tired recently. I should have told her, shouldn't I? It's lying not to tell her. I wouldn't tell her about the baby or being what I am. I would just tell her I couldn't see her. Maybe I could just tell her I couldn't see her for a few weeks. But why would anyone say that?

Danny comes in, upset because he thinks I'm ill. I go to his bed with him and sleep for a bit, then wake up around eleven, throw up in the toilet, go back to my bed and sleep again. The phrase 'morning sickness' is a total misnomer.

Football tomorrow. That's good. It'll take my mind off it. Although if anyone asks me to run backwards, bend over, or collides with my stomach I will upchuck all the fuck over them.

Sylvie

'Come on, keep it up, boys!' Mr Harvey booms across the field. We're playing netball on the courts, but I'm sat out on the sidelines with Carla Hollis, waiting for our teacher to call for a substitute. Carla's nice, and pretty weird, but we don't take many of the same classes, so we don't spend that much time together. We just hang out in Art and Games. Carla is sprawled on the cement next to me, making a sculpture out of gum that she is legitimately using for her Art GCSE.

'You're weird,' Emma tells her.

'I know,' says Carla.

I smirk.

Over in the top field, the boys are jogging around in a group. Max is with them. I wave to him and he waves back. Carla nudges me and smiles. I told her about the other night.

'So, Sylves,' says Emma. 'How good is Max?'

'Huh?'

'You *know* . . . Like, in bed,' she says, winking.

I make a face. 'I don't fuck and tell.'

She nods. 'I knew it. You haven't done it, have you?'

I roll my eyes. 'Why?'

'No reason,' she says, looking at Laura. She shakes her head with an expression resembling audacity, and looks out over the field at Max.

'He's a good kisser, huh?' murmurs Carla, from the ground next to me.

I nod. Carla got with Max last year.

'He's really nice,' says Carla. 'I like you two together. I think it's a good thing.'

'Why did you break up?' I ask.

'Ours was a temporary love.' She sighs. 'We met, we loved,

we lost, and for about three hours we drove each other crazy.'
She grins at me. 'I was on a brief break from Dean.'

'Dean who works at the pizza place?'

'Yeah. Like a really brief break. Like I left for three hours. He was so mad at Max, but they had a conversation and Max made him purr like a puddycat. He's so the will-be politician.'

'Who, Max? Nah.'

'Like, totally,' says Carla, pretending to be Emma. 'Liiii-aaaiiike, toooooooootallyyyyy.'

Emma looks over and gives me a weird, sad look. She shakes her head and whispers something to Laura.

I shrug and look back at Max. 'He's just nice, that's all.'

I'm trying to compose lines in my head. It's harder when you like someone to write stuff. It's easier when you hate someone. Hate breeds good material.

The guys are way over in the back field now, but I can still see blond hair mixing in between all the brunettes in my peripheral vision. There are very few proper blonds in our school.

I turn towards the netball game decisively, trying not to become one of those girls who stare at boys. I sure as shit do not want to become Emma *et al*. I have a life.

The ball bounces towards Carla and me, and we shrink away like it's a bouncing bomb. I hate playing netball, especially in the cold. Your fingers ache. It's hard to feel anything but pain when you catch the ball. Plus the girls who play it are super aggressive, like, steroid-aggressive. They whisper things to you under their breath and shove you whenever the umpire isn't looking. Crazy, butch try-hards. I used to be good at netball at my old school, but ever since I came to secondary school I suck. Everyone's bigger, faster, meaner, crazy-eyed. I don't mind most of the time, but in sports class it's really annoying. Last week I got tipped over by the centre player. My knees are still all scratched up. Still, that makes me look cool and punk.

'Oi, Walker! Stand up straight and get running!'

As if involuntarily, my head snaps ninety degrees to my right and I stare over my shoulder. Max has stopped a little behind the group. He's bent over double, as if he has a stitch. Mr Harvey comes closer to him.

'Get on with it, you bloody wimp!'

He steps in next to Max and Max flinches away. Mr Harvey says something to him and he shakes his head, still bent double.

I hear the words 'fucking hernia, have you?' and 'little queer' drift across the field. Mr Harvey is a dick. A complete and utter dick. I have no idea why he is still employed. Even if it weren't for the fact that he's a dick, there are all the paedo rumours. But maybe every PE teacher has those, because they all did at my last school too. Maybe it's expected. Maybe it's a *prerequisite* for the job.

'Weeeak!' Mr Harvey hisses at Max, and points directly off the field. Max is still clutching his stomach with one hand, the other pressed against his knee, keeping himself steady as he bends over. He shakes his head and moves slowly to the side of the field. Mr Harvey points again back at the school, telling Max to go inside.

Then Max yells at him. I can't hear what he says, but Carl and Marc come over with some more of the boys and they start shouting at Mr Harvey.

I see Max getting more and more pissed off. His face is redder and his jaw is more . . . locked up kind of. Then, when he looks like he can't take any more, he whirls around and spews on the ground behind him.

'Oh, just great,' I hear Mr Harvey say.

Carl leans over Max, with one hand on his back, but Max wipes his mouth and stands up and Carl's hand falls off him, and Max leans towards Mr Harvey and cracks, his face meaner than I've ever seen it (come to think of it, I've never seen it mean), and shouts something at him. It's short and sharp, and I don't catch all of it, but what I do hear everyone across the field and on the courts hears, because no one ever says it:

'Cunt!'

Literally everyone turns to look.

Mr Harvey glares at all of the boys on the field. 'Detention!' I hear him say, amongst a tirade of insults. Marc puts his arm under Max's shoulder, and Carl continues shouting at Mr Harvey as Max grips his stomach and they begin to walk him slowly in. Max is loved, it has to be said. The other boys crowd behind the threesome and block Mr Harvey off from Max's path. They are laughing and flipping Mr Harvey off, but Max looks in agony.

They're nearing the courts now. I will Max to lift his head, but he doesn't. He knows I'm here, and I deduce he's avoiding me because he doesn't want me to see him like this. Now, he doesn't look angry. Now, his face is absolutely drained of colour. He looks exhausted.

'D'you need to throw up?' Marc asks.

'Yeah,' Max says quietly, in a kind of weak, confused voice.

I look over at Emma, and she raises her eyebrows at me and pouts her lips. I shake my head at her.

I have no idea what you mean, Crazy, I say to her silently.

I watch through the strands of my hair as Max and his friends walk slowly down towards the school.

Max

'Are you OK?'

I can barely look up. I think if I do, I'll be sick. I hesitantly raise my eyes anyway. It's Sylvie. Behind her, Emma approaches. I look away quickly.

I'm sat outside the school office, where you wait when you're going to go home when you're ill. The receptionist is trying to get hold of Mum.

'Don't talk to him, Sylvie,' Emma calls from down the corridor.

Sylvie ignores her.

'Hey, Max, you alright, kid?' Sylvie whispers, sitting next to me, putting her arm around me. I smell her perfume and lean into her. I can't help it. 'I saw you go off the field.'

'It was just a stitch,' I mumble, not looking up, hoping Emma will just walk by. I can hear her getting nearer and nearer with her little crowd of followers. I can hear them whispering.

Shit. She's going to say something to Sylvie about the test. I know it. A lump rises in my throat.

'Then why are you sat outside the office?' Sylvie is asking me. She bumps my knee with hers in a soft, teasing way. 'Idiot. Just tell me what's up.'

'Hey, Max,' we hear. Sylvie and I both look up at Emma, who stands above us, hands on hips. Laura and Fay are behind her. 'Is your tummy hurting? Sympathy pains?'

Why can't you mind your own fucking business? I yell in my head, scowling.

Instead I say, dripping with sarcasm, 'Oh hi, Emma. Thanks for the little rumour I heard today.'

Best to meet it head on now that I know it's coming, and try and deny it upfront.

'You're welcome.'

'What rumour?' says Sylvie.

'Nothing, it's OK,' I say, and I slip my arm under hers about her waist.

I'm not looking at her but I can feel Sylvie studying my face. 'I have to go to IT,' she says.

Emma seems to be waiting for her.

'OK.' I grind my teeth, then I whisper into her ear, 'Just don't believe anything she says, OK?'

'Huh?' she frowns.

'I'll tell you later,' I murmur. 'Please don't believe her.'

Sylvie frowns, but she nods, and gets up to follow Emma to IT.

'Come on, Sylves, you can sit next to me,' says Emma.

Sylvie looks kind of exasperated with Emma but I worry anyway.

I call after them, as a cramp makes me almost double over: 'She's not your friend, Sylvie.'

Sylvie

'What does he mean?' I turn to Emma as soon as we're in the IT room. We sit down at a row of computers and we all log on.

'I saw him buying a pregnancy test on Saturday,' she says immediately, as if the info has been pressing against her lips, trying to escape. 'I told him that if he just up and left you after he'd like, got you in trouble, then I wouldn't let him get away with it.' She lowers her voice. 'Only I, like, totally knew he was cheating on you. He's a slut. He said it wasn't for you. That's why I asked you on the field whether you had done it or not. And then when you were like "no", then I knew he was. He's a total arrogant cock, Sylvie, and he doesn't deserve you.'

Frozen, my mouth open, I watch her face for a moment, not knowing what to say. 'Well . . .' I say, finally, the air escaping over my teeth. 'I never said we didn't do it.' I look down at my keyboard. My eyes are misting up.

Don't believe her, I say to myself, remembering what Max said.

'Sylvie,' she says, pityingly. 'He bought a *pregnancy test.*'

'Emma, this is really, really important, OK? This isn't the kind of thing you lie about.'

'I'm not *lying!*' she hisses. 'I would never do that to you.'

'Look me in the eye,' I say. 'Do you swear *on your mum's life* that you saw Max buying a pregnancy test?'

'Sylves, I swear on my mum's life.' She holds three fingers up and puts her hand on her heart, like a frigging Brownie. 'I sold that kid a pregnancy test. I handed it to him in a plastic bag and he gave me money for it.'

We hold each other's look as water fills my eyes.

'I swear to you,' she whispers. 'Oh, Sylves!' Emma suddenly, dramatically exclaims, and hugs me.

'Get off!' I splutter.

Fay leans in. 'Don't presume anything, Sylvie. He could have been buying it for a friend.'

'Does everybody know?' I hiss, looking at Emma.

'I was asking people because I didn't know what to do with this *crucial information*,' stresses Emma. 'And like, yeah, right!' She turns to Fay. 'That's so ridic. Who would ask Max Walker to do that, unless he'd potentially knocked them up?'

I think, biting the tip of my nail off. I almost gag on the black nail varnish. 'When did you see him buy the test?'

'Saturday morning,' Emma says immediately.

'Fuck.' My mouth falls wide open and I say instantly, without thinking, 'He was with me Friday night.'

'Maybe he got a text from someone he'd been with in the last few weeks.' Emma puts her arm around my shoulder. 'I can't believe he did that to you.'

I turn away and log into Facebook aimlessly, trying to hold back tears.

It's just a mistake. He's going to explain later, I try to reassure myself. *He said.*

'I wonder who he did have sex with,' Emma says, more to the room than me.

'He might not have . . .' Fay is saying.

'Of course he did!' Emma says. 'He must have had unprotected sex too!'

'The condom could have broke . . .' Fay says doubtfully.

'This is Max Walker,' Emma says sarcastically. She shakes her head ominously, and says, deeply, forebodingly, seriously, like some sort of soothsayer, 'He's going the way of Todd Z. Meaning: boy-slag.'

I try to wipe my eyes discreetly but the all-seeing eye of Emma notices everything.

'Don't worry, Sylvie. We'll tell everyone what he did and then no one will touch him with a barge pole.'

'Um,' says Fay.

'Don't,' I interrupt her.

'Huh?' Emma whispers.

'Don't tell anyone.'

'Why not? He deserves it, Sylvie! He can't just sleep with everyone and lead you on and get away with it!'

'Don't tell anyone, OK?' I repeat.

'I have to warn other women!' Emma basically yells.

'Emma.' I turn to her, wiping the last of the tears from my eyes. The black kohl eyeliner comes away all over my hands. 'If you tell everyone that Max had sex with someone other than me, or even that Max had sex with me, then I will tell everyone you had anal sex with Todd on the school field.'

Emma gasps and Fay shrieks. 'What?' Emma bellows.

'And that afterwards,' I add, 'you shat yourself.'

'Oh my god,' murmurs Fay, putting her hand to her mouth.

'Do you understand me?' I say. 'I swear to God, Emma, I will.'

Emma gives me an eye-over. She sees it: I am totally serious. 'You are so weird,' she tells me, but she nods, probably because right now I look like I could murder her.

Fay and Laura gape at me as I stand up, pull out the plug to Emma's computer and then storm out the room, like a kid with a mission. But Max is no longer outside reception. I look around helplessly.

'People like that deserve all they get,' I hear Emma mutter from the open door to the IT room.

Max

The receptionist couldn't get hold of Mum or Dad. Mum was in court, and Dad wasn't answering his personal mobile, so I end up staying in the sick room, occasionally throwing up into the adjacent toilet until the buses came at four in the afternoon. By the end of the day it seems everyone at school thinks I knocked someone up, apart from Marc and Carl. As I walk towards the common room to get my bag, guys keep holding their hands up to high-five me and girls keep looking at me like I'm dirty.

Even Maria comes up and says, 'Are you OK?'

'Yeah, I'm fine,' I mutter, trying to get my stupid dud key to go in my locker.

'Do you . . . need help?' she asks.

'Huh?'

'Like, with advice? On what to do?'

I stare at her blankly.

'Like, with abortions and stuff?'

'Oh my god.' I turn back to my locker. 'It's a rumour, Maria. There is no truth in it.'

'But everyone is saying Emma saw you buy a test.'

I slam the locker open. Finally. 'Yeah, fine, that part's true, but I was buying it for a friend, so can you please tell everyone that?'

Maria backs away from me. 'Sure I will. But you don't have to shout at me, Max. I was just trying to help.'

I rustle through my locker and keep my mouth shut. When I've found my books I pull them out and feel bad. I turn to say sorry but she's already gone.

'Fuck,' I hiss to myself. I close my eyes and lean my head against the cool metal of my locker. 'Fuck.'

I slide my books into my bag with a sigh, sling it around my shoulders and wander off to the bus stop.

The petrol smell on the bus seems soaked into the seats. I sit up at the front, feeling vomity, and run home when it drops me off. I hate how everybody looks at me. I hate that everybody looks at me at all. I used to like it, people looking at me like I was amazing, awesome, captain of the footie team. Now I realise popularity sucks for one very good reason: you can't turn it off.

I go straight up to my room, feeling shit about Sylvie, Emma, Maria, Mr Harvey and pretty much everyone I've pissed off.

Mum is in my room when I get up there, sat on my bed with a book that, upon closer scrutiny, appears to be entitled: *Parenting Practices: Gender and Sexuality*.

'Oh, hi Max,' she says, like it's a surprise to see me in my own bedroom.

'Oh, hi Mum,' I say, a bit sarcastically. We haven't really talked since we went to see Archie. She's been kind of . . . angry with me, I guess. Like, furious. She won't even look at me. It's like all she sees is me being knocked up, over and over. I know she thinks about it. She can't stop quietly swearing whenever I'm in the room with her.

Tonight, she smiles at me uncertainly and holds out the book as an explanation. 'I thought you might want to discuss some things.'

I dump my bag on the floor and my jaw gets tight. 'Like gender and sexuality?'

'Yes, sweetie.'

I stare at her like she's fucking insane. 'Why the fuck would I do that?'

'Max, don't be aggressive. I'm just suggesting we discuss whether . . .' She gets quieter. 'You might have been sexed wrong as a baby.'

'Oh my GOD! What is this? Shit all over Max day?' I hold back a shout of frustration, conscious from the sounds of imploding zombies and various beeps that Daniel is nearby.

'Honey, I just thought you might want to think about if you do want to be, you know, not a boy—'

'Like I have a choice what I am?'

'Many intersex children reject their assigned gender later in life—'

'JEE-sus, just because I'm pregnant doesn't mean that I'm going to suddenly become a completely different person.'

'Well, I wasn't aware you were dating boys. I thought there might be other things you were afraid to tell us.'

'I don't like boys! I'm not dating them! GOD! Haven't you been here my whole life? Do I have to spell it out for you? D'you think my whole existence is a lie? That I'm, like, covering up a secret obsession with dolls and hairstyles and Justin Bieber by working my arse off getting onto the first eleven and playing video games and watching *Hanna* with Saoirse Ronan like ten times?'

'How do I know when you don't tell me anything, Max?' she says tearfully. 'I feel like I don't know you anymore.'

'There's nothing to tell! I have told you everything!' I whine.

'I'm just saying you don't have to accept a male gender identity if you don't want to.' She gestures to my stomach and I put a hand protectively across it without thinking. 'If this has got you feeling differently. Has it, Max?'

'No, Mum, it hasn't. And I'm not faking about liking football and girls!' I come towards her, angrily. 'Now get out of my room!' I practically shove her out the door. 'And don't come in again without knocking!'

I hear her grumble in the hallway and the creak of Dad's footsteps coming up the stairs.

'Max, did you just slam that door?'

'Don't,' Mum warns.

'I've got people downstairs.'

'It's pregnancy hormones.'

'Not everything is pregnancy hormones . . . wait, what are you doing?'

'Nothing! I just thought—'

'Karen, what's that book?'

'I just thought we could discuss his gender and whether he wants to, you know—'

'Is this what Max is slamming the door over?'

'Stop growling at me, both of you, you're both doing it, I'm just trying to fucking help!'

'You're overreacting and it's winding him up. Come on, it's Max; he doesn't have to choose gender or change gender because of this. He's fine as he is, as long as you leave him alone!' His voice drops to a whisper. 'Sorry, I didn't mean that. I'm tired.'

'Well, I'm tired too,' says Mum. 'I'm tired of taking care of him and picking up after him and trying so hard to get everything right for sixteen years and then watching him *fuck it all up!*'

'Shh!' Dad says, mindful not of me, but of Lawrence and Debbie downstairs. He cautions Mum, 'Calm down. This is the first and only thing he has ever done wrong.'

Mum makes a snorting sound.

'Karen, it'll be over soon,' Dad says. 'We just have to ride out the storm. This isn't going to change anything. He's still Max. We'll go into the hospital, get rid of it and everything'll be back to normal. He's not going to change sex just because of an accident. He's still Max, OK?'

Mum is crying. 'He's *gay.*'

I suck in a breath and lower myself to the floor, leaning my head against the wall. I breathe out unsteadily. I hate Hunter. I hate him for everything he's doing to my mum, and to me and to my family.

'Who's he been *doing it* with?' she moans.

'Come into the bedroom,' I hear Dad murmur. 'Stop making a stir in the corridor.'

Then their door shuts and the voices stop.

I feel a tear roll down my cheek. I wipe it away and concentrate on my breathing. My bedroom's cold. I hear nothing but the rise and fall of my breath.

Dad means well. But everything has changed. Or maybe nothing has changed, except that everything is different now we acknowledge it. It, being me.

Daniel

'Max, are you content wearing what you wear?'
        'What?' says Max. He is watching the screen, not taking his eyes away from it. Tonight has been a very good night for me. Max seems a bit better, although he was sick at school today. He has played three hours solid of *Deadland 2*, though, and he doesn't seem ill to me. He is playing better than ever, and concentrating very hard, which is good because sometimes I have to tell him off for being easily distracted by things around my room. He is inquisitive, that one. He likes to poke things.

'You're wearing a T-shirt that says "Occupy", chinos and converse,' I inform him.

'I know what I'm wearing. I meant why are you asking?' he says. 'And don't call them chinos. It sounds gay.'

'Like homosexual?'

'No.' He shakes his head and moans. 'Um.' He pauses the game and puts his controller down and looks at me. 'People say something's gay when it's stupid. But really I shouldn't say it because it's not nice. To gay people, I mean.'

'Why not?'

'Well . . . you're comparing them to something lame. Like the word "chinos".'

'But what do you call them?'

'I dunno.' He shakes his head and presses the play button. 'Trousers. Chinos is just a dumb word.'

'Does that make me gay?'

'What?'

'Because I said something gay?'

'No. It's not gay, it's just stupid. Forget it.'

'What would make me gay, though?'

'Liking boys would make you gay.'

'Do you like boys?'

'Oh my god,' Max mutters, putting his hands in his hair and scratching. 'Aaaaaargh.'

'What?'

'Nothing. No, I don't like boys.'

'OK.' We pick up our controllers again and play the game but I keep staring at him in the screen and he notices and becomes slowly more agitated. I can tell because he is killing less zombies and getting shot more.

'Why did you ask me that?'

'If you liked boys?' I ask.

'Yes.'

'Because Mum was talking about stuff like that. Like, what it would be like if you were a girl and wore dresses, or if you were gay or something. I heard through their bedroom wall.'

'She's not serious!' Max says loudly. 'She – she was joking.'

'Why would she joke about that?'

'Because Mum's insane, Daniel.' He takes out a zombie leader. 'She has serious psychological problems.'

'Really?' I say, worried.

'No. I mean . . .' He looks over at me. 'She has psychological problems but . . . they're not serious.'

I kill a zombie midget and a zombie dog with a razor blade to its gut. I'm still confused, though. 'Does she think you want to be a girl?'

Max goes reddish and is quiet for a bit. 'Kind of.'

'You couldn't be a girl.'

'No.'

'You're a boy.'

'Well . . . yeah.'

'That would be impossible,' I say.

'Well . . . urgh,' says Max. He takes out a Pterodactyl.

'What?'

'Nothing.'

'Why did you say urgh?'

Max pauses the game.

215

'Don't freeze it!' I cry in dismay. 'I was just about to nuke the living dead HQ.'

'Do you want me to tell you something important or not?'

'Oh. Yes. I always want to hear important things.'

'OK.'

'Because they're important.'

Max groans. 'Of course. Alright. So. Sometimes men dress as women, or women dress up as men.' He looks at me to see if I'm following, which I find insulting because this is really simple so far.

'OK. I am following,' I say, which is the thing that Max asks me to say so he doesn't spend half an hour explaining something then have to backtrack, like that time I asked him what was going on in outerspace, and then after he had explained for 35 minutes about the Milky Way, I told him I meant Outerspace, in *World of War*, which is the fifth level of the game.

'Because sometimes people feel that they have been born in the wrong body.'

'Have they?'

'Err, I don't know. But anyway, um, they feel that way, and then they sometimes try to make themselves look that way, by wearing dresses and make-up, and sometimes having operations.'

'Operations?'

'Like, on their bits. Their male or female bits.'

I take this in. 'Eww.'

'Er, yeah. Anyway—'

'How?'

'How the operations?'

'Yeah.'

'Well, like if a guy wanted to be a woman, he would have his thing, um, taken off, and they would make lady parts.'

'EWW!'

'It's not ew—'

'THAT'S SO UNBELIEVABLY DISGUSTING!'

'Will you shut up? No it isn't, it's just sometimes people are born with something that's not what they want and they decide to change it.'

'But it's gross!'

'No, it's like plastic surgery; like if someone wants a facelift, they get it.'

'But that's disgusting too!'

'No it's not! Shh! Mum and Dad will hear you yelling.'

'But what about Sylvester Stallone?'

'Huh?'

'His face!'

'What?'

'It's disgusting! Is that what happens to your bits?'

'Urgh. Don't be so stupid. You don't get a facelift on your crotch, do you?' He puts his hands over his face and moans again. 'Jesus! I came in here to get away from all this shit.'

I pause. 'You swore.'

'I know,' Max says, like he's impatient with me. 'But haven't you been listening? I'm trying to tell you, some people are just born wrong and they . . .'

'What?'

'They feel sad or wrong until they get put right. And bad things can happen when people have things that don't fit them. So everything has to be removed, so that . . . so that people aren't sad anymore.' He sits with his hands over his face and we are quiet for a bit. 'You wouldn't want anyone to be sad, would you?'

I think about this, because Max seems very serious.

'No, Max,' I say, after about thirty seconds. 'I wouldn't want anyone to be sad.'

'OK,' he says, hands still over his face, and he swallows as if he has a Haribo in his mouth, except he doesn't have a Haribo, unless he has one without my knowledge, but I would be able to smell it. 'Then sometimes there are situations where it's not exactly that, but . . . it's like that.'

'Max?'

'Yes?'

'I am not following you.'

217

'Like . . . sometimes people have to choose whether they want to be a boy or a girl when they are kind of both.'

'What, people who look half like a girl and half like a boy?'

'Kind of.'

'Wow. I'd love to see one of them. I wonder what they would look like.'

'Yeah.'

'Probably totally weird.'

'Um.'

'So why do they have to choose?'

'Whether to be a boy or a girl?' he asks.

I nod.

'They just do,' he says, taking one hand away from his face and looking at his shoe and scratching it with his fingernail. 'That's just the way things are.'

'Like, how?'

'Oh god, I don't know.' He drops his other hand from his face and reties his shoelaces on his converse. 'Like how when you fill out a form it says male or female, or when there are changing rooms and they are male and female, or toilets, or clothes, or like on your driver's licence and passport, or when they do school uniform, or when you play a game and it's boys versus girls. Or when you get married and you have to be a boy or a girl because same-sex marriage is not recognised by some countries.'

'Isn't it?' I ask, but Max doesn't seem to hear me. He keeps talking to his shoes.

'It's just weird and people don't know how to treat you if you're halfway in-between. They think you're going to fuck with their head and corrupt their children and . . . stuff like that . . .'

'You said the "eff" word.'

'Sorry.'

'So, anyway, you're a boy, and you don't want to be a girl?'

He picks up his controller, looks down to the bottom left-hand corner of the screen, even though there aren't any zombies in it, and then back up to his viewfinder. 'No. I don't want to be a girl.'

'You want to be a boy?' I ask.

Max stares very still at the screen and then frowns, as if he has remembered I'm there. 'Um,' he says, and unpauses the game and kills another zombie. Then he looks confused, as if he has lost one of the zombies, except I look to check, and he hasn't, he has killed them all, five out of five.

I pick up my controller and nuke the evil HQ. This game is brilliant because it's the only one where I am nearly as good as Max. You can pick out of lots of characters too, and get them all through the levels. I usually pick Xylar, who is a small boy whose special weapon is fire coming out of his hands. Max usually plays Defender, who is a woman with big breasts and dark skin. I look over at my brother.

I decide to try a different tack with asking him questions about what happened earlier, because Max says when you are torturing the truth out of people, this is a good way to go.

'When we play this game,' I say, 'you always pick Defender, and she's a girl, so do you want to be a girl like Defender?'

Max sighs, like he is deeply, deeply irritated at me, and I realise I've been doing that thing where I ask questions all the time to him, which he has politely asked me not to do several times before, so I say, 'Sorry.'

He looks at me as if he has just noticed me and shakes his head and mumbles, 'It's OK.' Then he sighs again and says, 'No, I don't want to be a girl like Defender.'

'OK,' I say. 'But why do you want to be Defender every time we play, then?'

He looks at me, and then looks at the screen. 'Err, because she's hot.'

'What does hot actually mean?'

'Oh my god!' Max throws his controller on the floor and leans back against the bed like he's really tired and he whines and yells at the same time like I'm really annoying. 'It means sexually attractive! Stop asking me questions!'

219

I go quiet, which I do when people yell because I don't like it. Now it is Max's turn to apologise, but he doesn't.

'You yelled at me, Max,' I say.

'Well,' he grumbles. 'You ask stupid questions.'

I throw my controller down on the floor because I'm angry. I hate Max for being so moody and whiny this week. He's never moody and now he's being it with me and I haven't done ANY-THING and all I've done all week is worry about him being sick and now he's being horrible to me and I can't TAKE it anymore, so I shout, 'Well, you give stupid answers!' and I pick up the controller and throw it hard at Max's face and it hits his eyebrow and then I turn around and get on the bed and tell him to get out my room and I keep screaming at him to get out.

'Hey!' Max gets up and comes over and grabs my shoulders. 'Hey! Stop!'

At first I think he is fighting me, so I kick him really hard, but then I realise he is trying to hold me still, so I kick him harder.

'Ow! Daniel, calm down, I'm sorry! It's OK, Daniel, it's alright!'

I scream at him, 'I don't want a sister, I want a brother!'

'I know, I'm sorry!' says Max, like he is distressed. He looks like he will cry.

'I want a brother!' I howl.

'I'm sorry! I am your brother, I'm not going to be a sister. Ow, stop fucking kicking me, Daniel! OW!'

Max lets go of me and goes over to the telly-wall. I turn around and pick up a book and throw it at him and it hits him in the forehead but he is holding his stomach.

When the book hits his head he puts an arm over his head as well and crouches down. His eyebrow has a scratch on it that I made with the controller. There is a bit of blood but not a lot.

'I told you my tummy was hurt,' Max says quietly, with a scratchy voice, like he is catching his breath. 'I told you the other day. Why did you kick me?'

I stop screaming and even though my chest is heaving, I get really quiet, really quickly.

'I can't fucking handle you when you're like this,' Max says.

'Yes you can,' I say.

'You really hurt me.'

'Well . . .' I frown. 'You're big.'

'I'm not that big, Daniel.'

'You're as big as Mum and Dad.'

'No . . .'

'Yes you are.'

'I am almost, size-wise, but I'm way, way younger than them. You can't yell at me like that and shove and kick me. It hurts, and I'm not old enough to deal with it,' he says really quietly, like he is totally, completely tired. 'I just don't have the energy to fight you. And you can't ask me to do that. I'm not your parent.'

I shrug. 'You're old enough to be one.'

'No!' And then it's Max's turn to shout at me. 'I'M NOT.'

I'm still angry at him, but he seems to be very upset so I walk over to him and crouch down next to him and put my arm over his shoulder.

'OK, Max, you're not,' I say to comfort him, but it does the opposite because he cries once, loudly, under his arm. Then he gets up and walks out of my room, and I have no one to play *Deadland 2* with anymore.

I sigh, very deeply, like Max did earlier, and notice how our sighs sound very much the same, and I think this is probably because we are brothers, and we are the closest people to each other genetically in the world, and so even our sighs sound the same, and I think this is a very profound realisation, so I write it down in my notebook.

Archie

'I want to know,' I hear as I walk in my office on Friday morning, and I jump, realising Max is standing next to my examining table.

'Max! You scared me.' I heave my files carefully onto the desk. Max steps forward to help me balance the pile, picking up several that slip off the tabletop. 'What are you doing here? We have an appointment next week.'

'I want to know now,' he says, almost petulantly.

I sigh and glance at the clock on the wall. 'Look, you have to schedule an appointment. I have so many patients to see today and they all need my help too. I know what's going on in your life is overwhelming, but—'

'Archie! Please! I want to know!' Max can't look me in the eye. He puts his hands over his face and speaks quickly. 'Please, Archie. This is so embarrassing. I don't know anything about myself, and I've *never* asked anyone, I've *never* made an issue out of it, I just want . . . I want to know. Please.'

He takes his hands off his face, as if he needed them there just to speak.

I think, and then feel ashamed of myself, embarrassed for being in such a rush. I shut my door and sit down at my desk. 'What do you want to know?'

'I want to know . . . whether I'm a boy or a girl.'

He looks wrecked, as if he hasn't slept in weeks. *Somebody should have told him the truth,* I think. I sigh and decide to address the issue simply. 'You're neither.'

'No.' Max shakes his head. 'I Googled it. Being intersex means that you don't look like one or the other to a doctor. It doesn't mean you aren't one.'

'That's . . .' I rub my lips together, trying to find the right words. 'Not always true. Sit down,' I say, nodding to the chair opposite me. Max is standing rigidly, his arms crossed. He swallows, looks around and then moves to the patient's chair.

'Sorry for busting in,' he mutters.

'That's alright,' I reply. 'How are things at home?'

He looks up at me, like it's a stupid question.

'I see,' I say, nodding. 'Max, before we talk about this, I wanted to ask. The boy who assaulted you . . .' I falter. 'Has it happened again? Do you think it will?'

'No.'

'Are you sure?'

'I'm sure.'

I nod.

Max looks around the room and chews the top layer of skin off his lip.

'OK,' I begin. 'If a doctor can't decide whether a newborn is a boy or girl, they can check three things: the sex chromosomes, meaning whether you're genetically a boy or a girl; the gonads, meaning whether you have testes or ovaries; and how the body responds to hormones. Sometimes they do gender assignment surgery straight away. Sometimes it's necessary, sometimes it's . . . not.'

Max clears his throat.

'Do you want to ask a question?'

'No. Sorry,' he looks down at his knees and wriggles uncomfortably. 'Keep going.'

'In instances where intersex people have surgery at birth, some people aren't happy with their assigned sex, some people say surgery is genital mutilation, some experience reduced sensitivity, and many people require further surgery later in life.'

'But I didn't have surgery.'

'No, you didn't.'

'Why not?'

I pause. 'Your father didn't want you to have it.'

'Dad?'

'Yes.'

'Not Mum?'

'It just says your dad in your file.'

223

'So . . . did Dad not want me to have it because they would make me a girl?'

'I don't know, Max.'

'I can't imagine my dad wanting me to stay like this,' Max says, more to himself than me. 'He's such a, like, family values person.'

'What do you mean?'

'I don't know. He always seemed the more traditional one. He's the one who wanted to get the big house and to have the two kids and stuff. That's what Mum said.'

'Do you and your mum talk a lot?'

Max's eyes slip to the side. 'We used to. I don't know. We haven't recently.'

'So,' I continue, but Max interrupts me.

'What sex did the doctor want to assign me?'

'A girl when you were born, then they suggested that you be assigned to a male sex at nine, and again pressure was applied to do this at thirteen.'

'Why?'

'A lot of the surgery is done based on what you have on the outside, which is why many intersex people lose their ability to have babies. When you were born, in the mid-nineties, surgery was getting more refined, and so doctors still wanted you to have surgery, but instead of wanting to assign you a male gender based on your outward appearance, they advised assigning you a female gender based on your sex organs. When you were born, you had a vagina. Inside your body you had two gonads. One was an ovotestis, meaning half ovarian tissue and half testicular. As far as I can understand, ovotestes very rarely work, and are thought to be prone to certain tumours, so many doctors choose to remove them. Yours, like many people's, was removed shortly after birth. You *also* had a uterus and an ovary, but you had no testicles at all. Are you following?'

Max is groaning. 'Yes.'

'Max?' He looks up.

'I know you are a little embarrassed, but remember I am a

224

doctor. I deal with all sorts of embarrassing things, mucus and pimples and warts and I also run an after-hours clinic here where I talk to many young people about these issues. So, for me, this is not really an awkward conversation. OK?'

He nods shyly. 'Thanks, Archie. Sorry.'

'Don't apologise, please.'

He makes an effort to smile.

Poor kid, I involuntarily think. Then, *Don't get emotionally involved.*

I clear my throat. 'When you were born, you also had a small phallus, and couldn't immediately be assigned a gender. Your father wouldn't allow you to be operated on, except to have the ovotestis removed. It says in your file that your parents chose the name Max because they felt it would be gender-neutral. Then you grew up and you acted like a little boy and everyone treated you like a boy. This is all according to your notes. So, at nine, the doctors suggested you have the surgery to turn you into a boy.'

'Why at nine?'

'Well, firstly, the phallus looked more male by then.'

Max blushes. 'Oh.'

'They knew because—'

'Because of the photographs.'

'You remember that?'

Max rolls his eyes unhappily and shrugs.

I continue. 'You were relating to boys, acting like a boy and, crucially, you weren't growing like a girl. You weren't showing any signs of breasts, your penis was bigger, so a specialist suggested surgery to remove all your internal female organs at nine, and then again at thirteen. Then when your parents wouldn't consent, a course of male hormones was suggested, which they agreed to.'

'Yeah, I remember that. Why did my parents agree to the hormones if they didn't agree to the surgery?'

I think back. 'I don't know. It didn't say in your file. Perhaps it was a compromise.'

Max nods, and we sit in silence for a moment as he thinks.

Then he looks up at me through his hair and lets out a long breath. 'So,' he asks, 'what am I?'

He watches me nervously, his green eyes marred with turbulent thoughts.

'Firstly, I just want you to know that I think your parents haven't told you this because they didn't want to overwhelm you. Because intersexuality is rare, parents can often feel isolated and confused themselves, and I think they didn't want you to feel like that, growing up. Also, Max, maybe the reason your parents didn't do the surgery when you were younger is because sometimes when parents pick the baby's sex, the baby grows up and feels like the other sex. Or they don't feel comfortable being either. A lot of doctors and parents get it wrong.'

'Archie,' Max interrupts me. 'Tell me what I am.'

I pause a moment, then nod.

'I can't tell you why you are what you are, but you are what is known as a true hermaphrodite, born with both ovarian and testicular tissue. People with true hermaphroditism can have three different karyotypes, meaning the combination of chromosomes. The sex chromosomes, X and Y, define whether you're chromosomally male or female or both. For true hermaphrodites, possible karyotypes are 47,XXY, 46,XX/46,XY or 46,XX/47,XXY. Intersex people, just like people of male or female sex, are born in all shapes and sizes, so even a similar diagnosis to another person could mean you look fairly different.'

'Wait . . .' Max begins, then falters, holding the sides of his head with his hands as if he cannot concentrate. 'So, is female XX?'

'Yes, and male is XY.'

'Can you please,' Max lowers his head miserably, 'just tell me if I'm a boy or a girl?'

'Max, I told you, you're neither. Your karyotype is 46,XX/ 46,XY.'

He puts a shaking hand up to his lips and looks at me. He lets out a choking noise.

'My personal opinion is that your parents held out on surgery, not because they couldn't decide whether you should be a boy or a girl, but because they knew you didn't have to choose either.'

'Fuck.' Max leans over his knees and puts his hands to his face. 'Fuck,' I hear, mumbled, coming through tears. 'Shit. Sorry.'

'Are you going to be sick?' I ask.

'I . . . I don't know.'

I get my sick bucket from the corner of my room and hold it on the floor underneath him. I crouch down and touch his hair awkwardly. He shakes beneath my fingers. Tears fall off his face and pat the metal bucket like rain.

'Max,' I whisper. 'This is a good thing. You don't have to make choices, you don't have to have surgery, you can just be you.'

'I don't want . . .' he whispers, then his voice fades away and he shakes his head. He sits up, and his cheeks are streams of water. 'I don't want to be me.'

'Oh, Max.' I struggle to find words to comfort him. 'I'm sorry. Look, I shouldn't have told you this way, I should have let your parents do it, but I thought you should know, particularly with the baby.'

'Oh shit, the baby,' he sobs.

'Max—' I take hold of his hand and he grips mine fiercely.

'Jesus, I was so sure I could just come in here and solve all the problems and have the surgeries and just be a normal brother, you know?' He rubs his eyes with his other palm and I notice how pale he looks, how red they look. 'I looked intersex up on the internet last night, and I saw how girls could look like boys and boys could look like girls, and I was just so fucking sure I'd come in and you'd tell me yes, I was a boy, and everything else was just a mistake that I could ignore and get rid of. I want to get rid of it.'

'The baby?'

He wipes his arm across his face. 'No. I don't know. I mean

everything. I want to get rid of everything that makes me a complete freak.'

'You're not a freak, Max! Don't say that.'

'Archie . . .' he cries, and I put my arms around his head.

'Alright, OK . . .' I say soothingly. 'Please don't cry.'

'Is my appointment scheduled for the abortion?' Max asks quietly, wiping away his tears, calming himself down. 'Sorry about the crying,' he mutters.

'It's fine,' I say. 'I was going to ring this evening. The appointment is next Friday at nine a.m., at the hospital.'

'Good. I want it all removed.'

'You want a hysterect—?'

'Everything.' He cuts me off, checking his face in the mirror above my desk. 'Like Mum said.'

'OK,' I say doubtfully. 'If that's what you want, I can arrange for you to see a specialist to discuss a removal of all your female anatomy. Then perhaps they can schedule an operation before Christmas.'

'What's going to happen to me?'

I frown. 'In the operation?'

'No.' He sits silently, struggling. He looks exhausted.

'How do you mean?'

'Am I, like, going to get more boyish? Am I going to get facial hair? I don't know anything. Am I going to get more girlish?'

'Honestly, Max, I don't know,' I reply. 'Perhaps there are some tests—'

'Forget it, it's fine,' says Max abruptly, blushing. 'I'm sorry. I have to go.' He wipes his face on his sleeve one last time. 'Thanks for telling me and sorry to barge in. I just wanted to know. It was bothering me.'

He stands up. 'Sorry for the crying,' he murmurs again, hurrying out the door.

I leap out of the chair and grab the door before it closes after him.

'Max! Come see me anytime!' I call down the corridor. But it's empty. He's already run out.

Max

After I see Archie, I decide to bunk off school. I was gonna go back in, but I walk out of the clinic and clock the wall of the graveyard at the end of the car park and walk towards it like a zombie. I grab the top of the wall, grazing my palms, pull myself up and over the little buckling, rusted iron fence, and lie down in the cold grass. It's freezing, but I can't move, flat on my back in my blue parka with the hood up, and fake fur all around my face. My chest heaves but I force my eyes to stay dry. I swallow it up, all of it, choking on it as it goes down. I don't think about anything, just concentrate on nothingness, the shapes that move across my eyelids when I close my eyes. I really want to go to school to see Sylvie and try to explain things to her, but I feel too miserable, too eclipsed, too unable to function.

Sylvie finds me anyway.

With my eyes closed, I feel a body moving close to me and I jump, thinking it could be Hunter.

'Thanks for the welcoming reaction, Walker.'

'Sylvie . . .' I try to sit up.

'Don't,' she says, placing a hand firmly on my chest. We share a look and I settle back down on the ground. She lies on her side, her face turned in to mine, her breath in my ear, in the same way Hunter lay with me in my bed after the thing.

I watch the sky, the clouds sliding across it. Everything seems grey and bleached out. After a minute Sylvie murmurs, 'What's wrong?'

I wipe water from the corners of my eyes. 'Nothing. I'm sorry.'

'Arse.'

'Arse?' I look at her.

She nods. 'Arse.'

229

I wriggle around onto my side. 'OK. There is something wrong. But I can't tell you what it is.'

Her mouth squidges up and moves to the side. 'Did you get someone pregnant?'

'*No*,' I stress, closing my eyes. 'No, no, no.'

'OK, Max, OK,' she says, shaking me gently. 'I believe you.'

'The test was for . . .'

'It wasn't for a friend, was it?'

'Um, I can't tell you.'

'But it wasn't, was it? So what else is there? Did you have sex with someone else the other week?'

'Oh,' I realise something suddenly, taking my hands away from my mouth, noticing a fingernail is bleeding. 'You think I've had sex.'

'Errr . . .' she says.

'Oh my god.' I get wide-eyed. '*You've* had sex?'

'Well, yeah. I thought you had too.'

'No. I thought you *hadn't* too.'

She thinks for a minute. 'How have you not had sex? You get off with everybody.'

'Get off with,' I clarify. 'Means kissing.'

She props herself up on one elbow and leans away from me doubtfully. 'You some cray cray Christian, now your dad's a big politician? Is it no sex before marriage? Is that the freaky deal here?'

'No.' I smile slowly. 'I'm not *cray cray*.'

'So you didn't knock anyone up?'

'No, I couldn't have,' I reply truthfully.

'So who was the test for?'

I hesitate. 'I can't tell you. But . . . I hope that's OK because . . .' I bury my head in my coat. I shouldn't be saying it. I should be telling her she shouldn't hang around with me, that it's disgusting. I mean, I'm *with child*. Urgh.

I get tearful, but I look up into her eyes, because I don't want to be cowardly. I wet my lips and kiss her once quickly.

'Because I really like you,' I say, with a little sigh of tension coming out and making the air steamy. 'I like you more than

230

I've liked anyone, ever. You're pretty amazing, and I think about you a lot – a *lot*, a lot. And . . . I really, really don't want you to hate me or think badly of me.'

'I couldn't think badly of you,' Sylvie says. 'Annoyingly.'

'Why annoyingly?'

'I don't like depending on people. I don't like it when they can affect my emotions.'

'Wow,' I tease. 'You're so sophisticated. You have commitment issues already.'

'Well, I am an older woman.'

'By, like, a week!'

'I'm cleeeearly way more experienced.'

I knock her knee with mine, laughing. 'Shud urrrp. You're so weird! Someone tells you they like you and you tell them it's annoying and you've had more sex than them.'

Sylvie shrugs. 'I'm bad. A badass.'

'You are.'

'It's sexy.'

'Yes, but I think I'm supposed to say that.'

'Go on then.'

I pause, shyly. 'You're sexy.'

'You're sexy, Max.'

'Thanks.'

'Let's get off.'

'OK.'

Karen

Max walks in from school through the main door. It's still a surprise when anyone walks through it, as we've used the back door for so long. I'm in the large living room, having a coffee, reading a brief. I see Debbie walk past him spryly.

'Hi, Max, how are you?' she says, all bounce and joy and idealism-fired energy, which I find very exhausting to watch at the moment.

'Good, thanks, Debbie,' I hear Max say politely. 'How's everything going?'

'Oh, *so* well,' she replies. 'Everybody loves your dad. He's pretty much a cinch for MP, but he wants to get out there and shake everybody's hand anyway. It's like, Stephen, you can't shake *everyone's* hands!'

I sometimes wonder if Debbie has a crush on Steve. I sometimes wonder if Steve notices. He's not like that, really, but . . . I don't know. Power corrupts, so they say.

We haven't talked about Max having the abortion or a hysterectomy since the appointment with Archie, because Steve has suddenly become even more busy. I think it's on purpose. I have too, I suppose.

'Are you excited about the debate at the Lloyd George Centre?' she is asking Max.

'Yeah, sure,' he replies, not sure at all.

'So many people are coming. Two candidates, battling it out in front of such a big audience, all livestreamed to the web. It's so exciting, how new technology has transformed politics. It's really about creating drama for the debate. If Stephen comes across as the most exciting prospect for MP, you've got people. That's really our tactic. You're going to be there to support Stephen, right?'

'Steve,' Max corrects her, absent-mindedly. 'But yeah. Great.'

I see him go past the open door of the living room and up the stairs.

Five minutes later, he comes back down, in different clothes: a purple zip-up hoodie from Topman that I bought him for his birthday, a blue T-shirt, and grey cords from All Saints. I expect him to walk straight past but he stops and dips his head into the living room.

'Mum?' he says calmly. 'Can we talk?'

I put my brief down shakily, smile at him and nod. A week ago, I felt I knew everything there was to know about him. Now I feel like I know nothing. He's been having sex with boys, or maybe just a boy. He's been lying to us, to me.

Debbie walks past the door again, and Max and I eye her suspiciously.

'My room?' he suggests.

I follow him up the stairs, smoothing out the lines on my face, calming myself, even as my heart beats so fast. He will apologise, I think. I will forgive him, but I will set new boundaries, a curfew, I will make him admit when and where and who he has been with.

He opens the door to his room and gestures to the bed. I sit on the end and he sits at the head of it, on his pillow.

'So,' he says.

'So,' I say, my smile fading. His expression is icy. Max has never been cold a day in his life, but today he looks at me as if I'm not Mum and not on his side – as if I'm an enemy.

'Why did you call me Max?'

I hesitate. 'What?'

'Why did you call me Max when I could have grown up as either a girl or a boy?'

'I—'

'Do I just feel like a boy because you treat me like one?'

'I . . . It was a compromise. We—'

'I just went to see Archie.'

'Who's . . . You went to see Dr Verma?'

'Yes. I did,' Max says, quietly.

233

I wet my lips. 'We've never kept it a secret from you that you were both, Max.'

'Yes,' he says, and leans forward, imploring me with his hands. 'But you never told me what *type* I was. I didn't know that I was so rare, that I was one of the only ones that were truly intersex. I didn't know that really I don't have a choice, that I'm both and neither, and could never be one or the other. I never knew exactly what I was, that I could never have kids as a boy, that my gender is just constructed by how you treated me.'

'Max, I don't know . . .' I look towards the door, thinking of Steve. 'Maybe your dad . . .'

'*Why* didn't I get surgery?' he says, his voice cracking.

I panic. 'I wanted you to have surgery so you'd be like everyone else! It was your dad—'

'You wanted me to have surgery?'

'Yes! I told him, but then . . . we agreed that we would wait.'

'For what?' Max explodes. 'For me to decide what I was? I wasn't anything! You should have made the decision and not left it up to me!'

'Your dad was worried that we would make the wrong decision. I thought the worst when we decided you wouldn't have surgery until you were older. I thought that you'd be so confused, but until now, you've been fine—'

'Well, I'm not fine now, am I, Mum?'

'Max!' I shriek, the veneer of calm breaking. 'You can't blame me for that! You've been having unprotected sex!'

Max looks shocked, as if it's a surprise, as if I'm not supposed to say. He opens his mouth to say something, but I interrupt him.

'Don't you remember we had a conversation when you were about to turn fourteen and you said you didn't want an operation?'

'No!' Max says, but he looks uncertain.

'Well, you did. You'd had the course of hormones, and we were all in agreement that because there hadn't been a problem before, and because they were making you feel sick and aggressive and unruly, you were going to stop taking them.'

'I don't remember that.'

'You hated taking them. And in fact . . . even though your dad talked me round to not having surgery earlier, by that time I agreed with him, because you were always so happy, and then the hormones . . . I was worried the hormones would make you feel like we didn't love you the way you are . . .' My voice breaks. 'I'm sorry, Max. Maybe I was wrong.'

'Why the hormones when I was thirteen?' Max is frowning. 'Huh?'

'Why did the doctor say I should have them?'

'He wanted you to have an operation, but we all said no. They told us you might grow breasts if you didn't have the hormones. We thought it would be distressing.' I let out a sob.

'For who, Mum? Me or you?'

'Oh, Max.' I shake my head, wiping my eyes. 'Don't be like that. I tried so hard for you. We were under so much stress. This was your *life* we had to make decisions about. We didn't want everyone talking about you, staring, saying things. Do you think we should have carried on with the hormones?'

I look at Max. He is staring at me with an unreadable expression.

'Do you?' he says, after a minute.

'Maybe now,' I say softly. 'Yes. Maybe we should have done the surgeries when you were little. But they wanted to make you a girl when you were born. It would have been awful. Or it might have been fine.'

'I don't feel like a girl,' Max murmurs, frowning. 'But . . . I don't know. I feel like I don't know who I am anymore.'

'But you've been with a boy,' I say. 'Haven't you?'

'Mum . . .' Max balls his hands up. 'Stop saying that. It was a mistake, OK? It was . . .' He sighs deeply, turns crimson and mutters, 'It was just the one time and it was a mistake.'

Thank god, I think. *Thank god*. He's different already. I don't want him to be any more different. I watch him for a minute to ascertain whether this is the truth. He doesn't move. I nod.

'Do you want to do the operations to be a boy?'

Max stays silent.

'Max, what are you thinking?' I say, soothingly.

'What does that even mean?'

'It means that you have everything taken out. The . . .' I struggle to say the words. 'Ovary, the womb, everything like that. I don't know quite how they do it but they get rid of the . . . the vagina and then you can have another operation to give you male things, like the fake testicles that men who have testicular cancer have put in.'

Max puts his hands over his face and speaks through his fingers. 'I asked Archie to book the operation to have the womb and stuff removed.'

'Oh! Good, well done, sweetheart,' I say, relieved.

'But I don't know if I want it!' Max says. 'It's . . . I feel . . .'

'I know it's a lot, Max, but you have to make these decisions at some point. Isn't it easier to get them over and done with?' I smile at him, encouragingly. 'It'll be like ripping the plaster off. You think it will be painful but then afterwards you'll wonder what all the fuss was about. You've always been a boy. We always tried to bring you up so you could become who you wanted to be.'

Max doesn't look at me and is quiet for a moment, instead concentrating on balling up loose thread from his T-shirt between his fingers.

'I've just never thought about all this before,' he mumbles.

'I think you should, Max. I think you really should,' I say. 'You're so upset. We're all upset for you. Everyone's unhappy.'

I notice a tear drip down from his bent head. 'Come here, honey,' I say, and I go over to hug him. He leans his head on my chest and sobs, and I feel sorry I've been so distant since the clinic. 'I'm sorry, baby. You're right. We should have been more responsible. We should have made this decision a long time ago and not left it up to you to deal with. We thought we could leave it until you were eighteen, but we just made it your burden. I'm sorry. We'll do the operations and make you a . . . a proper boy.'

Steve opens the door.

'Hey, I just got in,' he says softly. 'Debbie said she heard yelling. Everything alright?'

I think about inviting him onto the bed to chat to Max. But then I think about how he feels about the surgeries, and what Max has decided. And I wave Steve away.

Max

'et your coat, we're going for a trip to London.'
'What, everybody?'

'No, just you and me.'

'Why?'

'Shhh!' Mum hisses. 'Don't ask questions until we're in the car and I'll get you anything you want from Topman.'

'I need some more T-shirts.'

'No you don't, but fine, yes, if you get in the car in the next ten minutes.'

I thought Saturday morning was going to be crap, because I'm not allowed to play football at the moment, so I'm missing the matches. I was just going to go and sit on the sidelines so I got up and washed and dressed and was just finishing the last of my homework on the desk in my room when Mum came in.

'Shh, don't wake Dad!' she whispers as I come down the stairs.

Debbie is already in the kitchen. She has a key now, and often comes before Lawrence gets here to get everything ready for their meetings.

'Hey Max, I hear you and your mother are going on a trip!'

'Hi Debbie,' I say, getting orange juice from the fridge. 'Yes, we're headed out. I'm getting some clothes for the new year.'

'You look great in what you've got on,' she says, her voice low, and I turn towards her, holding the juice and looking at her like, 'huh?'

She smiles. 'Have fun.'

'Thanks.'

'Max, get the sandwiches out the fridge; they're wrapped in tin foil,' says Mum, coming in with her coat on.

I grab the sandwiches and then lace up my Converse on the floor while she puts them in a cool bag.

'Do you want some treats?' She indicates the treat jar cupboard.

I nod. ''Kay. Cool.'

She seems better than before. I used to love doing stuff where it was just Mum and I. Because I was a bit older when they had Daniel, I had already got used to lots of time with my parents alone. Mum and I still sneak out together sometimes, so this isn't unusual, only this time it's a post-clinic, post-war outing. I am excited, but hesitant at the same time. I stand up and take her hand and squeeze it.

'Where are we going, Mum?'

'Surprise.' She winks, squeezing back.

I actually slept pretty well last night after my conversation with Mum. It seemed like a lot of noise was silenced in my head, when she made the decision for me. I would be a boy. It was resolved. After we talked, she put me to bed, and brought me a hot water bottle because it was cold. She stayed until I fell asleep, I think. I woke at eight, so I slept for almost ten hours. It's funny how refreshed one good night of sleep can make you.

I slip in the car and turn the engine on with her keys to warm it up. She is still doing something inside the house. She must have already been warming the car, because the windows have clearly been splashed with hot water so the frost will melt. All the other cars in the street have iced-up blue windows.

Mum has a Jaguar. It's not the uber-flashy kind, it's an X-type, with white leather heated seats in the front. I turn ours both on, so Mum will get into a warm seat, and flip the passenger mirror down in front of me so I can check my face for spots.

None. Not even on my hairline. I haven't ever had many. Although, now thinking about it, I got a few when I was on the hormones. My skin is really soft and has no blemishes on my face. My tan is going though. It's just kind of milky-gold now.

I wonder what I would have looked like if they had given me the surgery to be a girl. Somehow, after yesterday, it doesn't seem as horrifying a thought. Not that I'd want to be one, just that I cried everything out last night and now I've no more energy to be afraid. Plus, now Mum's kind of on my side, I don't feel so alone. Even if I don't know exactly what I want, Mum has my best interests at heart and she's seen me grow up and knows what will work. I guess she's right. I need to make a decision to be one or the other. It'll make everything so much easier: dating, growing up, signing official documents. Whatever.

I pout my lips and pull my hair over to one side of my face, so the blond is like a half-fringe, like a lot of the girls at school have. I tilt my chin up and give the glass a defiant look with my left eye. I could probably have done androgynous-looking girl. I look way more like a boy though. Especially my body.

Mum gets in the car and hands me the bags. Her door shuts with a resounding clunk and she sighs, before touching her hands to the wheel. She looks across at me and reaches up with her left hand and strokes my hair around my face.

'Do you want anything else, honey, before we leave?'

'No, I'm fine.'

'Yes, but you always say that. Are you sure?'

'Yeah.' I grin.

'OK.' She beams at me, pleased with me, and buckles up.

'Mum?' I say, as she backs out the drive.

'Yes?'

'Was the only course of hormones I had the one when I was thirteen?'

She pulls the car out onto the road and floors the accelerator. The cool thing about living on the outskirts of Hemingway is that we get to drive fast on all the roads close to us. 'Yes.'

'So, I haven't had any more hormones?'

'Well, you have the natural ones.'

'So, right now I look almost exactly how I would have looked anyway?'

'Mmm, pretty much,' she says, not looking at me. 'You grew quite a bit on the course of hormones, but it wasn't height or anything, just your chest. You got to your full height on your own, I think.'

'I'm five-foot-ten.'

'That's a good height.'

'How tall are you, Mum?'

'Five-foot-nine.'

'You always look really tall.'

'I wear heels to work.'

We're speeding through the countryside, towards the A40.

'So . . .' I look at myself in the mirror again. 'I would never really have looked like a girl.'

Mum clears her throat. 'Probably not.'

'You're thinner than me,' I say.

'Yes, thank goodness.'

'Huh?'

We laugh giddily, like when you've been holding a breath too long.

She gives me a once-over. 'It was a good idea to get you involved in football. You've bulked up with muscle since you started on the regional squad.'

'Yeah,' I agree. There's a silence, while I look down at my chest. 'So what would have happened if I'd had the surgery to make me a girl?'

'Um . . .' Mum flits a glance at me.

'You said last night that you wished I'd had it when I was born.'

'Oh, I don't know. I was upset. I suppose I'm glad we didn't. You'd probably have had a lot of hormone treatments.'

'Because I didn't grow tits?'

Mum frowns. 'Don't say tits.'

I look down my T-shirt.

'I don't like thinking about it,' she says.

''Kay.'

This shuts me up for a bit. A few minutes go by, and she starts to talk again.

'The thing was, with the operations, your dad was worried because the doctors said you'd lose, um . . .' She sighs, like she really doesn't want to talk about it. 'Feeling tissue. You know, down there.'

'Yeah but . . .' I bite my lip, thinking of how I'll probably never do it with anyone apart from Hunter. 'Sex isn't everything, is it?'

'Well.' She smirks. 'It's a pretty big deal!'

I shrug and look out the window glumly, thinking of all the sex I'll never have. 'So why are we going into London?'

'We're going to see one of the specialists that used to work with us.' She looks across at me. 'We're getting a second opinion. Don't worry. I'll stay with you.'

'I'm not worried.'

I watch her look over her shoulder and knock into sixth gear, getting on the M40. She's wearing a long camel trench coat, a lilac scarf and gold stud earrings, and her hair is up, very nicely. Mum has dark-blonde hair that she dyes caramel streaks into. She has it done at the hairdressers. I have lighter hair than her, like her dad had. Mum's dad's family is from Sweden originally, so they have light green eyes and blond hair. Daniel has reddish hair, a bit like a cross between how Dad's hair used to be and Mum's hair, and blue eyes. Dad has silver hair now. It used to be a dark chestnut.

'Mum?'

'Yes?'

'When did you book the appointment?'

'I called this morning at seven, when they open. It was easy to get you an appointment. He remembered you. You're a celebrity to the specialists.'

'Wow,' I mumble. 'How fucked up are these specialists?'

Mum looks over at me and tuts. 'Max, don't swear.'

'Sorry.'

'Get yourself a sandwich. I made your favourite. Have you had breakfast?'

'No,' I reply, rustling through the cool bag and finding a tuna mayo and brown bread roll. I take a bite. 'Thanks, Mum.'

'Listen,' Mum says, looking across at me. Rain has started falling on the window and the wipers are squeaking. 'Can I ask you a question?'

I chew slowly and swallow. 'Um, about what?'

Mum purses her lips. 'About . . . who you've . . .' She sort of grits her teeth. 'Been with?'

I look at my knees.

The raindrops race each other to the bottom of the glass. I think about how many holidays we've taken with Leah, Edward and Hunter, and how many we will take in the future; Mum and Leah laughing and going off together to sunbathe, my parents and Hunter's parents talking late into the night on the verandas of various villas while we listened from our beds, the windows wide open, the night air cool and refreshing. Hunter and I used to climb into bed with each other and talk until we fell asleep, years before Danny came along. I wonder what those times meant to him.

'Who is he?' Mum asks again.

'No one.'

'Max . . . I really need to know.' She looks at me, and then back to the road, then back to me again. I watch the rain. 'Is it someone from school?'

I shake my head slowly.

'Is it . . . is it someone I know?'

I think about this.

'Max?'

I shake my head again.

We sit in silence. The rain gets harder and lashes down on the roof of the car.

'Can we have the radio on?' I ask.

Mum looks over and watches me. I keep my face very still. She sighs, like she's impatient, but says, 'Yeah, OK.'

Archie

The phone rings twice before a female voice answers.

'Walker residence.'

'Hello. Who am I speaking to?'

'This is Debbie Mackenzie, Stephen Walker's assistant. May I ask who is calling?'

'This is Dr Verma from the clinic. I'm looking for Mr Walker. Could you put him on the phone, please?'

'Oh, I'm afraid he's on the other line at the minute—'

'Could you just tell him who's calling?' I say, a little impatiently. 'It's urgent.'

'I'm not sure—'

'Debbie, it's about his child, so please put Steve on the phone.'

'Oh! I'm sorry, yes, I'll just get Stephen.'

I hear her shoes tapping on the floor and then a brief, quiet exchange.

'Is everything OK?' Steve says immediately.

'It's . . .' I falter. 'I know I shouldn't meddle. But I couldn't help calling.'

'It's fine. What's wrong?'

'I just wanted to check . . . I don't suppose you would know why a private medical centre called Flint, Stamford and Associates on Harley Street would have requested Max's files this morning, do you?'

I hear a sharp intake of breath down the line. 'No,' Steve says. 'No, I don't.'

Max

'If you want the operations here, that can be arranged. We would remove the foetus, the uterus, the vaginal passage and the ovum. Obviously the ovotestis has already been removed. Of course, it would have been better to have this gender assignment surgery before school age, as was recommended to you, because adult hermaphrodites are very often confused as to their gender, with a high risk of depression and suicide.'

'Woh,' I mutter, but Dr Flint does not look at me.

Mum nods at him.

As cold and uninviting as Dr Flint's office is, his monotonous manner of speaking is way worse. I try to listen to him talk about how fucked up my life is.

'Of course,' he says, as if what he's about to say is so obvious we must be retarded for not knowing, 'it is a wonder Max can bear children at all. Very unfortunate that you have found out like this.' He scratches his dirty white moustache, then literally points to my stomach with his index finger, like, 'Counsellor: Exhibit A'.

He does this without looking over at me. Dr Flint addresses everything to Mum. He's a pale old man with a gravelly voice, pinched lips and black heads in his skin. He picks at his lips and scratches his face on and off the whole time he's talking to us, only glancing at his notes while continuing his tirade against the lack of surgery on my crotch.

'Now, I would have had you assigned as female before the age of four, and had a clitoroplasty and vaginoplasty carried out. My reading of the situation is that when Max was born, there was a degree of masculinisation of the genitalia – a phallus – which led to a nonconsensus between yourself, your husband and the doctors on how to proceed. However, my view is that even if Max was not assigned a specific gender at that stage, the vagina should have been closed up and menstruation later medically prevented. As I said to you during your child's many visits with us, I do wish that I had been around at birth and not brought in at the infant stage. This tragedy could have been avoided.' He waves in the general direction of my stomach, not having looked at my face since I came in, when he eyed me once and muttered, 'High cheekbones.'

'Max has always acted like a boy,' Mum says quietly.

The doctor hums between his teeth and concludes, 'Probably more nurture than nature.'

'Um,' I say, looking at my mum.

'Shh,' she says, listening earnestly.

He continues, gesturing again in my direction, this time with a pen, while addressing his speech to Mum: 'I would really say this type, presenting with working female sex organs, must be reared up as girls, because they have fertility potential, and that is what we try to preserve as much as we can, although really there are very few true hermaphrodites with any level of fertility. Perhaps this is why the doctors thought that doing nothing was acceptable. But obviously it wasn't right.'

'But Dr Verma said that hermaphrodites are infertile mostly because they have surgery,' Mum says quietly.

'General practitioners are very ignorant about the treatment of hermaphrodites.'

When did you train, dude? I think. The sixties?

'You should have been warned that because of the feminine looks combined with the course of hormones, the intersex child,' again, he gestures to me, 'would have an androgynous air, which is very attractive to young people, particularly teenagers, because it is less threatening than fully-developed men and women, and therefore he or she may well be more sexually active in this middle period of adolescence. Hopefully this will tail off towards the end of adolescence when his or her peers start to develop tastes more towards the ends of the spectrum of masculine and feminine. However, it is a much safer decision to opt for gender reassignment surgery now, as soon as possible.'

'Mm,' Mum says.

I start to feel pretty crap, thinking about the tailing off of people finding me attractive.

'Mum,' I whisper, nudging her. She takes my hand but doesn't look at me.

'If it had been done earlier, then Max would have been female and this would be a simple case of teenage pregnancy.'

This is the only thing Dr Flint has to say that resonates with me. If I was a girl, this wouldn't be an issue. I'm just not normal. I'm natural. I've not had any operations. This pregnancy is natural. But not 'normal'. So it has to be terminated. It's a weird thought.

'I'd recommend a strong course of hormones,' Dr Flint is saying to Mum. 'Maybe two or three courses, to make sure his chest doesn't feminise, etc.'

'Wouldn't it have done that by now?' Mum asks.

'Perhaps, perhaps not,' Dr Flint says, and finally turns to me. 'Do you ever talk to someone in your head?'

'Yeah, sometimes,' I mumble.

'That's a sign of gender dysfunction. You are confused. Gender dysfunction has been known to lead to schizophrenia.'

'But . . .' I say. 'Doesn't everyone talk to themselves in their head?'

'Or,' continues Dr Flint, ignoring me again, 'it could be that you absorbed your twin in the womb, giving you both your own female genitalia and his male genitalia and you are talking to your dead twin, who you still remember.'

I stare at him, aghast.

Dr Flint's mouth turns up at the corners and I realise he is smiling at me. 'You'll never get a girlfriend like that, will you, sonny? We'll get that thing sewn up.'

I can feel my face crumbling and try to hold it still.

The room is silent for a moment.

Then a voice comes from the doorway. 'This is such bullshit.'

I look around, shocked, at Dad.

Karen

We walk down the corridor of Dr Flint's practice in silence, looking at each other behind Max's head, as he walks slightly in front of us. Steve has dressed in a rush, wearing his old jeans and a thick brown jumper, a scarf, and thin raincoat slung around his shoulders. He strides formidably down the corridor. Despite his height, our strides are the same length. I have longer legs.

'How did you know we were here, Dad?' Max asks lightly, swinging around and walking backwards. His hair falls over one eye. He looks pretty and girlish. I think about what Dr Flint said.

Steve smiles at him, tightly. 'Dr Verma called me to tell me your files had been requested by Dr Flint's office. She thought I might like to know.'

I frown.

'Oh,' says Max softly, turning back. 'I like Archie.'

'Me too,' says Steve, as we walk into the lift. 'So, Max, what did you think of Dr Flint?'

Max shrugs. 'I don't know. What did you think, Mum?'

'It was interesting,' I say, pressing the button for the ground floor, glaring at Steve. The lift jolts as it begins its descent.

'Yeah, I guess.'

'I never liked that old trout,' says Steve, putting an arm around Max. He looks at me. 'I don't know what Mum was thinking, coming here.'

'Well, this was why you weren't invited,' I mutter.

'Yes, I noticed that,' Steve says quietly.

When the lift doors reopen, Max bolts out like he can't wait to leave. I follow him, but Steve grabs my wrist.

'Karen,' he begins.

'Don't,' I say, whipping around. 'I just wanted a second

248

opinion. Archie Verma doesn't know anything about intersex people, and I don't like her attitude. What is she doing calling you at home to let you know what I'm doing with *my own son*? Does she think she's *telling on me*? Bad Karen, who doesn't want Max to have to live through this charade, who'd rather he be normal and happy. Max shouldn't have to deal with this.'

'Shh,' he murmurs, as we walk slowly after Max, out of earshot. 'Firstly, Karen, if you wanted a second opinion, you could have told me, and I would have come, no questions asked. Secondly, Max chose Archie. He likes her.'

'Stop touching my arm,' I hiss. 'I don't want to talk to you right now, racing after me like you don't trust me, talking to Max like that about me. Steve, the hero, swooping in to rescue Max from the wicked witch.'

'You took off without telling me!' Steve counters. 'We had an agreement about these doctors. They want to cut him up and look at what's inside!'

'I think your personal feelings are getting in the way of what's best for Max. If we get this over with now, it may never be an issue again!'

'Karen!' Steve cries in exasperation. 'You can't control everything! He's always going to be intersex and have to deal with those issues. Just because some knife-happy surgeons get their hands on his genitals, doesn't mean everything goes away.'

'Urgh! Don't say that.'

'I just feel like it's ten years ago and you're trying to control everything again, and we both know how well that turned out.'

'Don't!' I whip around and stop him. 'Don't you dare bring that up. That was a long time ago. I'm not going to leave again. Just stop.'

'I'm just saying,' Steve growls, 'that you can't control who he is with a scalpel, and you *bloody* better not take him to that crank's office again without first informing me where you are taking our child.'

I turn away from him and we walk in silence, approaching Max, who is waiting at the door to the street. We catch each other's eye. Steve opens his mouth, closes it, and looks away from me. 'We need to talk.'

I shake my head, but I answer in the affirmative. 'Yes.'

We reach Max at the door.

'Everything OK?' he asks in a small voice.

'Of course, honey,' I say, smiling at him. 'Why wouldn't it be?'

Max

After the consultation with Dr Flint, Mum says we're going for lunch. Dad seems to not want to, but he comes anyway. They even let me have some wine with them, and then we head for Regent Street to do some Christmas shopping.

The conversation petered out over lunch, and then my parents started arguing about some case Mum's working on. It felt like they weren't arguing about that really, though, but about me. I zone out, thinking about operations and scars and stuff. It occurs to me that I don't really know much about Mum's work. It's Dad's stuff we all go to and know about. All I really know about Mum is that she loves Daniel and me. And now maybe not me, sometimes.

No, that's probably not true, I think. *You couldn't hate your own child.*

I start to think about my child. Would I hate it because it was Hunter's? Would I hate it if it came out dark-haired and Hunter-looking?

I chew my fingernails as we walk in a line of three towards Oxford Circus.

'So . . .' I say, in a pause between them talking. 'We're not going to do it with Dr Flint in London?'

'Maybe,' Mum says, just as Dad is saying, 'No. We'll just do it at Oxford, where everyone is sane.'

They look at each other, then at the ground. They both look really tired.

'What do you want to do Max?' Dad asks.

I shrug.

'He doesn't—' says Mum, as Dad says, 'Come on, Max.'

I fold my arms and I say, 'Well, the appointments are already set up in Oxford . . .'

'Do you want to have it there?' Dad asks.

'OK,' I say, really quietly.

'Max, don't cry, it's OK,' says Dad, and pulls me under his arm.

'Sorry,' I say.

We walk on for a bit and Mum says, sort of to herself, 'I wonder if all parents freak out so much when their kids grow up.'

'You're admitting you're freaking out?' Dad asks.

'You're admitting I'm growing up?' I say, and Dad laughs.

Mum looks over at him, ignoring me. 'No one gives you a rulebook to tell you how to deal with it all. Terrible twos, the first school fight, puberty, angry teenagers.' She looks off across the street, evidently thinking of Daniel. 'And angry ten-year-olds.'

'We're a handful, I guess.'

'Mmm.'

'It would have been better if I was normal.'

'Oh, Max,' Mum says. She hesitates.

'Yes,' I say.

She shakes her head. 'Only for you. I wanted you to have an easy life.' She leans in and whispers, 'If it were just for me, I wouldn't change a thing about you.'

Which is nice but confusing at the same time. I smile anyway.

We walk on and reach Hamleys, where a girl is dressed as Cinderella, stood on a platform, blowing bubbles at the kids. The crowd around her slows us down. It's a sea of faces at knee-height, and suddenly I start to see them all individually.

There is a tiny Chinese girl standing shakily in shiny, buckled shoes and a purple dungaree dress, watching Cinders with uncertain eyes. She reaches out a hand to point at the princess and looks back to her parents. Her mum smiles and nods, and her dad takes a photo.

Next to her there are two black children, a boy and a girl, with little knitted jumpers and grey hats. They are all wrapped up in scarves and coats, with just their white teeth, big brown eyes and teeny little noses visible. They smile in delight at each other.

In front of Mum and I are three blond kids. One is almost Daniel's height, one is about five and one is around three.

I look at the Swedish-looking kids, the black kids, the Chinese girl. It's like a fucking Gap ad, I think. My face feels warm. Maybe it's the wine.

There are loads more kids, an entire unbroken ring around Cinderella. A woman holds a baby up to watch her blow the bubbles. The baby kicks its feet and gurgles happily. It looks back at its mum questioningly, then at Cinderella, as if to say, 'Do you see her too, Mum?'

The baby looks young, and yet its face is so intelligent. It's like a full-grown person, trapped in a tiny body it can't control, looking out at a new world where it hasn't been before. The personality is all there. It frowns, follows a bubble as it grows from her wand, then laughs, and turns back to its mum, to check she's laughing. It could be only six months old or so.

There's a pregnant woman too, the mother of the black brother and sister, I think.

Suddenly I realise I have my hand on my stomach. I snatch it away, but then I wonder – did I feel a bump? I slide my hand under my jumper self-consciously, watching Mum and Dad to make sure they don't see. It's been almost three months since Hunter came into my room, but under my rib cage there is a slight rise to my stomach that wasn't there before. My cheeks grow hot as I spread my fingers over it. I look down at my jumper. I look up at the pregnant woman. I look across at the baby.

I think about how the potential for an entire life, the dream of it, is inside me right now, and that terminating it not only gets rid of a problem, it gets rid of that potential. I think about what Dr Flint said, how if I was a girl, this would be just a teenage pregnancy, just something I had wanted, maybe, but a bit earlier than expected. I feel suddenly sick.

'Mum,' I murmur, so Dad can't hear. 'That baby might only be a year older than mine.'

She turns to me, gives me a look, and guides me away from

253

the crowd. Dad walks behind us. I take my hand out from under my jumper and watch the tiny Chinese girl clap her hands as we pass her. We continue up Regent Street, past another young girl, in Wellingtons and a blue coat.

'Max, it will make the termination more difficult if you think about it as a baby,' she murmurs, takes my arm. 'I never told you this, but we had an abortion when I was younger.'

'Oh,' I say softly.

'It wasn't a big deal, really Max,' she says. 'I was twenty, your dad and I were still studying. But the ultrasound technician and the doctors kept saying "baby" and I just . . . It made me uncomfortable. So . . . call it the foetus or something. Do you understand why?'

I nod. 'Did you ever think about not having it?'

'The abortion?' She shakes her head, then changes her mind. 'Well, a part of me did romanticise about it for a few minutes. But I've always believed that you should have children when you can make a good life for them, shouldn't you?'

'Yeah,' I say. 'I didn't think I would ever be, like, pregnant, so I didn't ever think about if I had to have one.'

Mum nods and we walk on. A minute later, she asks, 'Is that girl you brought to Daniel's birthday party your girlfriend?'

'Um, sort of.'

'I really liked her. She was lovely.' She turns to me. 'But Max, it's a bit wrong to be hanging out with someone when you're . . . like this.'

'I know.'

'Just wait until you've had the operation.'

'I'll still be intersex afterwards.'

'Not after gender reassignment surgery.'

'Well . . . I'll still be intersex inside.'

She frowns. 'But what does that matter if you look and feel like a boy?'

'Um,' I mumble.

'You've always felt like a boy, haven't you?'

I shrug.

'Haven't you?'

I look over at Mum. She looks worried. 'Yeah, I guess,' I say to calm her.

To be honest, though, I've never really thought about it. I've just been Max. And Max is a little different. Not quite a boy.

'What are you talking about?' Dad says, leaning in. 'I can't hear with all this noise.'

'Nothing,' Mum says.

He nods and straightens up again.

'Mum,' I hesitate, whispering. 'Why didn't Dad want me to have an operation when I was born?'

'Oh . . .' She looks away.

'Did he want a boy and he didn't want them to make me into a girl?'

'No, of course not.'

'Well, he'd obviously like it more if I was a boy.'

'That's not true,' says Mum. She sighs.

We walk into Topshop and get on the escalator to Topman.

'Now I can hear you. What are you talking about?' says Dad.

'You,' replies Mum, curtly. 'Tell Max about what you did when he was born.'

'What I did?'

'About him being intersex.'

'Well, nothing. We decided you were alright how you were.'

Mum sighs again when we get upstairs and leans against a rail of jeans. She looks at Dad regretfully, like she's about to say something nice about him, but doesn't want to. Instead, she turns to me.

'I went to pieces when you were born. Dad dealt with everything: the doctors, the examinations, the hospital appointments. I couldn't come with you to them. I found it too upsetting. I was worried you'd grow up and everything would come back to haunt us, which,' she shrugs, 'has happened.'

I bite my lip. 'Probably wouldn't have happened without . . . you know.'

'It would have someday, though, Max.'

'Maybe not,' says Dad.

I shrug. 'I was fine, though. I've been fine.'

'Well . . .' Mum purses her lips and fiddles with the label on a pair of twisted cords. 'You know your dad painted Daniel's room yellow because it was unisex?'

'Did you?' I ask Dad.

'Yes. We wanted Danny to be whoever he was too. We shouldn't talk about this here,' he says, looking uncomfortable. 'We'll talk about it at home.'

'Yes,' Mum agrees, feeling a T-shirt sleeve. 'That's soft.'

'Dad's always got the campaign team round when we're at home,' I tell Mum, when Dad has wandered off towards the belts. 'What else did he do?'

'He . . .' She walks around aimlessly. 'Stopped them from taking pictures of you without your pants on. After the hormones you had when you were thirteen, he convinced me we shouldn't take you back to the doctors. He said they just wanted to document you and watch you and write papers on people like you to forward their own careers. He said they were sick perverts, wanting to poke and pull and stare at you. And—' She sort of winces. 'He was the one who said you couldn't have operations until you could decide for yourself. He said it was mutilation. No one was going to cut up his perfectly functioning baby.' She throws her hands around when she says this last bit, like she is imitating him word for word.

'Dad said that?' I stop walking. Mum turns back to me, avoiding my eye, feeling the black denim skinny jeans next to me.

She shrugs. 'He wanted you to be able to have children if you wanted to.'

I must look stunned, because she says, 'Obviously he thought you might be more androgynous than you are.'

'He knew it was a possibility I'd be more of a boy, though,' I say.

'Max,' Dad says, coming back to us. 'Come on, we can talk about all this at home.'

'No one's going to recognise you here!' Mum hisses at him venomously, and struts off.

Dad walks off in the other direction.

256

'Dad wanted me to be able to have kids?' I say to myself.

I stay where I am, shocked, frowning, thinking. Sarah McLachlan's "Angel" is playing on the sound system. I put my hand to my lips and bite my nail, and feel my eyes tearing up at the corners.

Dad was OK, in principle, with me having a baby. He thought it would be OK, even when he knew I could be a total freak, even when he knew I could be a boy, a man. He thought . . . He thinks . . . Does he think that now?

'Max,' Mum comes rushing back, looking remorseful. 'Don't cry, it's OK, I'm sorry.' She takes my hand and leads me out of the shop. 'I shouldn't have told you in the store, I'm sorry.'

'What about Dad?' I say, looking back.

'I'll call him,' Mum says, taking out her BlackBerry. I look at her and open my mouth, but I shut it again and wipe my face, feeling tears sliding between my fingers.

'He just . . .' She strokes my hair off my face and I struggle away from her. She looks hurt. 'He just didn't want to have to decide without talking to you. He said if it all worked, why not let you be . . . you.'

'What did you think?' I mumble.

'Steve, we're outside the shop. I think Max is tired.' She hangs up. 'To be honest, when I had thought about it for a while, I agreed with him . . . in principle. But the world doesn't work that way. We thought we were doing well because nothing had gone wrong so far. Then something like this happens . . . Max, I'm sorry. I've been going crazy thinking about it, about everything, about you having sex, being pregnant. It's just overwhelming for me too.'

I blush. 'Shh,' I mutter.

She continues, stroking the hair off my face. 'We can't change the world we live in, in our lifetime, anyway. We can't all be idealistic like your dad. We have to live in the real world.' She touches my chin. 'I want you to be normal so you can have the best chance at a nice life. Do you understand why I want that?' Mum is almost crying now. 'Do you understand what I mean?

Max? I love you, but I want things to be better for you. You understand?'

'Yeah, Mum,' I nod, drying my face, tired, my body aching, sore, exhausted, drained, sick and sighing. 'I do. I really, really do.'

She puts her arms around me. 'Oh, my love,' she whispers, and I close my eyes to the streams of shoppers walking past, eyeing us inquisitively.

Karen

When we get back from London, Daniel rushes into the kitchen to see if we've bought him Christmas presents, and Debbie and Lawrence greet us warmly.

'The family is back!' exclaims Lawrence. 'Excellent. Tuxes and dresses on in the next half an hour, please. Magdalene College Christmas Ball won't wait for its guest speaker.'

'I'm tired,' says Max.

'You don't have to go,' I tell him, emotionally exhausted myself.

'Ready to talk?' Steve murmurs.

'Now? Really?' I say.

'Stephen, I have Holden on the line for you,' Debbie says excitedly.

'Is this bag for me?' Daniel says, grabbing at a Hamleys carrier we dipped in for at the last minute. Steve holds it aloft.

'Not until the twenty-fifth!' Steve says, taking the phone. 'Sorry, always chaos in my house on a Saturday. How can I help you, Holden?'

'I can't WAIT for Christmas!' yells Daniel. 'Lawrence had the tree delivered today.'

Lawrence smiles, looking at me. 'You were so busy.'

'Thanks Lawrence, how thoughtful.'

'Can I call you back in ten?' Steve murmurs. 'Thanks.'

'Come see the tree,' Daniel says, grabbing my hand.

'Karen?' Steve sits down at the kitchen table, folds his arms and waits for me to join him.

'Sure,' I say to Danny, ignoring Steve, and heading through to see the fir that I neglected to order, dwarfing the room, branches bursting jollily out across the carpet.

'Soon,' Daniel says, 'there'll be loads of presents underneath it!'

'Let's decorate it tonight,' says Max quietly, from behind me.

I see him brush something off his face, and he walks past me, lowers himself onto his knees, and rummages through the box of tiny bells and ornaments by the tree.

'Cool,' Daniel agrees, and kneels down beside Max.

Max's blond head and Daniel's light red one bend together before the tree, and I take a deep breath and think about how it will soon be Christmas, and everything that's tearing me up inside now will be behind us.

I feel Steve put his arm around me, from behind.

'Karen,' he murmurs. 'We should talk about this. I know you're upset.'

'You always know.'

'Stephen?' Debbie calls from the kitchen.

We wait, unmoving, feeling each other breathing, feeling the pull of our busy lives; lives that revolve around home and work and other people. Steve dips his head to my shoulder and kisses it.

'Get off me,' I whisper.

'Stephen?' Debbie calls.

He holds me close and kisses my neck. 'Karen . . . I love you,' he whispers to the nape of my neck, rather hopelessly.

Sylvie

Monday morning
Homeroom's boring
All I do is think of you

I'm busy writing these pretty mundane but genuinely felt lyrics when my phone buzzes.

'Hey.'

'Hey. You mind me pranking you?'

'It's not pranking if I pick up.'

'Good point. Why did you?'

'Teacher's late again,' I say.

'Terrible.'

'She's an addict.'

'Yeah, to crack. I heard.'

'So, why are you calling me rather than coming to get me?'

'I'm standing outside the window.'

'What?' I stand up. 'Why?'

'Come see what love looks like, kook,' Max's voice says into my ear.

'Love?'

He giggles. 'You know.'

'Christ,' I say. 'I see you. You're naked.'

'No I'm not! Which window are you looking out of?'

'I'm joking.'

He spots me and waves. 'Are you coming down?'

'Yeah, OK.'

'We're bunking off again.'

'Golden boy, what are you doing with your life?'

'I'm rebelling.'

'You're throwing it all away, like a modern day James Dean, but with an even nicer arse.'

'Why, thank you.'

'Are you really bunking off again?' I say doubtfully. 'I mean, I can get away with it because I'm so good I don't need to be here to get As, but, like, I've noticed you work super hard.'

'I'll survive. I can't be in school. I'm a fugitive now. Everyone thinks I knocked someone up. It's pretty unbearable.'

'Everyone but me, huh? That's why you're hanging out with me.'

'That and your rack.'

'Oh my god, Max Walker is being rude! I'm telling everyone I've ever met right now.'

'No you're not.'

'Yes I am. I'm tweeting it.'

'No you're not!'

'And I'm tagging it with the hashtag "Stephen Walker's son".'

'Urgh, don't say that. Dad's doing a press day.'

'So?'

'Um, nothing. Hurry up, kook.' I hear his breath shudder.

'Are you freezing your balls off waiting for me?'

'Well . . .' he says. 'Kind of.'

'Why did you just look at your crotch?'

'Are you still at the window? I can't see you! Will you just freakin' come down?'

I run up and hug him from behind.

'AH!' he screams.

'Got ya!' I yell. We turn to each other, hold our phones aloft and both hang up. They both lock at the same moment.

'Oo,' I say looking at them. 'It's fate.'

Max grins happily and hugs me. 'You make me feel so good, Sylvie.'

'Alright, don't be cheesy. You know I'm a commitment phobe.'

'Sorry.'

'Come on, let's go fool around on a grave.'

'Gross.'

Max

Tuesday the eleventh is the day of the first appointment at the hospital.

The doctor is called Dr Jones. He's tall, has greying brown hair, and a kind face.

'After the termination, it is usual to have some mild bleeding and some abdominal pain. If that gets to be too much, just come back and see us,' he says. This is one of the only things I pick up on. Mum and Dad listen attentively as I watch Dr Jones' mouth moving and zone out.

'Shall we have a chat about post-operative contraception?' he asks, turning to me.

I shake my head.

'No?' he says, turning to my parents.

'No,' I say.

'OK.' He hesitates for a moment, then recovers. 'Let's get on with the pelvic examination, shall we?'

Mum and Dad leave the room for that. It's horrible, but it's over quickly, and the doctor says we should do an ultrasound because it's hard to tell with my anatomy if we'll be able to get the foetus out in the normal way.

I nod.

'Is that OK?' he asks.

'Sure,' I say in a small voice.

Mum comes in for the ultrasound, and the technician sets everything up and rubs the scanning thing across my stomach. I watch the technician, but she doesn't seem to think anything's weird or wrong. She turns on a monitor and watches it intently. It's angled away from me, but I watch the flare of light dance on and off across her face, and realise those flares of light are the closest I'll ever get to seeing what mine and Hunter's child looks like. The technician catches my eye.

'Can I see?' I ask quietly.

She hesitates. 'You want to watch the scan on the monitor?'

I bite my lip as Mum says, 'No.'

I can feel Mum staring at me.

'Might as well see,' I mumble, not looking at Mum, and the technician angles the monitor so I can watch. The door opens and Dr Jones enters, with a couple of other white coats.

'Can you tell the sex?' I ask.

'No,' she replies. 'Not until between twenty and twenty-eight weeks.'

I gather the weeks into groups of four in my head. Five months.

I'm finding my voice again, looking at all the lines on the monitor, so I ask another question. 'Why was my stomach hurting so bad?'

'Early uterine cramps,' the technician says, looking at me sympathetically. 'It's just your uterus stretching to accommodate the foetus.'

'It all looks relatively normal, Max,' Dr Jones murmurs kindly. 'Perhaps a bit smaller around the vaginal passage, but I think it should be possible to do under general anaesthetic.'

'Can I have the picture?' I ask.

'Pardon?' the technician says, just as Mum is saying, 'What?'

'Don't they usually do a picture?' I look from the technician to Mum. Mum is looking at me like I'm insane.

'Sorry,' I say.

The technician doesn't reply, just leans over to a printer and, after a bit of whirring, the machine spits out a small piece of paper, which she hands me.

Then Dr Jones tells us on the way out that he'll see us on Friday for the abortion, and that's the entire visit. It takes forty-five minutes total.

When we get home, Mum puts her head in her hands on the kitchen table and won't speak. I go to my room and sit in the dark, but for a nightlight.

There is a little broad bean shape in the picture. After a little while I can't look at it, so I hold it in one hand and cover my eyes with the other and lie there, curled up in the top corner of my bed, thinking and breathing and trying not to think.

I continue to do pretty much this all week.

I am a normal guy. I am a normal guy who would never have a problem like this. Like what? Like nothing. It doesn't exist. I am a normal sixteen-year-old. I listen to music. I wear my iPod. I laugh with my friends. I dream about kissing Sylvie Clark. I kiss Sylvie Clark.

I am a brother. I am not a sister. I am not an everything. I am not a nothing. I have no big choices to make. I am a teenager, and my biggest job is to be normal.

I can't look at myself in the mirror anymore, or at any reflection of mine in glass. And I don't know why.

Karen

I've been sleeping in the spare room since Saturday, after the trip to London, and I am in there on Wednesday, stripping the bedclothes, waiting for Max and Daniel to come home, when I hear the door slam. Today Steve and I came home from work at midday in order to make up and discuss Max. We sat at the kitchen table, too tired to talk, until we both, in silent agreement, stood, walked up to the bedroom, and lay down beside each other. We both slept for four hours without waking up, until the telephone rang, with news.

I walk out onto the landing.

'Boys?'

'Hi Mum!'

'Your dad has something to tell you. I think he's in the front room.'

Steve appears at the doorway as I descend the stairs, and Max and Daniel take off their shoes.

They shuffle in together in their socks. They both have on their school uniforms. Max's is basically an entire suit, with a black V-neck underneath his blazer. Apart from the uniform, he wears a watch on his left wrist, a nice one we bought him for his fifteenth birthday. His hair is tousled and his cheeks are red from the cold. Daniel has his version of tousled hair, with tufts sprouting comically on his crown, and a red face, except because his hair too has a hint of strawberry, he looks like a little peach. Daniel wears a knitted navy blue jumper with a white shirt underneath, a red tie and grey trousers. They look completely different but somehow alike, just in the face, a hint of an upturned nose, some freckles, wide eyes, long eyelashes.

'What's up?' Max asks, in a soft voice.

'Well . . .' Steve looks at Max with a hint of concern, then turns to smile at Daniel. 'Julie's baby was born today, in the early hours of the morning, so we're going out to the hospital to see it.'

'If you'd like to,' I add quickly, looking at Max.

'Cool,' our eldest son says.

'Daniel, would you like to see the baby?' asks Steve.

'Yes, excellent,' Daniel says, nodding.

'Good, then let's jump in the car and we might miss the rush hour traffic on the way to London,' Steve tells them.

They both stand up and head for the door.

'What was it?' Max asks, turning back.

'A boy,' Steve says. 'He's called William.'

Daniel

Max comes in my room tonight. He hasn't really come in much lately and I was missing him. This week it has seemed as if he's not listening to what I am saying and I have to keep telling him to pay attention. But tonight he comes in shortly after we get back from seeing William and eating the pizza Dad picked up on the way back, and he looks like he's happy to hang around for a bit, which is pleasing. He hovers over me for a bit, watching me play *Zombieland 4*, which is a new game I got for my birthday that's even better than *Deadland 2*, and giving me pointers. Then he stands up, wanders around my room looking at stuff, like my pictures of robots, and then he picks up my yellow bear, and strokes its bum, which is really soft.

'What's this guy's name?'

'Yellow Bear.'

He laughs even though it isn't funny. 'Right.'

'Doesn't Auntie Julie's baby look weird? It's like one of those dogs with too much skin.'

He sort of smile-laughs. 'It'll grow into it. It's just been born. Didn't you think he was cute?'

I make a face and kill five zombies in my game – four with a bazooka and one with a knife, because he's within a metre of my character.

He puts his arms around Yellow Bear and cradles him like a doll.

'I think babies would be cute if they looked like bears,' I say.

'Yeah,' he says back, sort of quietly.

'Like Ewok babies. I'd have an Ewok kid and then they would be cute but also I wouldn't have to buy them clothes and they could kill chicken-walkers.'

He says something really quiet and I go, 'Huh?'

Then he looks at me like adults do when they're acting like they know way more about something than you, but smiling, like there's a secret you'll know one day and it'll be great and aren't we proud of you and the potential you have, although we're not going to tell you about it because we don't think you'd understand.

'I said you'll have babies one day, little dude. When you meet someone nice.'

'I guess.'

I stick out my tongue, like 'yuck' but I suppose I will have them one day, only way later. Adults always talk about babies like they're the centre of the universe but William didn't look anything except kind of gross and asleep. My kids would be like superheroes, though. I'd train them up and fit robotic extensions to their arms with uzis and lasers in them that cut things like the ones used in laser eye surgery, which I will Wikipedia, I think, after Max leaves.

This brings me back to Max, who's watching me kill zombies in a glazed-eyes way, and I realise he's way older and leaving school in two years and then he'll have university, and after that maybe he'll have kids. That would make me an uncle. Maybe I could fit robotic extensions onto his children to make them super-powered. Maybe I'll reserve that for my own kids, though, because that will give his kids a power over mine, but then I realise since I'm having mine after he has his, the extensions and modifications in my offspring will be more advanced, so I could modify his offspring and not worry.

'Will you have children?' I say.

He's gone into a sort of daze, resting his chin on Yellow Bear's head, holding and looking at Yellow Bear's paw for no reason, which must be out of focus so close up, like when I get stuck staring at something and Mum is like, 'Move! Do something!' and then she tickles me out of it.

He shrugs, looking kind of grumpy. 'Probably not,' he says.

'Why?' I say, executing a ghoul. 'I mean why not?'

He adjusts the collar of Yellow Bear's T-shirt so it's all the right way round and then strokes his back. He makes Yellow Bear look up at him.

'I don't know,' he says. 'Why d'you think, Bear?'

'You shouldn't force his head like that,' I say.

'Sorry.' He puts the bear down like he knows he was being stupid.

'Hey.' I suddenly have a thought. 'Will my kids be like you or like me?'

'I don't know.' He ponders, like when you think for a while. 'I don't know what genetic things you pass down.'

'Like in your DNA?'

'Yes.'

'Like in *Jurassic Park*?'

He looks to the side, as if remembering. 'Yes.'

'What is DNA?'

Max frowns. 'It's like a code. Um. And that code is a description of you, that your mum's body builds your body out of. It's like instructions, like a building plan for a house.'

'Oh. I see.' I nuke a zombie crack den. 'But why would my instructions say that I had to be ginger? Was it a mistake?'

'No,' Max says firmly.

'Did my instructions go wrong?'

'No.' He shakes his head. 'You're perfect, Daniel. You're wicked.'

'So, what happened?'

'Well . . . if all the people in the world were the same, it wouldn't work.'

'Yes it would. It would be like *The Matrix*, except the cool bad guys would rule the universe.'

'Err, OK.' He looks at me and I look at him and wait for a explanation. He takes off his school tie and unbuttons some buttons on his shirt and lets a long breath out and looks very much like Dad did last week when I was waiting for him to explain alien warfare when he had just got in from some sort of lawyery conference.

'Imagine,' starts Max, 'that there is a great big power

270

controlling everything. No one knows what it is, but loads of people have different names for it.'

'Is this like God?'

'Yes, some people call it God, and some people call it Nature. But we think it's there because there seems to be an order to things.'

'OK. I am following you.'

'OK, good. Um . . . so when it comes to different species—'

'Like humans, dogs, etcetera?'

'Yeah. Well when it comes to species, the order seems to be that the species sort of tries to make more of itself, without really knowing it's trying, you understand?'

'Subconsciously?'

'Yes. Good word. OK, so the species is also trying to make itself better and stronger, so it can survive longer than all the other species. It's like a race. Like in *DeathMatch 4* on the PS3, where you have to be the last group to survive in your category. And on Earth, the humans are kind of winning, in our category.'

'What's our category?'

'Warm-blooded mammals,' Max says, the story getting faster. 'So one major tactic humans have used in the race is variation. Variation is where you make lots of different people, using lots of very complex DNA codes, with loads of tiny parts, including some called genes. The more genes, the more complex we are, and the more we can produce different types of people.' He frowns. 'Basically, it's something like that. So, when we produce different people, we find out which types of people are stronger, because they live through childhood, which are the years where you are small and weak and you're tested by the elements, like weather and starvation, and then after childhood, the different people who are stronger survive to produce kids who are like them, so their variation is proved strong and their kids are born with that variation too, and the humans get stronger as a group. And since humans are a social animal too, like wolves in a pack, when you get different people, they are all better at different things like hunting and homemaking, so

271

they help the group to survive. So your code made you who you are, because the codes are designed to spit out different people. Differences are part of a gigantic race to win as a species, so we all play a very important part.'

'Ah,' I say, nodding. 'So I'm special.'

Max grins. 'Yes, you're very special.'

'Good,' I say, but I still feel a bit strange, so I have a think a bit more, and then I say, 'But if I'm not like you and not good at school or popular, it means I lost some things when I was growing in Mum, didn't I?'

'You . . .' Max trails off. 'The thing is, Daniel, we're all different. We can't all have everything everybody else has.'

'So, kids?'

Max looks up and he looks very startled, suddenly, like I've just given him a neck-squeeze shock. 'What about kids?'

'Will my kids be like me or like you?' I ask. 'I think I want them to be like you. Or even better, like Dad, because you're a little bit small.'

He huffs and says, 'You can't always pick what your kids are going to be like.' However, he says this in a way that makes me think he is maybe thinking about something else.

'Are you sure?' I ask, just to be sure.

He thinks. 'I think if I had kids, they'd be as likely to be like you as your kids would be likely to be like me. Maybe.'

'Oh good,' I say, cheering up a lot. 'Then our offspring would have a fair fight when they battle.'

'Yeah,' he says, his voice sounding tight and tired. 'Well, glad to know you're comforted.'

Max

After my talk with Daniel on Wednesday night, I get into bed, switch all the lights out and start to cry hysterically. I've been feeling so weirdly uncomfortable over the past couple of days. I've been thinking, *This is it, the only time I'll be able to have kids. The only time I'll look at a baby and it will be mine. I'll see me in its face, see my mum and dad in it too, see my grandad and my nan.* The thought makes me feel really frightened and upset. I never thought about it before. I never thought about whether I wanted kids. When I was little, I presumed I would, someday, but then I realised when I was a bit older that that probably wasn't in the cards. I thought I was infertile, but I just didn't think about it often. I'm sixteen – why would I think about that? But now . . .

Am I thinking about keeping it? Am I seriously thinking about keeping it??

It's just that they won't let it happen again! Everyone's talking about getting everything taken out like it's a done deal. It was me that asked Archie to book it, but I was just so scared. Mum looks at me like I'm a time bomb, Dad avoids me and works all the time, and I just nod to everything. Hysterectomy, check, yes, whatever. But do I want that? I don't know.

I'm not sure. Oh my god. I'm not sure.

Even without them taking everything out, I'll never get knocked up again because . . . well, because I like girls, but also because who the fuck would go down there? Apart from Hunter, I mean. They'll never let me get artificial insemination. They'll probably never take eggs out and let me have donor spunk and a surrogate, because come on, who's going to let a single, sort-of-male he/she have that on the NHS? Then I can only do it if I get massively rich. So there are no other options to have children, ever, and now it's suddenly up to me, counting down in hours, to make a decision about something that could shape my whole life. Is this my only chance to have a baby? Am I going to end up lonely Uncle Max to Danny's kids, the uncle who is old and alone and doesn't have anyone coming to visit him at the nursing home, who has this weird semi-sexual problem that means he never married, and that we don't discuss, but all of Danny's grandkids whisper about? What will my life be like?

I hate you, Hunter. I fucking hate you!

I punch the pillow and turn over, mushing my hot tears into my duvet and choking quietly on sobs.

Is there even an option to keep it?

Whenever I even let my brain drift into the future nine months and imagine them with a baby, I immediately think NO. No, no, no, no.

But teenage girls have babies all the time. Is it so abhorrent just because it's me and I'm not a girl? I'm not a boy either. I have a stable family, we have money. Maybe Mum and Dad could bring it up as their kid and no one would ever have to know what I am.

This is insane. How can I even think about this? I mean, how would I even survive the pregnancy? People would see me around town. I can't just stay in my house for six months. And how would the baby survive it, being the child of a he/she? Oh my god.

NO. I can't do it. I can imagine it. Everything. The humiliation, embarrassment, my parents totally upset, friends either blatantly freaked out or subtly freaked out and the awkwardness means we drift apart. All my guy mates would think I fancy them. All my girl mates would think I'm gay. If I say I'm not, it doesn't matter. It's as bad as being gay if they are wondering about it.

Then there's the biggest thing: Sylvie. I like her so much it hurts when I think about her finding out. Sylvie, Sylvie, Sylvie. Oh my god, I can just imagine her face, her backing away from me, her looking disgusted, her reaching down and grasping and feeling stuff that's not supposed to be there. I really, really don't want to lose her. But it feels inevitable. It is inevitable. *I*

274

just want to hold onto her for a little bit longer, I plead to the universe. *Please, just a little bit longer.*

She won't even want to kiss me anymore, because she'll be worried I'll want it to go further, and if I explain that I don't want that then she'll leave me anyway because she's already had sex and she'll want it.

Me: 'Don't worry, I don't want to go further than kissing because it's a mess down there. Also, I'm pregnant.'

Her: 'Errr . . . I'm not sure I feel like kissing right now, but thank you', or 'THAT'S SO FUCKING GROSS GET AWAY FROM ME!'

Oh my *god*, I don't want to think about it. I don't want to think about it at all. Breathe. Breathe. Try and ignore that there's now a slight bulge beneath stomach muscles I used to be proud of. Try not to look at it. Don't touch it. Try not to think that there is a tiny baby in there. It's just a problem, and it'll be gone in a few days. As problems go, this is a fairly simply concluded one.

You're lucky. It's easy. You'll go to sleep, then you'll wake up and the next day life will be awesome again. Life will be awesome and you can make out with Sylvie without feeling guilty because she's unaware that she's making out with something gross (OK, still a he/she but not knocked up and maybe, if I can stomach it, just a he. Kind of.), you can blast through the league and make the top spot with the team, you can finish up your GCSEs and have an awesome summer, then start on your A Levels. Maybe they will find a way to get you laid, sew up the hole, put fake balls in (something inside me shudders every time I think about this. Never having seen bollocks in real life, I think of them as gross. I didn't look when Hunter had his out, but I felt them slapping me, and it freaked me out. Rank, gross, sick.), and though my dick is fairly small, the doctor once said it's not far below average. I remember on the way home from that appointment – I was about thirteen – Mum told me in the car that Dad is really well-hung, so this saved me. Again, how sick is my life that people feel the need to tell me these things/show me stuff/compare etc. It's like, 'Oh, you have odd genitalia. Clearly I can now talk to you about anything and you won't think it's that gross, because being you is an all-out sickfest anyway.' Or maybe for women it's also like, 'Oh, you're sort of a girl, I can tell you this'. And for the few guys that know it's like, 'I can tell you stuff that makes me feel vulnerable because you're way more of a girl than I will ever be'. Which I guess is technically true.

I can't believe what Mum said about Dad the other day. I always thought he was uncomfortable with me. We don't spend a lot of time together. I guess he doesn't spend a lot of time with Mum or Daniel either. He's so busy all the time, and he often seems distant. When I ask him his opinion about things, he just asks me how I feel, or what I think. The problem is I don't know how to feel or what to think about this.

In fact, Dad has never talked to me about being intersex, not even now I'm pregnant, not without Mum there too. I've always thought I'm not the boy that he wanted from a firstborn. It's a bit easier for him because I do like football, girls, etc., but I've always thought he seemed like . . . he can't forget that I'm a bit of both physically. I've always had that thought, but I've just ignored it.

He gets into our conversations when we're talking about how fit Jennifer Aniston is and we're laughing and stuff, and then you'll just see this thought pass across his irises and a twinge follows in his face and he starts off on 'but if you like other people, maybe even not women' – only he doesn't say that. He never just comes out and says what he's thinking, so I don't know what he's thinking. And I watch him and I think what I'm seeing is his heart breaking because I'm not his little guy. I'll never be his boy.

Then they've got Daniel, and he's into killing things, which is very boyish, but he also loves teddy bears and finds Dad annoying.

I don't think either Mum or Dad would understand why I'd be hesistant about having the abortion, why I feel so torn up about it. They wouldn't get it. How could they? They could have kids anytime. They never had to worry about finding someone to love them as they were. For them, it was as simple as falling in love and shagging. I don't like to think about it or verbalise it, but I'm not going to be able to offer that to people, and at some point, after Sylvie has left me, the number of available girls I can hang out with is going to dwindle, as they all fall in love and shag people. Soon they'll all be taken, partnered up, having babies.

I'm going to be alone, and older, and the choices and options are going to get fewer and fewer. So, I'm lying here, unable to stop the tears from coming, and I'm wondering – *Is this it? Is this my only chance?* And this bit I can't believe I'm thinking about because I'm sixteen, I was basically forced into it, Hunter would know it was his baby, I would get kicked off the team, no friends, no more girl prospects ever, and fuck, think of the fucking media and Dad . . . but . . . is this my only chance to have a child? Do I care? Because I think I might. I think I might care about that.

Sylvie

'Hey, Max!'

He keeps walking. It's the end of school on Thursday. I'm following him through crowds of people waiting for the buses.

'Hey! Hey, Walker!'

A bunch of boys near him laugh at me.

Max turns around and flips them off.

'Hey, were you ignoring me?' I ask.

'No, sorry,' he says. 'I was just thinking. I didn't hear you.'

One of the boys says something and they laugh again. He looks over at them and I shrug.

'Do you think I care what you think?' I yell to them.

Everyone has been talking about who Max has knocked up, why, how. Half of them think it's me. They keep coming up to me and slyly asking me things.

Max grins at my angry face as I too flip off the boys.

'What?' I say.

'Nothing,' he says softly. 'Kook.'

I study him for a second. 'Hey, green eyes. Something's wrong.' He opens his mouth to protest, but I shake my head. 'No, no, no. No lies. Come home with Sylvie. You don't have to talk. We can just cuddle and such things.'

Max looks around kind of blankly, then hangs his head like he's tired, and nods, looking lost. Then I notice something on his cheek and I make him tilt his head up. His eyes are full of tears.

'I'm sorry,' he mumbles. 'I really like you.'

I let go of his head. 'What do you mean you're sorry?'

'I just . . .' he wipes his face subtly and whispers: 'I don't think you should be going out with me. You're so awesome and . . .' He trails off and shrugs.

278

'And?'

'I'm just . . .' He mumbles something.

'Huh? You're scaring me, Max. What is it?'

'I'm going through some stuff.'

I wrinkle up my nose and stare at him. He looks really upset. I'm worried he's about to say something horrible, something that will mean we can't be together.

'Aren't we all?'

He shakes his head. 'No, like, really.'

I look around, thinking. 'No.'

'No?'

'No.' I shake my head. 'This is not how it goes.'

'I . . .' He looks confused.

'Have you knocked someone else up?'

'No! I swear.'

'Have you done anything wrong?'

He opens and closes his mouth, then shakes his head. 'I don't think so.'

I breathe out, unaware I'd been holding my breath, and say, panicked, 'OK, so, why are you trying to make me unlove you? Because I'm telling you now, Max, I can't do that.'

He blinks.

'Let me tell you something about me. Are you listening?'

Max nods.

I try to hold it together and not cry until I've finished talking. 'I'm not gonna make you stay with me if you don't love me. I get that sometimes people fall out of love and I don't want to be with you if you don't love me the right way because someday, someone will. D'you get me?'

He nods sincerely.

'Secondly, I only go out with people if I think it's going somewhere. Hence, if I have hung out with someone, say six times, or maybe for a couple of months, and I don't think they are super wicked, then I break up with them. And I think that's fair, because it doesn't waste someone's time, right?'

'Right,' he murmurs.

'But if I'm with someone, and I'm asking if we should end it,

279

this is how I do it. I say to myself, "Sylvie, are we (you and I) done?" and sometimes it's obvious that we are done, and sometimes we are not done, and if I still love someone, if I am not done, then I will hold on to that dying flame until it's all burnt out and it's taken me with it. I'm a week older than you, Max, so listen to a sage survivor of several long- and short-term relationships and learn.'

He's watching my mouth and eyes.

'Do you understand me, Max?'

He nods slowly. 'Yeah. I mean, I think I do. I've never really been out with anyone seriously.'

'Of course you have,' I say, trying to joke. 'You've been out with everyone!'

He laughs, but blushes. 'No, I really . . .' He looks around at the people passing us and lowers his voice. 'I've just kissed people.'

I wait and watch him for a moment. He looks nervous and tired, but he keeps looking at me as if he can't stop. He stares at my lips and bites his own, then looks down at my hands.

'So Max?'

'Yeah?' he murmurs, looking up with his eyes, his head still hanging low.

I gulp down nervousness, aware my chest is heaving up and down as I try to control my breathing. 'Are we done?'

He thinks.

'Are you and I done?'

Suddenly I get a lump in my throat and I realise I really, really, really care about this guy, about Max.

Please, please don't say yes, I think.

Max Walker looks at me, squinting in the low sun, golden hair lifting in the December breeze, his cheeks pink, and his green eyes bloodshot and dull. He looks at me like he's desperate, like he wants to kiss me so bad but he's fighting something. His eyes flick back and forth from the ground to my face.

'Max!' I say, and he looks into my eyes.

We hold each other's gaze. He sighs, as if he has to say this: 'No. We're not done.'

280

Confused by how fraught he looks, I ask, 'Are you sure?'

He nods. 'I didn't mean to make you think I was unsure.'

'OK,' I say nervously.

And suddenly in a rush, as if he was holding it in and had to burst out and say it, he comes out with, 'You're so beautiful, Sylvie.'

I grin, unable not to, at his pure earnestness. Then I roll my eyes to prevent the tears from coming. 'OK, then.'

He giggles.

'Come on, you weirdo,' I say, shoving him teasingly. I grab him by the hair and push him towards the school gates.

'Where are we going?' he asks.

'Back to mine, of course.'

He looks at me and smiles gratefully. 'I'm sorry,' he says.

'Stop. It's OK,' I say, putting my arm around him. As my own fear subsides, I notice Max looks as shaky as ever. He leans into me. 'You look so upset,' I murmur into his ear.

'I'm really sorry, Sylvie. I've been having a really, really bad two weeks.'

'It's OK. But that OK has conditions. Like, it's OK to try to dump me, but only if someone's died.'

He puts his hand up to his face and makes a choking sound.

'Shit! I'm so frickin' stupid!' I hug him again. 'Come on, let's get home.'

Back home, I leave him in my bedroom and I go downstairs to make tea, then come up with a trayful of goodies my mum gave me.

'What's all this?' he says, smiling at me like an excited kid. It's amazing what sugar can do to lighten people's spirits.

'I raided the treats cupboard. I said you were really upset so Mum said we could have anything. We've got muffins and homemade chocolate chip cookies. Go on, have one.'

He takes it from me. 'Thanks. I'm starving.'

'So what's up? Did someone die? I'm so sorry.'

'No. I mean . . . well, no,' he mumbles incoherently. 'To be honest, I've had a really bad autumn.' He pauses. He sniffs. 'I do really like you, Sylvie. I'm sorry I was mean to you. I just thought you'd be better off . . . well, not with me.'

'Why?'

He puts the cookie down on the bed slowly.

'Um, OK,' he says. 'OK.'

'OK, what?'

'I think I'm going to tell you.'

'Alright.'

'I . . . It's just, um . . . no one knows, so . . .'

'You're being very quiet.'

'Sorry,' he whispers. 'I've never talked about it.'

I move over to him and kiss his neck. He leans in and kisses my lips once, quickly.

'Sylvie, I want to tell you one thing before I tell you about *the* thing, OK?'

'OK.'

'Just, you can't say it back. You have to promise you won't, because I don't want you to regret it.'

'Scout's honour.'

'OK, so . . .' He nibbles his lip. 'I love you.'

I smile. 'Wow! I really want to say something in reply!'

'You can't,' he says sweetly. 'You promised.' He leans forward and kisses me gently.

Suddenly Max smiles, really big. 'There have been times in my life when I thought I would never, ever get to say that.'

It dawns on me. 'Oh my god, you have child cancer.'

'Er, no.'

'Are you dying?' I panic. He thought he would die before he loved someone! Oh my god! I put my hands to my face, unable to stop tears from escaping. Lovely Max dying. This is the stuff my fears are made of and they *can't* come true, they just can't. He can't die! I choke up and grab his sleeve. 'Have you always known?'

'No! I'm not dying, I'm not dying!'

'Oh my god,' I say, halfway to hyperventilating. 'Shit, you *scared* me!' I hit his arm hard, then hug him. 'Don't fucking *do* that, OK?'

'OK, I'm sorry,' he says, a little taken aback.

I sit up, getting myself calm again. 'OK, hit me. What is it?'

He hesitates. 'I'm not sure if I should tell you now.'

'No, tell me,' I assure him, kissing his lips. I just want to know now, whatever he is holding in. I want it over with. 'It's OK.'

He presses his lips to mine and we kiss for a bit. Then he moves in further and we're hugging, his face in my shoulder/ neck region.

His voice breaks and he mumbles quickly, 'I can't talk to anyone about it. I want to, like, discuss it with someone but . . . I just wish I could talk to a friend about it, but I can't tell anyone.'

'Wait, Max, slow down, slow down.' I pull his head back gently. Tears are streaming down his cheeks. Max . . . he just isn't the kind of person you expect to see crying. He's not a self-pitying person, and you can tell that from knowing him only for a little while. He's one of those try-hard, brave-faced, stoic people that you sort of have to love because they're so sweet. So I know that crying means something super bad. I put my other arm around him and hug him. Our foreheads press together, and he looks up at me and I look into his lovely emerald eyes, and I kiss him.

'Oh god,' he murmurs. He pulls away. 'Shit, Sylvie. You don't want to do that.'

'Shh,' I soothe. I kiss his cheeks, kiss all the tears off his face. He hugs me tighter and breathes in, with his face tucked into the curls on my shoulder.

'Max,' I say. I take a deep breath and gather all my strength, like I'm turning into the rock Max can count on. If he needs someone to talk to, I won't let him down. 'Look at me. I cross my heart and hope to die, anything you tell me will never leave this room, and I promise that I will still like you and I will still want to be your girlfriend. If you want me to be.'

'Well,' he sits up, wiping away tears and trying to calm down. He smiles. 'Sorry for crying.' He holds my hands and strokes them. 'I really do it's just . . . just only promise to be my friend, OK? Just in case you don't . . . want to be my girlfriend. And it's OK if you don't. I understand. So . . . just promise to be my friend.'

'I can promise to be your girlfriend,' I offer.

'I don't want you to. It'll just make it awkward.'

'OK.' I nod solemnly. Inside I'm flipping out. What the fuck is he going to tell me? He killed someone? He's a whore on the weekends? He does heroin? He has AIDS? Shit . . . I bet that's it. He has AIDS. His parents are these crazy do-gooders and they took him to Africa when he was a baby and he has AIDS. Outside I stay calm. 'I swear I will be your friend.'

There's a long pause, and he bites his lip.

'No one knows.'

I nod again.

He mumbles something that I don't hear.

'Huh?' I say.

'I'm, like, both,' he mutters quietly.

There's another silence. He swallows, looking into my eyes like he's guilty of a massive crime, looking ashamed. He tries to mouth something.

'Both what?'

He's still quiet.

'Bisexual?' I whisper.

He shakes his head. 'No. I'm . . . I was born . . . I'm not a boy or a girl. I'm in-between.'

Max

'Are you serious?'
     She lets go of my hands and I literally feel my heart breaking.

'So, you . . .' She shakes her head and looks briefly, for a millisecond, at my crotch. 'What do you have?'

I can feel my cheeks turn red. 'Um . . .'

'Never mind,' Sylvie says, holding her hands up like she doesn't want to know. 'Forget I asked. That was . . . stupid.'

I open my mouth but there's nothing I can say. She's backing away on the bed, minutely, trying to find the words to tell me to go, and I realise what I've done. I've told her. She knows. There is a leak in the seal of my secret. Sylvie knows and she's backing away, standing up, struggling to say anything at all and she's going to talk to people. She's going to talk to people at school about me and everyone will know. Everyone will know. Every day I'm there, everyone will know and look at me differently and talk about me.

Sylvie gets off the bed and wanders away a little in the room, her neck bowed, thinking earnestly.

'Wait, listen.' I stand up too, and come towards her. 'Please,' I plead with her. 'No one knows apart from my family and my doctors. Even my brother doesn't know, so . . . please don't tell anyone.'

Her eyes search the floor, then look up to me.

'Sylvie, please, I'm begging you.' *I am horrified*, I think. *I am an idiot.* 'It was such a stupid idea to say anything. I'm sorry. I'll go.'

'No, it's . . .' She falters, looking like she's having trouble speaking between breaths.

'It's OK, I understand,' I say, picking up my bag.

'Max,' she says, and catches my arm. 'No, just . . . wait a minute.'

So I do. I stand there, one hand on my bag, watching her face as she stands on the spot and just breathes in and out, concentrating.

After what seems like forever, she turns and looks me in the eye. 'This is huge, OK? I can't just . . .'

Thoughts wander across her face. I try to put myself in her shoes and guess what she is thinking. *Does this make me a lesbian? What's in Max's pants? How can I get him out my house?*

At this point I just want to be rejected, as fast as possible. *Cut me off, Sylvie, do it, because I can't stand it.* Even standing here, trying to say something, looking me up and down, making me feel queasy, she is stunningly beautiful. Her eyes are so intense and so thoughtful. Full of thoughts about me.

'Please don't tell anyone,' I murmur.

She looks at me like I'm insane. 'I'm not going to.'

'Thanks,' I whisper.

'So . . . um . . . how?'

'Normal people have XY or XX chromosomes. I have XX and XY.'

'Yeah but, like . . .' She trails off again. I can't tell if she looks grossed out or just incredibly confused. 'How does that happen?'

'Um . . . I don't know. Nobody knows.'

'Do you have, like, a . . .' She pauses. 'Penis?' She puts a hand to her mouth to cover a grin. 'Sorry. I can't say "penis" without wanting to laugh.'

'Oh my god . . .' I exclaim, wondering what she's thinking, if we're now in friend-zone, making jokes about penises, or whether . . . she still likes me. 'You're so inappropriate,' I say.

'I know,' she agrees. 'Penis.' She laughs a bit too hysterically.

'You think it's . . . funny?' I say, feeling my throat tighten with nervousness. *Please please please,* I beg the universe, not knowing quite what I'm asking for. *Please please please.*

Sylvie shrugs. I don't know what that means.

I shrug back and look down at my feet, still holding my schoolbag.

'Yeah, I have one.'

I glance quickly at her through my hair. Her reaction is a swallow, followed by a nod. 'Okaaay,' she says. 'Do you have, like, other stuff?' She wrinkles her nose and looks down at her own feet.

'Like what?' I say, playing dumb.

'Like a . . .' She makes a 'V' sign with her fingers.

I hesitate. It's fine to have a penis. But this is kind of the deal breaker. 'Yeah,' I murmur softly. 'But it's . . . smaller.'

'Oh my god,' she utters, and sits back down on the bed.

Neither of us speaks for a while and I slowly sit down on the bed too. She leans into my shoulder and whispers, 'Max.'

I turn to look at her, and then, in tentative staccato movements, she puts her arms around me, pulls me to her, then leans back and pulls me further onto the bed, so we're lying down lengthways, and she's cuddling my head into her neck.

'I don't know what to say,' she whispers.

'You don't have to say anything,' I whisper back.

We lie there for a while.

'So . . . are you more girl than boy?'

'Um,' I turn to her and frown. 'Why are you covering your mouth?'

'Breath.'

'You don't have bad breath.'

'I might,' she mumbles from behind her hand. 'I ate a burger.'

'I'm half and half and you're worrying about your breath?' I try to joke.

She nudges me with her knee and smiles weakly.

I half-heartedly smile back. 'I'm pretty much half of each. I can't . . . have children in the guy way, though. I'm infertile.'

She thinks. 'That's sad.'

'Yeah.'

Sylvie frowns. 'Do you have balls?'

'Ew,' I whisper, without thinking. 'Um, I mean, no.'

'To be honest,' Sylvie says after a bit, 'you're not missing anything. They're the most ugly part of a guy's anatomy.'

'Really?' I am mildly fascinated. 'You've seen them?'

'I've had lots of sex,' she whispers. 'Lots and lots.'

'Sylvie . . .' I raise my eyebrows. 'You're such a slut.'

She grins a little but doesn't look at me. Then she asks, 'Is that why you haven't done anything with girls? Other than kissing, I mean.'

I look off to the side and open my mouth, but I don't answer.

'You know everyone calls you a clit tease.'

I smile, kind of sadly. 'I've heard.'

More silence.

She strokes my hair but she doesn't press her body to mine like she usually does. I think, *Sylvie will never kiss me again. She will never grab my arse again,* and I study her face and her ringlets and I hold back tears.

Sylvie

I thought I knew you well
Fucking hell

is what I am thinking as I stroke Max's blondie-bear hair.

My brain is on overdrive, trying to make my face look comforting while having a crazed monologue firing questions off inside my head.

How is this even possible? He always looked totally boyish before, but now I'm looking him over and thinking 'this is a girl' and trying it on for size, and I'm noticing, yes, there are some major similarities between being seductive in a pretty-boy way and in a girl way. I knew the guys I had dated before were more . . . *guy*-ish, but I thought that was because they were in uni and older and more mature. Max has no facial hair at all. Didn't I think that was weird? Why didn't I? What does this say about me?

Well, I just thought that blond people don't have much excess hair, and he was younger than all my other boyfriends. I just thought he was sexy, super sexy, and I didn't stop to think, like I am now, that if you brushed his hair over to one side, and those amazing green eyes with their bambi-long lashes, and those pouty lips, and that big, sweet smile, and the soft, soft skin, and the kind of thin-ish neck, and the not massive chest, and the delicate, long fingers and cute, round arse . . .

'What are you doing with my hair?' he asks, kind of defensively.

'Nothing,' I say immediately.

I have to acclimatise to this. I feel like I need an hour or two just to walk alone and have my thoughts, but how do I have my little moment of shock without him here, without making him feel like I don't want him here?

In a way, I feel like I can't believe it until I've seen it. You know what I mean. Because it's so strange, beyond the sphere of my experience, that in a way I can't believe anything has changed between Max and me. Has anything really changed? Perhaps it hasn't.

I look back at him and bite my bottom lip with all my teeth.

'Ow.'

'Huh?'

'Nothing,' I murmur.

Max blinks at me. There are tears in his eyelashes. He's so beautiful. He's still Max. Isn't he?

There must be other people who are like Max, and for each one of them, a person like me who lies beside them and goes through the thoughts I'm thinking. I bet there have been tons, in the history of the world. Hermaphrodite is a Ancient Greek word, isn't it? So they had to have been around then. I bet tons of people go through this and come out the other side. Tons and tons. Or maybe just the one ton.

'Is it pretty common?' I ask Max.

He falters. 'Um, I have no idea.'

'You wanna Google it?' I say. 'We could find out.'

'I have done. It's, like . . .' He sighs, looking really tired and like he kind of wants to leave. 'It's confusing. Some of the stuff about intersex conditions on the internet is just . . . totally wrong.'

'Is that what it's called? "Intersex"?'

'Yeah. People used to say "hermaphrodite".' He mumbles the last word as if he doesn't want me to hear and be weirded out.

'Why don't we Google "intersex" and "how common"?' I suggest. We are both kind of silent, just lying there, waiting, I guess, for me to come to a judgement. It feels like something to do, to move on in my head beyond shock. To make Max feel like I'm still here with him, trying to understand.

He looks at me unhappily and plays with my hair. His eyes linger on mine, then trail down to my lips. 'OK,' he says softly.

I search around on the floor next to my bed and find my laptop. It's a white MacBook, covered in stickers. I sit up on the bed and Max leans up on his elbow, flicking his hair out of his eyes, hugged by my left arm. I type into the search box on the safari browser and click on the first link that comes up.

' "To answer this question in an uncontroversial way",' I read, ' "you would first have to get everyone to agree on what counts as intersex – and also to agree on what should count as strictly male or strictly female. That's hard to do. How small does a penis have to be before it counts as intersex?" '

'Not that small,' interjects Max. I look down and he's grinning shyly, not looking at me, so I nudge him playfully, tenderly, and read on.

' "Do you count sex chromosome anomalies as intersex if there's no apparent external sexual ambiguity? (Alice Dreger explores this question in greater depth in her book, *Hermaphrodites and the Medical Invention of Sex*)." I bet that would be an interesting book to read. I mean, why do we have two sexes if we aren't actually all part of the two sexes?'

Max leans back on the bed, as if he doesn't want to listen, or like he's tired of hearing about this. 'Right,' he says.

'Wait, here are some statistics.'

He sits up and we stare at the screen together.

'Whoa, there are a lot of complicated words here,' I mutter. 'Which ones do you have?'

'Hang on,' he says, reading, frowning at the screen.

'I guess you'd maybe be under this category?' I say, pointing to 'Not XX and not XY'.

'I guess so. Wow. One in one thousand, six hundred and sixty-six births. That's a lot.'

'Yeah, it is,' I murmur. 'So, if the population of Britain is . . .' I Google it. 'About sixty-two million, that, divided by one thousand, six hundred and sixty-six is . . . Wow. Thirty-seven thousand, two hundred and fifteen. That's loads!'

'Yeah. Though, I had an ovotestis when I was born, and it says here that's one in eighty-three thousand.'

'That's still, like, seven hundred and fifty people in the UK who have it. That must be loads in the world.' I say. 'Wait, what's "ovotestis"?'

'Um . . . where you have tissue of both an ovary and a testes in the same gonad. But they take one out in an operation,' he says quickly. 'So now I just have one ovary.'

'Oh. Wow.'

'Check this out, though.' He reads, ' "One in one hundred people differ from standard male and female." ' He thinks about this and looks pleased. 'That's so many.'

'You didn't know any of this?'

'I had no idea.'

'How do you not know?'

'My parents never told me much. We don't talk about it.'

I nod. 'Oh my gosh. One in a thousand people – not intersex people, just regular people – have surgery to correct stuff. Did you have surgery? I mean, besides removing the ovotestis?'

'Er, no.' Max gulps. 'This is insane. I can't believe there are so many intersex people. I thought no one was.'

'Well,' I say, watching Max, open-mouthed, moisture on his lips, staring at the screen. 'I guess you were wrong.'

He looks at me. Our faces are so close together. He swallows. 'Why have you never talked about this with anyone?' I say.

'Because . . .' He blinks. 'It's gross.'

'Max, you are not gross.'

'Well, it's . . .' His eyes flit to the screen. 'Improbable.'

I watch him. Max Walker: golden boy, smart, sexy, funny, sweet, smiley, supportive, cool, popular, kind, fun, great boyfriend, great kisser, secret strange person. An intrinsic weirdo, and you wouldn't even know it.

'Max,' I whisper. He looks at me; once at my lips, then into my eyes. 'You are improbable.'

He smiles warmly, gratefully, relieved. The corner of his mouth rises first, showing a little of his teeth, widening his grin. His eyes are lit up by the low winter sun coming in the window, and I am just, just, just . . . falling.

'Sylvie,' he says, 'you are probably more improbable than I am.'

I lean forward, and he leans forward, and we kiss *extremely* slowly and sexily.

'You know,' I whisper, 'you're not a freak. And no girl who was really cool would think you were.'

Max looks down and presses his lips together. 'Um, maybe they would if . . .'

I put my arm around his shoulders and pull his head towards mine and he closes his eyes and stops talking.

He puts his arms around me and we twist so we're both lying facing each other, propped up on our elbows. He pulls me to him and gives me the kind of amazing, scintillating, ridiculous, insane, wicked, cool, awesome kiss. I roll on top of him and slip my hand between his legs. I can't help it.

Max's forehead crinkles, and he reaches for my wrist and holds it. 'I'm not ready yet.'

'Max,' I murmur, and kiss him again. He moans and lets me touch him for a minute. I feel him getting hard beneath his trousers. Then I reach for his belt and undo it. I feel for the waistband of his boxers and I am just hooking my fingers beneath it when he backs away suddenly, grabbing for his belt. He scoots up the bed, away from me.

'I'm not ready,' he says quickly.

I think for a few seconds, then nod. 'I'd like to, though. Not now, but, you know, someday.'

'Maybe, I guess.' Max chews his lip. 'Sylvie . . . can I tell you something else?'

'Of course,' I say. I feel calm now. I feel OK.

He buckles his belt.

'Truthfully, I've always been OK about being intersex. I know that's weird, but that's just the way . . . I mean . . . Fuck. Look, I never wanted people to know and sometimes I've worried I'll end up alone, but I never felt ashamed about it.'

Max starts to shake and I frown and reach out for him, putting my hand on his knee. His teeth chatter a little and he has this funny reaction that's making everything shake, like shock after an accident.

'Until September, because . . .' His eyes start to fill up with tears and he wipes them away angrily. 'Fuck. Sorry.'

'What happened in September?'

'Someone . . .' He gathers himself and says quietly, 'Someone made me have sex with him.'

I am silent. It takes a minute for information like this to go in. You expect people to be joking. Sometimes people are not joking.

'He was, like . . . bigger than me. I don't know. He threatened me, kind of. I was in shock. I couldn't do anything.'

We sit in silence for a minute and I stroke his wrists without thinking about it. This is so surreal. I look up at Max, and he is watching me, clearly worried.

Then I remember what he said about the way his anatomy is.

'How small are you?'

'Um,' he says, and I see this, *What does she mean?* thought flash across his face right before I see the, *Ohhhh, that's what she means,* right before I see, *How embarrassing* flash up there. 'I'm pretty small.' He winces and holds up his little finger. 'Like, about that wide.'

'Jesus. So this guy . . . Were you hurt? What happened?'

'I bled quite a lot. I went to the doctor. She gave me a stitch.'

'Oh my god!' I start to cry, watching the tears in the corner of Max's eyes, my body getting over the initial shock. 'No! Oh my god! Max!' He looks so innocent and unassuming, and he shrugs, and the only thing I see is that he's worried about what I'm thinking, so I throw my arms around him and hug him. 'I can't believe someone did that to you! That's so horrible!' I cry. 'You're such a sweetheart.'

'Thanks, Sylvie,' I hear him mumble into my shoulder. 'I didn't know if I was overreacting.'

'What?' I turn to face his neck, pressed against him with my arms still wrapped around him.

'Only the doctor knows and she didn't react that much. I didn't know . . . I mean, I guess she believes me but I wondered if . . . if it happened to a lot of intersex people or something. You know . . . because people are curious.'

'It's fucking horrible,' I say, and I hug him closer. 'It's fucking horrible.' I pull back and look at his face.

'Sylvie,' he whispers.

'What?'

He looks up, opens his mouth, shakes his head and smiles, but he looks really sad. 'Nothing.'

'What is it? Tell me.' I slip my hand around his back and down, so my fingers are touching his bum, and my lips are almost brushing his. My sobs suck in and out a little too quickly, my breath a bit too staccato, but I'm not thinking about me. I'm thinking about Max. He looks at my lips, then up to my eyes, and he's never looked so sexy and sweet.

But then his lips part, he looks down, he looks up again, and says, 'Not today. But maybe tomorrow.'

'No, Max, come on, it's me!' I hold his face. 'Tell me.'

He looks down. He swallows.

'I bought the pregnancy test for me. The guy . . . he didn't wear . . .'

'Oh . . .' I say. 'You're pregnant.'

Max looks up. 'Thanks for letting me tell you.'

I gasp, finding it hard to breathe. I take in a breath but it's sharp and short and not enough oxygen. Uh oh. Jesus. Fuck. 'I can't . . .'

'What?'

'I can't . . .'

'Sylvie, are you . . .? Is it OK?'

'No, I'm sorry, Max.' I stand up, my hands out in front of me. I turn around and search for the brown paper bag I keep around my dresser. 'I really can't . . .'

'I'm sorry,' he pleads.

But I shake my head, totally overwhelmed, about to have a serious panic attack. *I want my mum,* I think. *I'm going to cry and not breathe and pass out. I can't breathe!*

The boy I love is a broken idea. This is too much. It's too much. He touches me. I back away, push him off, panting heavily.

'I'm sorry,' he begs me, the light hitting his hair and eyes, lighting him up like a proverbial, sexless angel.

I look at him and have this thought: 'You're going to get rid of it, aren't you? Max?'

His cheeks turn a deep red. 'Yeah.'

'Oh thank god,' I gasp. 'I just can't . . .'

I kneel on the floor and he stands over me, not knowing what to do.

'Are you OK?' he asks. 'Sylvie?'

He kneels beside me and puts an arm around my shoulder.

'Oh Max.' Quietly, I murmur: 'I'm sorry, I'm sorry. I get these panic attacks. I get scared I'll lose things. I'm just glad you're not . . . that you're not . . . I just want things back to normal.' I cough into the paper bag, my heavy breathing slowing ever so slightly.

He stands up.

'Normal?' I hear him say.

I look up. To my surprise, he looks furious.

'If there's one thing I'll never be, Sylvie,' he says darkly. 'It's normal.'

'Wait, Max, I didn't mean—' I gasp, breathing into my bag. 'You have to believe me, I'm OK with the whole intersex thing, it's just the—'

'Forget it.' He cuts me off, almost growling the words. 'It was stupid of me to think you'd get it.' He heads for my door, then turns back, seeming panicky, his face red and miserable. 'I thought you were different.'

'I am different!'

'No you're not, you're just like everybody else. You think I'm a freak,' he says, almost cruelly. 'You think I'm disgusting. Well, I hope you like being alone on your high horse.'

'Don't say that to me,' I gasp angrily. 'You come in here telling me all this shit, Max, it's too much! I'm not perfect! I can't react like a perfect fucking angel to what you're saying! It's overwhelming! It's too much!'

'You think it's too much for you? How about *me*? You think I like dealing with this, asking myself these awful fucking

296

questions all the time, having to make choices that *no one* else has to make, having *no one* to talk to? Fuck you!'

'Stop shouting at me in my room!' I feel dizzy and sick, like I'm about to pass out. 'You have to go!'

Max looks like he's about to cry. 'Don't tell anyone,' he says miserably.

'You have to go!' I moan, feeling my chest crushing me. I start bag-breathing again.

Max flies out the door. I hear the sound of his footsteps down the stairs, followed by the slamming of the door.

This is too fucking much for me.

Daniel

Max and Mum come home at the same time. I am looking for them in the big window that watches over the driveway. Max walks in the driveway just as Mum's car passes him, and she honks. He waits for her and she gets out the car and puts her arm around him. He shakes his head and shrugs Mum's arm off his shoulders. I go downstairs to meet them but the stairway is so big that by the time I'm at the bottom (I bump down on my bum step by step) they are walking through to the kitchen, so I follow them in. Dad is there.

'I HATE YOU, MAX!'

'What?' says Mum. 'Daniel, don't say that!'

'I do hate him! He said he would always tell me everything and then I find out he has a girlfriend and he has got someone pregnant.'

'What?' Max says, his head snapping up like a flip phone.

'That's not true,' says Mum. 'Where on earth did you hear that?'

She looks over at Max and Max snaps, 'Of course I haven't!'

'It's just on the rumour mill at the moment. We're dealing with it. We think it originated from a student's blog,' Dad says quietly. 'I didn't know Daniel had seen it.'

'My friend Mouse told me at school, 'cause her big sister told her, stupid,' I say to Dad.

'Don't call me stupid, Daniel,' Dad says in a deep, scary voice.

'Well, have you got them to take the blog down?' Mum says to Dad. 'That could be really harmful.'

'Lawrence is on it.'

'Whose blog?' Max asks.

Mum looks over at him. 'What did you say?'

He looks at Dad. 'I . . . which student?'

'You don't need to know, Max,' says Dad.

'Dad!' Max whines.

Dad looks at Mum and then Max. 'We're threatening to sue the blog site itself for publishing slander and trying to get in touch with the student. They'll most likely take it down shortly.'

Max moans like he's ill.

'AND,' I shout over them, angry that they're ignoring me, 'he said I was special and different and vital to the human species' winning position in the race and he was LYING!'

'Daniel, stop yelling at your brother!' Dad says, growlingly.

'Why do you think I was lying?' Max says, exasperated like he's annoyed with me.

'YOU WERE LYING!' I scream. 'I'm not special. Everybody wants to know about you, Max, and they never use pictures of ME in the papers, and no one is interested in ME, and I don't play for a sports team because I'm not good enough, and I never win anything. It's all about YOU. EVERYTHING'S about you, and I'm sick of it!

'Oh, sweetheart,' says Mum. 'Of course you're special. You're special to us. Max is only being blogged about because of a bad thing.'

'This isn't between me and you, Mum,' I say. 'This is between me and MAX THE LIAR!'

Max sort of sinks onto a chair at the table like a boat capsizing, and he says, 'I didn't lie.'

'Yes you did! You lie all the time now! I never know what's going on! I HATE YOU!'

'Daniel!' Max takes his hand away from his mouth. 'I'm sorry. I didn't lie. I just didn't want to tell people Sylvie was my girl-friend in case something happened. And I haven't gotten any-one pregnant. Sylvie and I . . . We're not going out anymore, anyway.'

Max and Mum glance at each other then look away im-mediately.

'Well what about me being special?' I ask him. 'That wasn't the truth, was it?'

'It was, 'cause—'

'It WASN'T! Everyone loves you!'

'OK! It wasn't! Stop screaming!' Max shouts at me, standing up and picking up his bag. 'Fine, it wasn't the truth. You get to be normal like everyone else. I'm sorry that's so awful but you'll find out one day that it's way, way better than the alternative.'

'You think I'm too young to know ANYTHING!' I shout back as Max walks towards the kitchen door.

'That's not true,' Max says angrily. 'I tell you about loads of stuff!'

'Sometimes things are too complicated for people to understand when they're young, sweetheart. That's why you explain things to people slowly so they can take everything in,' says Mum, sighing at me.

Then Max looks at Mum and Mum looks at Max and then Max looks away, at me, and Mum looks over at Dad, who looks at the kettle, and I realise they are all ignoring each other.

'What is going on here? What has been going on for the last month?'

Max looks at me like he knows I know something, while Mum does a fake laugh like she doesn't know what I'm talking about, and Dad makes the tea and ignores us all, shaking his head like he doesn't know what to do.

'You're all much more educated than me because you have all been to big school, you know way more words than me, you all know ALL OF the words to tell the truth with, but instead you lie to me and twist truths so I MISINTERPRET THINGS!' I scream this last part.

'Daniel!' Dad says, and he shoots Mum a look and she shoots Max a look and Max shoots her a look and their eyes meet and Max looks confused and Mum looks guilty and Dad looks sad.

'All of you communicate increasingly poorly as you explain more complex things!' I shout, and then I am very, very tired, and I give everybody a weary look and I leave the room.

Max

Everything is breaking apart.

It's Thursday, the night before the operation, and I'm in bed. Downstairs I can hear music playing. Dad has some people over, working to delete the blog and clear up the rumour before it's reported by the papers. Mum is with him. Daniel is playing a computer game. I can hear the muffled gunshots from his room. It's as if tomorrow isn't happening. It's almost Christmas. I'm wearing my Christmas pyjama bottoms, which are soft and red tartan, and a light jersey jumper, and my socks.

I'm lying in bed, on my side, thinking, feeling horrible. Feeling crushed and empty and spent and aching. I touch my stomach. It's just a small bump. I feel it sometimes now, to see if it's grown, when I'm in private. I've been having these fantasies. I've been feeling torn. I wanted to talk to Sylvie about it so much. But her face, when I told her. She was just . . . it was too much. She couldn't take it. She raised her hands to her head and muttered 'no no no'. She was panicked. She was gulping for air like a fish out of water.

I was so embarrassed. I felt like I could just die, right there on her carpet.

I saw her grasping for this bag, then she put it to her mouth and she said she just wanted things to go back to normal, for me to get rid of the baby, as if it was nothing, as if by a quick operation we could right all the wrongs. I thought about how all the doctors have always said that about me: that surgery could make me normal, get rid of the 'problem'. I felt suddenly angry, angry at her for having such a huge reaction when I've been keeping it all inside for months, angry at her for not holding me, angry at her for knowing what I am. I shouted at her. Then I ran. I just ran.

Tears slide down my face in the bed. They leak out of me. I

feel like it's always dark in my head these days. Everything has gone sour.

Even now, I want to talk to Sylvie more than anything, so badly. But I can't. I can't talk to anyone. I need to talk to someone who will get it, maybe someone else who's pregnant. I thought about asking Auntie Julie, but I don't want her to know. I'd rather as few people know about it as possible. So that leaves Mum and Dad, who won't get it, and Archie, who might, maybe. And one more person: Hunter.

Could I talk to Hunter? He'd probably just freak out. But I don't know. He didn't seem to think what he did was wrong. He seemed to think *we* did it, together, when we were talking. He seems to really like me. It's so weird. All the years we were friends and I never thought about us in that way. We were always hugging and stuff, but we were little kids. Little kids hug each other. We've shared bedrooms on every holiday our parents have taken together since we were babies. We used to go camping all the time. Maybe if I told him he would . . . I don't know. I could at least talk to Hunter about everything. About how I'm feeling. Maybe I could just talk at him, let it all out. There's no one else.

He'd probably want it. Because he likes me, and because it will be like me and him, mixed together. We're both smart. We're both attractive. He'd probably love to have a baby with me; it would tether me to him.

Oh my god. This is insane! Hunter held me down! Hunter held me down and still managed to look me in the eye and tell me I enjoyed it, that we had fun. Screw Hunter. He gave up his rights to this conversation when he walked out the room back in September, and left me there alone. Screw him.

It's not going to happen. It'll be over tomorrow.

Although I'm smart enough to know nothing will really be 'over', that nothing will 'solve' the problem of the baby, or me. There is no right way to do this. It's all guesswork.

I guess that's parenting for you, I think bitterly.

At least a part of it will be over. Maybe the rawness of it will go away too. I touch my stomach. I don't want to think about this anymore. I don't want to think about tomorrow.

I turn over on my pillow and try to shut my ears to my mind.

But I start to think instead about what Daniel said, how angry he was at me. I think about how little he and I and Mum and Dad have talked recently. About how little Mum and Dad have talked to each other recently. About silences when we're together while Daniel chatters on. I used to go hang out with Daniel all the time, but now I feel like I can't stand to be around him. I know why, two reasons: I'm jealous of him, for being normal, for not having these problems, and secondly, I don't want to lie to him, and something about everything just doesn't feel right. I feel like I'm as bad as the people who would think being intersex was weird. There's something about the whole situation that doesn't feel honest.

I've always thought people should just be as they are. Daniel's perfect, even being so weird and awkward. So's Sylvie. They are great. Part of the reason I love them both is because they are so kooky. So, am I fine as I am? Should I just be half and half and tell people to deal with it? And if I am fine as I am, then is this baby fine as it is?

I cover my head with the duvet. Every thought I think convinces me a little bit more that I'm either insane or halfway there. My head feels so full of shouting voices that I can't tell which one is my own. Which opinion is truly mine? Who am I? Does the fact that I don't have a gender even matter? Or does it mean I am absolutely alone? Will anyone ever understand me just wanting to be me, or will they all think I'm a freak, forever?

Can I keep this secret always? Or will the secret slowly poison my family?

I think about Mum's face and Dad's face, if I told them I wanted to stay this way, to be able to have kids when I grow up, be able to do all the normal things, just . . . differently.

I'm an idiot. I feel sick at myself, getting this confused. It's just my hormones. This is what happens when you get pregnant. You get emotional and hormonal. But aren't our hormones part of what give us feelings in the first place? Aren't those feelings valid?

Archie called the house today and spoke to Mum about the hysterectomy etc. Dad made out he was busy so he wouldn't have to hear it. The surgeon who will do the corrective surgery is going to be present during the abortion to look at my insides close up, and see what he can do and when he can set up the hysterectomy and other surgeries. Then he's going to talk to us about it when I wake up from the anaesthetic.

I keep imagining the conversation in my head, wondering what he's going to say. I wonder how they sew vaginas up. I wonder what it will feel like when it's done. This is what I've had, all my life, and now they're telling me I have to have a scrotum and testicles. I imagine how I'd feel if I were a woman, and I was told I'd have to be changed like that. I know I'm not one but . . . I'm not a man either. Let's face it. I'm not a man. And I don't know if I want to be.

I have until tomorrow to think this all through, and it's too soon. It's too much, too soon, and I feel like I'm being pulled in different directions, because I'm so panicked too about Mum and Dad and how much I want to make them pleased with me, make them happy again. Mum has been weird with me lately, but then she was so nice to me on the day in London. Dad keeps trying to talk to her but she won't speak to him, then she tried to speak to him about my surgeries and he won't talk to her. It feels like our family is falling apart. Daniel must be so upset.

I wish we could have talked about this more as I grew up. There are so many things we haven't said, that I don't know about how they feel. About how I feel. I feel like this point of view needs to be more developed before I make decisions like this. But Dr Flint, somewhere in his monologue, made a good point. If I don't have the operations now, I'll start to look different. Or rather, everyone else will start to look different, and I'll stay the same. This is the turning point. This is the time when whether you are a boy or a girl counts. And you have to pick one. Why? Because those are the rules. Everything else is a non-entity.

I wish I could just tell everyone. I wish being me was normal, or if not normal, then accepted. I wish I didn't have to hide all these thoughts. I wish I didn't have to be alone with this, to worry that I'll always be alone. Maybe that's the worst thing about being intersex. That I can't tell anyone. I don't want to be alone anymore.

There is barely any energy left in my body, but I get up and go through to Daniel's room.

I open the door softly, and whisper, 'Danny?'

'Max?'

'Hey, are you crying?'

'No,' Daniel says in a muffled voice.

I push the door almost shut, and he lifts up his duvet cover. I climb underneath and tuck him in.

'I'm sorry, Max.' Daniel sniffs.

'It's OK,' I whisper.

He sobs. 'I was so mad you didn't tell me 'cause you don't talk to me anymore.'

I watch him sniffle and rub his eyes for a bit and then I give him a hug and he settles down.

'I'm sorry too, Daniel, OK?' I say. 'I promise I'll talk to you more. There's been a lot going on.'

'But you're my brother!' he says. 'You can't lie to me anymore.'

I regard him solemnly, and I say, 'I won't lie to you anymore.' I hold up my little finger. 'Pinky promise?'

'Pinky promise.' He nods and takes my finger.

I settle my head on the pillow.

'What has been going on, Max?' Daniel asks me.

'Just . . . a lot of real stuff.' I turn to him. 'You know how we always battle on those games like *World of War*?'

'Yeah.'

'I feel like I've been battling in real life. I feel exhausted and sometimes I get too tired to talk.'

'You've been sleeping a lot.'

I ruffle his hair. 'It takes a lot of energy to fight against real things.'

'More than pretend things?' he says.

'Yes. Way more than pretend things. Big, scary real things,' I say, and I close my eyes.

Daniel

Max falls asleep for a bit, but I want to ask him a question, so I poke him and he wakes up.

'Errr, what?' he says.

'What's the scariest thing in the world, Max?'

'Poltergeists!' Max hisses funnily at me, and then does a big yawn. 'Do you want me to get the torch?'

'No, no torch.' I put my hand on his mouth to stop him from speaking about spooky stories. 'I mean the scariest real thing in the world.'

'Poltergeists are real,' he mumbles from behind my hand.

'No they're not.' I frown at him. 'And neither's Santa.'

'Ouch,' he says, and half-laughs, even though this is totally inappropriate because it's disrespectful to the memory of Santa, who was real when we believed in him.

'Mum and Dad are so whispery these days. I want to know about grown-up stuff,' I tell Max. 'What is the scariest real thing, Max? And you have to tell me out of loyalty. I must know. You promised never to lie to me again and you did a pinky promise.'

Max looks at me. In the dark, his seaweed-colour eyes are black with one small, thin oval of light from I don't know where. He breathes out and I know he's going to tell me, so I take my hand away from his face and I wait. He looks straight in my eye for a long time then swallows and moves a little forward on the pillow.

He thinks for a bit and then he opens his mouth.

'The scariest thing is a secret,' he says very slowly and sort of rhythmically.

'How can a secret be scary?' I ask scornfully, but wanting very much to know.

Max swallows and breathes again, and looks at me. He thinks a bit and bites his lip.

'Secrets are like invisible maggots,' Max says slowly. 'No. They're like zombies, OK? They eat away at your brain . . .' He touches my wrist. 'You know, like the zombies in *Deadland*. And then they get out, and they eat at your guts so you've got none, you've got no guts, and you can't be brave. And they eat . . . your vocal chords, so you've got no voice. You can't speak. And they eat . . .'

'What? What else do they eat?'

'They get out of you and they eat the air around you. They make it all thin, so you can't breathe. Then they eat the other people around you. They eat . . . they eat Mum and Dad.'

'Is that what's happening now?'

He pauses. 'Yes. But you can't ask them about it, OK? Because then they will know I've told you all this, and they'll be mad at me.'

'I swear I won't tell them.'

'What do you swear on?'

I think. 'Both their lives.'

'Wow. OK.'

We're both quiet for a minute, but then I have a question. 'All of them?'

'Huh?'

'Will it eat all of Mum and Dad until there's nothing left?'

'No . . .' He looks around, like he's thinking. 'It eats bits of their souls and worries around . . . like, goes around their brains, nibbling at their brain cells. So they get mean and snappy, because that's what happens when your soul gets eaten. And . . . and the eating keeps them up at night, because it hurts, so they get tired. It . . . it eats at love, and empathy, so the things that bind you to other people get gnawed away at, until they're thin and easily breakable.'

'What's empathy?'

'Empathy is where you understand other people, but . . . you feel the understanding, rather than think. It's different from sympathy. It's like where you can imagine yourself as that person. You know what I mean?'

'Like me and you? Because I sometimes imagine I'm you.'

'Do you?'

'Yes.'

'Why?'

I think. 'Because you're Max.'

'And who's Max?' Max asks.

'Max is . . .' I get confused. What doesn't he understand? Max is Max. He's the best at *World of War* and he knows everything.

Max clears his throat. 'Anyway. Yeah. Like me and you.'

'Does the secret get your heart?' I ask. 'When it eats everything?'

'Yes. Bits of it.'

'Does it get what's beneath your heart?'

'What's beneath your heart?'

'The centre. Your . . .' I think. 'Your You. The thing that beats like a drum and says "I am Daniel, I am Daniel" or "I am Max, I am Max". You know, how you know you're you. Does it get that bit?'

'I . . .' Max's mouth is open and he looks at me and breathes in, like a little whoosh. 'I don't know.'

'Max? I want to know everything from now on. Even if it's scary, and even if you can't tell me right now and you take a bit of time, you *have* to tell me.'

Max stares at me for a minute like he's going to say something, but when he opens his mouth, he just says, really quietly, 'OK.'

'Why are your eyes wet?' I ask.

'Allergies,' he says, and turns his face away from me, and we go to sleep, and I dream of assassinating secrets with bombs and nukes and a rifle with a silencer on the end.

PART THREE

Karen

The early morning light moves across the waiting room. Max and I are silent, both watching the floor, as if waiting for it to do something.

Steve didn't come. He wanted to. We argued about it. All we seem to have done recently is argue through gritted teeth and fake smiles because, of course, we can't shout, we can't even really talk. Lawrence and Debbie are in the house all the time, and sometimes I think it is perhaps on purpose; that Steve runs his campaign from home not to be close to us, but to avoid us. To avoid me.

In the end, we agreed that since the termination was scheduled in Oxford, Steve might be recognised, so he couldn't be with us after all. In some ways, sitting here with Max, I think Steve is lucky. What would I say to even a daughter of mine in this situation, never mind a son? It's the right thing to do, and soon the waiting and worrying will be over, but it's never pleasant. No matter how much you know that you could not provide a home for a child, that it's the wrong time, that it's not right, it is never something that is easy to do. If someone saw Stephen Walker sitting in the waiting room of an abortion clinic after the blog about Max yesterday, it would only make things ten times worse. So I'm here, de facto parent, the one who has sacrificed more – more time, more love, more heartache, my physical body – to bring them into the world and take care of them, and will always be the one that they will blame, that they will resent for the sway I held over them, for making them into who they are, the one they will remember sat beside them at their worst moments. I hope that when Max remembers, he thinks of me as being on his side and not snapping at his heels. But kids live in such small worlds, really. How can they see things like this objectively? In all probability, he won't until he's much older. Now he just sits, glumly, obediently, as if I have dragged him here. It feels like that, in a way, to me too.

'Do you want a drink ready for after, Max?' I ask quietly. 'Can of Coke?'

'Huh?' Max takes the headphones from his iPhone out.

'Something to drink after? You'll be thirsty.'

'No,' he says, adding, 'Thanks.'

He fiddles with his earphones and looks out the window.

'What are you listening to?'

He shrugs.

'Why don't you read another magazine, love?' I suggest. 'We've got twenty minutes before the nurse can take you in and get you ready.'

Max shakes his head. His fluffy hair swings around. There is a tuft at the back he has had since he was little. I sigh and turn back to my reading. I can't look at him anymore without wanting to fall apart.

Max seems to have completely lost his voice.

He nods to everything, halfway between utterly terrified and utterly robotic, compliant, moving when I say, agreeing when I say, signing the forms when the doctor and I point to them.

We were up this morning at six; dressed and ready to go by six-thirty. We didn't want to be late for the appointment, so we went early to get ahead of the rush hour traffic.

Max was downstairs, waiting for me in the kitchen. He had his rucksack, a T-shirt, jeans, boots, his jumper and coat on. He was sitting at the head of the table, just staring at the wood. The light was pale, diffusing through the room in a grey-blue glow that drained out the colours.

I don't think he said a word until we were walking out the door. Then he muttered, 'Hang on', and ran back up the stairs for something.

Now he sits in the waiting room blankly, his eyes like two opaque circles of green slate.

'I'm going to get some air,' I whisper, afraid of disturbing him, of having to deal with more than we already do today.

Max

Mum has stepped outside for a few minutes. I can see her through the glass door. She stands in the corridor, looking away from me.

I have been leaning forward, but I sit back, and feel in my pocket for the little bit of paper I ran upstairs to get. I leave it in there.

Why did I bring the picture from the ultrasound?

I don't know.

Dad asked about it the other day. Mum had told him I had it. He asked if he could see it. I said I didn't know where it was.

Liar, liar.

I don't even know why I asked for it at the appointment. Maybe because it was the only picture there will ever be of my family, in a way. The one I could have made. The one I could have if I wasn't intersex, if I was just a girl, or even a boy, with a girlfriend, who had made a mistake.

But I'm scheduled to talk to the surgeon when I wake up about starting the gender reassignment process next week. So, I guess that's the beginning and the end of my little family.

I met the surgeon who will be sitting in on the abortion to look at my anatomy this morning. He said the hysterectomy is going to be on Monday, barring complications in the abortion procedure. Then they will schedule other operations in January, to 'fix' bits of me. Then I'll take hormones to make me look more masculine and develop like other guys. He said he was glad I'd thought everything through. Except I haven't. In fact, I've been trying not to think everything through as much as is humanly possible.

He said that I am being very brave. I couldn't think of a bigger lie.

The picture had been in the drawer beside my bed but then

this morning I just thought I should have it. Why did I think that?

It's burning over my heart, in my chest pocket. It's burning but I have to keep thinking why I'm here. I run a movie trailer of terrible reactions in my head: Sylvie's face, Mum's anger, Dad not knowing what to say, me feeling like I want to die of embarrassment and shame for the last few months.

I'm sweating and shaking but maybe you can't tell on the outside.

I feel like I've lost my life over the past few weeks. I've just reverted to how blank I was the night Hunter came into my room, the night all this started, and got worse and worse. I felt incapable of interrupting, of asking questions of any of the nurses or doctors as they talked to us, as they told me to sign the forms. I feel that my intersexuality is the main part of me, which is exactly what I never wanted growing up. I never wanted to be seen and judged on my inbetweenness alone. But that's just what I am now. A product of my body, what it does, what it was made for. That's why we're here.

But I don't want that to be why we're here. That shouldn't be the reason. I mean, there are other reasons why I shouldn't have a baby right now, but I've been so caught up thinking about being intersex, I haven't had time to think about them, or come to terms with where I am, what I'm doing today. I'm starting to understand, sat here in this room, that being here because of this reason, because I'm intersex, feels wrong. I wish I had more time to think.

I fiddle with my breast pocket and feel terrified, horrible, nervous.

I wanted to talk to someone earlier, when they did the pre-op pelvic exam, but I felt like asking more questions of the doctors would be impolite, like they're all looking at me like how dumb and young and stupid is this kid? I've interrupted all our lives – Mum's, Dad's, Daniel's, the doctors', Sylvie's – and now I've just got to nod apologetically and get through the next few hours without passing out in shock, or breaking down.

If only someone knew how the baby came about. Maybe they

would give me more time if they just knew. But it's just me here that knows the truth. And I'm an inconvenience, even to myself, that I don't want to be. I shut my mouth tightly, feeling dizzy and faint. I shake my foot violently under my seat and press my lips together until they hurt.

The operation is called a surgical termination. Archie told us about it. It's going to be done under general anaesthetic, so I'll be asleep. That's supposed to be in forty-five minutes.

'Just get rid of it,' I heard my mum whisper to my dad the other day. 'We'll just get rid of it and everything will go back to normal.'

Man, I've heard that said so many times in my life.

The tiny black and white picture seems to burn my skin through the fabric of my T-shirt. I look down at my body and hate myself.

When you think about it, all nouns are also definitions. The word 'it' and the word 'normal' spin around in my mind, like opposite fates.

Karen

The nurse who comes to collect Max is a different nurse to the one we signed the papers with, and the one who took us to the pelvic exam an hour ago. This one is young, slim, with dark brown hair, and she reminds me of the nurse who took care of me through my labour with Max. I see her walking towards us through the glass, then she slips her head into the waiting room.

'Max?' She smiles.

He visibly jumps, but does not move off the chair. She frowns and I stand up and catch her attention.

'Yes, that's us,' I say, as if it could be anyone else.

'Oh, good,' she says, looking over to Max again. 'Are you alright, Max?'

Max bites his bottom lip, before nodding and standing up. He wraps the headphones around his iPhone, looking guilty and nervous. His face is white and clammy.

'Give me that, Max,' I murmur, and he hands it over, then follows the nurse, both fists clenched, his fingers digging into his palms.

'You've signed everything, you're happy with everything?' she asks quietly.

Max looks at me. I nod and he nods at the nurse.

'Yes?' she nods.

Max emits a tiny murmur of agreement from between tight lips. 'Yup.'

The nurse glances questioningly at me and I make a 'what can you do, he's nervous' face. She nods sympathetically and leads us down the corridor to a small room. We fill it uncomfortably and she gestures to the bed and pats a sealed plastic bag with a hospital gown in it.

'Don't worry, we're not staying in here. If you just want to

318

pop this on, I'll be back in about ten minutes and then we can get off to theatre, OK? Is Mum coming in?'

Max looks at me.

'Yes, I'm coming in.'

'We don't allow family in the operating room after the patient has gone under, but you can be there until Max falls asleep,' the nurse explains.

Again, Max looks at me. I nod, and he turns to the nurse and nods.

'Alright then, these are some scrubs for mum.' She opens a wardrobe and pulls out some blue overalls, laying them on the bed. 'Put the shoe covers on too, please.' With this she smiles and leaves the room.

Max sits on the bed and puts his head in his arms.

'Come on, now,' I say as sunnily as is appropriate. 'You have to get changed, OK?'

He nods, but doesn't move.

'One step at a time, Max.'

Max

I'm on the bed. I'm on the bed in the operating theatre and all I can hear is myself breathing. The cannula – the plastic tube the anaesthetic is supposed to go down – feels weird in my arm. The anaesthetist is going to put the drugs in me through the tube in a few minutes. He'll tell me when. Then I'll have a minute before I fall asleep.

How did we get here? How did this become my life? How did we get to this terrible place that's tearing apart my family?

'Max, don't,' Mum mutters, pulling my hand away from my tiny bump. I didn't even notice I was touching it.

I think about this potential for life inside me, the fact that my body can make life. I feel like I'm burning up. I feel so scared. It's not my fault that I'm intersex and it's not the baby's fault how it came to be. It's just different. Just like me. It just came to be in a different way and now it's here, and I just . . . I feel like all choices have been taken away from me. I feel like I'm being stripped of all the things I am. I don't want to be a parent but I don't want to be here today either, and I feel so frustrated and weird and angry that Hunter made that choice for me, that I was robbed of it, that because of the way my body works, I no longer have a say in something so important. I feel like I'm crazy, or even if I'm not, I feel like this decision is about to do something so against what I want that it's paralysing me. I never thought I would have to make a choice like this. How can I know I'm making the right choice? In the end, how am I, or Daniel, or kook Sylvie, or this ill-conceived baby, or anyone any different from a 'normal' person? If you love someone, you love them. It doesn't matter where they came from or if they're a boy or a girl, or if you fight, or if they're weird, or if they find it difficult to communicate with you, you just fucking love them.

Oh shit. Oh my god. I can't do this. I need more time to think.

Oh fuck.

I have to say something. I have to say something.

Karen

The blue scrubs are uncomfortable, but the facemask is worse. My breath is hot and I'm overwhelmed by the heat of the room. I stand on Max's left side. There is the doctor, the anaesthetist, the surgeon observing for the corrective surgery next week, and two nurses in the room, all readying themselves for the op.

I look everywhere but at Max. There are a number of frightening-looking metal implements on the doctor's tray and I'm thankful Max is lying down and can't look at them.

Before we went in, and while Max was changing in the bathroom, I thought about calling Steve. I checked my phone. Two missed calls, both from Steve, and a text message: 'I feel like I should be there.'

Frankly, I didn't know what to say. Yes? Perhaps.

Max came out, carrying his clothes. He looked at the phone as I typed a reply.

'Who is it?'

'Just Dad.'

'Oh.'

He looked at me, then looked away again. Max seems so much smaller than I was at that age. Small and soft-skinned and blond, like only toddlers and chicks should be. He looks like some of the girls I saw waiting in the other waiting room we passed; much too young to be dealing with this.

I pressed 'send' on my message. I had written, 'None of us should.'

Max sat next to me on the bed and I stroked his hair and neck.

The nurse called us in to a side room next to theatre and they put the cannula in Max's arm.

Now we're here, and soon it'll be done, and we can go back. We can go back to our lives.

They will remove the uterus in a second operation next week. Max has signed the consent form, even though Steve frowned and argued with me about it. I would have liked Max to have children. He's such a kind, sweet, happy little person. It would have been nice, in the future, to have had grandchildren, but not like this. Now it's happening, I realise this is the only way Max could have had children. I had tried not to think about it before. But we should have had these operations a long time ago. It wasn't right to wait this long. It's upsetting us, everyone, Max.

'My poor babe,' I murmur, stroking his hair, as he lies on the operating table. 'It'll be over soon.'

'OK,' says the anaesthetist. 'I'm sending you off now. You'll feel drowsy and in just under a minute I expect you to be asleep.' He smiles at Max, and Max looks panicked.

'He's just nervous,' I say quietly.

Max

Sixty seconds. That's all I have. Sixty seconds to say what I have to say. About not doing this. Not right now. I just need some more time to think about it. To be ready.

My eyes dart around the room. My mouth opens. I swallow.

Who do I tell? How do I say it? What can I say to make this stop?

There's the doctor, but he's not looking at me, not at my head, at least. There's the nurses, but they are looking at the doctor.

Mum's not looking at me. I panic. She's not looking at me!

I look over to my right. One nurse is above me, leaning against the wall. She is watching me carefully. When I look at her, she comes over to me.

'Alright, Max?' she asks.

I open my mouth. I have to say it. I have to tell someone. Fuck. I find it so hard to talk to strangers about this. I never have before. Shit.

Then, suddenly, there is a flash of blue to my left, and Mum is there. Thank fuck.

I give the nurse a small nod and a weak smile. She squeezes my hand, and turns slowly away from me, and I wait until she has walked away, down the other end of the room, watching the doctor.

I turn to my left. 'Mum,' I whisper.

She frowns at me questioningly.

I gesture. A minute movement with my head and mouth that signals 'come here'.

She comes over and dips her head down to me. 'What, Max?'

She touches my hair. She looks non-human in the mask. My eyes look down.

I have to say something. But no words are coming. I feel

324

myself getting fainter, moving away from consciousness and reality.

I have to say something.

I look up at her.

'Mum,' I whisper.

It's the only thing I can say.

'Mum . . .'

But she gets it. Her eyes widen, my eyes beg her, and Mum nods. She looks over at the doctors, then back to me.

'I can't, Mum. I can't. I need more time, Mum . . .' I murmur. She nods again, stroking my hair across my forehead, and I slip off to sleep.

Steve

I am in the recovery room, wearing sweat pants and a hooded jumper, trying to look not like myself.

Max is looking unlike himself too. I've always thought of him as such a confident, successful young man: a leader, a reliable person, a mature person, particularly lately, with how he has dealt with all of this, how little he has complained.

But in the bed, he seems to be a child again, his hair ruffled on the pillow, asleep more deeply than simple sleep, pale and vulnerable. His lips are parted, his skin is hairless. He seems to have sunk not simply into the bed, but back through the last five years. He looks eleven to me.

I stroke his hair, feeling a peculiar mix of ownership and intrusiveness, holding my child without his knowing.

I should have been here for the operation, but I couldn't be, for Max's sake, because someone would have known me. We were worried, as it was, that someone would recognise Karen. We thought me going would have been too much of a risk. There is always someone who will have a quick visual memory of my face on their paper, or on the evening news broadcast from Oxford. It flits across their face like a shadow, followed by a light, and then they move towards me, shake my hand, look with keen interest at the faces of the people around me. At my family.

Perhaps I should never have run. Perhaps I should have let politics go when I knew I had a family that needed protecting from the limelight, like Karen let go of vying for the top spot when she knew the boys needed her at home. She always found work easier than me, and perhaps we should just have taken each other's roles. But she was their mother, and somehow, as modern and educated as we were, it seemed to make more sense for Karen to take the more active parenting role. Even when we knew that sometimes she could not handle it. She could have had my job. She could have already been an elected MP. That's the thing about Karen: logic, academics and objectivity always came easily to her. She never had to try to be the best barrister we had; she just was. But achieving a balance between objectivity and the subjectivity at home was always hard for her. She felt every blow Max felt, but keener than he did, because she saw the bigger picture, knew what it would mean to him growing up, knew how people would treat him. Max's happiness has always been more important to her than, really, anything.

But this meant that she could not make medical decisions for him when he was born, found it hard to take care of him without worrying she was hurting him and making the wrong choices for him. After those first few years of turmoil, Karen found a coping strategy. When things go wrong, she sits back, being too objective, too cold. It's not her fault. She didn't have a real mother figure growing up. She didn't expect to have an intersex son. Everybody copes in the way they were taught to cope.

Not very many people see it, but cool Karen Walker has a huge, warm, endlessly giving heart, and it beats almost entirely for our children.

She was wary of the campaign, and she was right to be. The work for the campaign is taking me further away from my family when I thought it would bring us closer, and I feel myself using it as a barrier, using it to distance myself when I don't want to comment on what Max is going through, what he should do.

I am a politician, at the end of the day. I don't like to announce an opinion until I have properly formed one. The only thing I can honestly say to Max is that I don't know what he should do – about the hysterectomy, about the gender reassignment procedure, about anything – so I haven't said anything to him.

It has been Karen driving us towards the operations, because she knows time is running out, and I've been thankful to her for taking the reins on this occasion, for being the strong one. As I watch Max sleep, I realise I need to be there more, for my children, for my family. You cannot take your family for granted.

I had thought we would all come together on the campaign. I thought the kids would be proud, I thought Karen would be excited. Perhaps I didn't think it through enough. Perhaps I didn't think a lot of things through, as Karen said the other night in bed.

'Did you ever think about what would happen if Max had children?' she murmured, her back to me.

'I wanted him to have the option.'

'Seriously, Steve?'

'He could have used a surrogate. He could have grown up wanting to be a girl,' I offered diplomatically. Then, when she was silent, I said, 'Karen, I didn't know this would happen.'

'We should have made these decisions for him.'

'I don't think we should have.'

'Don't you? This is our fault.'

'It's—'

'It's our fault.'

'These things happen. Teenage pregnancies happen.'

'This isn't just a teenage pregnancy.'

'How is it different, Karen?'

'Because . . .'

'Because?'

'Because he's a boy!'

'What do you want me to say, Karen?' I grunted. 'Of course I didn't imagine it like this. Of course I didn't!'

'Keep your voice down!'

'Of course I didn't want this for him, but now it's happened, we have to let him make his own choices.'

'He doesn't know what he wants. You don't know what you want.'

'And what do you want?'

'I want him to have a good, normal life. I want him to not be treated differently.'

'Doesn't that sound so cynical? So awful? Do we care that much about what other people think?'

'That's a strange question for *you* to ask.'

I ignored the remark. 'Making decisions based on what other people think just seems plainly wrong to me.'

'Plainly wrong? You get to wander around on your high horse being the hero politician and you don't see how our lives are! You don't live the day-to-day life of a parent. You're never here, and when you are here, you're with Lawrence or Debbie. You don't live like a regular person. You're surrounded by sycophants and people who worship you.'

'I thought you would be proud of me. You knew this is what I wanted. We talked about this years ago, in our twenties.'

'Well, I was stupid in my twenties, Steve!' Her voice was low and hoarse. 'I was ignorant and young and I said things and wanted things without knowing what they would really be like. I had no idea what it would be like to raise a child with an illness, who needed privacy, who needed us both to be there.'

'It was just an accident, Karen,' I said quietly. 'If we did anything wrong, it was not getting the doctors to figure out how Max's fertility worked. If he had known, then he would have been careful.'

'Just an accident . . .' Karen muttered.

We were quiet for a moment, both lost in our thoughts.

I sighed regretfully, and spoke softly, trying to get her to understand how I was feeling and what I had been thinking. 'I just want the world to accept Max the way he is, for him not to have to compromise one way or another. It's not his fault he's born this way. It's not life-threatening, it's not something that's wrong.' I turned to her. 'Karen?'

She stood up.

'What are you doing?'

'Spare bedroom,' she muttered.

'I just want him to—'

'I *don't* want to talk about it,' she snapped, her voice breaking and filled with tears. She left the room with her BlackBerry in hand.

I sigh, in the hospital room.

Max takes a long time to come around, which affords me a lot of time to think. I have not seen Karen here yet. One of the nurses suggested she might be in the canteen. I have a feeling she is avoiding me, and I choose not to disturb her.

Suddenly Max takes a deep breath in, which turns into a yawn, and his eyes open. He blinks, with a particularly unreadable expression in his eyes. I'm sitting back in the chair, slightly behind the head of the bed. He doesn't notice me. His lips part, and he lowers his hand to his stomach, touches it and frowns, seeming dazed. He lifts the sheet.

'Max?' I say.

Karen comes in. She looks beautiful, but older than I remember her. I suppose I look older than I remember me. Her hair shines in the light, the blondes mingling with caramels and chestnut. I wish we wouldn't fight. I wish I could talk to her. She moves over to Max with trepidation. Then she smiles at him.

'Did you stop the termination?' Max says.

'What?' I murmur, turning to him.

Karen pauses momentarily, faltering, her hand hovering in the air, halfway towards touching Max. Her hand stops hovering, and she retracts it. She shakes her head.

Max looks confused. 'But you . . .' His eyes flit from side to side and frown at Karen. 'You . . .' He stutters a little, then seems to realise something and he stares at Karen as if in horror. His mouth slowly opens at the same time as his face changes, the eyebrows frowning deeply in anger, the mouth buckling in sorrow, the eyes boiling from blank to furious.

'No!' he says, louder than before. 'No! But you knew! You knew!'

'Max!' Karen says, her hands once again dancing in front of her.

'NO!' Max moans now, trying to sit up in the bed, but still groggy, gasping and holding his stomach. 'NO!'

'Max, I told them we weren't going to have the rest of the operations,' Karen says nervously, quickly, in a shrill voice. 'I cancelled the appointment for the gender reassignment talk, the hysterectomy, everything. You can choose about all that in your own time. I just, we had to—'

'I can't believe you! I can't believe you!' Max protests.

'What's going on?' I say, standing.

Karen shakes her head. 'It's for the best, honey.' She stumbles over her words, becoming redder. 'Now everything can go back to normal, and we can forget all about—'

'I'm not normal! I'll never be fucking normal! Can't you get that into your thick head? Give me up now if you want something normal, because I'll never be right for you!' Max leans forward, snarling now, like a dog. 'You knew what I was asking! You fucking knew!'

As Max is saying these words, I rush over to the door and shut it quickly.

'Shh!' I say, but Max and Karen don't hear me. 'Max, what's going on? Everyone can hear you outside. Stop yelling.'

They ignore me, and Karen tries to put both her hands on Max's yellow mop of hair.

'Don't touch me!' he screams.

'Please, Max,' she says desperately.

I turn to her and notice how much she is shaking and how her hand flutters to her mouth and throat and back to try to touch Max, then away from him again.

'What are you doing, Karen?' I ask quietly.

'I want her out,' growls Max, not taking his eyes off Karen. 'Get out!'

She shakes her head sadly. 'I did it for your own good.'

'I just wanted some fucking time, some breathing space!' Max shouts. 'How could you do that? That was my choice to make!'

'It's better this way, sweetie,' Karen says softly. 'I'm sorry.'

'Don't call me sweetie!' he says, as she walks towards him. 'Get away from me.'

'Max—' she says, touching his hair.

He pushes her hands away and leans forward and screams so loudly that the water in the glass beside him ripples.

'GET AWAY FROM ME!'

Max

Dad drives me home from the hospital on Friday night. When we open the kitchen door, Mum is there, in her coat. Her hair is wet. It's raining outside.

I tense up immediately, wanting to throw something at her. But tensing hurts my stomach, and I wince painfully.

'Go up to your room, Max,' says Dad.

I look at him, register what he's just said, and run upstairs. I change my clothes from the hospital, and I sit on the bed.

It's quiet. Daniel is staying with Hunter's parents. I hope they don't come round to drop him off. I feel shaky and weak thinking about it.

I hang my head over my knees.

After a few minutes, I hear Mum and Dad's voices murmuring downstairs. I open my bedroom door, creep down the stairs and up to the kitchen door, and sit just beneath the keyhole. Everything is too quiet, and I look through the hole, just to check that they are there.

They are stood at either end of the table, not saying anything, not looking at each other.

After a while, Dad says, 'What the hell were you thinking?'

Mum looks out the window at the black night. She doesn't look at Dad.

'Karen,' Dad starts again. 'All he wanted was some more time to decide. He just needed time.'

'We might have assigned him the wrong gender,' Mum says finally.

Dad shakes his head. 'No. We didn't assign him a gender; he decided who he wanted to be. He always has, up until this point.'

'If he'd said it to you, what would you have done?' Mum says quietly.

'I don't know! Given him some—'

'More time! More time, like he wanted? For *what*? For him to show? For it to be an even more invasive operation? For him to panic and end up keeping it and ruining his fucking life?'

'He wouldn't have kept it! He just wanted to talk about it more, think it through.'

They wait, watching each other warily.

'He never talks to you about it,' Mum murmurs darkly. 'It's always me who has to make the hard decisions.'

Dad lowers his head, like he's stopping himself from saying something.

'All I know is that we've always told him he could be who he wanted,' he says finally. 'And every time that we've tried to impose something upon him because those bloody doctors have told us it's realistic and it's for the best, I have deeply regretted it.'

'Steve, I did what I thought was right,' Mum says.

'You weren't there, Karen!' Dad suddenly shouts. 'You weren't bloody there in the beginning. You didn't have any *right* to make these decisions without *me*!'

I frown, surprised and annoyed. What's he talking about? Him? How is this about *his* right to make decisions for me?

'It's been sixteen years,' I hear Mum say, in this bitter, strained voice. 'When are you going to forgive me?'

There's a silence and then she starts to talk again. 'One year, one year of his life when I couldn't take care of him, when I was overwhelmed and couldn't cope thinking about how fucking difficult his life was going to be. I'd just been pregnant for nine months and then to be asked to deal with the intersex issue . . . To think the hard slog is over and then suddenly—'

'It wasn't just one bloody year, Karen. Every time there was a problem, you refused to deal with it and Max saw that, even when he was little. And he learnt never to complain, never to ask for help. That time you up and left, when he was five and we found out you were pregnant with Daniel, and I had no idea where you were for *two months*.'

Mum kind of gasps. Her face looks horrible, through the

keyhole. I look away, thinking about what Dad's just said. I remember that time. I remember being frightened until Daniel was born, because I thought she would leave again. But then he came and it felt like we had been a rickety table of three legs and he was the fourth, and then I knew Mum couldn't leave, because the baby would keep her with us. I felt safer.

'*Two months, Karen!*' Dad shouts. 'I thought you were never coming back. I was worried you were dead! I had police out looking for you!'

'I was exhausted—'

'Well, so was I! I had a full-time job, I had a five-year-old that wanted to know where his mum was . . .' Dad's voice breaks, and tears immediately come to my eyes. My dad's voice never breaks. He's as sure and steady as anything. 'Since then, you've been much better, Karen. You've found a way to cope, but it's to be so objective as to cast aside Max's feelings, his choice today, to make a choice you thought logically was for the best. Every time you have to deal with something, Karen, you move away, you create distance. It's almost instinctual. And Max has barely had a bad mood since you left for those two months, because he didn't want to rock the boat and make you leave again. Do you know what that's like to see in the eyes of a five-year-old?'

'I—'

'No, you bloody don't, because you weren't there. Since then he's just gone along with everyone else, done whatever he felt he had to to please you, to make you not leave again, and you don't know how hard that is for me to watch. You've made our son a pushover. He doesn't stand up for himself.'

'He's not a pushover, he's amicable!'

Dad sighs and I glare at him through the keyhole. *I'm not a pushover.* But then I think, and I turn around with my back to the door, and I wonder, *Am I?*

Dad speaks again, and sounds at the end of his tether. 'I'm so tired of it, Karen. Maybe I shouldn't have run for MP. Maybe I need to find a better balance. Maybe I stepped away from our home and our family, and that's my fault, but I was so . . . I just wanted to have it all. To be able to show the boys that you don't have to sacrifice to have a family.'

'Well, maybe you do,' Mum snaps sharply.

Silence.

They seem to both be exhausted from yelling. I look through the keyhole.

Mum suddenly smacks the table with her hand. 'We've always had this family story, Steve: "Karen's the bad guy, Karen's the fuck up". Well I've been trying to be the perfect wife, the perfect mother, I've dedicated my bloody life to trying to make up for being so useless when we were young and when we had Max, and I'm done. I'm *done*.'

She walks around the kitchen, picking up random things, looking like she's about to do something with them, then banging them down again on the counter like a mental person.

'I stand by my decision. It was a difficult one, but I think I did what was right. Don't tell me, Steve, don't *tell* me it would have been a good thing to let Max decide that he couldn't go through with it, to let him ruin his life.'

'I understand it was a hard decision, Karen.' Dad's voice is muffled. He's rubbing his face with one hand. 'I'm glad he felt he could talk to you. I'm sad he didn't feel he could turn to me.' Dad sniffs, and I realise he's wiping away tears. He says more quietly, 'I thought if we just showed Max that we accepted him, that we . . . But I can't believe you did that to him, Karen. And I cannot believe . . .' he breathes in and out rapidly, '. . . that you didn't tell me immediately about what he said, or tell me even when I'd got to the hospital. Because you knew what I'd say. You knew, didn't you?'

'Why did you come to the hospital?'

'That's not the point.'

'Don't you trust me?'

'Answer the fucking question!' Dad shouts. 'Tell me you knew!'

There is a silence, and then Mum speaks, and her voice is hard and quiet. 'Yes, I knew. I still think in the end it will be for the best. He's only sixteen. He has so much going for him.

There is no right in this situation,' she whimpers. 'I realise, Steve, that maybe Max won't forgive me for a long time, but he will forgive me. And I knew you'd probably never forgive me. And of course I didn't want that, because I love you, Steve, but . . .'

She trails off and there is silence for maybe half a minute. I peer through the keyhole. Mum stands with her hands leaning on the kitchen table on one side of it and Dad is opposite her, around the other side, sat down, arms folded, both of their faces dark and still.

'I'm just going to say what all parents know and never say. I love you, Steve, but I love Max more. And I did this for him. And I'm not sorry I did it.'

Then there is an even longer silence. Mum's face is ashen, tired and eerily dead. But she looks strong. Strong and used to bearing something.

My secrets, I think. My secrets are pulling this family apart. I slump down onto the floor by the door and thumb my lip.

'Well,' Dad's voice murmurs. 'Then there's nothing left to say, is there?'

'I'm going to go,' says Mum.

'To Leah's?' Dad asks.

'No. Leah and Edward have their hands full with Hunter. He's getting detention after detention at moment, cutting classes. I meant . . . maybe I should go somewhere . . . for a while.'

Then Mum whispers something that catches in her throat. I comprehend, 'I should stay at my sister's', at the end of her sentence.

I look back up through the keyhole. After her last word, she moves quickly, her head down, slipping carefully past Dad, scooping her keys off the counter into her handbag. She stands with her body facing him, not looking up from behind her hair. She's wearing her jeans, a green jumper and a tan leather jacket. Her lips look really pink and wet, and so do her cheeks. Her hair is all messy and looks dark blonde from the rain. She actually looks really pretty.

'I agree,' says Dad.

Mum raises her head, and her eyes are cold. 'Daniel's still at Leah's,' she says. 'I'll pick him up.'

'No,' says Dad. 'I'll do it.'

Mum looks as if she's about to say something. Then she shakes her head wearily and lets herself out. The back door shuts gently.

There is silence for a bit, then Dad puts his two massive hands over his face and lets out a big sob, carefully, trying to hold back, hold it in. He gets up slowly and stands very still. His hands go to his hips and he takes a few deep breaths. His stomach and big chest move in and out as he gasps. I've never, ever seen my dad cry.

I remember once, on Mum's birthday years ago, before Daniel was born, he got her this beautiful necklace. It was a heart, a gold heart, and she's worn it ever since. And she cried when she took it out the box and he said, 'For the love of my life.' I remember all the occasions when Dad seemed at all soft and they are all images of him and Mum. Him hugging her, him dancing clumsily with her, their wedding photos where he was looking at her like she was the most amazing thing in the world. Now he's thrown her out because of me. He picks up a tea towel and wipes his cheeks. Then he moves towards the door and I sit back from the keyhole and freeze.

Steve

I open the door to see where Max is. It's at times like these you need your kids most, to hold them in your arms.

I open the door, planning on heading for the stairs, but on the floor right in front of me is Max.

One look at him sets me off again. The same mop of yellow hair he's had since he was a baby. Little green eyes poking out from under it, wondering if I'm going to yell at him or whether he's going to get away with snooping. Little bugger.

He's not broad and bulky like me, but he's not thin either. I notice for the first time how much he's grown. I was right. It all goes by so fast. You always think of your kids as 'the kids'. I still imagine him small and wet from the bath and listening to a bedtime story in his pyjamas, even though he's sixteen and nearing a good five-foot-ten now. It doesn't matter to me.

I look at his little body, the one that Karen and I created, and I hunch over him, put my arms under his shoulders, kneel down in front of him and pull him up into a hug. I feel his hands on my back, and remember when they were little paws.

Max

I basically sleep for the entire weekend, go back to school on Monday, and throw up at school on Tuesday. I know I'm going to do it about five minutes before I do. It's a build-up of thoughts inside me that somehow creeps from my brain into my stomach. It's in a break between classes, and I'm walking towards the Geography block. Then I make a sudden right out of the main corridor and down the dead end where the loos are. I walk in and no one is there, so I go into a cubicle, put my bag down, lift the seat up and heave into the bowl. I puke up my breakfast and then I dry heave twice, but nothing else comes out. The remnants of a bagel float half-digested in the loo water. I wait a minute until I'm sure it has all gone and then I flush, walk to the sinks, wash my face, then go to Geography.

The entire time I'm thinking how I went to the hospital with something inside me and I came out alone, with nothing, as if nothing happened, with no choice or thought required from me. I'm a passive observer to the pain around me. I'm the fuse of the bomb. I don't even light myself. I don't choose when I go out. I don't explode. I just am.

After Geography, I go to the common room. When I walk in the door, Olivia and Marc are snogging. I make a sick noise and go over to the lockers to dump my books. Kerry is there. She's new.

'Hi,' she says, and smiles at me.

'Hi,' I say half-heartedly.

At first break, Marc and I went into town and got vodka and mixed it with orange, because it's going to be our last day of term soon, and it's nearly Christmas, so we thought, why not?

Now he thrusts it at me and we drink it all, going back and forth between us. I get drunk quicker because my stomach is empty. Carl refuses to join in because we have an exam later, even though it doesn't even count.

Then Marc suggests we play spin the bottle, winking at Olivia like, 'I can't wait to see you lezz up'.

I say no at first, but then I see Sylvie. She walks in the door right next to us. I turn away from her quickly.

'Hey, Sylvie,' Marc says. 'Do you want to play spin the bottle?'

My eyes flit over to her and I watch her from beneath my hair.

'No thanks,' she says to Marc, looking at me.

Marc shrugs and moves away to Olivia, leaving only Sylvie and me by the door.

Hey,' she says. 'Um, how are you?'

'Great,' I say. I'm embarrassed, trying to make a joke, but I lose faith halfway through and it comes out sulky.

She hesitates.

'I meant, do you know what you're gonna do?'

She looks slightly uncomfortable, and I think about how she reacted, how it was this big deal for her to have such a disgusting boyfriend.

'I had an operation on Friday,' I murmur in a low growl, then add sarcastically, 'So you don't have to worry about me anymore.'

She nods. 'I wondered . . . when you weren't in school. I'm so sorry, Max.'

I start walking away.

'Wait.' Sylvie catches my arm and I shrug her off. She looks flustered. 'Wait, Max! Are you OK?'

'I said I'm great.'

'Let's go somewhere we can talk,' she says, reasonably, moving towards the door. She clearly expects me to follow, like the little sheep I am.

'Forget it. It's over,' I say, meaning everything. That everything is over. 'So you can just go back to normal and I'll go back to whatever the fuck I am.'

'Shit. I didn't mean that "normal" thing I said on Thursday. I was just having a panic attack. I get them sometimes.'

'I feel so sorry for you,' I say coldly, and she stops talking abruptly. I look her in the eye, aiming at a defiant glare. 'Have you told anyone?'

'No.'

'Are you sure? Not even your mum?'

'No!'

My throat catches and I feel my face curling up miserably. 'Swear you won't.'

Sylvie frowns, watching me closely. 'Are you drunk?'

'Get lost,' I reply lamely. I walk over to the game dizzily.

Marc looks up at me and beckons me over. 'Come on, you twat.' When I sit down next to him, he says more quietly, 'What's up with Sylvie?'

I shake my head. 'Not going out anymore.'

I knew she couldn't cope, I think, taking the drink bottle from Marc. I knew it.

The real problem is me, anyway. Not her. I'm just tired of being in people's lives. I make everyone hate everyone else. Everyone thinks I'm disgusting. I am disgusting. I'm a catalyst for hate and confusion. I just show up and fuck up everything. Look at Mum and Dad. I'm weak and cowardly and I don't stand up for myself, just like Dad said. I'm weak.

I get paired up with the new girl, Kerry, in spin the bottle. We have to kiss in front of everyone. She grins afterwards.

'You're an incredible kisser,' she says.

Marc laughs. 'Practically every girl in our year knows that!'

Olivia looks over at me. It occurs to me that Marc might be jealous.

Good, I think bitterly.

'Max, it's you again,' Olivia says.

I look up. Kerry is giggling. The bottle has landed on me again, and we get off again.

The whole time Sylvie is watching and I feel bad, bad, bad. But at the same time I hate her. I hate everything that makes me remember.

Anyway. She's better off not liking me.

'Kerry's kind of . . . um . . . a player, Max,' says Maria, at the end of lunch, as we're walking to our lockers. 'I mean, seriously, she cheated on her last boyfriend at her old school loads. My brother told me. He's friends with a guy who goes there.'

'So?' I say.

'So, what about Sylvie? I thought you really liked her?'

I yank my bag out my locker really hard, so the whole row shakes. 'What about Sylvie?'

'You're totally drunk,' says Maria.

'So?' I ask, and laugh.

'You're an idiot,' Maria says, affectionately but firmly, giving me a sisterly hug. 'I dunno what's going on with you, but I'm here if you need to talk, OK?'

I rub my eyes and nod.

'OK, Max?'

'OK.' Maria shakes her head sadly at me and walks away. I hear her feet tap out of the common room and the door creaks shut. I don't look up as she leaves.

Then I feel pissed at myself because I'm being so horrible to everybody, but I feel like I can't stop, so I punch my locker really hard and hurt my hand. I look down and there's blood on my knuckles, and a dent in the locker door, so I get out of there before someones comes to see what the noise was.

Everything seems to be carrying on. Except Mum is staying with her sister, Auntie Cheryl, and her husband, Uncle Charlie. I think she thinks I hate her. It's half true.

She came back yesterday, on Sunday, to get some of her stuff. My aunt came with her. She clearly knew about everything that has been going on with me. I opened my bedroom door to see what was going on in Mum and Dad's room, because I could hear whispering and things being moved, and Cheryl was stood at the door to their room. She turned towards me, and her face fell into lines of sympathy.

'Oh, Max,' she said. It's an interesting thing about Mum, that she feels that, because I'm her kid, because I 'belong' to her, that she can make very personal decisions about my life, like who to tell my secrets to; when to come in my room without my permission and 'tidy up', i.e. mess with my stuff; whether to let surgeons operate on me when I've made it clear I don't want the operation.

I know exactly what I would have done if she had stopped the operation, and she would have got her way in the end. I would have ummed and ahhed about it, like I always do about any decision, tried to talk to her and Dad a bit more about it, then panicked and had it anyway. So it would have been exactly the same as before. I wouldn't have had the baby. I'd have been too scared and pathetic about how I felt, about wanting it a bit, about feeling so torn, worried about what everybody would think, and I would have freaked out and done what everyone wanted me to do. My body freaks me out, and hence . . . Hence, what? Hence I'm paralysed. I feel like nothing is ever going to change.

A bit later, Mum, again without my permission, pushed open the door to my room. When I saw her head peeking through, it took all my strength not to just jump off the bed and scream at her, shake her, hit her. She took away any control I have over my life. She took away my choice. Just like Hunter took away my control, my choices. Really, which one is worse? Just add her to the list of people who think they know what's best for me. It's almost full, with Hunter and all the doctors, but there's just room for her too.

'I don't want to see you,' I said immediately.

'Max,' she said. 'I'm your mother.'

'You're not me.'

'What?'

'Are you me?'

'Max,' she said, placatively.

'Fuck off saying my name like that! No! The answer is no! You're not me! So you don't know what it's like. You shouldn't choose for me, and you shouldn't come in my fucking room without knocking!' I shouted, barrelling towards the door. I shoved her out, and slammed it shut, narrowly missing her fingers.

'Max, please!' I heard her in tears on the other side of the door. 'Please come out.'

Her voice sounded lower to the ground. I heard her weeping, and then Cheryl's voice said softly, 'Come on, Kaz. He just needs some time, you said so yourself. Come on, love.'

Then I heard the sound of floorboards – my mother getting up – and they shuffled away on the carpet, into Mum and Dad's room, and shut the door.

I sat down against the wall next to the door and scratched my head back and forth until it hurt. Then I bit my knuckles until they hurt. You don't know why you're doing these things when you're doing them. It just feels like you're going crazy, that you have no control over what happens in your life or how you feel, and you have to do something to get the energy out, to get back in control. I took deep breaths, huffing them away. I sat on the floor and tightly held my knees with my palms, until I was calm again.

Sometimes when I need to let off steam, when I'm angry or upset or something, I play football. I've never been really good at letting out emotion. I've been thinking recently that Dad was right, that I don't like to rock the boat.

I remember Mum leaving when I was little, but I didn't know it was for two months. I guess the way I remembered it, it seemed like a few days to me. I was terrified she wasn't going to come back, and afterwards I used to get scared a lot when she left the house, even if she was just driving down to Hemingway to get the shopping. I would sit, totally still, in the window, imagining horrible things, imagining that she would die and never get home or know how much I loved her. I would whisper, 'Mummy, Mummy, Mummy', over and over again, like a little prayer. If I could just prove myself by being a good boy, by waiting for her, by not crying, by sitting quietly and whispersaying her name, then she would come back. I realise now that maybe this fear started after she left that time.

But Dad was wrong about one thing, because Mum is not really to blame, not alone. Really, I know I've always been scared of rocking the boat, because I always thought that being intersex was the thing that was difficult to cope with, and that if I piled anything else on top of that, everyone would stop loving me. Maybe my parents didn't talk to me about being intersex because they didn't want it to be an issue, just in the same way Hunter's parents were trying to do the right thing when they told him I was intersex when he was young. Maybe they thought by introducing him to it at a young age, he'd grow up OK with it. But you can start out with all the good intentions you like and still everything can go wrong. Hunter and I, we both got confused.

I wish I could let all this out by running onto a muddy field and kicking a ball about, but I'm not playing football until January. Doctor's orders. Marc and Carl think I had my appendix out. The teachers must know, though, mustn't they? It feels like my secrets are leaking out as the circle of people who know widens. Mum got a note from Archie and gave it to the school office. I watched it being handed over, one of the last things I did with Mum. It was white and folded and slipped into an envelope, twirling through the air, as Mum presented it to the head teacher. The head teacher looked at it, then back at me, shocked. Her face said, *Oh, that's why*.

Maybe I was just imagining it. I never asked Mum what the note said. I didn't say a word to her.

It was going to be my last day on Friday for the Christmas holidays anyway, but after getting drunk yesterday, I get up on Wednesday morning and I get dressed into my uniform, then I sit on the floor in my room with my bag, feeling like nothing, like crap, exhausted. I'm supposed to leave for the bus at ten past eight but I can't stand up. I physically can't. I feel so tired.

I think back to what Sylvie said, about only leaving, only letting go when you're done. I feel so done.

Dad comes in at half past eight. He says it's OK. That I don't have to go in if I don't want to.

He waits.

'Do you want to?' he asks.

I shake my head.

He goes downstairs. I think he's taken a day off work.

Lawrence and Debbie aren't here. No furious planning going on downstairs. Dad just sits in the living room.

At lunch he brings me tomato soup, like I'm sick. I don't feel like eating, but I eat it because I don't want him to feel bad. I'm such a hassle. I'm an emotional bomb for him and Mum now. I'm the child that, when they think about me, they think about what's beneath my pants, they think of me having sex with someone, some stranger. When they think of me they think of gross words like: 'genitalia', 'womb', 'phallus', 'gonads'. He's being so nice to me. I feel bad that I can't feel much for anyone right now. I feel bad that I don't feel worse that I know Dad is lonely without Mum.

I shrug, in my head. I get selfish.

We're all lonely, I think. I'm always going to be alone.

I watch movies, endless DVDs. I don't wash. My hair gets all greasy and looks almost light brown. I sit about in my boxers and a T-shirt. I lose a bit of weight.

It's Friday afternoon when one of the movies finishes, and I get up. I'm bored. I think my body wants to move. I think about maybe watching *Con Air* in the living room, like I did with Dad one night.

I stand up out of bed. I'm wearing a grey T-shirt and blue boxers. I look at myself in the mirror vaguely. I hate what I see now. I look rough, and dirty, and ambiguous. Not quite androgynous. It's not quite the right word. The right word is ambiguous. Once you're aware of something you see it everywhere. Like how I was thinking about red-haired girls this summer, when everything was normal, when nothing had gone irrevocably wrong, and I saw them everywhere.

My dick in my boxers is too obvious. I put on long cotton jogging trousers. My chest isn't big enough. I pull on a jumper. I sit on the floor and put on socks, because it's cold.

'Max!'

I wait.

'Max!'

I hear Dad coming upstairs. He opens the door and the bright light from the hallway makes me shield my eyes.

'Marc and Carl are here.'

'What time is it?'

'It's almost five in the afternoon. Aren't you going to open your curtains?'

I don't answer.

'I told them you're upset because your mum's moved out,' he says softly.

He never calls her Karen in front of me anymore. He used to call her Karen when he talked to us about her.

'You could go to the cinema with them. It's a Friday, have some fun.' He hesitates, then says gently, 'Just make a bit of an effort, Max.'

I scowl at him as Marc and Carl come up the stairs.

'Alright?' Marc says. 'They're doing a medley of Johnny Depp films at the cinema tonight. We're going to see *The Rum Diary*. It's on at six.'

I brush my hair out of my eyes. 'I'll shower,' I murmur.

Sylvie

I always take things too far down the road of brutal honesty. I've been with guys before who have told me bad stuff. When Toby told me about all the drugs he used to take I kept asking him and asking him all these questions, drawing the pain out bit by bit. I always want to know everything, every detail, because I feel then like it will be cathartic, I won't be scared of more pain, it'll be done. But every time I do that it spells the death of my relationships. After, Toby told me it just wasn't the same. I should just have not made Max tell me about the baby. But I prodded and poked.

It was everything at once that made me have the panic attack. Every fact was a blanket of heat and oppression that became a pile of blankets that smothered me. And I don't care if Max is a boy or a girl or not at all. I seriously don't care. I know Max. I know who he is. *What* he is is just a detail.

After he left I started crying because I felt like I couldn't say anything to anyone about it. I couldn't say anything to Mum or Dad, because it's a secret. I promised I'd keep it. I'm not that great at talking to my parents – they're both kind of academic and 'elsewhere' sometimes, but when I'm scared, or when there's a problem, generally I can go to them. But I can't talk to anyone about this. Then I realised that's probably how Max feels, but way worse.

He can't say anything to any of his friends. Marc and Carl would have a fit. The only people who know are his parents, and I think he doesn't want to talk to them about it because it would upset them. So I want to talk to him, but I don't know if I can handle it, being the only person he can talk to. That's why I had the panic attack in the first place. It's way too much for one person. I don't know what to do.

Max

On the way to the cinema, passing all the Christmas lights in town, I make an effort, like my dad says. I smile at stuff and Marc and Carl tell me about the game I missed on Saturday and the training I've missed all week. I smile and say, 'Great'.

'He doesn't want to hear about the game he couldn't play, does he? You dick,' Carl says to Marc. 'Tell him about Olivia.'

Carl looks over to Marc and he grins slyly, like they're both part of this pact, this cult that has access to secrets I'll never comprehend.

I'm sure that's me being paranoid, I think, and look away, straight ahead, then when Marc doesn't say anything, I ask, 'What about Olivia?'

Marc clears his throat and Carl says, 'She's his girlfriend now.'

'Oh,' I say casually, pulling the door to the cinema back for them.

'What happened with you and Sylvie?' Carl asks.

I join the queue for tickets. 'Didn't work out.'

We're practically alone in the cinema. I guess it's early. The 'Johnny Depp Medley' turns out to be a Hunter S. Thompson medley. They've already shown *Fear and Loathing in Las Vegas*, so we watch Johnny Depp faff about in Puerto Rico. When we're in the dark, I remember what it was like to kiss Olivia. I don't want to think about it, but it keeps creeping back into my mind. Then I think about kissing Sylvie. How she was warm and soft and had a loud laugh and groped me. How she smiled with the right side of her mouth only and joked all the time. I remember how her tongue flicked in and out of my mouth. I think about Sylvie's lips. I think about other girls I've kissed. I think about all of them.

I eat my popcorn. It tastes like cardboard.

One day, all kisses will be memories.

'Psst.' A guy in the front row is waving at us. There's a Christmas film on in the other auditorium, so it's just him, his friends and us in the showing. They come over. It's some guys from the sixth form college. I watch while Carl and Marc talk to them.

'What you think, Blondie?'

'Huh?'

The college guy laughs. 'Haven't you been listening? You've been staring at me the whole time I'm talking.'

'Nope.'

'No?'

Normally I would have been pseudo-aggressive back, but I can't be bothered. I shrug and turn back to the movie. 'Whatever.'

'Don't mind him,' says Marc jovially. 'He's had a shit week.'

'It's fifteen quid for one.'

'Nah, we're OK.'

'One what?' I ask.

The college guy turns to me. 'A joint, deafhead.'

He stares at me like it's some sort of challenge. I watch him back.

'Are you trying to stare me out or something, kid?' he says, and I laugh at him, and throw him fifteen quid. He gives me a plastic bag with a twisted-up cigarette in it.

'Serious?' says Marc. 'We're at the cinema.'

'What if we get caught?' Carl whispers. 'You can smell that stuff even with it not being lit.'

The college guys move off.

'So we say it was him.' I shrug petulantly. 'Whatever. Give me your lighter.'

'I don't smoke,' says Marc.

'Yeah but you always carry a lighter. Hand it over.'

I light the joint and suck in lightly.

Marc starts to giggle and takes it off me. He tries it too, and soon we're both slid way down in our seats, smothering laughter. Carl gets up and walks out.

350

Sometime during our chatting and giggling the movie ends.

'Shit!' Marc says. 'I totally didn't watch that.'

'The book was better.'

'There's a book?'

I give him a sideways look. 'You're kidding, right?'

Marc stands up. 'Come on, let's go to Pancake Café.'

'Nah, I'm staying here.'

'What?'

'I'm just gonna sit here for a bit.'

'Why? The people for the next film will be in soon.'

'I know.'

He falters. 'I want to go out. Olivia's going to be in town.'

'So go, Marc. We're not attached at the hip.'

'What's up with you?'

'Nothing.'

'You've been acting weird for two months.'

'I said nothing, Marc,' I hiss. 'Just fuck off.'

He waits for a moment. I watch the credits rolling. When I look over to my left, he's gone.

My buzz from the pot is turning into being irritated and melancholic again, especially with the cinema going quiet and dark.

The trailers start up for the next film, and people start walking in. I sink low into my chair and try not to meet anyone's eyes.

Max Walker, son of Stephen Walker, stoned in the cinema.

I wish I was more sorry that I'm not being an upstanding citizen, Mum, Dad, I say in my head. *But I guess being perfect didn't work out for me.*

My lips curl up and I almost sob in the cinema, but I hold it back and sigh, biting my lip hard to keep myself quiet. All I ever wanted was to be perfect. That sounds like a pretty big ask, but perfect means bland, inoffensive, likeable. I wanted other things too. I did want to stand out, be smart, be nice, but I tried so hard for those things that it wasn't really like I was asking anyone for them. Really what I wanted was to be something more than the sum of my male and female parts.

I concentrate on the screen in front of me. The first trailer is for an action movie that looks pretty cool. Then the second is for this arty film about this really horny guy who can't talk to women, but gets with loads anyway. It made me think of phalloplasty. It's an operation where they make your penis bigger. I remember when I was younger they said they could do it to me for free, on the NHS. I asked Dad about this the other day, when we were talking about operations. He had asked me if I still wanted the hysterectomy and all that shit. I said no. I had to come a long way to say that tiny fucking word, didn't I? But I asked him what had happened that time when I was offered the phalloplasty. He said I was near average size anyway, and that I could have lost all feeling in it if I'd had it done. I nodded, took one of the soy banana shakes out of the fridge and went up to my room again. I didn't know I could have lost *all* feeling down there.

There were so many other occasions I wanted to ask him about, but I was embarrassed. I wanted to ask about that night when I was thirteen, what the hormones did, why exactly the ovotestis was taken out. Instead I went up to my room and played *Sonic* on the old Sega, like I used to when I was little.

I think about what he said. How would I know if I was average size? The only hard one I've seen is Hunter's. Everybody's soft at urinals.

I shift about uncomfortably. My head's so full of the pot, it's like a fug of fog in my frontal lobe.

I'm ashamed of what I am and who I am, I think, looking at the back of the chair in front of me. *More who I am. What I did. What I let happen.*

I think about Sylvie and how, when you really like someone, you just want a few more minutes with them. You just want to talk to them a bit more. You just want to walk them home. Even if you know it won't work out, you just want to listen to them and watch them a bit more because they're so nice and they smell so good. What will happen after all the girls stop talking to me? What will happen after all the minutes are over?

I have tried not to think about it before. I wonder what other people do when no one will have sex with them. Just not have sex, maybe. Or, I guess, maybe that's why some people go to prostitutes.

But I could never be the type of person who has sex with prostitutes because I couldn't do that to someone. Prostitution is so sad. Wouldn't you just be thinking about the girl the whole time? What happened to her to make her feel like she could let people do that to her? Why does she have to do this for money?

I don't really feel like I'm from the right background to get into hiring prostitutes. All the people in films with issues a bit like mine (but not quite like mine, because I haven't seen any films about intersex people) have something weird in their background, like alcoholic parents, or people that didn't love them. They're outsiders. But I'm not an outsider. I'm from a loving, supportive family, in the centre of a good community. No matter what Mum and Dad have done over the course of my life, I know they did things because they loved me. Even Mum. Even the operation. Even when I was angry, and saying things to hurt her, and thinking bad things about her . . . I know really that she didn't do it for her. She did it because she thought it was the right thing to do to save me. I think about what she said to Dad. About how she loved me more than him. I feel like the worst person in the world for doing this to my parents. For splitting them up and tearing them apart from the inside, for making them have to choose between me and them, and then not even being particularly grateful to either of them. Not acting appreciative at all.

Anyway. Prostitutes. I couldn't just let someone inside me if I didn't like them, particularly not now I know how it feels, after Hunter. I can't believe that some of them like it. It must be horrible to have sex with someone you don't like. It must be completely blank. Just empty.

Like I feel now.

But I guess I don't know what I'll feel like when I'm older. I couldn't see myself doing that now, maybe, but think about when I'm old and in my thirties. That's fourteen years away. That's a long time. Oh my god. What about my forties? Fifties? *Sixties?*

What am I going to do when I get older? Will this emptiness just grow and grow? Will I never be able to have sex with people because they'll all be grossed out at the way I look, and then will I go to prostitutes, just once, at first, because I just want to do it once, to know what it feels like to be inside someone, to be cuddled up to someone, and then what if I go more and more, because I feel so empty without that feeling, now I know how it feels?

I shift uncomfortably in the cinema seat. There are more people in for this screening. The trailers are still rolling. I don't want to cry in front of them. I start to panic a little, and my breathing gets faster as I think. As I realise that I am going to be intersex my whole life. Years and years and decades, maybe for seventy years, I'll be like this. And, unless I find someone who doesn't mind having sex with me, I'm going to be alone all that time. I'll probably be alone all that time. Think. How difficult it is for people to find someone they love, who likes the same things as them, who has the same values, who wants the same things out of life, and then imagine adding to that the fact that they not only have to be OK with having sex with a hermaphrodite, they have to like it.

Without being a totally weird pervert, I add to myself.

My cheeks are so hot, and I look up, and the movie's started, and it's this sex scene.

I look up and look straight down again. I don't watch stuff like this. Because I don't want to know what I'm missing, what I'll always be missing. I look up. I see breasts.

I look down. I feel weird. I feel like I want to get out of the auditorium, but there are people on both sides of me in my row.

I look up. I try to imagine me, in a scene like this. But I can't.

I look down again.

I look up. They're properly mashing. I imagine Marc and Carl in a couple of years' – no, months' – time, able to do that,

354

talking about it with each other, sharing in-jokes that I don't get. And they see I don't get them and they drift away from me and we stop being friends. There's a lot of moaning going on. I blush. I wriggle. I put my hands in my lap and pick my fingernails, watching the figures on the screen, in the dark.

I stand up.

'Excuse me.'

People tut. I sniff my sleeve. I smell really, overpoweringly like weed.

'Excuse me.'

I shuffle past everyone and walk quickly to the door and out. There's a toilet and I go in it and lock the door. The light comes on automatically, and it's just us again, me and my reflection. I turn away from him.

The bathroom is marble. The sink is set back into the wall, on a marble bench. I lean against the wall, with the mirror on my right.

The thing is, Dad, I think. *I'm trying to hold it together. This is me trying. I really am trying.*

I look down at my Converse. My feet are too small. My hands are too small. Soon everything will be too small, and too delicate, and maybe I won't make the football squad when I go to sixth form college, and then university. Maybe I won't be the Max that rules the school. Maybe I'll just be a loner, a too-androgynous, too weak to play football, too frigid to kiss loner. Then one day I'll be nothing of my own. I'll be an uncle to Daniel's kids. I'll be a provider for Mum and Dad in their old age because I'll never have a family of my own. I'll be the person who always has time to be there for other people. That doesn't sound so bad. Settling for not so bad sounds OK. But, you know, it's hard when you tried so much to make life really good.

I look down at my purple Converse again. I look at my face sideways in the mirror. In the bathroom light, it's much darker. It's much older.

I turn away and choke. I start to cry. I haven't the whole week. I didn't even after the operation. I try to wipe it away and be quiet so no one outside will hear and come see what's wrong. I reach for the hand towels and try to fix my face.

I'm such a fucking idiot. I'm an idiot for thinking it could ever be OK. I'm an idiot for thinking that if I just stayed in fucking bed I could forget it, and everything would go away. I'm a stupid idiot.

Sylvie

It wasn't my idea to go out tonight, but Dad wants me to get out and meet other people my own age. I think he's not happy about me having all older boyfriends. He doesn't know about Max.

'She should get out and have fun and make friends,' he said, turning to Mum. 'Shouldn't she?'

Mum shrugged. 'Ah, she's fine. I like her being a weird loner.'

'Thanks for the help,' said Dad.

Still, Carla Hollis had rung the house, asked if I wanted to come to the Town Hall, where everyone in Hemingway hangs out. It's basically a club. Kind of. There's a lot of crap metal played there, but some good rock and lighter stuff. It's not that great, but it's OK. She was being nice because I'd been upset at school during Games, and she'd heard through Emma (somehow Emma knows everything) that Max and I had broken up.

So I got dressed up kind of *Girl With The Dragon Tattoo*-y goth.

As I head out, I say bye to Mum and Dad, and Mum says, 'You look cool', just as Dad says, 'You look terrifying.'

Max

Outside the cinema I see Marc and the group of guys. They call me over and I feel like I'm walking into a different world as I cross the road to be with them. We head for the Town Hall, which is a Friday night club for sixteen-to twenty-one-year-olds, where local bands play. We hang out with the older guys from the cinema, who are complete wankers but think they're cool. They stink of pot. But then so do I. Everybody gets drunk.

Kerry is there.

She cuddles up to me in the club. She starts kissing my neck. I get drunk. Marc tells me he's had sex with Olivia. I get more drunk. I can hardly walk. Kerry pulls me outside. She pushes me against the wall and kisses me. I kiss her back. She puts my hand under her skirt. I touch her.

Then she unzips my jeans and slips her fingers between my fly.

'I'm on the pill,' she whispers.

I shake my head. She shrugs and pulls a condom out of the mobile phone pocket of her parka.

'No.' I shake my head, pulling away. 'Sorry.'

I practically run back inside.

As soon as I'm back in the dark hall, I see Hunter by the bar. The light there illuminates his face. He sees me and stares at me. I feel his dark eyes on my neck even when I turn away. I feel him walking up to me.

'Hey!' he says, loudly over the music. I face him. 'My sources tell me you just went outside like five minutes ago with Kerry Duncan. I guess you don't take that long, hey?' He laughs.

I shrug, look through him, look around him. There is a group of girls lined up against the wall. They are all looking at him like they fancy him. Some of them are looking at me the same way. Hunter follows my eyes and winks at them. He's dark and foxy. I'm blond and angelic. One of them giggles and waves at us both. I feel a lump rising in my throat.

Hunter turns back to me, licks his lips, grins darkly.

'Wonder what they're imagining,' he says, leaning in to me, his breath hot on my neck. His lips brush my skin and he pulls back and grins.

'I had to have an abortion,' I mumble.

'What?' He frowns. I guess he can't hear me over the music.

'Hey, Hunter,' Kelly Morez calls, walking past us.

'Hi,' Hunter says dismissively.

I shake my head, turning away.

'Max!' he yells, grabbing at my jacket, then at my waist to turn me around. 'What did you say?'

'Get away from me,' I say, feeling my eyes water. 'I hate you.'

'What's wrong?' he says, holding my coat.

'Pregnant,' I drunkenly mutter.

'Huh?' He looks at my stomach, then back to my face.

'I got rid of it.' I wipe tears from my face with my sleeve and push him off feebly.

Hunter looks confused. 'You what?'

I shake my head. He tries to grab me again but I push him off, crying. 'Get away from me.'

I walk out the hall.

'Wait,' Hunter calls, grabbing my arm and pulling me around the side of the hall, where Kerry and I were minutes before. 'What's wrong? Are you OK?'

'You don't care!' I almost wail. 'You just took what you wanted!'

'What the fuck?' he says. 'Look, calm down.' He puts his arms around me and it's like when we were kids again and he'd hug me if I fell over or lift me up when I was too small to climb onto the climbing frame with him. 'Calm down,' he says soothingly.

'People will see,' I say, trying to shrug him off. 'They'll write about me. Because of Dad.'

'There's no one here, Max. Look around,' he says. He's right. There's no one here but us.

I sniff and wipe my face. I'm properly crying, wiping tears away from my cheeks as he stands with his arm around my waist and watches me.

'What were you saying? In the hall?' Hunter asks.

I drop my hands to my side and sigh deeply and he uses his thumb to wipe under my eyes. I let him, feeling helpless again, feeling pinned by his authority in our friendship.

'No!' I say, thinking about this, batting his hand away. 'Get off!'

He steps back, holding his hands out and I shrink down to the ground, crouching, my back against the wall. 'You knocked me up,' I say, because it's the least crazy, embarrassing way I can say it. Because it's the phrase that least makes me want to cry.

'What?' Hunter says. 'How is that possible?'

'I'm half and half, you dumb shit!' I say, checking to see no one's here before I do. 'What did you think would happen?'

'Max . . .' Hunter sinks to the ground, kneeling in the mud and grass. He reaches out and puts his hands on my knees, as if to steady himself. 'Shit, Max, I'm . . . I'm sorry, OK? Shit. What are you gonna do? Are you gonna have it?'

I shake my head. 'It's gone. I . . . They made me get rid of it,' I mumble.

He looks off to the side. 'Fuck. I didn't mean to hurt you. I'm sorry.' He puts his arms around me. 'I just lost control, alright? I didn't mean . . . I thought that you . . . Max, please don't hate me, I'm so sorry.'

I'm frozen in a ball. I can feel Hunter's arms around me, his head leant against mine, but I ignore him, instead thinking about everything I've lost over the past few months. I feel his hands running down my back, stroking me. I feel helpless and trapped again. My fault. I shouldn't have come here. I shouldn't have got drunk.

I will never again be this vulnerable, I promise myself.

'Max, look at me,' he commands.

My head rises, despite myself. 'What?' I say.

Then, angry at myself again, I push his arms off me and stand up. He stands too and moves closer to me.

'I really never meant to hurt you,' Hunter explains. 'I thought you'd like it and . . . come round to seeing stuff my way. I've always . . . you've always been . . .' He searches for the right words. 'Think of how much fun we've had together over the years. Don't you want that? Don't you want to be best friends?' His hand brushes a tear off my cheek. 'Do you want to always be alone?'

I sniff.

'Do you want to always be alone?' Hunter repeats.

His dark eyes are black in the starlight. He moves towards me, his hands icy on my skin. His fingers brush my jaw on either side and I realise I'm paralysed again, and drunkenly swear and shout at my body inside my head.

'Look, if you can get over this . . . you don't have to be alone. We were so good together. I've always been in love with you,' Hunter whispers, his tone firm but almost shy. 'You don't want to be lonely, Max. It's horrible.'

His fingers reach the back of my head and pull me towards him. Our lips meet, and he kisses me softly.

Then I think about being alone and, just for a moment, I kiss him back.

But as we kiss, I also put my hand to his chest. I shove him off me. He falls backwards onto the dirt. I walk towards him and lean over him.

'You are a fucking nasty piece of work,' I hiss, and he looks at me like I'm crazy, then he grins, a grin halfway between malicious and as miserable as I feel, and then he makes a kiss noise at me. I take all the saliva I have worked up from our kiss and I get it in the front of my mouth and I spit at him.

Then something catches my peripheral vision, and I look up, and Sylvie Clark is standing there watching us.

I walk away from Hunter towards her, then I walk past her. 'Max!' Sylvie calls after me. 'Don't you want to talk?'

I don't turn around. *No, I don't want to talk, Sylvie. I don't want another friend. I wanted a girlfriend. I wanted all of you.*

I trudge past the houses, then down the country road towards home. It's freezing and I can't stop the salt rolling down my cheeks.

When I get home it's almost midnight. I let myself in with my key and go straight to my bedroom, then stand in the middle of the room, wondering what to do. What's my next move? Where can I go from here?

I find I can't cry anymore, so I just hate myself and feel drunk and dizzy and can't sleep. It's the night before Christmas Eve.

Daniel

It's the night before Christmas Eve. My brother came into my room tonight. He came in without me knowing. I was asleep. Then I wake up because there is a noise and when I look up it is Max. My light is on and the TV stack is shaking like he has just bumped into it.

'Sorry,' he says in a voice like his mouth is full.

'You've been even more upset lately,' I tell him.

'Yeah,' he says.

'I wasn't asking, I was saying,' I say.

He stands there and sways a bit.

'Do you want to play Top Trumps Dinosaurs?'

Max frowns and seems dizzy. 'Not right now.'

'I mean when I get them for Christmas, silly.'

'Oh, no.'

'Why oh no? Don't you want to play?'

'No, I mean. I mean, yeah, I'll play. Sorry Daniel.'

'OK.'

'Listen, Daniel,' Max says, and he comes up close to me and puts his arms around me.

'You smell funny,' I say.

'Listen,' he says very quietly and hugs me very tightly. 'I love you and I'm sorry for being a bad brother. I wish you just had a brother. A good brother. A normal brother. I wish it was simple.'

'Don't be sad, Max.'

'I'm really sorry.'

'I know, Max,' I say and I look at his face. 'I think you're just tired. Why don't you go to sleep here?'

He hesitates. 'No. I'll go in my own bed. I'm cold. I'm probably just tired. You're right.'

Max

I used to feel like I wanted to be somebody special. Now I just wish I could go back, and aim to be boring, uninteresting, normal.

It takes strength to be proud of yourself and to accept yourself when you know that you have something out of the ordinary about you. I had that strength. I had the solid foundation of a happy home, a good upbringing, a family that loved each other. We knew, collectively, where we were going. We were on the same page about who we were and how we dealt with things.

But we weren't as strong as we thought. We thought we'd been tested, and we hadn't.

Now I'm too tired and scared to say anything positive, to be proud of who I am, to be a good big brother to Daniel, to be anything but indifferent. I don't believe in anything I used to believe in anymore. Growing up, you believe the friends you have are good people, you believe your parents are always right, you believe that when the hard times come, you'll know what to do, you'll get through it, you'll be the hero.

But then the bad things happen and everybody lets everybody else down. And you realise that old friends can be bad people. Your mum and dad can't fix everything. You're not the hero you thought you were. It was just that you hadn't had anything that difficult to deal with yet, so you didn't know that you were really the coward. That you were really weak. No. I don't believe in the things I used to believe anymore.

I already have apathy about everything surface-deep, and everything deeper is changing for the worse and it's my fault: Mum, Dad, Sylvie, Daniel, all of it. I used to think I wasn't trying at all to be the best brother, the best son, the best footballer, the best friend. Now I realise I was trying really hard. I'm starting to understand that attempting to be perfect has been the goal of my life. Our lives. Attempting to be this fault-free, smiling person in this loving, happy family that fits so perfectly in this pretty, inoffensive little town. What was so bad about that goal, after all? Only that I couldn't do it. That I let everybody down. I've been so down about it, so depressed thinking about all the balls I was trying to juggle that I've dropped, and now the cogs are turning towards total apathy about it all, everything, and all I can think is that I am a shell of a human being. I'm a pushover. I'm to blame.

It's not Hunter's fault that I didn't push him off me, and it's not Mum's fault that I didn't stop the abortion before that last second. I guess I wouldn't have kept it, but I can't help thinking that I might have, if things were a little different, because I've spent so much time recently thinking about it and feeling sorry for it, and crying over it. Because it wasn't the poor baby's fault how it was conceived, no more than it's my fault that I'm intersex.

But it is my fault, how I've reacted to my diagnosis, how I've dealt with it. Who I've become.

It was my turn to make the hard decisions. I had to count on me and me alone to hold my life and my family together. But I let all the voices get too loud and I didn't listen to my own voice, that central thing at the heart of me that was beating like a drum, insistent, like falling rain on a window, saying that I should stop, give myself time, that I shouldn't just do what everyone else said, that I should fight back and be who I am rather than who everybody else wanted me to be. I'm not the hero boyfriend Sylvie deserves. I'm not the hero big brother Daniel needs. I'm not the perfect son my parents wanted. I'm not the champion, or the parent the baby needed.

I'm weak and I'm scared and I'm tired. I'm a coward. I left things unsaid for too long and now it's too late. I left a huge decision on Mum and then blamed her for it, when it wasn't her responsibility. I should have said something earlier. I should have done something.

It doesn't matter if I think like a boy or a girl. It doesn't matter anymore if I'm either or both or neither. All that shit seems so petty and immaterial now. There's so little difference between one human being and the next, it's just hypotheses, human ideas about life and the world and words, that mean nothing; about definitions that mean nothing to the earth, to nature, to the universe. Boys and girls and intersex people and me – we're just ideas, and when we're dead, the ideas will go with us. It all means nothing. But I was so self-absorbed with it all, so absorbed with being this object that Hunter made me, this thing, so absorbed with me, me, me, intent on closing my eyes to everything and not thinking for a second, just doing, just getting rid of the problem of me, acting like a victim, playing my role. I got rid of the wrong thing. I got rid of my dignity. I got rid of my autonomy. I deserve to be alone. I deserve for everybody to know what I am. Who I am. It doesn't matter anymore.

Now I can't stop thinking. I can't stop thinking that I let everybody down. I let Dad down. I let Mum down. I let Sylvie down. I let Daniel down. I let me down. I let the baby down. And for that I'll always be alone. I'll always be ashamed. I'll always be a coward.

Steve

I'd like to say it's a sixth sense that makes me knock gently on Max's door at two in the morning, but it isn't. I'm not like Karen in that way. I just worry about him all the time now. So I'm still worrying about Max when I knock on his door. I heard him walk up the stairs but he didn't say hi, so I didn't bother him. Maybe he didn't notice me. Debbie and Lawrence have been here for a meeting all evening, but since they left I've been in the living room, getting the house ready for Christmas, putting out some of the decorations, finally getting round to putting lights over the bannisters on the stairs. I did everything Karen used to do. The cards on bunting around the room, the evergreen plants on the mantelpiece, the berries everywhere. I wrapped some of the presents and put them under the tree. I'll put the big ones down there on Christmas morning. I'm terrible at anything to do with a stove, so I tried to buy mince pies off Nancy down the road but she insisted on giving them to me.

Everybody knows Karen is not living with us anymore, of course, even though we tried to keep it a secret. I don't know how they know. I've not told anyone. Since people found out, a number of women have come up to me. I was chopping wood in the front drive yesterday and Emily Forner pulled over to offer her condolences. It's . . . uncomfortable. They don't understand that I'm not not taken. I'm in love with Karen. I couldn't love anyone else. But this isn't about love. It's about principles.

I scratch my hair and yawn. Lots of late nights recently. Lawrence and Debbie have been coming for an hour or two after Max goes to sleep, just to talk everything through. Lawrence knows I'm withdrawing my candidacy. I'm having Debbie sort out everything we've worked on before we tell her. Don't want to make her feel terrible or take away her pay right before

Christmas. I'll keep her on as an assistant until she finds a new placement. After they leave every evening, I have the strangest feeling: like I'm shaking with energy and sadness. I sit up late into the night, sipping on a malt.

Tonight I put the stockings on the mantel and got all the church candles out of storage. I lit everything downstairs, to see how it looked. I fixed the fairy lights, put them on. It was all lit up like Santa's Grotto. I thought I'd go upstairs, wake Daniel up, give him a treat. But at the top of the stairs I found I really wanted to see Max. See him having fun again. See him smiling.

So I tap on the door softly with my knuckle.

'Max?'

I knock again, then enter. At first I think he's wide awake, but the way he's propped up against the wall is wrong.

'What's wrong with Max?'

I turn around. Daniel's standing in the doorway in his blue pyjamas, looking at Max.

'Daniel, go to your room.'

'I'm worried.'

'Go to your room.'

'But—'

'Go to your room, *now!*'

I hear Daniel scramble away, and I stride towards Max. He's cuddled into the wall with his hoodie over his hair, his arms curled up, his chin resting on his hands. His skin is pale and looks moist. I take one arm and shake him urgently. The hoodie is soft and warm, but when I take his hand it's cold.

'Dad?'

Daniel is behind me, the phone outstretched in his hand.

'I called nine-nine-nine.'

THREE WEEKS, THREE DAYS LATER

Sylvie

Now we're doing our mock exams we're granted town privileges. So the usual group wanders into town to buy strawberry laces and I trail after them, bored out of my mind, composing lines of poetry I scribble on my year planner, wishing I had a best friend who got me.

Emma *et al* have forgotten about the whole me threatening to tell everyone Emma had anal sex because she was spreading that rumour about Max thing, in the hope that I'll talk to them at some point about what happened. I just wander a little behind them, writing. I walk about more on my own now. I don't mind being alone. I used to be scared, but now I guess I'm growing up. I realise that there isn't any use for fear. If you panic, it doesn't get you anywhere. You just lose people and opportunities and the chance to get what you want.

I've been bunking off a little bit recently, but only when I have lessons where I won't learn anything. That's proving to be about fifty per cent of school hours, so I've made it my new mission to study the history of poetry, all the good, old poets, from the Greeks right through to the contemporary spoken word artists. My favourite so far is Edna St Vincent Millay.

I'm developing my style in my poetry. I'm not a rap person. I love it, but that's just not what I do. I was trying to steer my style towards rapped spoken word but I decided, in the end, to just listen to what came out of my head. That ended up being a lot of lyrics. Song-style lyrics. Maybe I'll become a singer like Debbie Harry from Blondie. I love that band.

The lyrics have a lot of emphasis on rhythm, and are kind of obvious in some ways, but it's instinctual. I just write the way I talk, and it seems to come out like that. I got a new desktop Apple Mac for Christmas, so I've started to sing my poems into GarageBand as I write them as well. It's been helping. I can type almost as quick as I can think, so I can listen to the words in my head while I write them, and concentrate on getting the exact structure down, just as it came from my brain.

It's funny, too, how the very best poems I've written seem to already exist in the air around me. I don't have to try to write, or think about what's going on in my life. I just have to listen, and if I listen carefully enough, I'll hear a poem that already exists, and my body will act as a channel for it, from my ears to my brain, through my fingers, to the page.

I think of it as listening to my inner voice. Maybe it's the me that's deep inside me; maybe it's outside me in my emotions and relationships and interaction with the world. It could be both. It could be neither. What matters is that I get some sort of truth out of it. Out of the whispering, beating and pulsing come little poems that fly onto the screen and spit out of my printer.

I think that was the problem with Max, now I've fit some pieces of the puzzle together.

Max didn't listen to his inner voice. I think there were too many voices telling him what to do, if you ask me. If I got pregnant now, would I keep it? Maybe, because I love kids, but maybe not, because I could have them any time, because I'd want to be able to support kids financially before I had them, because I'd want to be with the father. But if I was Max? If I couldn't just have a kid at any time? If this could be my only chance, because I was into girls, but had the reproductive system of a girl too? If I could never be with the father anyway, if all I wanted to do was be a good person?

We're sixteen. I don't want to know that there are choices that are that tough to make in the world, and I bet Max didn't either. One good thing about being sixteen is that you're supposed to come down on the side of optimism, of naivety and hope, and for Max, that's not a reality anymore.

We talked at his brother's birthday about kids. Just a bit. Max said more than anything he wanted to be a hero, for his little brother, for if he ever had kids, if he adopted. It seemed funny to me at the time, that he mentioned adopting. It's not something you think about. But I guess he didn't think he could ever have kids biologically then. He said he wanted to be a good person and do right by people, and that he didn't really care what he did for a career as long as he could play football, run around outside, and be around kids. Daniel came up to him then. Max said he was his best bud. They high-fived. Max laughed.

Yeah. He didn't know then.

So maybe he would have had it, if he could have chosen. But you make your choices, whether they're your own or made because other people pushed you to. Reasons are reasons. They're not excuses.

Everyone has heard, one way or another, about the Walkers. Not about the baby, or the fact that Max is intersex, but about what he did. I don't know who found out first. The papers reported it, and said their source was from inside the hospital. People are vultures. They'll find a way to get secrets out. It's probably just a matter of time before everyone finds out the rest.

Everyone keeps looking at me like I know something. I haven't said anything about why he did it. Emma and the others are waiting for me to spill, but I won't.

Max's mum came round to my house and I told her I knew about the baby. She didn't know Max had told me. Mrs Walker said she remembered me from the Halloween party, and that Max had really liked me. She wanted me to know that she was certain he really liked me, and she said he wouldn't have meant to be mean to me and that he didn't want to break up with me. Max's mum said she didn't want me to think of him as a mean person, that Max wouldn't want that. She came round because she wanted me to know that. She said I had been with him the night before the operation. She also said that I was the last person to talk to him on the night he did it, apart from his brother. That's not totally true. I don't think she knows that he talked to Hunter, or that Max never really spoke to me.

Her coming round was a bit insensitive to Max, I guess, but really I don't know what I'd do if I was a mum in that situation. I understand she didn't want me to hate him.

I wonder if he hated her. If he hated everybody when he did it. When he took all those painkillers. I wonder how she feels.

I wonder if he was scared. Not scared to die, but scared to live. I wonder if he thought no one would ever love him. He thought the idea of him being intersex put me off. I tried to tell him I couldn't care less, but I guess I didn't try hard enough. I wonder if he was scared of it getting out, of people knowing.

The only other person who knows everything right now is Hunter.

Hunter came up to me about a week ago. He spotted me across the town centre on a lunch break. I saw him coming. I was sat on a bench, alone, reading a book.

He came up to me in the periphery of my vision, a dark shape moving towards me steadily. He asked me about Max. I said I didn't have anything to say to him.

'I don't have anything to say to you. Go away.'

He sat down next to me, grinning at me. I wanted to smack him.

'Weren't you Max's girlfriend?'

'Fuck off. It's no business of yours.'

'You're pretty aggressive. I was just asking. Max's mum told mine what he did, 'cause they're best friends, and then I saw it on the news,' he added quietly. 'I just wondered if you knew anything.'

'I know everything.'

'Bet you don't.'

'I know what you did to him and the abortion and him being intersex.'

He gaped at me.

We sat in silence for a bit.

'You haven't told anyone, have you?' he said.

'No,' I said.

'Did Max tell you?'

'He told me most stuff.'

'Did he tell you about us?'

I put down my book and turned to him. 'Firstly, he didn't tell me your name, but I realised when I saw you at the Town Hall together. Secondly, Hunter, there is no "us" in the you and Max sense. He hated you. You forced yourself on him and he was very, very upset. Do you understand?'

'I was just asking if you knew anything else, you don't have to get—'

I cut him off. 'You really think I would share anything with you? You're not a part of this story, Hunter. You're not in the loop. Leave it alone.'

'I was in the loop for years before you came along,' he growled bitterly. He wiped his eyes with his sleeve but I couldn't see any tears.

'And now you're not.'

He seemed to be about to say something, then reconsidered it, stood up slowly and put his hands in his pockets. He started to walk away, then turned back and watched me for a while, waiting for me to look up.

'You think I don't care,' he said.

I kept my eyes studiously on my book and didn't reply. When I eventually looked up, he was gone.

Max's dad was on TV the other day, giving his resignation from his current office and stepping out of the race for Member of Parliament. Obviously he didn't say the real reason why. He didn't take any questions. He just said he was needed at home. He looked really nice, and genuine, and sad.

Max's mum has moved out. That's been spread around too. Everybody knows now.

I try not to think about it, but I guess I do a lot. I miss Max all the time.

As I walk through the car park behind Waitrose, on the way to the bakery with Emma, Laura and the rest of my halfway friends, I see him alone, leant against the little brick bridge over the dyke. He's pulling a sandwich apart with equal parts acute concentration and tired misery: the kind where you don't cry, you just look mean-spirited.

I watch him drop the packaging into the bin beside him. Then he peels the top piece of bread off the sandwich and puts the rest on the bridge while he tears bits off it and throws them to the ducks. I hear loud quacking.

Once he's done with that piece of bread he peels off what looks like ham and cheese from the other piece of bread. The sandwich filling sticks together, held by that disgusting industrial-strength mayonnaise you get in supermarket sandwiches, and we both look at it dubiously before Max drops it into the bin. He turns to the other triangle of sandwich, peels off the top slice of bread, and removes a similarly gross filling. It flies unceremoniously into the bin.

The girls are walking in two groups, one behind the other. The first must have hit his peripheral vision, because he looks across at them, squinting in the sunlight as if he's searching for somebody, wiping his hand absent-mindedly on his jacket. Then his head drops and his chick-yellow hair shakes as Maria calls over to him. Then he sort of goes to look up, but decides against it, pretending to ignore her as if he hasn't heard her, and he turns back towards the bridge. With one hand, pink with cold, he picks up the three slices of buttered bread left and trudges down the bump in the ground the bridge is on and around behind the bridge, to the muddy bank of the dyke, where the ducks are all quacking like an insane choir and we can't see him anymore.

I continue tramping after the girls.

I look over the bridge and see a bit of bread fly in the air then fall to the water, as a roar of arguing quacks peaks and then dies down.

The thing is, sometimes you have to be brave and say who you are and how you feel. Even if you don't know how you're going to do it. You just have to take a deep breath, and decide to start.

I sigh, steel myself and slyly duck (no pun intended) out of the group.

'Don't do it, Sylvie!' Emma calls after me.

Laura, beside her, murmurs, 'OMG.'

'He's totally gone off the rails,' Emma tuts condescendingly. 'Did you hear he practically did it with the new girl behind the town hall?'

I turn back as I'm walking away and flip her off. Emma shakes her head at me, like how juvenile am I, with a big old crush on Max Walker. I don't care anymore. I don't care about any of them. I don't care about any of it – the intersex stuff, the Hunter stuff, the baby stuff. I only care about Max.

I trudge down the little hill and stand above him, higher up the bank. Max is dropping bread near his feet and watching as the ducks come up to him and snatch it suspiciously. He stays very still, so as not to disturb them. When he hears the squelching of my shoes in the mud, he looks up.

'Hello,' I say, emboldened by the vision of myself as a shining knight come to save the poor little maiden. But then I think, *Oh, shit, what if he still hates me?*

'Hi, Sylvie,' Max says quietly.

'So, how's it going?'

I'm trying to be conciliatory but because I've drawn in my breath to 'steel myself', my speech is coming out in little brusque spurts. Max's face reacts to this by becoming even more miserably sober and unmoving. He looks at the ducks and sort of gestures with his bread, like, 'I'm feeding ducks, which is neither really joyous nor terrible', and he speaks, his mouth barely opening, and shrugs.

'Alright.'

I walk down until I'm standing beside him, in the soppy mud. It sucks at my shoes and a goose quacks alarmingly at me.

'Hunter came to talk to me the other week.'

He looks worriedly at me. 'What did he say?'

'He just wanted to know how you were. Don't worry, I told him it was none of his business.'

'Oh,' he says, turning back to the ducks miserably. 'Thanks.'

He thumbs the bread.

'I know he was the one who . . .' I say.

'Yeah, I guessed you had figured it out.'

'Yeah.'

He doesn't look at me or say anything further, and I hesitate. I start to walk away, sensing that he wants to be alone, but then, very quietly, so I almost don't hear at first, he speaks.

'I'm sorry about everything, Sylvie. Like kissing Kerry. It was a huge mistake. And I'm sorry for like . . . stuff I said, and . . . you know what I mean.'

I nod.

'You can't keep ignoring me at school,' I say.

He shakes his head. 'I don't know what to say to you. I didn't think you'd want to speak to me.'

'That's crazy, why wouldn't I want to speak to you?'

He shrugs. 'Didn't think you'd want to get involved. Everything's so complicated.'

There's a silence. Max throws another bit of bread at a mallard.

'I don't think it's complicated. It's pretty simple, really, isn't it? Hunter's a bad person who did something horrible to you. You were just trying to make sense of it.'

Max looks at me out the corner of his eye, like he's not sure what I'm saying. Then he looks down at the ducks again.

'I don't know.' He studies the crust of the bread that he's holding. 'I'm not sure.'

'Max . . .' I falter. 'Aren't you going to go to the police?'

Max shakes his head.

'It would kill my mum and dad,' Max mumbles. 'Mum's not living with us at the moment. They'd have to see it go through the courts. I don't want people to know. Besides, I'm scared of Hunter. I do anything he says, pretty much. I'm a pushover.'

'You're not a pushover.'

'Yes I am. I let everyone tell me what to do and I don't stand up for myself or ever take responsibility. The only reason I took those . . .'

'The pills?'

'Yeah. The only reason was because I just wanted to take

376

back control. I wanted to make a decision, even if it was just for things to stop.'

'You're not a pushover,' I whisper sadly. 'Do you . . . do you still want things to stop?'

Max looks at me. 'I was just drunk, Sylvie. I wouldn't have done it otherwise.'

I nod. 'Why are you so scared of Hunter?'

'He's just . . . I don't know. The way he acts, like he's in charge, like he owns me. He's always acted that way and I've always just done what he says. I just think . . .'

'What?'

'If you can fuck people and overpower them and there's no chance you'll end up hurt, then you're feared, and if you can't, you're vulnerable and you have to fear people.'

'That's . . . pessimistic. Doing stuff out of fear is always pessimistic.'

'I dunno. I've had a lot of time to think.'

'You missed the mocks.'

He shakes his head. 'I had to take them the same day you guys did, but on my own, later.'

'How did you do?'

'Pretty shit. Dad's not happy.'

'I guess you've never done shit at anything before, right?'

'Yep, I'm lowering all their expectations.'

We both look at the ripples on the water and watch a coot fight with a moorhen for some of Max's crust.

'So,' I say. 'If you can both do people and be done, what do you do?'

'I don't know.' He thinks. 'Accept that you're a bit of both, I guess. Or that you're neither.'

'Or just be you. What does it matter?'

'I guess. The bit beneath your heart,' he mutters, with a wry grin.

'Huh?'

'Something my wise little brother said.' Max hands me a bit of bread and gives me the first real look of the day. His eyes flit from my hair to my eyes, to my chin and he looks away shyly.

We both pull off bread and try and feed it to a little duck who isn't getting any because the bigger ones are faster and meaner.

'You should go to the police,' I say quietly. 'What Hunter did was wrong.'

'I just can't.'

'OK,' I murmur.

'Can we talk about something else, Sylvie?' Max looks up at me. 'Just, like . . . all everybody talks to me about at the moment is this stuff. Not specifically this stuff but . . . you know.'

'Yeah, OK.' I nod. 'Sooo . . . you know there's this half-guy I like?'

I see a tweak of a smile appear on Max's face. 'Really?'

'Yeah, he's like a suicidal wackjob, but blond and pretty with a nice arse, so you can kind of get past the screwed-up-ness.'

Max laughs, a giggle of hilarity. It's good to hear. His face lights up, just for a moment, but it's there – that familiar blast of sunshine. He pulls the last bit of crust apart and chucks both pieces into the water. Then he puts his hands in his pockets and murmurs, 'Kook.'

Archie

There have been many things that have gone through my mind since Max came in to see me in September last year, about being intersex, gender, my own ideology, and the ideology of my profession towards gender and intersexuality. We thought we understood gender – the idea of men and women as finite concepts with boundaries between each other, but lately I have come to understand that we are only just beginning to comprehend what 'gender' is, what it means to be allocated a certain gender, how much that informs the person a child becomes, and what happens when we don't talk about gender as a malleable thing, when we shy away from discussing gender with children and teenagers and even adults. Dealing with trans individuals in the clinic did not prepare me for dealing with Max, because being one gender and wanting to be another is a completely different thing, perhaps even the opposite, of feeling, as perhaps Max does, OK as you are, but forced to choose. As a doctor, most of the health issues we work with involve a clear-cut right or wrong way to be. It is not OK to be obese, it is not OK to have cancer, it is not OK to eat sugar all the time. Many moral issues are the same: it is wrong to be racist, it is wrong to pay men more than women for the same job, it is wrong to murder. Perhaps this is why intersexuality is so controversial. The 'norm' is to have two separate genders, and when someone presents as different from the norm, we think they are 'wrong', we call their condition a 'disorder'. But how detrimental is intersexuality, really, to a person's life? It's a conversation I wish, in a way, I could have with Max, but that is not to be. Distance prevents me from doing so, and also protects me from the emotion that must make this issue more difficult for Max and his family to discuss than for me. As much as I now know about Max, about this rare condition, I sense I can only begin to imagine what it must be like for a parent of an intersex child, understanding that physically your child is happy and healthy, perfect even, but that, due to societal pressure to be normal and the fear of differences, being intersex may just ruin their life. It's not the fault of the condition, but one can understand how 'fixing' the condition might seem to make the problem go away.

I found out about Karen leaving when Max and Steve Walker came to see me at the surgery to talk about the overdose. An ambulance had taken them to the nearest hospital in the middle of the night. Max used the painkillers I gave him and some of Karen's sleeping pills, but he was also inebriated. We don't know how much Max really meant to do any harm to himself, and I suspect Max himself does not entirely know what he meant to erase. They pumped his stomach at the hospital, kept him overnight and sent him home.

Steve wanted to do more for him, so they made an appointment and came in to see me just before New Year. Max said he took the pills because he couldn't sleep, but he also said he was depressed. He was confused and seemed disorientated. I arranged for a psychiatrist to meet with him once a week for an hour. We put him on a mild anti-depressant for two months. He comes off it at the end of February. Steve didn't want to put him on any medication at all, so he was insistent that it was mild and short-term. The psychiatrist tells me Max is doing quite well, and slowly coming to terms with everything. He didn't talk for the first few weeks, then one day he began, tentatively, to speak about his feelings.

I drove to the Walkers' house the other day. They live in a rather grand and sparsely populated area of countryside on the edge of Hemingway, called Oakland Drive. You have to squint at the house names on the gates as you pass. All the houses are set back from the road, beyond long drives.

Max lives at 'The Gables'. It's a large, white building set back from the road, and looks to be over a century old. It has a tall, wooden gate in front of it and a hedgerow around it, with a couple of tall trees in the back. It looks a nice place to bring up kids. I went because Steve asked me to come to talk to him, without Max, about the future.

I advised they continue with counselling, and talk as a family. I said that I could see Max adjusting well in time. I didn't stay for coffee, as Steve suggested. It's a natural impulse to become involved with patients' lives when you have been through something this important with them, but it's equally as important to stay objective. That's what they need me for. I don't suppose I'll see Max again for a while. In fact, I hope not. That will mean he's doing well.

With this in mind, when I see Karen Walker in the clothing boutique on The Promenade, my first thought is to subtly slip out of the store. First I have to remove the shoes I'm trying on. I pull them off, apologising softly to the shop assistant, but before I can dash out, I feel a tap on my shoulder.

'Hello, Archie,' says Karen, in her smooth but strangely cold voice. 'It's so nice to see you.'

I smile politely. 'How are you, Karen?'

'Good!' She nods, realising how she sounds: determined; a little crazed. She laughs. 'I've been thinking about drinking in the morning. It's something I've never done that I've always wanted to try.' She pauses, as if waiting for me to say something.

I take my cue. 'I'm sorry for calling your husband about the clinic in London—'

'Are you?' Karen cuts in, rather sharply. She drops her head. 'Sorry,' she mutters. 'It's . . . been a bad year.'

I slip my handbag over my shoulder. 'I really am sorry, Karen. I was concerned when I came in that morning. I didn't know the clinic. I thought Max might have gone on his own.'

'No,' Karen speaks over me again, but this time softly. 'No, you didn't. But that's OK. Maybe I was a little . . . bad with Max. I hope I'll get another chance but . . . how can I know?'

For a moment she looks like she might cry.

'Karen?'

She dips her long neck and her golden hair covers it as she

brushes her cheek with a finger. Her head bobs up again and she beams at me, just like Max used to do.

'Is everything going OK with Max? With his therapy?' she asks.

'Things aren't so bad.' I hesitate, wondering how much she knows. 'I hear he's doing well. Obviously Dr Evans and I don't share notes, but she tells me he's . . . on the mend.'

She nods again, earnestly. 'Mm, I think so. I don't know . . . Daniel tells me he is.'

'He is,' I say, and I reach out and touch her arm gently.

'I just wish he would talk to me,' she murmurs, looking off towards a rack of dresses. 'We used to talk a lot.'

'It'll happen.'

Karen shrugs. 'I don't know. He hasn't been telling me the truth for a long while, even before we stopped talking.'

It seems to me like she wants to talk. Perhaps she doesn't have many people she can turn to.

Then she sighs, and says something that makes me want to set her straight, despite my need to stay professional and distanced.

'He wouldn't even admit that he was attracted to boys at all. What am I supposed to think? I used to think he was so open and brave.'

'Isn't he going out with Sylvie Clark now?' I ask, trying to deflect this last comment.

'Sylvie? I thought they broke up?'

'Oh, I'm sorry,' I say pointlessly, because Steve had told me the day before that they are seeing each other again. 'I don't know. I just presumed.'

'Well, he's probably bi, but he won't talk to me about it.'

'Karen, really, Max isn't.'

'How would you know?' Karen says, almost disdainfully.

'Well, it wouldn't be a problem anyway, but I know he isn't.'

'I suppose he talks to you more than he talks to me now.'

'I haven't seen him in a long time, Karen.'

I turn to go but she grabs my arm. 'Wait!' she exclaims. 'How do you know?'

'I . . .' I've said too much. I see suspicion in her eyes and I turn away. 'Just take my word for it,' I say, heading for the door.

'I mean, if he isn't . . .' Karen's voice has become firm, and yet desperate, like her throat has constricted. She grasps my arm with both hands and looks me in the eye.

'Archie?' she whispers. The boutique owner stares at us, and together we step outside into the light.

I look around at passers-by. When we're alone, I say, 'I can't. Confidentiality.'

'Archie.' Karen pulls me to her. She looks stricken with grief. 'What is it?'

I open my mouth but I can't speak. Suddenly, Karen Walker doesn't need me to speak.

'Oh my god.' She drops my arms and steps away, her eyes wide in horror. She puts her hands to her mouth.

'I'm sorry,' I whisper, not knowing what to say or do.

'Oh my god.' A deep, hollow sound comes from her throat. 'Max.'

Max

Sylvie and I are making out in my room.

'I love you to the nth degree,' I mumble through her lips.

'I love you . . . with every fibre of my being,' she says back. It's a game we play.

'I love you . . . more than I love football.'

'Oh my fuck, how romantic. OK, I would love you even if you were covered in hair.'

'I would love you even if . . .' I smile, kissing her neck. 'You were some kind of goth-y, biker-chick freak who wrote poetry.'

She nods, grabbing my cheeks. 'That's so sweet! I would love you even if you were half-and-half.'

I grin and laugh. 'I would love you even if you had oral herpes.'

'That's disgusting. I would love you even if you had gonorrhea in your eye.'

'That's highly unlikely.'

'You're highly unlikely,' Sylvie says, and kisses me, stroking her hands down my back and grabbing my bum. I giggle and she slips her hands around to the front of my pants.

'Not yet,' I murmur.

'Not yet? As in, not right this second? How about this second?'

'Oh my god, stop.'

'How about now?'

'Stop!' I yell, tickling her.

We get entangled on the bed and kiss more, when suddenly I hear a voice shouting my name. I sit up.

'Wait, Sylvie, listen.'

'Ignore it,' she says, biting my jaw. I almost fall back onto the bed, but then I hear it again.

'MAX!'

384

'Sylves, I think it's my mum.'

'Shit, really?'

'Yeah. Come on.'

I take her hand and we go out onto the balcony of the landing, but she's not in the hall downstairs. I can hear shouting in the kitchen, so we run down the stairs.

When I push open the door, I see Dad stood by the kettle. Mum is stood at the other end of the table, shouting at Dad.

Everyone goes quiet when we come through the door. I feel a soft object bump my back and Sylvie puts her hand in my palm.

'What's happening?' I ask.

Mum turns to me. 'I . . . I . . .' she stammers. 'I just wanted to see you and your dad wouldn't let me.'

'Well.' I shrug uncomfortably. 'That's because I don't want to see you.'

'I thought we said you wouldn't come over for the next few weeks,' Dad says to Mum quietly.

'I have to talk to him!' Mum shrieks, looking at me. She's been crying. Her make-up is dark and pooled under her eyes.

'Come on, Karen, you can't just burst in and yell things at him. He's very unsettled right now,' Dad says. 'He needs to rest and take things easy.'

I go and sit at the table just in front of Dad, pulling Sylvie after me. He moves so he's just behind me and puts his hands on my shoulders. I don't want to leave Dad alone to have a screaming match again. It was horrible enough the first time.

'Come on, Karen, we said you wouldn't come here.'

'He's my son!' Mum says, and I suddenly feel really sorry for her. I look down at the table and pick at the wood. She puts her hands up to her face and covers a little gasp of pain. 'Maxy?' she says to me. 'Why won't you tell me anything anymore?'

I shrug and mumble, 'You know why.'

'No, even before that,' Mum moans. 'You didn't want to tell me, but you could have. I'm so sorry if I made it hard for you, but you could have told me.' She sobs and covers her face again.

I frown and look up at Dad. 'Could have told you what?'

She looks up at me and whispers, 'How the baby came about.'

'But I did,' I protest.

'Please, Max,' she begs. 'I want us to talk. I want you to tell me who . . .' She brushes away tears from her face and her voice gets ragged and breathy.

'I want you to tell me who, and I will lock them away . . .'

And I realise.

'No!' I shout loudly. I stand up, throwing my chair backwards. I don't want to hear it. Every cell in my body is trying to throw off what she is saying, stop time, change the course of present momentum. 'Shut up!'

Dad has to jump out of the way of my chair as I stand. 'Max! Be careful!'

'Tell me who it was, Max,' Mum says, like a lawyer this time, with both her palms flat on the table. 'Tell me who he was and I will make sure he never harms you or anyone else ever again.'

She looks as if she would kill him. Dad is staring at her like she's crazy. But then I watch it dawn on his face too, feeling the panic rise in my body until it feels like the blood is drumming in my ears, a cacophony of embarrassment, shame and, weirdly, guilt. I do not want Mum and Dad to know. I don't want it to be another problem. I don't want them to think of me that way.

No no no no no no no, I think. *No!*

'Karen?' Dad murmurs. She looks at him with tears in her eyes and confirms with a small nod. Both of them turn to me.

'Max, tell me,' Mum says.

I can't say anything.

'Max, you have to tell us,' says Dad. 'It's OK, Max. You can do it.'

'Be brave, honey,' encourages Mum.

There's a silence. Mum is waiting for me, Dad is waiting for me, Sylvie is gripping my hand so hard, and I look at her hopelessly. She looks back at me and it's like we converse with our eyes.

I can't, I say.

You have to, she says.

No. I shake my head. *I don't.*

And I realise I can't say anything. My mouth won't move, my voice won't speak. I'm paralysed again. I can't say anything.

I look down at the table.

'Hunter.'

Mum and Dad's heads both snap to Sylvie.

She says it again, softly. 'It was Hunter.'

Daniel

Mum and Max end up hugging in the living room for a long time, and then a police officer comes round and I'm not supposed to know anything but I listened from the stairs so apparently Hunter is being arrested. Everybody was crying for a while, but they're all alright now and everyone's happier now Mum is home. Dad says she isn't staying overnight though, she's just looking after us until Dad and the policeman have gone and dealt with Hunter and come back. But Sylvie is staying overnight. I don't know what happened exactly. It's hard to hear from the stairs. They had the door closed.

Mum and Dad had a fight, which is why Mum isn't staying here at the moment, which I can understand, because sometimes they are both very irritating. But sometimes they are really nice. Like when Dad builds a fort in the back garden with me or Mum takes me for ice cream in Oxford at the posh tearooms. She says I'm a big boy now and I won't misbehave. That's right. I won't. I'm grown up. I'm ten and two months and twenty-one days.

I hear a tap over my shoulder and when I turn around, Max is standing against the doorframe.

'Hey buddy,' Max says. He looks all red and jolly for the first time in ages, which is good because he wasn't even jolly at Christmas. He was just faking it for me, and it was so obvious. He kept going up to his room for five minutes and then coming down again, and then in the evening he was getting upset in his room and Dad came and gave him a big bear hug for ages and they talked a bit quietly, and then Max came downstairs and him and Dad watched action movies after I slept. That's what Max told me. He said they watched *Terminator* 1 and 2, and then *True Lies* and ate chocolate-covered raisins.

'Hi Max,' I say. 'Did Hunter hurt you?'

'Huh?'

'I heard he attacked you. I was listening.'

'Yeah.' Max nods, looking funnily relieved. 'Yes, he did. But it's all dealt with now.'

'OK,' I say. 'Have you come to play Top Trumps?'

'Yes,' he says.

'Cool. Do you want to play the two-player on *Zombieland 4* first, though, because I have to finish this level before I can play Top Trumps. It's imperative.'

'Oh, good word,' Max says.

'OK, hang on a minute,' I say, and I kill four zombies and get the powerpack.

'You're doing better, aren't you, Daniel?' Max says.

'What with?'

'You know, with . . . everything with me.'

'Oh, yes. I was worried when you tried to kill yourself, but then I found out you were different, and now I know you'll be OK, because we all know and now you can talk about it. I guess it was hard for you because you're not very different at all in other ways, but I'm sort of different to most of the kids in my class, so I know how to deal with being different. You can ask me anything you like and I'll help you anytime. It's OK. Plus, you weren't lying to me before.'

'Huh?'

'About being special. Sometimes I thought maybe you didn't know about being different but I guess you do, because you are, so you weren't lying when you said I was special. We're both special.'

'That's right,' he says, leaning against my bunk bed and grinning. He got even taller over Christmas.

'Like superheroes!'

'Yeah, totally.'

'Like genetic mutants.'

'Don't get carried away,' Max says, and he laughs even though it's not funny.

Steve

I go with DI Travers over to Leah and Edward's house to find Hunter. I shouldn't have come but I had to. I've just resigned my post, but my job as Chief Crown Prosecutor was to make sure little bastards like Hunter are locked up, and I'll fucking well make sure that happens tonight.

I called Paul Travers because he's to the point, unemotional and respectful. He'll keep the charges quiet. I'll ask for the court records to be sealed as it's rape of a minor, and Paul won't be tempted to beat the shit out of Hunter like I am right now, in the passenger seat of the car. Gripping the car door handle, staring at the Fulsoms' house, waiting for the moment when Hunter comes running out and I have to jump out the car and can legitimately tackle him to the ground and smash his face into the gravel.

This is a kid I watched grow up. This is a child we let sleep in the same bed as our child.

Karen was right. I can't forgive her. Not because of the abortion, but because she didn't listen to Max when he said something so important. If we don't listen to him, if we take away his right to his own choices, his own body, then he stops being an autonomous being and becomes a thing. He stops making decisions for himself, he forgets how to stand up for himself, and things like this happen. People like Hunter will happen to him.

The house in front of me is quiet. I see the light of the living room dim in the hallway. Paul must be in there, telling them what he always tells the families. Paul's good at this. I imagine for a minute Karen and I sat on our sofa, being told that Max had hurt someone like Hunter hurt him.

He'd just never do that. I know Max.

Suddenly, bright white light fills the car. I turn around. Two headlights swing into the drive, and the gravel crunches as Hunter's car comes to a stop.

I go to open the door but the only urge inside me is to beat the living daylights out of him. I stay put and shrink down in my seat.

Hunter switches off his engine and looks quizzically at the police car. I'm in shadow. He's parked to the right of me, closer to the house. I don't think he can see me.

I watch Hunter stepping out of the car. He stubs a cigarette out on the interior of the car door and leaves it in there. He shuts the door with a thud.

He walks slowly towards the front door. The kid is tall, proud and cocky. He strolls slowly, predatorily, towards the house, then stops near the front door. He looks back over at the police car. His eyes are black in the dark. He's wearing black trousers, a T-shirt and an open long-sleeved shirt. I won't forget this for a long time.

The front door opens and he turns towards it.

'Mum?' he says. 'Are you OK? What's happened?'

He's not even worried. He doesn't even suspect we're here for him, I think. I open the car door and slip quietly out.

'Baby,' Leah cries. She runs forward and throws her arms around him.

'Is Dad OK?' he asks.

'Hunter,' she cries, her voice hoarse. 'Why did you do it? Why would you do that?'

Hunter's hands go to her waist. He sees Paul coming out his front door. His mouth opens. He knows what's coming. Paul is walking towards him. Edward leans against the doorframe, bent over like an old man, his arms folded. He can barely look at Hunter.

'Hunter Fulsom,' Paul says softly but firmly. 'You're under arrest for rape of a minor.'

Hunter looks over at Edward.

'Dad?' he says. His voice is deep – deeper than Max's. As I get closer, I see dark stubble all over his chin. He's broader, taller, even more so than when I last saw him in September. Hunter grew up. He became different to Max. We should have noticed.

Paul gets his handcuffs out and holds one out for Hunter. 'It's best to come quietly, Hunter. It'll work out better for you that way.'

'Fuck that,' Hunter mutters.

'Hunter, you're going,' Leah says. 'You're going.'

'No.' Hunter moves away from Paul and Leah grabs for him. 'Mum, get off me! I'm not going! I didn't do anything!'

'Are you drunk?' Edward asks angrily from the porch.

'No, I'm not drunk,' Hunter says, shrugging his mother off him.

Leah reels back. Tears pour down her face. 'Why, why, why,' she murmurs repeatedly.

'I didn't do anything!' says Hunter. 'Mum, stop crying!'

As Paul comes towards him, Hunter backs away.

'You are under arrest for the rape of Max Walker,' repeats Paul.

'No, 'cause, he wanted it!' Hunter says clumsily. 'He wanted to have sex with me. He said it would be fun.'

Paul leans in towards him. 'Come on, now, your mum and dad are here. You don't want to say anything that will hurt them more, Hunter. Let's go down to the station.'

'Fuck you,' Hunter whines.

The kid's drunk.

'What have you been drinking?' Leah says. She walks up to him, holds his cheeks and looks him in the eyes. Leah's a nurse. 'Sweetheart, what are you on?'

Hunter bats her hands away. 'Nothing.'

'What's been going on with you this year, Hunter?' she cries angrily.

'Nothing, Mum!' Hunter yells.

'I feel like I've lost you!' Leah puts a trembling hand over her mouth and sobs. 'What happened?'

'It was Max! I . . .' Hunter anxiously runs a hand through his hair. 'Max and I, we . . . He wanted to.'

'Hunter,' Leah cautions.

392

Paul takes a step towards Hunter and Hunter backs away and turns towards his car.

But I'm stood behind him.

As soon as he sees me he stops, frozen. I hold out a hand, thinking I'm just going to stop him, thinking of blocking him from moving, but I reach forward and grab him by the T-shirt and hike it up around his throat.

'Don't you dare say my son's name!' I say, almost growling.

'Steve!' Paul darts forward and puts his arms between my body and Hunter's, just as Hunter grabs at my shoulder and tries to push me off. Leah rushes up behind him and puts her arms around her son's shoulders.

'Stop struggling,' I hear her tell him. 'Just stop.'

'Let go, Steve,' Paul mutters in my ear. 'Let go.'

I could break his neck right now if I wanted to. I could just reach out and snap it. But at the same time I realise I don't want to touch his skin. I'm suddenly afraid if I touch him, I'll break down completely.

Instead I pull his T-shirt so his face is close to mine and I whisper hoarsely, shaking through my whole body at the nearness to him, 'Do you know what you put Max through?'

Hunter holds my gaze. He swallows. He lifts his hands up over his head, off me, and Leah lets go of him. She turns, looking for Edward, but he is still unmoving in the doorway.

Paul is holding my arms. I release Hunter's T-shirt.

Paul takes a few seconds, looks at me, then steps away and walks around us. He stands behind Hunter.

Without taking his eyes from me, Hunter puts his hands behind his back. He looks back over his shoulder at his parents. Leah is crying loudly, walking back into the house. Edward stands on the porch, keeping his distance. Typical Edward, always keeping out of situations, with that snooty air, when he should be in the thick of it, protecting his family. No wonder his son has such a warped sense of right and wrong, of loyalty, of morality.

Hunter turns to me, away from his parents, and leans in close.

393

'Mr Walker, I really . . .' he whispers, his lips trembling, his pupils dilated. Hunter grunts, feeling the cool, stiff handcuffs lock in place. 'I really care about him. And . . . the baby,' he adds quietly. He thinks this will help, that he can explain, like there is an explanation, like there is an excuse. He opens his mouth again. 'Please, I—'

'No,' I say. 'No you don't.'

Paul holds Hunter's cuffs with one hand and opens the back door of the police car with the other.

I shake my head. 'You don't care at all.'

Hunter continues to look at me. A sliver of understanding, of guilt, dawns on his face. His eyes fill with tears. Paul places a hand on Hunter's scruffy hair.

I watch him coldly, analytically. We thought they were kids, but they weren't. Where was I when they grew up?

I'm giving up work, I tell myself. I'm going to be at home. I don't want to turn around in five years' time and not know who my children are.

Leah and Edward watch Hunter like he's a stranger. I feel a flash of empathy for him. He's alone now.

But then it's over. Empathy is like that. It's a two-way street. Someone dehumanises you by violating your child and every human thought you had for them is broken, undermined, then gone.

I shake my head at him in disgust. 'Get in the car.'

Daniel

Max sits down on the floor and takes a controller and I start him up on two-player.

'Um, so,' Max says, getting ready to shoot. 'Did Dad tell you about . . . my being different?'

'No.'

'Oh. Mum?'

'No.'

'Daniel, stop making me ask questions. How do you know about it then?'

'Oh, I heard Mum and Dad talking, so I went and found some copies of your medical records in Mum's bedroom and I looked all the scientific words up. It's so stupid how they do everything in Latin. We're English. The Romans should get over themselves.'

'Um . . . Yeah.'

'Yes. Not yeah,' I tut. 'Anyway, I wouldn't worry about your variation, Max. The statistics about how common intersexuality is are very skewed and they think that the rate of intersexuality now could be as high as four per cent. Some cultures register eight sexes. One in one hundred live births are checked for some sort of ambiguous genitalia. Also, there are over a hundred videos online of hermaphrodite pornography, although, to be honest, I think they are faking because they don't look like you. You may be different like me, Max, but the good news is that we're living in a world of different people. Sylvie's weird too.'

'There are over a hundred videos online of hermaphrodite pornography?' Max says in a loud voice.

'Max?'

He looks at me like he's just noticed me there. 'Yeah?'

'I thought it was inappropriate of you to try and hurt yourself before asking me what I thought about it. 'If you want to know what I think, I think it would have been absolutely the worst thing in the world if you had died.'

'I'm sorry, Danny,' Max says, and looks down like he knows it was bad to do that.

'You didn't try to talk to me about it. I could have helped.'

There is a pause and the zombies approach us because both of us are a bit distracted.

'What about Mum and Dad dying?' Max says thoughtfully. 'Wouldn't that have been the worst thing in the world?'

'Well, they're older and I guess it's preferable that they die before us.'

Max puts his hand to his mouth but it is obvious he is smiling, although yet again it is a serious topic. He is just weird sometimes.

'Thanks,' he says.

'You're welcome. We're siblings. I don't care if you're a boy or a girl or neither. We're best friends.'

'I'm your best friend?'

'Aren't you? Or is Sylvie?'

'I didn't mean . . . Yes. Yeah, I'm your best friend, Daniel. We're best pals.'

'OK. Good.' I kill two zombies. 'So what's Sylvie? Is she your girlfriend now?'

Max smiles. 'Yeah, she's my girlfriend.'

'Cool.'

'I'd better get back to her in a bit. I was just coming in to say goodnight.'

'It's OK, we can play another time.'

We nuke a temple in the game and thousands of zombies run out and we throw hand grenades at them.

'So, like,' says Max. 'Did you read up on the types of . . . like, gender variation?'

'Yeah.'

'I find it really confusing about what I am. I couldn't find exactly the right thing on Wikipedia before the doctor told me. They said it was really rare. Now they've told me that they

396

didn't want me to know earlier because I assigned myself a male gender role, or whatever, but apparently I'm 46,XX/ 46,XY. They still don't know what it means for me exactly, like, how I'm gonna grow and stuff, because everyone is different. Even with the same chromosomes, your hormones can be different and how you present.'

'Oh right,' I say, and shrug.

'D'you know what that means?'

'Of course I know what that means. Your code says you're not a boy or a girl because you're sort of both.'

'Which one do you think it is? Both or neither?'

'Why?'

'Um.'

'Do you give a shit?' I ask him, nuking another zombie base.

He shrugs. 'Not really, I guess.' He shoots the zombies that run out of the base.

'Aren't you going to tell me off for saying "shit" when I'm only ten?' I ask.

'No. I'm going to kill you,' he says, and he goes into the on-screen control panel and puts himself on another team that also kills zombies, but is my enemy.

'Daniel?' he says as he annoys me by shooting my character's second-in-command. 'I've changed my mind about something. I'm not saying you should do anything that would make them, well, not *who they are*, if you know what I mean . . .' Max takes out half my team, then chases my attack Puma over a rocky waterfall. 'But I'd totally let you modify my kids.'

I grin widely. 'Yes! With robotic extensions?'

'Yeah. I bet you'd do a badass job.'

'Thanks, Max. That really means a lot.'

'No worries.'

'And Max?'

'Yeah?'

'I'm sorry about the baby.'

'Thanks,' he says, glancing at me. He sits in silence for a

minute, his thumbs going crazy on the controller, then he swears. 'Shit! Sorry, I killed you. I wasn't thinking.'

'It's OK, Max. I'll let you have that one. You only killed my sphinxfighter. I've got to a higher level with the dwarflord anyway.'

Max

'Come on, hurry up!' I yell.

'Why? We have like eight hours till the sun goes down!' Danny shouts back.

'We have to make a stop first at the garage and it closes at four! Are you ready?'

'I'm ready.' Danny appears from his bedroom. 'Sylvie's downstairs. I heard her bike.'

'Is she?' I ask, looking out the window. Down on the drive, Sylvie, in a short purple dress and long grey socks, looks up at me. She lifts up her Ray-Bans, squints, and waves. I wave back and she blows me a kiss.

Daniel comes up behind me and tugs on my T-shirt. 'Come on.'

He turns and bounds down the stairs and I follow, lifting the latch for him on the front door.

'Hi, Sylvie!' Daniel calls. He speaks to me over his shoulder. 'On your bike, then!'

This is a literal instruction, not an idiom in his case. I have my provisional driver's licence but I'm not seventeen yet so I have to drive around car parks or fields with Dad.

'Max!' Dad calls from the porch as I pick my bike up off the gravel.

I turn. 'Hey. I thought you were volunteering today.'

Dad used to work weekends a lot, and every weekday without fail. But since everything happened, he has stopped work, and just volunteers now, giving talks in community centres. It's been nice to have him around more.

Dad smiles. 'I decided to book today off. Do some things around the house. Are you going for a bike ride?'

'Yeah,' I nod.

I'm glad Dad didn't run for MP. He told me he's happy not to, because he gets to spend more time with us. Since Mum left, he's started to cook again too, and he seems to really enjoy it. We had a barbecue the other day, just the three of us. We see Dad a lot more than before. We talk about being intersex now sometimes; just about how I'm feeling and how the therapy is going. I go every fortnight. Dad's wearing a jumper and jeans today. He's been wearing fewer suits. So has Mum. They both look more relaxed than they used to.

'Alright then,' he says. 'Will you be home for tea?'

'I think so.'

'What would you like?'

I look at Daniel but he looks back at me and shrugs.

'Um,' I say. 'Lasagne or something would be great, Dad.'

'Done. Sounds good. I'll have it ready around five.' He nods and turns back to the house. Before he shuts the door he says, 'I'll be here if you need me, OK, Max?'

I am embarrassed, but I smile gratefully. He knows what day it is.

We wanted to go it alone today, just Sylvie, Daniel and me, so Daniel and I pumped up the tyres on our old bikes last night in preparation. Daniel doesn't know why we're going. He thinks it's just a nice road trip.

He found out about the baby, because he's a lot smarter than anybody gives him credit for. I admitted everything he worked out for himself, and eventually, after he had asked again and again, I gave him a tempered version of events, about what happened between me and Hunter, and how the baby came to be. Obviously I omitted certain things.

I don't want him to know about today, or why we're going where we're going. He asked me to tell him everything, and as much as I can I have, but there are some things I just don't have the words to explain. I figure if I'm not ready or able to understand them yet, then it's not fair to heap the confused thoughts in my head onto my little brother. Growing up is overwhelming enough without doing it before you're meant to.

I woke up last night at one, four, and again at eight.

At one I heard Dad in his bedroom, making notes into a dictaphone. He's thinking of writing a book, and he makes notes late at night.

Mum was still working until a few weeks ago. She's actually a great barrister. Daniel and I have been to see her in court. Afterwards, she took us out for scones, which Daniel went crazy over. We're kind of rebuilding a relationship slowly. That was last month, but she's taking a long sabbatical from practising law over the summer. She has a little townhouse in Oxford and she's reading a lot and just hanging out, really. She's a lot more fun with Daniel than she used to be. With me she's kind of less fun than she used to be, but more real. We're working on it.

Last night I listened to Dad speaking passionately into the dictaphone. I imagined him waving his arms around. Daniel and I thought Mum and Dad would get back together, but they haven't. I don't think either of them is seeing anyone else. I feel bad about that. That's probably the last side effect of everything that happened in autumn that's remained, hung around, leaving a bad taste in the air. I think sometimes of that note Dad gave Mum, 'To the love of my life', and I think about how they probably are the loves of each other's lives, that they had something like Sylvie and I have, and that I've taken that away from them. Dad's voice lowered to a murmur, then started up again, loud and righteous. Just another night. I put my iPod headphones in, turned over and shut my eyes.

At four I sat up, startled, drenched in sweat, Gang Starr repeating 'Take It Personal' in my eardrums. I pulled the headphones out and took my T-shirt off. My chest hasn't grown or feminised or whatever dumb term Dr Flint used. I guess if it hasn't by now it never will, so there's another theory debunked. Doctors know nothing. Well, that's kind of unfair. Let's just say the world is unpredictable. Science is unreliable. It can't tell you who you are or what you'll want or how you'll feel. All these researchers are going crazy in their labs, trying to fit us into these little boxes so they can justify their jobs, or their government funding, or their life's work. They can theorise and they can give you a mean, median and mode, but it's all standardised guesswork, made official by arrogance. You have to be pretty into yourself to think you can play a part in defining the identity of a bunch of people you don't know, of human beings with complicated shit going on in their bodies. They still don't know what certain parts of our brains do, they still don't know how to cure a common cold, and they claim to know about sexuality, about gender. Well, you're not a man because you like football and you're not a woman because you're attracted to men, and you're not not a chick because you like to be the one that gives, and you're not not a dude because you like to receive or because sometimes you cry at dumb movies. Daniel cried all the way through *Rise of the Planet of the Apes.*

I wiped the sweat off my chest with my T-shirt. Still no hairs, but my chest is actually pretty hard at the moment. Daniel wanted me to teach him to work out so we've been doing reps every morning before school. I mean, I guess I'll never be a bodybuilder but compared to my friends, I'd say I'm keeping up.

I sat like that for a while, my T-shirt crumpled in my hands, just staring blankly at my bed covers and feeling my shoulders lift and drop with every breath. It's quiet in my head now. Just my voice, no one else's.

I'm alive. It's a good thing. I'm glad about it. I'm intersex, and I'm coming to terms with that. One thing that does cross my mind from time to time, between all the talking about being intersex with my therapist, is the fact that I conceived a baby, and that I could again someday. I never thought before how life is so accidental, how it can so easily and quickly be made, and then gone again, in the space of minutes. It makes me appreciate everything more, but it also makes me think about how much of our fates are set by chance, and how many little accidents had to happen to make me what and who I am.

I'm still hung up about what I had to do, what Mum had to do for me in the end. Nobody should have to go through a pregnancy when they don't want to, and I'm glad that I didn't. But even though it was an accident, and even though it was bad timing, and a bad situation, it was so hard for me to make that choice. I guess it's always hard to make that choice and I don't envy anybody that has to. But what's even worse is that I didn't. I just let it happen. I never fully came to terms with it before it was done, and perhaps I haven't, even now. In any case, it's a fucking heartbreaker of a thing to go through, and I don't know when or how you're supposed to get over it.

I don't know how you deal with it.

But I do know that I'm so, so glad I didn't have the other surgery in the end. I really don't think I could have come back from that. I just wouldn't have felt like me. It would have felt like not only do I not make my own choices, but this body isn't mine either. My whole body would be a reminder, every day, that I wasn't brave enough just to be myself.

I throw the covers off my bed and feel my head. It's hot and slick with sweat. I wait. I watch the room become more visible in the dark. I decide it isn't Sunday yet. I decide it's still Saturday night. I know I'm lying to myself. I sink back into the pillow, turn on my side and fall asleep.

At eight. At eight . . . At eight I wake up and this time it's Sunday morning.

We take our bikes away from the houses and into the narrow roads through the fields. The sun lights up Sylvie's caramel hair and Daniel's red hair in front of me.

'Come on, Max!' Daniel shrieks excitedly, and I speed up ahead of them. We go up and over the hill, then fast down the side of it. The petrol station is on the edge of the road, standing alone.

'Why are we stopping?' calls Daniel.

'Just wait here,' I say.

Sylvie and I lean our bikes against the building, not worrying to lock them up, while Daniel waits impatiently on the tarmac.

This is the Oxfordshire countryside. No one would steal bikes here.

'Hello,' says Sylvie. 'Some of your best flowers please.'

Sylvie leans on the counter, her arms brown and her wrists small and delicate. She wears a watch and a friendship bracelet I gave her. I wrap my arms around her soft waist and kiss the nape of her neck, slipping the money for the flowers onto the counter.

When Sylvie and I were biking around at the beginning of the summer, we found this cute little church up on a hill. It's in a tiny village, but all the houses are spread out beneath it in the valley. The church was sweet enough, but none of us are religious, so I said I didn't want to come to the church when we did this. But then Sylvie said wouldn't it be lonely all by itself in a field somewhere?

I couldn't argue with that.

'Come on!' yells Daniel ahead of us, pedalling furiously up the hill with the church on it, finding it easier going with his four or five stone, however heavy he is.

'Careful of cars,' I caution, pumping my legs to catch up to him.

The three of us track our bikes around the graveyard wall. The wall is low and stone, and built a very long time ago. The church itself has grey-green stone, and moss all over it. Flowers fill the yard: nice, bright hollyhocks and vines and sweet williams. We park our bikes in the shrubs at the back of the church and then we climb around the back, up a very narrow path with a series of wooden arches over it, all with honeysuckle growing up their sides, creating a sweet-smelling corridor up to a spot that overlooks the valley beneath the hill. Cute little red-brick cottages are below, along with fallow fields filled with wildflowers and poppies and buttercups and daisies.

There is a bench here that is dedicated to a child who died six weeks after she was born. Her name is Matilda.

I look at it, unsure. Daniel sits down.

'This is a lovely place,' he says cheerfully.

'Hey,' a soft voice says from behind me.

'Hi, you,' I say, not turning around as she puts her arms around my shoulders and kisses the back of my neck. Then she takes my hand and I squeeze it gratefully.

'Now what?' I murmur.

Sylvie's bare shoulder brushes against mine as she comes to stand beside me. She looks out over the vista. 'I don't know.'

We listen to the crickets whispering, and watch the heads of the poppies nod in the breeze, down below us.

'I'm gonna take Danny down the hill to play,' says Sylvie.

'What am I supposed to say?'

'Whatever you want,' she replies softly. She moves forward and tickles Daniel, taking his hand and running a little way down the valley in front of me.

It's a smooth but steep slope, and I sit down on the bench and watch them playing in the wildflowers, in a great expanse of speckled green.

I brought the picture from the ultrasound to the bench over the valley. Perhaps it's stupid or sentimental, but I wanted to come here to say goodbye, if only to an idea of a person that helped me to realise that I might not be so broken, that I do have a future, that maybe one day I will have a family, and that maybe I won't be afraid.

I think I had romantic notions of me being over it at last, in a timely, Hollywood fashion, conveniently on the day the baby was supposed to be born, and setting myself free from past mistakes by leaving the picture on the bench in the graveyard, propped against it. But I can't do it. It's in my pocket the whole time I sit there, just looking at the grass.

Sometimes I still feel that there are two of me: one clean, flawless picture, the other imperfect and cracked; one boy, one girl; one voice that speaks aloud and one that whispers in my ear; one publicly known to have been troubled but be on the mend, the other who has privately lost something to do with innocence and gained something to do with knowledge and adulthood that can never be undone. I feel sometimes there are things that tear me in two directions, that there are two sets of thoughts that grow side by side. But then I realise that I am

405

whole, whatever that means and does not mean; I am complete without the need for additions or alteration.

'Nice spot,' Sylvie murmurs, coming back to me and sitting beside me.

'Thanks for coming,' I say, putting my arm around her, feeling her warmth. I stroke her soft skin with my fingers, and we both look out over the valley. 'I know it's weird.'

Sylvie leans her head on my shoulder. 'No, it's not.'

Acknowledgements

Firstly, thank you for reading. I have been very lucky in my life, and my particular brand of luck has been to be surrounded by clever, warm, passionate people. Of those people, there are a specific few I would like to thank here for being supporters on the road to telling Max's story. These are:

The Authors' Foundation and K Blundell Trust for awarding me a grant to write this book, and the Brocklesby Trust for several grants over the years. It can't be underestimated what a difference financial support makes to someone trying to find their feet, or in this case, voice.

My wonderful editor and publisher, Arzu Tahsin, who stepped up to the plate to make an unknown, part-time writer into a novelist. This did nothing less than change my life, and I'm eternally grateful. Thanks also to everyone at Weidenfeld & Nicolson and Orion for doing such a beautiful job with the edit and cover of *Golden Boy*, particularly Sophie Buchan for all her hard work and clever thoughts, and also Mark Streatfeild and Jennifer Kerslake. I'm so looking forward to working with you all over the years, and books, to come.

Everyone at my lovely literary home, Conville & Walsh. Jo Unwin, my brilliant agent, saved my first manuscript from the submissions pile. Jo, thanks for being my support and teammate, always having faith and for all the fun we had with *Golden Boy* at LBF 2012. It's been, and I know will continue to be, a great pleasure. A big thank you also to Carrie Plitt, Jake Smith-Bosanquet, Alexandra McNicoll, Henna Silvennoinen, Alex Christofi, Patrick Walsh and the rest of the team.

As always, I would like to thank my amazing family and friends for being the absolute best. In the world. Ever. I credit your example, encouragement and love with making me who I am today. Particularly I'd like to thank:

Andy Squires, for being enthusiastic about *Golden Boy* (and all my stupid ideas) from the beginning; Rosie Cannon, for suggesting I write something along the lines of *Golden Boy*; for their love and generosity, Karina Cornell, Coralie Colmez, Becky Preston, Melissa Hollis, Coco Quinn, Carla Evans, Sarah Mosses, Liv & Tim, Rhys & Sarah, Richie B, Tom & Tam, David & Kit, Joyce Walker, Kate, Brian, John, DJ, Bridge, Neil, Billy, Lucy, Luke, Geri, Georgie, Ben, Lottie, Spesh, Andrew Walker, Kate Squires, O and Stan, Nan D; the inspiring Michael Reeve; graphic artist genius Cassie Leedham; Phoenix editor and friend Hannah Kane; and my English teacher, Garrath Ellershaw. Very, very importantly, I'd like to thank the lovely Chris Goldberg, without whose support, belief, unwavering faith and very clever notes, this book would not exist in its current form.

Finally, I would like to thank my parents, to whom this book is dedicated, for being really, really cool.

GOLDEN BOY

Reading Group Notes

WHY I WROTE *GOLDEN BOY*

By Abigail Tarttelin

The summer before I wrote *Golden Boy*, I was thinking a lot about gender. How does it affect us? How do other people treat us differently because of it? How does our experience as a certain gender shape us? For example, in general women are smaller and physically weaker than men – might years of living with this vulnerability make us more cautious?

There were several factors in my life that made gender a theme at that time. Like many writers, I am inspired by reading, and that summer I read *The Women's Room* by Marilyn French in a quiet park opposite my flat in Camden Town. It was also a bit of a summer of love, and I was thinking about the roles men and women traditionally

411

play in relationships. I also grew up being friends with a lot of guys and was experiencing surprise at that time in realising that there *were* differences between us, caused by something as arbitrary as the chromosome combinations we were born with. Gradually, these themes developed, and sometime in late September I started to write an email, sending it back and forth to myself, about two brothers, one of whom was not quite, or only, a teenage boy.

A big fan of Spanish-language cinema, such as the films of Pedro Almodóvar, in 2009 I had taken myself to see an Argentinian film called *XXY* about an intersex teenager living in a remote coastal village. Three years later, I wondered if a discussion on the different experiences of the two 'accepted' genders could be approached with a narrative about an intersex individual. I wondered how someone who had grown up as a male might cope with finding out that, due to the capabilities of their body, they must deal with an important and often frightening part of the female experience. How would my lovely protagonist, who I now named Max, cope with his body's insistence on exposing his secrets? Would his family treat him differently? Would he have the courage to live with an undefined role in society, or would he seek out definition?

When it came to writing *Golden Boy*, I realised that many depictions of LGBTQIA individuals in contemporary culture show them living on the periphery of society. I questioned why this was, as intersex and trans individuals can be born to anyone, anywhere, and the matter of gender impacts on most people's lives at some point or another. It became very important to me that Max live within an 'average' family and community so that *Golden Boy* had the best chance of reaching, and speaking to, mums, dads and adolescents everywhere.

Later, after I had written the first draft of *Golden Boy*, I became aware of a new generation of bloggers and subculture internet icons subverting old ideas of gender identity. Their identity was informed by gender, but by alternative genders or nonconformist attitudes to their own gender that they had chosen. These bloggers were as young as 14, and they weren't afraid. They were out, proud and completely self-confident – at the pinnacle of a progressive, worldwide movement towards embracing the idea that identity and gender are things we have to take into our own hands and not absolute concepts we are born with.

The example these young people offered proved that characters such as Max and Sylvie were wanted and perhaps needed in literature and mainstream culture. At the same time, press coverage – the front-page articles on trans children in *New York Magazine* and *The New York Times* in 2012, for example – made me ever more confident that a novel such as *Golden Boy* could contribute to a discussion on gender by making the subject accessible, addressing families and readers, and not solely those already at the forefront of progressive thinking about gender and sexuality.

Culture tends to lead the way for society as a whole to progress, and we are undoubtedly seeing a more fluid vision of male and female emerging in contemporary art, writing and fashion. With publishers willing to go wild over books such as *Golden Boy*, the hiring of women such as Tilda Swinton and Casey Legler to model menswear fashions, Sweden's argument over the sexless pronoun, ample magazine coverage, and TV shows such as *Hit or Miss*, everything seems to be pointing towards a freer idea of she and he, in what could be the biggest cultural and social phenomenon since the sixties.

FOR DISCUSSION

- What would you have done if Max had been your child?

- Did *Golden Boy* change the way you think about gender?

- What might have happened if Max had kept the baby?

- Did Max's parents do the right thing by not assigning him a gender earlier on? What were their true motivations? Did they have his best interests at heart or were they sticking their heads in the sand?

- Why is Max drawn to Sylvie when he could have his pick of the more popular girls at school?

- How would you have reacted to Max's revelation in Sylvie's shoes?

- Was Max hiding in plain sight?

- Did Daniel's maturity towards the end of the book surprise you?

- Should Steve have put his political ambitions to one side sooner?

- Is Hunter an out-and-out villain, or is he a more ambiguous character? What did the author intend us to make of him and why?

- How is the medical establishment portrayed in *Golden Boy*? Do you think Archie is a representative figure?

- What does *Golden Boy* tell you about the nature of family? Was Steve a better parent than Karen?

- What did the author gain by setting this story not on the margins of society but in a very established household?

- What does Max's intersexuality represent in the book?

- Sylvie writes, 'I thought I knew you well / Fucking hell'. Do any of the characters in *Golden Boy* really know each other?

- How much do we rely on ideas of gender in our own lives? Are some of those ideas outdated?

- What does the future hold for Karen and Steve?

- Max writes, 'Science is unreliable. It can't tell you who you are or what you'll want or how you'll feel.' Do you agree with Max entirely?

FURTHER READING
AND WATCHING

Middlesex by Jeffrey Eugenides

Annabel by Kathleen Winter

Wasted by Kate Tempest

The Women's Room by Marilyn French

Flick by Abigail Tarttelin

XXY directed by Lucía Puenzo

C.R.A.Z.Y. directed by Jean-Marc Vallée

Tomboy directed by Céline Sciamma